REBEL EMPIRE

A NOVEL OF THE SPANISH-CONFEDERATE WAR

BY

BILLY BENNETT

Published by Saber Books

Billy Bennett

*This novel is lovingly dedicated to my beloved
Grandmother Florence Bennett.
Thank you, Granny for your love. All my life I have
been awed and inspired by your great strength and
perseverance. You taught me to never give up.*

PROLOGUE
1895

Commander Blake Ramsey stared at Havana harbor from the deck of the CSS Mississippi. The sun was well off to the west, there were only a few hours of daylight left. Lieutenant Ray Brisk, the ship's chief engineer came alongside so that he could also get a look at the island. For Confederate sailors, Cuba was an island paradise.

"Looks like we get to enjoy a night in Havana," said Ramsey. Brisk smiled wryly. They'd been stationed off of the African coast for weeks on the antislavery patrol. They were ready for a little rest and relaxation. Brisk spat a brown stream of tobacco juice into the sea water.

"Don't make no sense, us having to take part in keeping people from trading niggers. Seems almost hypocritical." Ramsey knew Brisk well enough to know that it was the CSA's participation in the international patrol off the African coast, and not it's keeping of African slaves itself, that had him all riled up. Like most white people in the CSA, he still clung defiantly to the institution of slavery. Ramsey chose his words with deliberate care.

"We're the last slave holding nation in the Americas. That makes our foreign relations difficult enough as it is. If we didn't participate in the patrol, we probably wouldn't have any foreign relations at all." Brisk rolled his eyes.

"Our constitution forbids importing niggers from outside the Confederacy. It always has. You'd think that'd be good enough for them." Ramsey shook his head.

"Not good enough for the Europeans, especially the Brits. The way they look at it, ninety percent of slave smugglers are bound for the CSA."

"You know as well as I do that the demand for slaves is going down. A good, healthy, buck nigger is barely worth half what he was in 1890. Smuggling isn't as big a problem as it was ten or twenty years ago, when the western territories opened up and the demand was sky high."

"I guess they figure there wouldn't be a smuggling problem at all if we didn't exist to tempt the smugglers," said Ramsey. "The British are tired of paying the brunt of the cost of the patrol. If we didn't chip in, we'd have a serious international problem."

Now it was Brisk's turn to shake his head.

"No, they're just all high and mighty and self-righteous." He swore disdainfully to show what he thought of the British. "You ask me, we shouldn't care what the Brits, the Yankees or anyone else thinks."

"We have to be careful Brisk. If we snubbed our nose at the rest of the world like you want us to do, then we'd likely find ourselves with no one to trade with at all. That would be disastrous for the Confederacy." The CSA had developed a lot of home industry since the War of Confederate Independence and the War of 1869, but it still hadn't developed near what it needed to support itself, not nearly half. Most Confederate industry was military related. They could manufacture, rifles, cannons, and ammunition—but little else. Ramsey turned his eyes to the battleship on which they stood. The warship was one of the finest vessels in the Confederate States Navy. She had an all metal hull. Her steam engines made her one of the fastest battleships afloat. Her twelve inch guns were both long range and deadly accurate. The Confederate Battle Flag fluttering at her bow declared that she was the pride of the Confederate Navy. But her hull and engines had been manufactured in England. Her guns had been manufactured in France. Her massive propeller screws had been forged in the Kingdom of Prussia. Like virtually everything else of high industrial quality in the CSA, she was an import. The point was lost on Brisk who again shook his head.

"The Brits need our cotton. Without it their textile factories would shut down."

"The British get a lot of their cotton from India these days," replied Ramsey. Brisk, like a lot of people in the Confederate States, failed to realize that cotton wasn't quite the king that it used to be. The Confederate economy had peaked in the 1870s and 80s. The early 1890s had seen major economic downturns on both sides of the Atlantic and especially in the Confederate States. Boll weevil infestations, soil depletions and an increasingly hostile foreign market were all insuring that 1895 was looking to be the worst year for Confederate cotton sales since the War of Confederate Independence. Back in 1863 cotton exports had been hindered by blockading US warships. Now they were being hindered by an incensed European public opinion. Even doing business with the CSA carried with it a stench in most European circles. It brought with it accusations of not only condoning slavery, but of aiding and abetting it. As a result, more and more European venders were declining to do business with the Confederacy.

"France does plenty of business with us," said Brisk.

Ramsey nodded. The French Empire and her main allies, the Empire of Mexico, the German Confederation, and the Austrian-Hungarian Empire were all allied with the CSA and therefore had no problems trading with the Confederacy. The problem was that France had a much smaller textile industry than Britain and her allies like Mexico and Austria-Hungary had virtually none. Ramsey reflected that it helped that Emperor Napoleon IV was not answerable to his people in the sense that the governments of Britain and the United States were. Like it or not, a dictatorship had certain advantages over democracy.

The CSS Mississippi cruised into the narrow channel that led into Havana bay. The bay divided into three main natural harbors. On the eastern side of the bay, the La Cabana was an impressive sight. The Spanish built fort was one of the largest fortifications in the Americas. The red and gold Spanish flag fluttered proudly above it.

"I've heard that Spain is reconsidering the agreement allowing our ships to make port here," said Ramsey.

"They'd be fools to," said Brisk. "Cuba's right off our coast and Spain is a long ways away. If we wanted to take Cuba for ourselves they'd have a hard time defending it against us. Richmond's been trying to pressure Spain into selling us Cuba for twenty years. Just let them give us an excuse to take it by force." Ramsey nodded. The CSA definitely had its eyes on the island.

"The way I figure it, they've already given us plenty of excuses. The locals here are tired of Spanish rule. This island can be a dangerous place." He cursed derogatorily. "It took the Spanish three years to put down the last insurrection."

"And it took ten years to put down the one before that," said Brisk. "I'll bet there are plenty of Cubans who would gladly trade the la Rojigualda for the Blood Stained Banner." Ramsey couldn't argue. He pulled a cigar from the inside pocket of his dark gray uniform coat, struck a match and got it going. Brisk continued: "You'd think with all the problems here the Spanish would be eager to get rid of it." Ramsey blew out a long whiff of smoke.

"I wouldn't say that. Spain's empire has been in decline for a long time. Cuba is one of the few prize possessions that they have left. They won't ever let it go easy."

Ramsey smoked down his cigar and tossed the butt overboard. He then prepared to take charge of the deck crews that would secure the ship to its moorings while Brisk made his way back down to the engine room. Once the ship was docked and fully secured, Ramsey made his way up to the bridge where the Captain was waiting in the wheel house.

"All secure, Mr. Ramsey?"

"All secure, sir." Captain James Macneer was a good Captain. He was a much older officer, nearing or even past retirement age. He'd commanded a blockade runner during the War of Confederate Independence and a commerce raider during the War of 1869. He'd earned his position as the commander of one of the CSA's finest ships. Serving as his executive officer had been Ramsey's honor, but the younger officer desperately desired a command of his own.

"Inform Mr. Brisk that he'll have command of the ship this evening. After that you may organize the shore leave party and the skeleton crew. Then you may go ashore yourself."

"Won't you be going ashore tonight, Captain?"

"My chest has been giving me pains again. I'm going to turn in early tonight and get some rest." Ramsey nodded. The Captain had been turning in early for half the voyage. Ramsey had just about been able to run the ship as if it were his own, which was good if you wanted the experience needed to merit your own command.

"Enjoy yourself in Havana, Commander. You've earned it."

"Thank you, sir."

"I do have three small tasks for you."

"Anything, sir," replied Ramsey.

"First, draw some funds from the quartermaster's office and buy us some fresh fruits and vegetables. I'm blasted tired of the canned monstrosities that masquerade under the name." Ramsey smiled.

"I'll see to it, sir." Next the Captain held up his binoculars.

"My binoculars are broken. They hit the deck during that storm we went through a few weeks ago and haven't worked properly since. See if you can find me a cheap pair. I'll get these repaired when we get back to Mobile. Have the quartermaster give you all the necessary funds."

"Very good, sir."

"And here…" Captain Macneer pulled a five dollar gold piece from his coat pocket. He tossed it to Ramsey. "Get me a couple bottles of the best rum you can find."

"Yes, sir!"

After taking his leave of the Captain, Ramsey set to work. He found the quartermaster and signed a receipt for sixty-five dollars. Once he'd pocketed the funds, he ordered the crew to assemble on the deck. The whole crew rushed to their places like wild men. They were ready for some leave. Ramsey was thankful that he didn't have to pick and choose the poor souls who would have to stay aboard that night based merely on his own whim. He'd worked hard to cultivate a reputation of fairness among the men. He held a clip board in his hand with the disciplinary record from the voyage. Men who had gotten drunk, who had been involved in brawls, had been late for duty or who had otherwise performed their duties sub-standardly, would now pay by having to stay aboard ship while the rest of the crew enjoyed the night in Havana. Ramsey selected a young Ensign with a bad habit of turning in sloppy paperwork to serve as officer of the deck for the night. He didn't mind telling Lieutenant Brisk that he would be in command for the evening. Brisk, like Ramsey, wanted a command of his own one day. He was grateful for the chance to take command, if only for a night in port.

"Now you men have a good time, but be warned you are expected to be here come morning and you are expected to be fit for duty. I swear any man that is too hung over or injured to do his job, or heaven forbid, any man that isn't on board and makes us late, will wish that he had never been born. Dismissed."

The assembled sailors whooped and hollered as they broke up and headed ashore. Ramsey wasn't long following after them. The sun had begun to set when he made his way onto the streets of Havana. The city didn't go down with the sun. The streets were well lit by gas lamps. Ramsey found a nautical supply store where he purchased a new pair of binoculars for the Captain. Afterwards, he had no problem finding a liquor store to buy the Captain's rum. When he slapped the Captain's five dollar gold piece down on the counter and the Cuban storekeeper saw Robert E Lee's reverent face staring up at him from the coin, he smiled a smile that was missing several teeth. With his own money, Ramsey bought himself a box of cigars. Virginia tobacco was good. Cuban tobacco was better.

As good a reason as any for Cuba to be part of the CSA one day! With the binoculars, rum and cigars in a bag, he made his way to the city market where he made arrangements for a large number of vegetables and fruits to be delivered to the ship. Finally free to pursue his own vices, he went in search of a casino. The one he found, Miss Dixie's, was actually owned and operated by a Confederate proprietor.

There were a lot of Confederates doing business in Cuba. With Spain in debt up to her ears, and the added problems of the recession, Madrid had had no money to invest in the Cuban economy for years. Confederate investors had largely picked up the slack.

Ramsey played roulette and cards for a couple of hours, but when he found himself down ten dollars he decided to call it a night. When he returned, he was pleased to see that the sailors he'd detailed for the night watch were alert and at their post. In fact they had stopped someone who was apparently trying to board the ship. As Ramsey advanced on them, he saw that it was a man in a Confederate Naval officer's uniform. The guards had decided to let him aboard. Ramsey viewed his face for a brief moment as the man turned around to pick up his duffle bag. It was no one he had ever laid eyes on before. By the two stars on his hat he could tell that he was a Commander. Most notably, the officer had a jagged scar that went down the side of his face. By the time Ramsey had made it to the dock, the strange officer had already gone up the rampart escorted by one of the sailors.

The remaining sentries stiffened to attention at his approach and brought their rifles up in a salute. Ensign Ruck, whom Ramsey had left to be officer of the deck, also brought his arm up in salute. Ramsey returned it.

"Ensign Ruck, who was that officer?"

"Sir, he said he was Commander Smith."

"Smith? What's he doing coming aboard our ship? For that matter what's he doing in Cuba alone? We don't have any other ships in port here. Did he have his papers in order?" His tone said they would pay dearly if the man's papers hadn't been spot on. Shoddy paperwork was the reason Ruck was stuck on the ship doing night duty.

"Sir, they were all in order. He had orders from the Navy department to board the first Confederate vessel bound for Mobile. He says he's a naval engineer. He's been in Cuba doing some sort of joint work with the Spanish on their coastal fortifications. I didn't have any reason to suspect anything, so I sent Seaman Corry to show him to a spare cabin in the officer's quarters." The explanation was perfectly plausible. Still, Ramsey wanted to check it out for himself. He didn't like strangers on his ship. He made his way up onto the deck of the Mississippi. The mysterious Commander was nowhere to be seen. He did catch sight of Lieutenant Brisk standing near the bow.

"How was Havana?" he asked.

"I lost ten bucks," replied Ramsey.

Brisk winced.

"I'm glad I stayed here."

Ramsey sat down his bag and pulled out the box of Cubans.

"I wouldn't say the entire trip was a waste." He opened it up and handed his friend one of the fresh cigars. He also took one for himself. A few moments later, when they were both puffing happy clouds, Ramsey asked, "Did you see our guest?" Brisk looked confused. Ramsey explained about the strange officer that had just come aboard.

"When we're done, we'll go to the cabins and find him."

Ramsey nodded. He took another long drag on his cigar. Just then, he caught sight of a man running along the ship. At first he didn't recognize him.

What's that fool doing running on deck! Then he recognized the face. The scar was unmistakable. It was their strange visitor. He had divested himself of his uniform coat and hat. He had even kicked off his shoes. Before Ramsey could so much as holler at him, the man jumped over the side of the ship and into the dark water below.

"Man overboard!" cried Ramsey. He and Brisk rushed to the spot where he had gone over. Brisk cursed.

"I swear he went over on purpose!" They looked down at the water below. The stranger had jumped off on the bay side of the ship. It was dark and hard to see. Several men from the skeleton crew had begun to come up onto the deck, hollering questions about what to do. Ramsey wasn't sure. Over the sound of the shouting sailors, he thought he heard the sound of the man swimming away from the ship as fast as possible.

Why would he want off the ship in such a hurry? No sooner had the thought occurred to him, than he heard a loud explosion under the deck and felt it vibrate through the whole ship.

Brisk blasphemed and swore profanely.

"What was that?"

Suddenly to Ramsey the whole world seemed to explode. The sound of the blast ruptured his eardrums. For the briefest instant all he saw was fiery red. The heat of the flames seared him. Miraculously the blast sent him flying off the ship like a kicked football. He landed in the sea. Whereas a split second before all had been red, now all was black. For a moment he thought he was dead. Up above him, a fiery red light made its way into the dark depths below. Ramsey summoned all of his remaining strength. His uniform weighed him down, but he kicked and clawed for the surface with all his might. As he broke the surface, he filled his burning lungs with fresh air. He looked over towards what was left of the CSS

Mississippi. She was burning. The explosion had nearly cut the forward third of the ship from the rear two thirds. Ramsey could tell that the ship's powder magazine had gone off. Most of the superstructure had been smashed by the explosion. The hull belched a torrent of fire and smoke. As sea water flooded the hull, the mortally wounded ship began to sink at her moorings. There was nothing that could be done to save her. Here and there, a few sailors had been thrown from the ship and were splashing in the water. Anyone who had been below decks when the explosion happened was surely dead. As Ramsey swam away from the burning ship and towards the shore, one thought raced through his mind.

Somebody's going to pay for this...

I

Cole Allens, the editor of the Covington Gazette barked orders at his newspaper minions like a General ordering an army on the field. Some said he had gained his commanding demeanor from his time spent with the army, covering the Second War of Rebellion back in 1869, when he was little more than a kid. Others said he had inherited it from his uncle who had been the paper's founding editor. In any event, no one slacked while he was around.

"Hey chief, have you decided what's going to be page one?" Cole silently ridiculed his own inaction.

"Not yet, Jack! You'll be the first to know!" The printer darted back down to the print room while Cole seated himself at his desk and lit a cigar. He had two descent stories for the morning edition. One was about the continuing Nevada dispute between the Republic of California and the Mormon nation of Deseret. Both sides were again threatening war over the mineral rich desert territory. The story would have been likely to sell more papers if it hadn't been going on so long. California and Deseret had been arguing over Nevada for twenty-five years. Both had seized a chunk of it. Both had claims on the other's chunk. Both had threatened war a dozen times in the past two decades. People just weren't that interested anymore, no matter how eerily menacing Cole found the most recent round of saber rattling.

The other story was about the enormous cost over runs and construction delays that the Franklin capital project was experiencing. The United States had finally decided to take action and build a new Federal capital city. Being situated directly on the border of the Confederate States as it was, Washington DC was far too vulnerable to be the US capital. The Federal government had mostly elected to hold sessions in various other US cities over the past twenty-five years. In all that time, Washington had been little used. No one wanted to sit under the shadow of Confederate guns. Congress had passed a resolution authorizing the construction of a new federal capital further north on a piece of land generously offered by both New York and Vermont. The new federal capital city would be called Franklin, after Benjamin Franklin, who had been one of the only prominent founding fathers who hadn't been from the South. Upon Franklin's completion, Washington would revert back to Maryland but be a historical national park under the administration of the Federal government. Many were also saying that it would primarily be utilized as a massive military base. But if Congress couldn't get Franklin's construction back on track, and deal with the cost overruns, it would be forever before the U.S. government officially took up residence in its new capital city.

One problem was its grandiose size. Many of the politicians in the US government had decided that a good way to make up for the large amounts of territory that had been lost in the First and Second Wars of Rebellion, was to build the largest, most expensive capital city possible. On his desk, Cole had a sketch of what was being dubbed "the US Presidential Palace." Many in the nation decried the word "palace" as being to "royal" and therefore inappropriate for the head of a democratic republic. They were clamoring for the title Presidential "mansion." Still others were demanding it simply keep the title "White House" (even though the current plan was to paint it a creamy beige color). Whatever name it ended up having, or color it ended up being painted, "palace" aptly described the future residence of the President of the United States better than any other. Compared to the White House in Washington, it was the Palace of Versailles.

In the end Cole settled on the Franklin story. The people were eager for the new capital to be built. If they were properly informed, then maybe they'd put the pressure on the politicians to get it done.

Cole had risen and was headed down to the print room when the telegraph started clicking. He paid it no particular attention. There was no reason to believe that anything of greater consequence than what they already had would come in. He had just set Jack and the other printers to work on the front page, when the telegrapher hollered down to the print floor from the newsroom.

"Hey chief, something came in that you'd better see!" Cole recognized the tension in his voice. It was the kind of tone that said it was a big story. Cole turned to the printers.

"Hold off on page one!" he said.

"Chief, the paper's going to be late hitting the street!"

"Just wait!" One thing his uncle Perry had taught him, was that it was okay for the paper to hit the stands late as long as it contained a blockbuster story that none of the other papers had. *If the story is big enough!* Cole crossed his fingers as he marched himself back up to the news floor. He practically snatched the wire out of the telegrapher's hand. CONFEDERATE WARSHIP, CSS MISSISSIPPI, BLOWN UP IN HAVANA HARBOR. CSA THREATENS WAR WITH SPAIN! DETAILS FOLLOW…

"Yes! George! Come write this up! Cover! We need an illustration! No time to draw one up just find us a map with Cuba and the CSA on it. Then get to work on a good picture of an exploding battleship for the afternoon edition." A while later the presses were rolling. The Gazette hit the stands nearly an hour and a half late, but they were the only paper with the story. They sold out, leaving their competition papers in the dust. Cole didn't slow down to savor his success. He sat down at his desk, lit a new cigar and started soaking up the details of the Havana crisis. He then started writing an editorial for the afternoon edition.

In the aftermath of the disaster that has unfolded in Cuba, it is still unclear exactly what has transpired and who is to blame. The Spanish are blaming Cuban rebels. The Confederates are blaming Spain for failing to maintain control of the island. In any event, the Confederate States have, predictably, seized upon this tragedy as an excuse to further expand their territory. As anyone familiar in the least with the Geo-Political climate of the past quarter-century can attest, the CSA has long desired to add the island nation of Cuba to its territory. Indeed, when one considers the Confederate seizer of the Isthmus of Panama from Columbia just a few years ago (with the aid of their militaristic ally the Empire of France) one may be surprised that the Confederacy has not already taken the island of Cuba by force, except perhaps that Spain is a harder nation to pick on than Columbia. In any event, the destruction of the CSS Mississippi in Havana last night, seemingly by Cuban Rebels, has provided the Confederates with a most convenient and almost too perfect opportunity to renew their demands on the Spanish government to part with its prize island. Had an older or more dilapidated vessel and not the pride of the Confederate Navy met its demise in Havana, one would be tempted to believe that the Confederates had themselves engineered this whole fiasco to justify their annexation of the island. We concede, however, that that is extremely unlikely given the loss of life and the fact that the Confederacy spent a fortune on the late warship, a fortune that it is demanding be repaid in gold, gold which Madrid's coffers is sadly lacking these days. And so Richmond is demanding that Spain immediately cede the entire island of Cuba to the CSA. As our own nation will attest (as will the nation of Columbia), the CSA will not hesitate to declare war and to take away territory by force of arms at the least provocation—(or in the case of Columbia, none at all). The Confederates have twice shown in the past thirty-five years that they are willing to make war to achieve their ends. The leaders in Madrid would do well to remember that the CSA has twice prevailed in war against a larger and stronger power and if they fared so well in their wars with the United States of America, what prospects does tiny Spain have of standing against them? The Confederate States are larger and stronger. They are also perfectly situated geographically to take the island. Cuba is only eighty miles from the Confederate state of Florida. Our own government is extremely unlikely to intercede on Spain's behalf in any way. Grover Cleveland, like all Presidents of the past twenty-five years, was (in addition to being a Democrat, Republicans being considered by all, except possibly the

*legally insane as being unelectable) elected on the promise to
keep the United States out of military conflict with the
Confederate States—indeed out of the troubles of the outside
world period. While President Cleveland has clearly been
stronger than his immediate predecessors in all matters foreign
affairs, his modernization of the US Navy being a perfect
example, he has never shown any inclination whatsoever, that
he would be willing to enter into a confrontation with the CSA,
especially on the behalf of another nation. The horrors and
humiliations of the Wars of Rebellion, even after more than
twenty-five years, are still too fresh in the mind of the nation.
Make no mistake, Spain will find no help from Washington or
New York, or wherever our distinguished leaders are meeting
right now. One wild card in this unfolding drama is Britain.
The British have taken the lead in recent years in pressuring
the CSA to abandon its institution of slavery. The British will
undoubtedly oppose any expansion of the Confederate States as
an extension of slavery. What remains to be seen is whether the
British will be willing to take any action on Spain's behalf. We
must admit that it is not very likely. The Confederacy has been,
since 1869, close military allies with the Empire of France—an
alliance that has driven a sharp wedge between the British and
French. Relations between Britain and France are now the
worst they have been since the battle of Waterloo. Most experts
believe that Napoleon IV has his own territorial ambitions in
Europe and elsewhere. If France were to declare war on Spain
along with the CSA, than to put it bluntly, Spain is doomed.
While we need not remind our readers that this paper is no
friend of the Confederate States, we must regretfully
recommend that Spain accede to the Confederate demand. This
will have the benefit of allowing Spain to receive at least some
payment for the island of Cuba, and most especially of sparing
many lives from being lost to the horrors of war.*

Cole looked up from the finished editorial and looked at
the clock. It read twelve fifteen.

I'm late! He grabbed his hat from the rack and dashed
out the door. He was fortunate that Marie's Café was only a ten

19

minute walk (for him a five minute run) from the offices of the Covington Gazette. Cole would turn forty-four years old the next year. He ran like an eighteen year old. The beautiful young woman waiting for him at the tables outside the café was fifteen years his junior. If she was angry at his tardiness, she didn't show it, indeed she lit up with a smile and giggled at the sight of him, a distinguished newspaper editor, running at breakneck speed down the street. She rose to meet him. He took her into his arms and kissed her. There were audible coughs from several of the people seated outside the café. Such public affection was taboo in polite society. At the moment he didn't care.

He'd met Helen a year earlier. He'd married her six months later. They'd taken their honeymoon in New England. Though they'd long since returned from the trip, the honeymoon still hadn't ended. The past six months had been the happiest of his life.

"You've had a busy day, I presume," she said as he held the chair for her to sit.

Taking his own seat he replied, "You might say that." She smiled and held up a copy of the paper.

"You were the only one to hit the streets with the big story. Everyone everywhere is talking about what's going on." At that moment the waiter appeared.

"I'll have coffee and a ham sandwich," he said. Helen ordered soup. As the waiter walked away he asked her, "How has your day been?"

"I went to the art gallery before coming here. There are some beautiful paintings there."

He smiled.

"There are indeed."

She smiled and playfully swatted his hand.

"I wasn't talking about mine." She was an aspiring artist. He'd bought her plenty of paints, brushes and canvases. Of course he adored everything she produced and even discreetly sent some of his employees to the art gallery with cash to buy some of her paintings. Not enough to give her the false impression that she was the next thing to Leonardo Davinci, but enough to keep her confidence up. She had in fact sold some paintings that he hadn't been the shadow buyer of.

"There was a beautiful painting of some place called Hawaii. Have you ever heard of it?" Cole nodded.

"It's a group of islands in the Pacific. They're usually called the Sandwich Islands. I think the British own them." She looked at him with a dreamy stare. "I would love to go to an island, or at least to a beach." He winced. She'd wanted to go to a beach for their honeymoon. The problem was that the United States no longer possessed any beaches in warmer climates. With the independence of California, the US Pacific coast was limited to the coasts of Oregon and Washington State. Most of the US Atlantic coast was similarly inclement accept during the warmest of summers.

Of course, I could have taken her down to the CSA. The Confederate States had plenty of warm beaches, even during the fall and winter. They both had passports, they could have gone. But Helen's father had been killed during the Second War of Rebellion when she was only three years old. He'd thought it unwise to suggest they take their honeymoon in the country that had killed her father. *Should I offer now?*

Thankfully she changed the subject. Holding up the paper she asked "Will there be a war?"

Cole lit a cigar and looked at her.

"I hope not."

II

"Move it you filthy niggers!" cried one of the overseers on horseback. Ebenezer and the other slaves took the verbal lashing in stride. The white man had a leather whip that was far more intimidating. Fear of that whip kept the black men moving, even though their feet were tired from walking for four hours. Ebenezer's back bore manifold witness to the awful

21

work a whip could do. So did the backs of all the other negroes marching with him. They were on their way to a slave auction. Under most circumstances that was one of the most terrifying places for a negro to go. Under present circumstances, Ebenezer, and the other black men he was chained to, counted it a blessing. Any slave from Sharpstone Plantation just north of Natchez Mississippi could tell you that it was hell on earth. Mr. Fitch Haley was known to blacks and whites both as the cruelest planter in south Mississippi. The man beat his slaves at the slightest provocation and sometimes just because he enjoyed being cruel. He'd once had Ebenezer whipped with twenty lashes just for sneezing too close to him. Haley was feared by blacks and disdained by whites. Fortunately, he was as short on business sense as he was on human decency. His plantation was running in the red when most of the others around Natchez were breaking even. A few were even turning a profit, despite the recent economic downturn. Despite the way he drove his slaves, production was down. Sharpstone had three times as many runaways as other plantations in the area. Haley had more bills than he knew what to do with and so now he was selling off some of his slaves to raise some much needed cash. Ebenezer thanked Jesus he was one of the ones up for sale.

"Pick up the pace, boy!" cried the overseer at the black man taking up the rear. By the silver mixed in with his black hair, the slave had to be twice the overseer's age. That didn't stop the overseer from popping him with his whip. The black man wailed in pain.

"I's sorry boss! I sho' is!" he picked up the pace and quickly caught up with the others. There was a creek off to the right. Ebenezer wanted desperately to take a drink. He didn't dare ask to. As if to make his pain of thirst worse, the overseer opened his canteen and took a long gulp of water. He sighed in pleasure, then turned to one of the other white men riding along with him.

"How much further?"

"Not much, another two or three miles maybe."

"Shut up, both of you," came a harsh and commanding voice. The white men practically came to attention in the saddle. The blacks kept walking, eyes forward, mouths shut, trying as much as possible to be nothing more than scenery. Fitch Haley had come riding up. "I pay you men to watch my niggers and make sure none get away. Quit your yapping and pay attention."

"Yes sir, Mr Haley!" they chorused.

"Now speed it up," he said. "The auction is about to begin." The overseers set on the slaves with renewed vigor. They didn't have to use the whips though. The slaves were more anxious to arrive than the overseers. All but one.

Ebenezer looked ahead to try and see how his friend Cap was doing. The slave walked with slumped shoulders. Ebenezer knew he still had tear filled eyes. But his stride was not diminished. Cap's woman and little one were not being sold. He would probably never see them again. Ebenezer hoped little Zeke belonged to Cap. A lot of the little negroes running around Sharpstone had skin that was just a little too light. Several bore striking resemblances to Mr. Haley. Ebenezer didn't think Zeke fell into that category. He had his mother's looks for sure, but his skin was as black as midnight, just like Cap's.

Before long, they passed a sign. Ebenezer exercised a secret skill that no one there knew he possessed. He read the sign. SLAVE AUCTION TODAY! Ebenezer had been taught to read by a slave named Caesar. Ebenezer had only been ten years old at the time. Caesar had taught him at night by candlelight in absolute secrecy. Caesar had run away not long after that. As far as he knew, the white folk had never caught him.

Not long after that, they came to a cross road. Off to the left, there was a large field. A large number of people were indeed gathered for the auction. A wooden platform had been raised. Several groups of slaves were chained up behind the platform under heavy guard. Wagons and carriages were still coming in from all directions. Most of the white men assembled in front of the stage were planters in fine suits. Some were buying. Most were selling. The downturn in slave prices that was sweeping the CSA was causing a lot of slave owners to sell off their excess slaves before their value diminished further.

In addition to the men of the crowd, there were also a few white ladies in the mix. They were dressed in fancy dresses with hoop skirts and carried parasols to shade their delicate complexions.

Suddenly, Ebenezer heard a sound that he'd never heard before in his life. In a way, it sounded like a miniature train engine. Down the road, he caught sight of a carriage moving on its own without any horses pulling it. Ebenezer had heard of such things before, but hadn't believed a word of it. He did now. When a horse drawn carriage didn't move fast enough to suit the white man driving the horseless carriage, he picked up speed and the contraption sped past its horse drawn counterpart leaving a trail of dust behind it. When the horseless carriage turned onto the field, all eyes were on it. Some were in awe of it. Many more made fun of it and its driver. In any event, Ebenezer had no chance to look at it closer. He and the others were quickly marched off to the back of the stage.

As Ebenezer was being prepped for sale, along with the other negroes, a horse drawn carriage came riding onto the field. It was driven by a well-dressed negro. In the back of the carriage rode Mr. Mansel Dumas, the master of Twin Harbours Plantation, and his eighteen year old son, Mitchell. A horse drawn wagon followed behind them, with a couple of white overseers. As he came down from his carriage, Dumas turned to the slave driving the carriage.

"Take the carriage and get under some shade Berry, no sense you roasting out here in the heat. You can come get us when it's over."

"Thank you, Massa Mansel!" said the slave and happily moved the carriage under the shade of some nearby trees. Dumas was then greeted by his fellow planters, including Fitch Haley. Young Mitchell made straight for the horseless carriage, hoping his father would be too preoccupied with business to notice that he'd slipped away.

"I see you're buying today, Dumas," said Haley looking at the empty wagon and the overseers he had brought along. "I've brought some prime niggers to sell here today, so you make sure and check them out. They're hard working and well-mannered, I assure you of that."

Mansel Dumas nodded politely as Haley went on to make the same assurances to the other buyers in the crowd. He looked around for his son. Mitchell was busy examining the horseless carriage. Mansel marched over to him.

"Check it out Daddy, isn't it great! It's called a Benz!" Dumas waved his hand derogatorily. "They'll never catch on. Take my word for it son, these things are nothing but a waste of money. Besides, it's a Yankee machine."

"Actually sir," said the owner who was still sitting atop the contraption, "it is a French copy of one designed in Rhineland."

"Then I'll beg your pardon on that one point, sir," replied Mansel Dumas. He then turned back to his son. "Now come along. You're going to run Twin Harbours one day, and you need to know how to buy slaves. Now come with me and pay attention." They went back over towards the platform.

"There's a lot of westerners here," said Dumas to his son. He motioned at the number of men wearing spurred boots and cowboy hats. "The price of slaves has been down, but there's still a pretty big demand out west. These men haven't come here to mess around. They'll be high bidders." He lowered his voice so just his son could hear. "We've got two thousand dollars. We need some strong bucks and they're going to be the most expensive." At last the auctioneer ascended the platform.

"Ladies and Gentlemen, thank you for coming out today. As you can see we have some excellent stock to sell to you this afternoon. I'd like to remind everyone that all slaves sold at this auction come with government issued papers so that there can be no future question as to rightful ownership or natural origin of your property."

Back in the 1870s, the huge demand for slaves in the western parts of the CSA had not been met quickly enough by domestic supply to suit some people. Smuggling from Africa had become a bad problem in those days. Slave markets in New Orleans, Natchez, Vicksburg and Memphis had seen a raft of black slaves in the 1870s that could not speak any English at all and many of whom bore tribal markings from Africa. The Confederate government had taken swift action, requiring all blacks, slave or free, with origins in the CSA to be registered with the Confederate government. Selling or possessing slaves without government issued papers was a crime. The Confederate government's zeal in cracking down on the smuggling was due in part to a desire to appease an outside world that was fed up with slavery, and also in part to slave owners in the CSA who didn't want the value of their slaves driven down by new arrivals from Africa. The auctioneer continued:

"I would also like to remind you, ladies and gentlemen, that all sales are final. And now the auction will commence. First up for bid is this prime buck nigger from Mount Edmond Plantation near Baton Rouge." A big black man climbed up onto the stage. He stood over six feet tall. He had massive arms. "Luke here is strong as a bull. He's good for chopping wood, building barns, digging ditches, handling livestock..."

"Let's see his back!" someone cried from the crowd.

"Take your shirt off and turn around Luke." The slave complied and turned around. There were no marks on his back. There were nods and grunts of approval from the men in the crowd. No one wanted a slave that was a discipline problem, especially one that was so big and strong. The bidding started at five hundred dollars and rose quickly. Dumas bid eight-hundred for him but dropped out when a man from Texas bid nine. Another westerner, all the way from San Diego South California, bid a thousand. The two westerners bid against one another several times. In the end, the man from Texas bought

Luke for one-thousand-five-hundred dollars. Another big slave was next. Dumas was outbid on him too. He went to the South California man for twelve hundred dollars. Several women and smaller male slaves were sold next.

"Here comes the first of Haley's bunch," said Dumas. "This may be our opportunity."

"What do you mean daddy?"

"Watch and learn my son."

"Next up for bid is this buck nigger from Sharpstone Plantation from right here near Natchez. Another large black man climbed up on the platform. "Ebenezer here is not only strong, he's also skilled. He's good in the blacksmith shop and a good carpenter. He's healthy and young. He'll be an asset to his master for years to come. Now, what am I bid for this fine buck nigger?"

One of the men swore loudly at the man running the auction.

"Show us his back before you start calling for bids!" The auctioneer sighed.

"Show your back, Ebenezer!" Ebenezer turned his back to the assembled planters and pulled off his shirt. Gasps and curses came from the field below as the planters gazed at his back. He didn't have a few lash marks. Like all the blacks from Sharpstone, his back was a labyrinth of scar tissue.

"I'm not buying no uppity nigger!" cried the man who'd demanded to see Ebenezer's back. Not far away, Fitch Haley had turned several shades of red. More curses flew at the stage.

"Trying to pull a fast one on us! Who are you trying to fool?" Now the auctioneer winced. On the platform, Ebenezer's eyes closed in emotional pain. His hopes of leaving Sharpstone were going up in flames. If he wasn't sold, Haley would probably take out his frustration by having him beat. Down below, the auction was on the verge of coming apart. The shouts were growing louder and angrier. Over it all, Mansel Dumas hollered.

"Four-Hundred-Dollars!" His unexpected bid brought silence to the crowd. Mitchell stared at his father in confusion.

When the auctioneer recovered from his surprise he replied, "Four-hundred! Do I hear Four-fifty?" Silence pervaded the crowd. Most of them stared at Dumas as if he were insane. A few of the locals smirked knowingly, but kept their mouths shut. Haley had gone from red faced mad, to a look that said he was sick to his stomach. Even with slave prices down more than ever before, Ebenezer was worth more than twice that. "Four-hundred going once! Four-hundred going twice! Sold! Sold to Mr. Dumas for four hundred dollars." Ebenezer was as surprised as everyone else. He stood on the platform as if unsure what to do.

"Go on boy, go on to your new master!"

Dumas motioned to his men to take charge of Ebenezer. As they chained him and took him to the wagon, Mitchell looked at his father.

"Daddy, I'm confused. I thought you said never to buy an uppity nigger?"

Dumas quickly hushed his son. He leaned close so that only Mitchell could hear.

"Fitch Haley is mean as a snake. He beats his slaves just for the fun of it."

"Then Ebenezer's not really an uppity nigger." Dumas nodded. The crowd reacted the same way to Cap. Dumas bought him for three-hundred-dollars. In the end, Dumas bought all but one of Haley's slaves and still had a hundred dollars left over. For their parts, the newly acquired slaves were thankful they would be riding to their new home in a wagon. Ebenezer gave thanks to God that he was no longer the property of Fitch Haley. He wondered what kind of man his new master would be.

III

Nathan Audrey rode into Pine City just as the sun was climbing high to noon. A young, gun toting deputy Marshal rode alongside him. Depending on your political view-point, it was Pine City California, Pine City Deseret, or Pine City Nevada. After the Second War of Rebellion, the new Mormon nation of Deseret and the new Republic of California had torn the US state of Nevada apart like dogs going at a steak. The USA had since abandoned all claim to the territory but had not officially ceded it to anyone else. The Mormons controlled close to two-thirds of the territory. Pine City, however, was located in the western third that California controlled.

They rode their mounts down the two rows of pine wood, clap board buildings that made up the town and hitched their horses in front of the sheriff's office. After dismounting, he used his hands to rub his lower back. It hurt horribly. At sixty, he wasn't a young man anymore. He turned to the young deputy Marshall at his side.

"Wait here." He then walked into the sheriff's office. As he came in, the sheriff rose from behind an old wooden desk that, like Audrey, had seen better days. He glanced at the silver star on Audrey's vest.

"Are you Johnson?" asked the Sherriff. Audrey nodded, altogether unselfconscious about the lie. He'd been using the name Johnson for over twenty-five years, ever since California had become an independent republic. Even though he was wanted for a murder that had taken place thirty years earlier and, as it stood now, in a different country, he still clung to the alias. George Custer was thirty years dead. Surely in the United States they had long since stopped looking for him. But he was still unwilling to use his real name. For one thing, it would raise too many questions with too many people. For another, he knew that the past had a funny way of catching up with you.

The sheriff had a mirror on the wall. Audrey glanced briefly at himself. The silver beard and long silver hair would have kept anyone who knew him all those years ago in the USA from recognizing him. Audrey pulled out his papers and handed them to the Sherriff.

"In Sacramento they said you'd nabbed Black Dog himself," said Audrey.

The Sherriff nodded. He pointed to the cell across the room where a dirty unkempt man sat like a caged animal.

"Sacramento wired and said that they were sending someone to get him. I have to admit I expected you to bring along some help. We killed most of his gang when we broke up the bank heist, but three of them got away. I wouldn't want to travel alone with Black Dog."

"My deputy's outside." The sheriff, who was about Audrey's age, pulled the curtains aside for a peek at the deputy Marshal. "I'd want somebody besides a young pup like that watching my back with someone like Black Dog."

"Thanks for the concern, Sheriff but we can handle it. If he gives me any trouble I'll shoot him."

"The cold blooded murderer certainly deserves it. I reckon that if you don't shoot him before you get him there, they'll hang him in Sacramento." Audrey nodded.

"Higher than Ben Butler." The Sherriff returned to his seat.

"And that is what makes him so very dangerous. He has absolutely nothing to lose." Audrey looked over at the notorious outlaw. Black Dog was staring at him through the cell bars. He smiled a savaged grin that showed a mouth that was missing several teeth. Those that he still had were a nasty yellow color. Audrey turned back to the Sherriff.

"We'll be leaving just as soon as we've gotten a bite to eat and wired Sacramento that we've got him." The sheriff shook his head.

"I'm afraid you won't be able to send a wire. The telegraph has been down since yesterday."

"Has it?"

The sheriff nodded.

"And you know what Marshall? It's got folks around here on edge. What with tensions high with the Mormons and all the angry talk that's been going on back and forth between Sacramento and Salt Lake City, half the folks around here are expecting the Mormons to attack us any day. The telegraph just up and going out is too eerie to be a coincidence."

"I'll let Sacramento know." The sheriff reached into his desk drawer and pulled out a manila envelope.

"This will let the right people know what's been going on out here." As Audrey pocketed the envelope the sheriff continued. "We had a couple of Mormon preachers come through here several days ago. They went to preaching in the town square about a coming judgment. They said if we didn't leave or convert that God would destroy us all."

"You people had better be on your guard," said Audrey.

"Believe me, Marshal, we are. That envelope I gave you is a request for the army to send us some protection."

"I wouldn't hold my breath. California doesn't have a very large army," replied Audrey.

"I know that, Marshal." The sheriff swore. "I tell you Marshal it was folly, our leaving the Union to be an independent republic!" Audrey wasn't sure how to reply. California had declared its independence from the United States over twenty-five years earlier at the close of the Second War of Rebellion. He'd been down in Mexico fighting in the French Foreign Legion then. After murdering Custer, he'd had nowhere else to turn. He'd spent that short war fighting on the side of France and the CSA against his own former compatriots. California's timely secession had provided him with the opportunity for a new life. He'd started out as a bounty hunter and earned a position as a California Marshal.

"Seems to me that the USA didn't do a good job of protecting California even when we were part of the Union," said Audrey. California had seceded in the aftermath of the US defeat because the USA had failed miserably to protect it. They'd sent troops to fight in Virginia and Mexico and had left the rest of the nation open to attack. The Confederates had invaded and seized the southern part of California. Now that area was a Confederate State in its own right. The United States had also allowed the Mormons to secede and to cut the intercontinental railroad which had severed California from the bulk of the USA. Audrey wasn't surprised the inhabitants of California had felt betrayed and abandoned enough to go their own way. The sheriff didn't seem convinced.

"The problem wasn't that the USA didn't have the ability or the resources to protect us. The problem was they didn't know how to use them. Take my word for it. If we'd stayed in, we would have been better off in the long run." Audrey shrugged. It was water under the bridge. Things were what they were. Whatever the future held for California, it was a future apart from the Stars and Stripes.

"Come on Marshal, let me get you a bite to eat. We'll leave our deputies to watch this scum. Then we'll get you on the road." A while later Audrey and the Sheriff were walking down the town's center dirt road. The wooden frame of a large, partially constructed building loomed to the south.

"That'll be a new courthouse when it's done."

Audrey nodded.

"When it's finished we'll be able to try criminals like Black Dog ourselves without having to send them to Sacramento."

Again, Audrey nodded.

"You'll be able to hang them too."

"Don't think some of us didn't want to do the honors anyhow. They killed one of my deputies and one of the bank tellers in the robbery."

"Black Dog's murdered a lot of people. Out here, no one would have blamed you if you'd strung him up," said Audrey.

"I know that. But it sets a bad precedent. You and I are supposed to represent the law. Taking matters into our own hands only undermines our position." In a way Audrey saw his point, but he was, deep down, a practical man. He really didn't care how blood-thirsty, cold-blooded murderers met their end, so long as they met it. Of course he didn't include himself in that. The man *he* had killed had had it coming hundreds of times over. To Audrey, George Custer had been every bit as evil as Black Dog. In the end, Audrey had only killed him when pushed to the edge. Some men might find it hypocritical that a man on the run for murder had dedicated a substantial portion of his life to hunting down murderers, but Audrey had no such qualms. Audrey had made his peace with God and he was convinced the Almighty had protected him all the years he'd been on the run. Instinctively his hand reached up and felt the silver crucifix he wore under his shirt.

The Sheriff led Audrey into the Pine City Tavern. It housed a bar, restaurant and casino. Several men nodded to the Sheriff respectfully as they made their way to a table. The proprietor saw to them personally.

"Put all this on my tab, Joe." He then motioned to Audrey. "This is Marshal Johnson. He's here to pick up Black Dog."

"Then his meal is on the house." He looked at Audrey and cursed Black Dog's name. "Just make sure he keeps his appointment with the gallows and with the devil." A while later, Audrey and the Sheriff had plates of beans in front of them. They were nearly done with their lunch when someone came bursting in so suddenly that the two law men reached for their guns.

"Fire, Sheriff! The city stage is on fire!"

"Then don't just stand there, Samuels! Get a bucket team going!" As they rushed out of the tavern, Audrey immediately caught the smell of smoke. The men of the town were rushing to gather buckets. A building on the west side of the town was blazing and sending up a black pillar of smoke. Above the shouts of the men sounding the alarm and the roar of the fire the sound of gunshots reached Audrey's ears. Four men came bursting out of the sheriff's office. Even from that distance, Audrey could see that the one in the lead was Black Dog. Audrey drew his pistols and blazed away. One of the men that had come to rescue Black Dog fell over clutching a bloody wound. The sheriff turned to see what was going on. When he saw the escape in progress, he pulled his own gun and started firing. Another one of Black Dog's rescuers fell dead, just as he was about to leap into his saddle. Black Dog and his final rescuer leapt onto waiting horses and high tailed it just as Audrey and the Sheriff came running up. Both lawmen had fired their pistols empty.

The Sheriff ran into his office while Audrey ran to his horse. Inside the office both deputies were dead. The two outlaws were getting farther and farther away. Audrey reached into the saddle bag and pulled out a rifle stock. He reached in again and pulled out a barrel which he connected to the stock. Finally, he pulled out a scope which he attached to the rifle. He loaded three bullets and worked the lever. The sheriff watched the whole process. Each moment the outlaws gained distance. Audrey brought the rifle up to his shoulder and aimed through the scope. The rifle barked. Black Dog's henchman fell from the saddle. Audrey worked the lever again and once more brought up the rifle. To the sheriff, the shot was impossible. The rifle barked again, and Black Dog went to his appointment with the devil a little early.

IV

Joseph Whitmore took a last drag on his cigar as his train pulled into New York Central Station. He had the private Pullman car all to himself. That was one of the benefits of owning fifty-one percent of the stock in the railroad company. A brief knock came at the door and a butler in a finely tailored suit entered the car.

"Excuse me, Mr. Whitmore. We have arrived and a carriage is waiting for you." Whitmore nodded and after stubbing out the butt of his cigar he rose to his feet. The butler helped him into his coat and handed him his top hat. Several local railroad executives and other rich businessmen were waiting for him on the platform. There was also the usual mix of politicians and reporters.

"Welcome to New York, Mr. Whitmore!" they chorused. Whitmore let out a silent grunt. He wasn't in New York on railroad business. He had several other enterprises going that were far more interesting to him. Whenever he was in New York, he seemed unable to escape the barrage of business men seeking his investments or of politicians seeking his financial backing. Of course he wasn't without protection. His personal assistant, David Lovejoy, climbed down from the Pullman and moved in between the multi-millionaire and the crowd.

"Gentlemen, Mr. Whitmore is quite busy this week. He has much business to take care of. Requests for an appointment may be made at the Fifth Avenue Hotel with Mr. Whitmore's secretaries." While Lovejoy held off the rabble, Whitmore made his way to the waiting carriage. He sighed relief when he had climbed inside and closed the curtains. A few moments later Lovejoy climbed in with him.

"To the hotel, sir?" he asked.

"No David, to the shipyard. I want to get down to business right away." Lovejoy gave instructions to the driver and they were off. Travelling through New York City by horse drawn carriage was not easy. It was the middle of the day and the streets were very crowded. Whitmore pulled the curtains back slightly and watched the brick and mortar buildings of the city as they rode past them.

"I wonder how the construction is coming in Franklin," he said. His construction firms had bid for the job of building the new Federal capital. He'd been outbid. The Federal government gave the contracts to the lowest bidder. Now they were paying for it in cost overruns and a construction schedule that was falling further and further behind.

I may not have done it for the cheapest price but by jingo I'd have done it right and on time!

"Are the new steam engines really as fast as I've heard?" asked Lovejoy. Whitmore allowed himself a smile.

"They're faster. If President Cleveland will authorize it, I will build the navy the fastest warships afloat. Nothing the Confederates or the French or even the British have will be able to match them."

"If Congress authorizes it."

Whitmore nodded. "I have friends in Congress who will see that it passes." He folded his hand into a fist. "The problem is, I shouldn't have to resort to cronyism to get the fool politicians to do what needs doing. This isn't about profit. It's about my nation being secure, and having a fast and powerful navy is one of the best ways to make it secure." Whitmore owned lots of stock in the railroads, but his industrial empire was built on shipbuilding and arms manufacturing.

It wasn't long before the carriage was completely bogged down in traffic. Outside a newspaper boy was hawking his papers.

"Extra! Extra! Read all about it! Spain tells Confederacy no deal on Cuba! CSA threatens war! Read all about it!" Wanting to find out the latest about the crisis, and looking for an excuse to stretch his legs, Whitmore opened the door of the coach and stepped out of the carriage. He handed the boy nickel and then hopped back into the carriage with the paper and without waiting for change. The boy waived his thanks and then went back to hawking his papers. Whitmore quickly read through the front page article.

"Well, what's the latest?"

"The Confederate President, John Marshall Stone, has asked the Confederate Congress for a declaration of war against Spain. They are expected to vote on the matter this week."

"What has President Cleveland said?"

"He has made no official statement as yet." Whitmore folded up the newspaper and put it aside in frustration. "It torments me to no end."

"What is that, sir?"

"I own factories, shipyards, foundries and a substantial amount of railroad. I, more than anyone, know the industrial power of this nation." He pointed out the window at the great mass of people walking the streets of New York City. "We have a great population to match our industrial might. We should be the most powerful and feared nation on earth! More powerful than Britain and France and certainly more powerful than the CSA! When we speak, nations should tremble. Instead we keep silent like a timid mouse as if the Confederate States were a cat that could devour us at any moment! Balderdash, I say!"

Lovejoy removed his spectacles and wiped them clean. He sat in thought, considering what Whitmore had said. One of the things Whitmore appreciated about Lovejoy was that he was not a yes man. As a multimillionaire, Whitmore often found it hard to find someone who would have the fortitude to openly disagree with him. Lovejoy was someone he could count on to honestly discuss matters. Lovejoy replaced his spectacles.

"What you say is true, sir. The problem with the United States is not our resources or potential. The problem is psychological. The Confederates not once but twice defeated us against what seemed overwhelming odds."

"We were defeated because we had fools for leaders!" interjected Whitmore.

"Granted, sir. But deserved or not, the Confederate States enjoy an aura of invincibility. Until that aura is removed, our defeats in the Wars of Rebellion will forever haunt our national consciousness."

Whitmore nodded. Lovejoy had a point. Whitmore then looked up suddenly at Lovejoy with fiery resolve in his eyes.

"Then we must make certain that the aura of invincibility surrounding the Confederacy is shattered. If Spain stands up to the Confederates, it will go a long way towards showing the people that we need not fear the CSA."

"What are you proposing, sir?"

"That the United States does everything it can in making sure that Spain has all the arms and materiel it needs to fight the Confederates. If Spain and the Confederacy go to war, it will be a great business opportunity for the arms industry— my arms industry. Whitmore cannons and rifles are the best in the world. What better way to show that fact than by having them used in battle against the CSA?"

"If President Cleveland is unwilling to even comment publically about the situation between the Confederate States and Spain, why would he consider providing military aid to the Spanish? Such a move would certainly not be well received by Richmond. It would be a very aggressive foreign policy decision."

"He'll agree. I will use all of my considerable influence to see to it that he does." He looked Lovejoy in the eye. "The Federal government is presently meeting here in New York, yes?" Lovejoy nodded. "Then I think that my inspection of the shipyards can wait. Have the driver take us to Wall Street." Lovejoy smiled a wry grin.

"Sir, I doubt that even you will be able to see the President on such short notice."

"There's one way to find out," said Whitmore.

At Lovejoy's command the driver turned the carriage around and headed for Wall Street. Congress had taken Federal Hall as its meeting place in New York City. It was a converted customs house that stood on the site of the original Federal Hall where George Washington had been sworn in as the first President of the United States of America. It was one of the few examples left in the city of classical architecture. Most government departments had secured buildings nearby. The President and most of his cabinet had their headquarters in the building across from Federal Hall.

Joseph Whitmore climbed out of his carriage and walked boldly up the stairs to the entrance of the building. David Lovejoy followed him. They were met by a blue uniformed policeman.

"May I help you, gentlemen?"

"Yes," said Whitmore. Rather than just come out and say he was there to demand an audience with President Cleveland, Whitmore decided he would have an easier time getting in to see the President's secretary. "I am Joseph Whitmore. I am here to meet with Mr. John Garrison."

"Are you expected, sir?"

"I have come on a matter of urgent business. If you will give him my name, I assure you he will see me." The policeman nodded.

"Wait here, gentlemen." The policeman stepped into the building. Several minutes went by and Whitmore grew restless.

"Patience, sir," said Lovejoy.

"I did not earn my fortune by being patient, David," said Whitmore. "I earned it by being the kind of man who knows what he wants and goes for it." Finally, just as Whitmore was about to enter the building himself to see what was taking so long, the policeman emerged followed by John Garrison. Whitmore had only met the President's secretary a couple of times but he recognized him immediately.

"Ah, my dear Mr. Garrison!"

"Mr. Whitmore. To what do we owe this honor?"

"I have come to speak with the President on a matter of urgent business."

The policeman's eyes rose in interest. Garrison smiled an appeasing smile.

"I'm sorry sir, but I'm afraid that the President is not here. He left on a train this morning bound for Philadelphia. He's not expected back until the day after tomorrow. I'd be happy to schedule you an appointment."

"Yes, do that. I'm staying at the Fifth Avenue Hotel as usual. When you have scheduled the time, I may be reached there."

"What shall I tell the President is the nature of this meeting?"

"Tell him it involves the national security of the United States."

Garrison looked confused but nodded all the same.

"Very well, sir. Is there anything else I can help you with today?"

"Yes. Where may I find the Spanish embassy?"

With the question, the President's secretary received the first clue as to what the multimillionaire wanted to meet with the President about. The answer to the question gave Whitmore a clue as to where the President was and what he was doing. It was an encouraging thought.

"The Spanish embassy is located in Philadelphia."

"Is it?" said Whitmore. "It would seem I have come to the wrong city." He then tipped his hat to the secretary and the policeman. "I will see you soon, gentlemen." Whitmore made his way back to the carriage flanked by Lovejoy. A few moments later they were once again bound for the shipyards.

V

Lance Corporal Jefferson Case cursed the day that he'd ever been assigned to Fort Stick and Ship Island. He had imagined a lot of things when he'd joined the Confederate States Marine Corps. What he was going through at that moment, had not been one of them. He swatted a mosquito that had landed on his neck. He winced in pain. His fair complexion didn't take well to the sun and he'd been on outdoor lookout duty on a very regular basis. As a result, he was extremely sun burned. When he pulled his hand away there was a spot of blood on it.

Little devil's been eating on me. Not for the first time he lamented that Ship Island had about a billion mosquitos. With a sigh he raised his binoculars and dutifully scanned the horizon for what seemed like the hundredth time that day. The open sea to the south was clear. Case swung his gaze back towards the south and the Mississippi coast. Through his binoculars he could just make out the coastline. Off to his right was the port of Biloxi, to his left was Gulfport. Off to the west he spotted a plume of smoke. It was a civilian passenger ship, most likely traveling from New Orleans to Mobile. Such ships passed through the Mississippi sound on a regular basis.

"All clear, Corporal?"

Case turned to see Captain Fordice.

"Yes, sir. Just a small civilian transport off to the west. I'm keeping a sharp eye out for intruders though."

"There hasn't been any Yankee ships around here for years," said Fordice. "They know the Gulf of Mexico is our pond. They know better than to come trespassing." Case looked at the massive cannons sitting atop the fort. Anyone who came along looking for trouble would get a nasty welcome, but it was not Yankees he was talking about.

"After what happened to the Mississippi in Havana, I'm honestly more worried about the Spanish."

Fordice smiled.

"I wouldn't worry too much, Corporal. I don't think the Spanish navy is going to show up anytime soon to attack Gulf Port or Biloxi." His smile turned savage. "The same can't be said about our navy and the lovely city of Havana. Richmond could decide this week whether or not to declare war on Spain." Case let out a sigh.

"Take heart, Corporal. We may well find ourselves stationed in beautiful Cuba in the near future. I assure you, you will find it an improvement over this place." With that, Corporal Case wholeheartedly agreed. He'd heard from fellow marines and sailors about how beautiful the island was, how good its tobacco was, and most of all about how beautiful the women were.

That's the best reason I've heard for declaring war on Spain! Suddenly, he felt a familiar sting on the back of his neck. Instinctively he slapped the offending mosquito. Once again he winced in pain and just barely stifled a cry. Captain Fordice looked him over. Case's neck wasn't just red, it was blistered almost to the point of looking like it had been exposed to fire. His hands and face were also very much sunburned.

"Your hide's as cooked as a thanksgiving turkey," said Fordice. "You look like a red Indian. I'm gonna send someone to relieve you and I want you to go see doc right now." Case's heart skipped a beat at the idea of visiting a doctor, but he wasn't about to argue with the Captain. He said the only thing he could.

"Yes, sir." As the Captain headed back down the stairs to the interior of the fort, Case suppressed the shudder that went up his spine. He reflected that on the bright side it was good to have a commanding officer that cared about the wellbeing of his men. He'd stayed away from doctors all his life. His father had been a veteran of the War of 1869. The surgeons had taken his arm. His father had cursed doctors all his days since and constantly admonished his son.

All they do is make things worse! Case had therefore grown up with a natural aversion to doctors. His Latrophobia meant when he got injured he took care of it himself. When he got sick he toughed it out. His relief showed up a few minutes later. Case wasn't sorry to get off watch duty early. The private that had come to take his place didn't look happy about suddenly finding himself on it. Case handed him the binoculars and headed down into the interior of Fort Stick. The infirmary was a small brick room in the side of the fort. He found the door open but knocked on it as he entered. Dr. Andrew Richardson was the fort's attending physician and surgeon. He was younger than most of the doctors Case had seen in his life. Richardson looked to be about thirty and had a big bushy mustache. He wore a gray Confederate Army uniform. Only its black trim identified him as a member of the medical branch. He had a single star on his collar—the rank insignia of a Major.

"What can I do for you, Corporal?"

"I was ordered to report to you by the Captain, sir."

"Were you? Well, have seat." The doctor finished putting various bottles into a cupboard on the wall. He turned and looked at Case. "How long have you been stationed here?"

"About six months, sir."

"Strange, I don't think I've seen you before."

And you wouldn't be seeing me now if I wasn't under orders. "I don't get sick very often, sir."

"Well you're here now so it must be something serious." Case motioned to his neck. Richardson's eyes grew wide when he saw it. "That's just about the worst sunburn I've ever seen. Take off your hat." Case removed his kepi revealing the shock of red hair that covered his head. "Yeah, that explains it. You're a fair complected red head. One of those poor fellas who's skin just won't tan. Where are you from?"

"Norfolk Virginia, sir. I had problems with sunburn back home but never this bad."

"It's all the guard duty and watch duty during the day," said Richardson. "You're spending a lot of time in the sun and your skin can't handle it." He lifted Case's chin and stared at his face. "Your face is pretty bad too." Case held up his hands. The tops of them were blood red. Richardson examined them the turned around and grabbed his writing pad and ink pen. "Alright Corporal, here's what we're going to do. From now on I want you to take every precaution to protect yourself from the sun. When do you get to go ashore again?"

"Four days, sir."

"When you go ashore I want you to buy a new hat and pair of gloves in Biloxi. Get a felt hat with a big brim. Until then I want you to make a cloth drape and let it hang from the back of your kepi over your neck. The French forces I served with in Mexico did that, and it did a very good job of shielding them from the sun. This will give it a chance to heal up. You can use a cool wet compress to try and ease the pain." Case nodded.

"Thank you, sir."

"You're welcome. I want to see you again in a week and don't wait this long to see me the next time there's a problem."

"Yes, sir." Case took his leave of the doctor. He went straight to the barracks and used an old hand towel to make the drape. When he put his kepi on with the drape he thought he looked ridiculous but when he went back outdoors he noticed an instant difference in the amount of pain he felt on his neck. Within a few days his neck had healed considerably.

Runs were made to the island by steamboat every Friday and Monday to bring in food and supplies as well as rotate members of the garrison for weekend leave. After helping unload the steamboat and carry the cargo from the docks to the fort, Case finally climbed up the gangplank and took his place on the steamboat. It had been a month since he had last been ashore. Five other Marines also crowded onto the boat—four privates and a sergeant.

"How's the neck, Corporal?" The familiar voice startled Case. He turned to see Doctor Richardson.

Case reached up and felt his neck under the drape that hung from his kepi. It was still rough and leathery but virtually all the pain was gone.

"It's much better sir, thank you." The boat's single smoke stack started belching smoke as the steam engine rumbled to life. Case felt the deck vibrate under his feet. The boat chugged away from the docks. Case then headed to the front of the boat and stood at the bow. He breathed in the salty sea air as the wind blew in his face. He found it very refreshing. The shore started growing near very quickly. The boat's birth was just west of Biloxi. When Case finally made it ashore he wanted to kiss the ground.

I hate that island. He slung his duffle bag over his shoulder and started walking down the beach towards Biloxi. To his left he passed several plantation houses that faced the water. Compared to some that he'd seen when he'd been stationed in South Carolina they weren't very big. Off to his left he passed a negro mason working on a small brick wall that surrounded a plantation house quite a bit larger than the others. The black looked to be in his forties. He was at least twenty years older than Case. Case called to him.

"Hey boy, can you tell me a good place to buy a hat?" The negro stopped his work and looked over at Case. Case watched the negro take in his uniform. The black man reached up with a mostly mortar covered hand and wiped sweat from his forehead with its less dirty back.

"Well suh, dat depend on wat kine o hat you won't. Mister Jones, he own a nice clothin' sto' jus pass da lite house. He sell some mighty fine hats suh but deys' pretty 'spensive." The black man then hesitated a moment as if unsure whether to say more. He did. "If in you won'ts a mighty good hat wit a fare price though, and you don't mine gittin one from a free nigga you's can git one from Miss Ellie. She make good hats suh and clothes too suh."

"Where can a find Miss Ellie?"

"She sets up a stand on da beach jus a ways further down. Keep goin, you see her befo' you gets to da lite house."

"What's your name, boy?"

"I's Jeremias, suh."

"Well Jeremias, thank you kindly. You have a good day."

"You too, suh."

Case continued down the road that ran along the beach front. When he reached a point where it intersected with a road that headed inland to the north, he found a make shift wooden stand with a couple of wooden tables and racks. A beautiful young negro woman, probably Case's age or younger was busy folding clothes. The cream and coffee color of her smooth skin showed that she was a mulatto. In spite of himself and everything he'd ever been taught and raised with, his heart started racing and he broke into a sweat even though there was a light cool ocean breeze blowing from the sea.

She's beautiful... Catching his breath he started looking at the merchandise. There were various articles of common clothing laid out, mostly shirts and pants made out of cotton and wool. There were also quite a number of felt hats. They weren't the fanciest hats he'd ever seen, but they looked well made. Case spotted a black one with a large brim that would go well with his uniform. Suddenly the woman noticed him. She was visibly startled when she saw a uniformed white man standing by her stand.

"You must be Miss Ellie," he said in his friendliest tone. "Jeremias told me that you would be willing to sell me a good hat."

"Yes suh," she said, relief flooding her voice. The mention of Jeremias seemed to ease her apprehension.

Case pointed at the black felt he had eyed and asked, "How much?"

"A dollar twenty-five, sir." Case raised an eyebrow. Her speech contained only a slight trace of the uneducated dialect that was common to the negroes of the CSA. It only served to heighten the attraction he felt for her. Had she spoken with the harsh intonations of slavery it might have snapped him back to reality. He was a white man and she was—at least half black. The laws of culture, society and the State itself said that they were forbidden to be together. Such a thing constituted the highest form of social and cultural derision (although Ellie's light colored skin showed that somewhere in the not-too-distant past a slave master had had no compunctions about lying with one of his female slaves). If Case's mother ever knew that he'd been sweet on a mulatto girl she'd disown him. His daddy would probably shoot him. Case was suddenly thankful that a man's thoughts were his own. Only in the fantasy world of his mind could he possess her. In the reality of the world they lived in, he'd have to be content with that. He pulled out a gray-back and a half dollar coin and handed them to her. Then without waiting for change, he put the black felt hat on his head and walked away.

Biloxi was a beautiful and quaint little port city. Almost the entire beach front was lined with houses. There were a few docks, but all the larger ships made port at Gulf Port to the west. Having secured his hat, Case decided to get himself some decent food. As he went inland he passed several shops and other establishments. Many of the buildings were decked out in red and white patriotic bunting. The Blood Stained Banner or the Confederate Battle Flag flew from nearly every structure. Case found that he was hardly the only uniformed man in town. Several other marines, and soldiers from the nearby Army garrison were also in town as were quite a few Confederate sailors. Men tipped their hats to him and ladies curtsied. Young boys pointed at him excitedly. Slaves and other negroes likewise tipped their hats or nodded respectfully. One thing that could be said about the Confederacy was that it appreciated its men in uniform.

At last he found a restaurant called Randall's. It had a large wooden porch where tables sat covered by umbrellas. A negro in a white suit greeted him as he approached.

"Hello suh! Just one today? Right dis way suh!" The negro led Case to a table. "Can I git you sumthin col' to drink suh?"

"I'll have some sweet tea."

"Yes suh! Some sweet tea." The negro hurried off. A fantastic series of aromas was coming out of the building. Case found his mouth watering. He'd had almost nothing but hard tack and beans for weeks. The negro returned a few moments later with a tall glass of tea and a small dish filled with something cheesy. Whereas Case's mouth had been watering, now he was positively on the verge of drooling.

"Here's yo' tea suh. And dis is Massa Randall's specialty. He give all customers a little samplin'." Case dug into it like a starving man. It was some sort of cheese and vegetable casserole. He subsequently ordered a full serving of it, along with some grilled red snapper. After devouring the meal, he felt fuller than he had in a long while. He dreaded the bill. Marine Lance Corporals didn't get paid much. He was pleasantly surprised when the negro laid down the bill. The price was only half what he'd expected from the prices on the menu.

"Mr. Randall, suh, he say soldiers and sailors they only pay half, suh."

"Well you tell him I much appreciate it," said Case. "And tell him it was good. Best I've ever eaten as a matter of fact."

"Thank you, suh, I will suh."

Case pulled out a nickel and set it on the table. When the negro saw the coin bearing the image of John C Calhoun he smiled a big white toothed grin.

"Thank you again, suh."

After leaving, Case made his way back down to the beach. Off to the west the sky was red. The sun was getting low in the sky. Suddenly Case found himself, almost uncontrollably thinking about Miss Ellie. No matter how he tried, he couldn't get the Mulatto girl off of his mind.

She was so beautiful… He tried his best to resist the urge to take a walk out to where her stand was and talk with her. Nothing good could come from it, of that he was certain. In fact she'd probably misjudge his intentions. White men were usually interested in only one thing when it came to good looking Mulatto women. He made his mind up to forget her. As he turned to walk away from the beach, however, he found himself walking inexplicably toward the west and Miss Ellies stand. As he drew near, he saw a cart that was hitched to a horse. Ellie had apparently loaded up her stand for the day. As he got closer, he realized that she was not alone. Three men seemed to be giving her a hard time.

"I'm telling you missy, you don't want to set up here no more," said one of the men. "Niggers ain't got no business selling to white folks, you understand?"

Ellie didn't answer him. She did her best not to look at him, and tried to load the last of her merchandise on the cart.

"You answer me when I talk to you, wench!" said the man and grabbed Ellie.

"You let me go!" she said. "I'm free! And I can do business here just like anyone else."

"You're gonna learn to watch that mouth of yours, nigger!" he slapped her and Ellie fell to the ground. The man had hardly landed his blow, when Case bull charged into him knocking him to the ground. They went down hard into the sand. Case wasted no time in pounding away at is face. He landed two or three blows before one of the fellow's friends grabbed him from behind by the throat. The other started kicking and punching Case with everything he had. Case brought his foot up and kicked the man between the legs. He went down, and wouldn't be getting up anytime soon. Case then slammed the back of his head into the one that was holding him by the throat. The man fell backwards with a busted and bloody nose. Case gasped for oxygen. He came around in a round house punch and landed a blow that knocked the man back a couple of yards. He, too, wouldn't be getting up anytime soon. Only a moment later, the man that had first attacked Ellie came crashing into him. Now Case was on the ground and being pounded away at. Suddenly Ellie leapt on Case's attacker from behind.

"Get off me you black witch!" he said and back handed her, knocking her off of him. In that moment, Case flung a handful of sand into his face. He swore. And punched Case right in the solar plexus knocking all the air out of him. He punched him one more time in the face for good measure and then stumbled to his feet trying in vain to get the sand out of his eyes. Ellie had risen to her own feet, and grabbed a heavy wooden plank that was part of her clothing stand. With all of her might she swung the board and hit the man upside the head, knocking him cold.

She made her way over to Case who had taken a terrible beating. He lay sprawled out on the sand half unconscious. Somehow, she forced him to his feet and laid him down on the back of her wagon.

Case awoke to bright sunshine, coming through a window. His head was pounding, but he was in a comfortable bed. To his left he saw Ellie. She was asleep in wooden chair by the side of his bed, with a wash rag in her hand.

She's been watching over me all night... He tried to get up, but as soon as he did, intense pain shot through his ribs. He let out a yelp, and Ellie shook herself awake.

"Don't you be trying to get up, you hear?" she spoke with a tone of authority. "You took a beating last night." She stood, dipped the rag in water, rung it out and then dabbed his forehead. "I do appreciate you coming to help me," she said.

49

"My pleasure…Miss Ellie."

"You remember my name…" she said and a flush came up in her coffee colored cheeks. She rose again and walked away for a couple of minutes before returning to his side. "I'm lucky you came along," she said. "How did you come to be back near my stand?"

"I was there to see you again…" he said. *I must have hit my head harder than I thought. I'm just spilling my guts here.*

She rose so hurriedly that he thought he'd scared her off. But suddenly, he heard the sound of a tea pot whistling. Now he did force himself to sit up in the bed, painful though it was. She'd removed his uniform coat and shirt in the night. His ribs were bruised a nasty black and blue color. Ellie returned a minute or so later with a bowl of broth. She sat back down in her chair. She would have spoon fed him but he didn't want to seem quite that helpless. He took the bowl and sipped at the hot broth. It felt good going down. As he finished it, he caught her out of the corner of his eye. She was looking at him, much the same way he'd looked at her the day before. While his heart soared, his mind warned him of the danger, the sadness, the hopelessness and the pain that waited in his future if he tried to give his heart what it wanted.

"Miss Ellie, thank you for your kindness. But I'm afraid I really must go. If I don't report in by a certain time today, I'm afraid I will be in a lot of trouble that will be minor compared to last night." She nodded and helped him to his feet. He hurt horribly, but he reckoned he'd live.

"Can I at least know my rescuer's name?"

He smiled at her. "Case, ma'am. Jefferson Case."

She smiled back at him. "Well Mr. Case, I am eternally grateful for your kind assistance. I do hope I will see you again."

"Jeff, Ma'am," he said. "Call me Jeff."

She smiled broader and looked up into his eyes. "Only if you call me, Ellie,"

Suddenly, almost magnetically and uncontrollably, they were drawn to one another. Case took her in his arms and their lips met in a passionate kiss. For better or for worse, his heart had beaten his head.

VI

Joshua Winslow let out a yawn as he put down his book. Gray's Anatomy was not easy reading. He rolled his neck to try and get the crick out of it. He'd never been able to sleep on a train and this trip had been no different. He'd tossed and turned all night in his Pullman's berth. He pulled out his pocket watch.

8:09 AM...I wonder if we'll arrive on time? He seriously doubted it. He'd made the train trip from Chicago to Lancaster several times now (and vice versa) and it had never once arrived on time. Sighing he picked the textbook back up. The racket and jouncing of the train as it moved along the track made it hard to concentrate, but it was by far not the only distraction. Across the aisle to his right, a white man and his wife were gawking at him. He wasn't sure if it was because they'd never seen a black man before or if they had never seen a black man in nice clothes on a train before. In any event, it bothered him. *Of course,* he reflected *it could be worse.* He'd had other passengers demand to be moved to another car because they did not fancy riding in one with a black man. It was as if his very presence somehow injured or insulted them. More than once he'd been denied passage on a train, though usually he was able to buy his way through most troubles. Sighing again, he resolutely went back to his reading.

A while later the steward came into the train car with a breakfast cart. Going from seat to seat he said things like "What will you have for breakfast sir...what can I get you mam..." The porter then intentionally passed up Joshua and proceeded to serve every other passenger in the car. When he finally stopped in front of Joshua he said, "What'll ya have Sambo?" Suppressing a grunt, Joshua put down his book and stared at the cart. He took a bowl of chowder and a muffin with a cup of coffee.

He asked the steward, "What time are we expected to arrive in Lancaster?"

With an irritated look the steward said, "Between ten and eleven o'clock."

Joshua nodded. If they arrived at ten o'clock they would only be about an hour late, which was unusually proficient for the railroad. Joshua put his book aside and started to eat his breakfast. He glanced out of the window to his right at the passing countryside. The beautiful green plains stretched as far as the eye could see. At regular intervals they would pass farms surrounded by fields of corn. They were definitely in Nebraska.

Joshua finished his breakfast. Instead of going back to the medical textbook he pulled out a copy of the Des Moines Register he had picked up when they passed through Iowa. WAR IMMINENT: CSA ISSUES DEADLINE FOR SPAIN TO CEDE CUBA. PRESIDENT CLEVELAND VOWS TO KEEP U.S. OUT OF CONFLICT. Joshua let out a sigh. Any expansion of the CSA also meant an expansion of slavery.

Of all the millions of negroes in bondage or abject poverty on this continent, how did I come to be what I am? To have the opportunities I have? His mother had always said it was by God's grace. Another article warned of another potential war further west, between the Mormon nation of Deseret and the Republic of California. Folding up the newspaper in disgust, he pulled his textbook back out.

At exactly ten-thirty the train pulled into the station in Lancaster Nebraska. The station was large and brand new. The state capital of Nebraska had boomed in size ever since the main line of the US transcontinental railroad had been re-routed through Nebraska in the aftermath of the Second War of Rebellion.

Joshua hefted his own bags and made his way out of the train car. His father was waiting for him on the platform.

"There's my boy!" Joshua dropped his bag and embraced his father. Jethro Winslow was a fifty-nine year old version his son—with the exception of Joshua's eyes. Joshua had inherited his slanted eyes from his Indian mother. "Let me help you with those…" said Jethro.

"I have it Father…" He again hefted his bags and he and his father made their way out of the station. As usual, they drew the looks of the white people that they passed. There were hardly any negroes in Nebraska and they stood out. Joshua stood out all the more for because of his formal clothes. Whereas Jethro was dressed in the flannel shirt and overalls of a farmer, his son wore a suit. Jethro's wagon was hitched not far from the train station. Another black man sat in the back. He was in his late thirties.

"Hello Obadiah!" said Joshua. The farm hand hopped down from the wagon and helped Joshua put his bags in the back. Obadiah then stared at him and smiled a smile that was missing a couple of teeth. He then melodramatically made as if to straighten the lapels of Joshua's coat. He turned to Jethro. "Look at de fancy nigga in the suit." Joshua made as if to knock his block off. He had grown up with Obadiah teasing him. Since Joshua had gone off to medical school the good natured teasing had only increased—at least when he made it home for end of the semester breaks. All teasing aside, however, Obadiah, like Joshua's parents, was immensely proud of him. Jethro took his place in the driver's seat, flicked the reins and the wagon headed off drawn by a farm horse.

"So how is school going, son?"

"Fantastic father! This past semester we got to dissect some actual cadavers."

"Cad what?" asked Obadiah.

"Cadavers," replied Joshua. "Bodies…human bodies." Obadiah looked over to Jethro with a look of disgust that he tried to hide from Joshua.

Ever so tactfully Jethro said, "I wouldn't share that with your mother son. It might be a little much for her to handle." Joshua nodded.

53

Disgusted though he was, the idea of dissecting a human body held a certain horrid fascination for Obadiah. He couldn't help prying a little deeper.

"Where do de' bodies come from?"

"A few people donate their bodies to science but not many. We get most of our specimens from state prisons. They let us take the bodies of convicted murderers that have been executed."

The mention of executions caused Jethro's mind to flash back to the Second War of Rebellion. He thought of the Mormon traitors he'd been ordered to hang. That memory immediately led to some others from the same time period that he wished to heaven he could forget but that would just not go away. He'd never shared with his son or with anyone else for that matter, much of what he had experienced in the war.

For the next three hours, Joshua regaled them with information about muscles, hearts, skeletons, kidneys, the endocrine system and a variety of other things that turned their stomachs just to hear about.

At least the boy is taking advantage of the opportunity he's been given, thought Jethro. When the wagon finally turned off the main road onto the approach to the Winslow's farm, Joshua breathed in the sweet smell of home. As he looked towards the field, he spotted his mother picking corn. When she spotted the wagon coming up the drive, she dropped her basket and ran towards them. Joshua leapt from the wagon and ran to meet her. He towered over her. He was as tall as his father. His mother pulled him down to her and held him tightly. She kissed him several times all over his face.

"Momma!"

"Don't smother the boy Lilia!" said Jethro with a laugh.

"I am forced to go without my son for months on end and when I finally get him back for a week you say don't smother him." Joshua hugged his mother tightly.

"I missed you too Momma." Jethro reflected that amongst his wife's people everyone one was one big immediate family. All generations lived together in the tribe.

The notion of a young man leaving his family and going off into the world was foreign to her. More than once he'd had to sit up in bed with her at night, consoling and reassuring her. The gold they had...*obtained*...at the end of the Second War of Rebellion had allowed them to buy their own land and start their farm. It had also allowed them to give their son a chance at a life that neither of them had ever had. A life that very few negroes on the North American continent could ever even dream of.

"Well let's get in the house," said Lilia. "I've got lunch waiting." Inside she had prepared bread, corn and green beans. Joshua scarfed it up. "Look how lean you are!" said Lilia to her son. "Aren't they feeding you enough?" Joshua smiled.

"They feed me fine Momma."

"Looks to me like a little farm work would do him some good," said Jethro to Obadiah. After finishing lunch, Joshua went upstairs to his room. He came back down a few minutes later dressed in some of his old farm clothes and immediately went outside to work alongside his father. He'd been in medical school for three years, but he still hadn't forgotten how to work on a farm or what an honest day's work was. He helped pick corn. He cleaned out the stables. He chopped wood. He was so happy to be home that the time flew by. As the sun was getting low in the sky, Joshua hefted the axe and chopped what must have been the one-hundredth piece of wood. Suddenly he felt his father's hand on his shoulder.

"That's enough for today son. You've done a day's work in five hours. Let's go eat supper and visit for a while." Joshua nodded and followed his father back to the farm house. The delicious aroma of a cooked pork roast reached Joshua's nose and his mouth started to water. Obadiah was already at the table.

"Good thing you showed up. I's gone eat it all fo myself." After dinner they sat in the living room around the fireplace while Jethro read from the Bible for the family devotion. It had always bothered Joshua's mother that there was no Baptist church (or any other church for that matter) for them to attend. The nearest Baptist church was over twenty miles away and the all white congregation had made it plain to Jethro and Lilia over twenty-five years earlier that they weren't welcome there. They had to be content with family devotions. If there were ever enough negroes in that part of Nebraska to form a congregation, Jethro and Lilia were willing to invest their own money in starting a church. For the present, and for the past twenty-five years it had just been them. After the devotion time, they just sat around the living room, basking in the soft glow of the fire and talking.

Taking her son's hands in her own, Lilia said, "Now my son, tell us what you have been learning."

Much to Jethro's relief, Joshua did not begin talking about organs and other aspects of anatomy. He certainly didn't talk about dissecting bodies. What he did do—at length—was tell them about all the different types of medicines he was learning about. In particular he told them about a substance known as Salicin which was extracted from Willow bark. In its refined form it would dull pain and even reduce fever.

"Another very interesting medicine is cocaine," said Joshua. "It is derived from the Coca plant. It's excellent for toothaches." Obadiah fell asleep in his spot in the corner of the room very quickly. As proud as he was of his son, Jethro almost fell asleep himself. When Joshua started talking about the effectiveness of iodine in treating cuts he did fall asleep, happy to have his boy home, if only for a little while.

VII

Former Confederate President Thomas Jonathan Jackson sat in his private railroad car reading his Bible. Lifting his head, he turned to look out the window at the passing trees before turning back to finish reading one last passage. After closing the Bible he rose to his feet and carefully made his way to the sink. At seventy one years old, he was no longer as steady on his feet as he once was and the jouncing train didn't do wonders for his balance. He pumped himself a glass of water and drank it down, wishing it was ice cold lemonade instead of bland lukewarm water from a tank. Suddenly a knock came at the door.

"Come," said Jackson. His assistant Sandie Pendleton entered the room. At fifty-five, Pendleton's hair was closer to the color of Jackson's white mane, than to the blond hair Jackson had known from Pendleton's youth. He'd been little more than a boy when Jackson had asked him to join his staff during the War for Confederate Independence thirty-five years earlier. He had subsequently served as Jackson's chief of staff for the ten years of his Presidency and had continued to serve him in the fifteen years since he'd left office

Where has the time gone?

"I'm sorry to disturb you, Mr. President, but we'll be pulling into Atlanta shortly."

"Sandie, I've told you not to call me that. I haven't been President for a long time and these past fifteen years I've been quite happy to be rid of the job. So call me Thomas."

"I don't know that I could ever get used to that, sir," replied Pendleton. The train suddenly started to break. Jackson just barely managed to catch himself and not lose his balance. The view of green trees outside the windows had been replaced with the sprawling brick buildings of Atlanta. As they neared the grand central train station, they could see and hear the crowds that were waiting.

As usual, word of my arrival has stirred up a hornet's nest, thought Jackson.

"It looks like a pretty nasty crowd out there, sir. Should I call the guards so they can get you off the train and out of here quickly?"

"Sandie, you know I've never flinched. I faced the Yankees on Henry House Hill, and I will face this crowd." Sandie nodded. He helped Jackson put on his black coat, handed him his cane and then opened the back door of the railroad car so that the former President could walk out onto the small open deck at the rear of the car. Since Jackson's car was the last in the train, he immediately came into view of the crowd. At first the cries that met him were so enthusiastic he thought Pendleton might have misjudged the crowd.

"Stonewall! Stonewall! Stonewall!" Most of the men Pendleton's age and older, who were veterans of the War of Confederate Independence and the War of 1869, loved him and revered him along with Robert E Lee and Jefferson Davis for helping to lead the Confederacy to victory in not one, but two wars. In their eyes he could do no wrong—even if they thought he'd become eccentric in his old age. To many other people however…

"Get out of Atlanta, nigger lover!"

"Go to hell you miserable Black Republican!"

"You're a traitor to the White Man!" Jackson let the insults and curses wash over him like a tide. The first time something like this had happened, Jackson had had to prevent Pendleton from drawing his pistol in rage that such people would dare to say such things to the great Stonewall. Now, though, Pendleton had become as used to it as Jackson. Some of the older veterans in the crowd, however, were not content to allow the insult to their great hero's honor go unchallenged. A brawl quickly erupted between the veterans and the firebrands. Though older by decades, the veterans gave several of the younger troublemakers a good thrashing. More than one of the hecklers was hit over the head with a cane. After a few moments the tussle grew so bad that Jackson thought that the crowd was on the verge of a full-fledged riot.

I don't want anyone hurt because of me. "Enough!" he roared as loudly and harshly as if ordering an army regiment to halt. "If my years of service to this nation has not proven my loyalty, and earned me the right to speak my mind about what is best for our country, then it is you who are acting like tyrannical Black Republicans."

"You want to let the niggers loose!" came a call from a young white man that, from the look of his shabby clothes, was not wealthy enough to own a single slave, nor was he ever likely to be. Jackson drew a deep breath then continued to address the crowd.

"Many of you have judged me not by my own words, but by what others have said and written about me. If you want to know the truth about what I believe and why, then come and hear me speak tonight—then judge me! The Confederate States are a free country. If you disagree with me then you can let your voice be heard with your vote—but at least hear me first, unless you are afraid!" The crowd stood there in silence.

Suddenly an old veteran cried out "You tell em Stonewall!" Suddenly the crowd started to part. Collin Hurston, the mayor of Atlanta approached the railroad car flanked by several policemen who began to disperse the crowd.

"Welcome to Atlanta, Mr. President, it is an honor to have you in our fair city."

"Thank you," said Jackson.

"Won't you allow me to escort you to your hotel?" Jackson nodded. He turned to his aid.

"Mr. Pendleton, if you will see to everything, I will ride with the mayor."

Pendleton looked uneasy at having Jackson out of his sight, but he said, "Yes, sir."

The mayor headed back the way he had come. Jackson followed after him as quickly as he could. A fine black carriage was waiting for them out front. As soon as they entered the coach and the doors were shut the Mayor exploded.

"I sent you a wire asking you not to come here!" said Hurston. Jackson fixed him with an icy cold glare from which the mayor recoiled.

"As I informed the men waiting for me on the railroad platform, this is a free country. I will go where I will. And I will caution you, sir, not to take that tone with me again."

"Sir, when you were in Chattanooga this past week you caused a riot!"

"No sir," said Jackson. "Fools such as the ones I just encountered started a riot. I did but speak what I feel to be the truth."

"That we should let the niggers go?"

"That slavery has outlived its usefulness and that it has long since gone from being an institution beneficial to us, to one that weighs us down and hurts us. It may even prove disastrous for us if something is not done."

"As I recall, Mr. President, you tried to do something about it when you were in office. You nearly tore the nation apart." What Hurston said was not an understatement. Jackson had inherited the Presidency after Robert E. Lee's death at the end of the War of 1869. He had finished out Lee's term quietly, spending most of it trying to fully secure the Confederacy's borders and trying to incorporate the newly acquired territories. In 1873 the Supreme Court of the Confederate States had ruled that it was constitutional for him to run for a six year term of his own. Like Jefferson Davis and Robert E. Lee before him, Jackson had received every single electoral vote. But then he started trying to deal with the slavery issue. At first he managed to get a few of his measures passed. But when it had become clear that he was trying to hasten the end of slavery itself, his Presidency turned into a nightmare. At one point South Carolina threatened to secede from the Confederacy, and over a third of Congress tried to have him impeached. Newspapers across the South had called him all manner of names. The six years of his own Presidency were six of the most miserable in his life.

"I tried to do what I felt was best for the country. What I still feel is best for the country." In the years since he left the Presidential office, Jackson had continued advocating something that was extremely unpopular and yet in his opinion vitally essential to the security and future of the Confederate States: the gradual, compensated emancipation of the negro.

The carriage came to a halt in front of the Theodore Warren Hotel. Jackson cautiously let himself out. Hurston called after him.

"Just be warned sir, there are a lot of people in this city who disagree with you and your views vehemently. I will not be responsible for any riots that might ensue." Jackson turned his back to him and walked into the hotel, leaning on his cane for support. The former President of the CSA was shown immediately to the Presidential Suite. Pendleton and the rest of Jackson's staff arrived shortly thereafter. They carried Jackson's things up to the suite. The Theodore Warren was the newest and most luxurious hotel in Atlanta. Jackson sat himself down at the fine mahogany desk in the parlor and reviewed his notes. In his younger days he'd been a military man of few words. Having the mantle of the Presidency thrust upon him had forced him to adapt. It had changed him in so many ways. A few hours later, Pendleton came into the parlor.

"It's time sir." Jackson removed his spectacles, gathered his notes and rose to leave. The Gladstone Theater was another of Atlanta's newest and most impressive buildings. It had an auditorium that could seat several hundred. The city had boomed in recent years, becoming one of the CSA's largest centers of industry. Jackson wished more cities in the CSA had followed Atlanta's lead. The Confederate States were still incapable of meeting their own needs for manufactured goods. Because of the perceived constant threat of the United States, the vast majority of the industry the CSA did have was geared towards arms manufacturing.

Large crowds waited outside the theater. Jackson's carriage turned down a side street and came to the back of the building so he could enter from the rear entrance.

The Confederate anti-slavery movement bore little to no resemblance to the abolitionist movements of other countries. Abolitionists of the outside world made their arguments on the idea that slavery was evil and inhuman. But the ideas of white-supremacy and negro inferiority were so ingrained in the mindset of the Confederacy, that such arguments were at best doomed to fall on deaf ears and at worst counter-productive. The Confederate anti-slavery movement, such as it was, was not motivated so much by conscience, as it was by the desire of rich men to preserve their wealth. Many believed that the Confederate cotton industry was on the verge of collapse. Thanks to boll weevil infestations, soil depletion, competition from other cotton producing regions like India and to foreign markets hostile to slavery, many plantations were running in the red and many more just breaking even. In a twist of irony, the main proponents of ending slavery were wealthy, slave owning planters who'd begun to see their profits and fortunes sink because of the declining cotton market and the ever decreasing value of their slaves. Those planters wanted an emancipation program where the Confederate government would pay them massive amounts of money to free their slaves, so that they could subsequently invest their new found capital in more profitable ventures—like industry. As such the Confederate antislavery coalition went by the misleading name of "the Confederate Society for Prosperity and Industrialization."

In the 1870s and 1880s Confederate "abolitionists" had been little more than mocked and ridiculed. Since 1890, however, many people had begun to take them more seriously, and more and more rich planters, threatened with the loss of their fortunes, were getting on board.

Opposing them was a powerful coalition of people who wanted slavery kept in place. Among them were a minority of planters whose plantations were still doing well, and also people who believed that keeping the negro in chains was a matter of moral principle. They argued that the negro was by nature inferior to the White man and that the master / slave relationship was the only proper relationship between the two races. Such people loudly proclaimed that freeing the negro would inevitably lead to "racial equality." To counter this, the vast majority of antislavery forces did their best to assure people that after emancipation, all means would be used to insure that the negro was kept in his place—a place of subservience to the white man. In a further twist of irony, the greatest opponents to emancipation were poor white people who had never been able to afford slaves. Such people were very much opposed to using tax payer dollars to bail out rich planters.

While a spokesman went out to introduce him, Jackson peered out at the packed hall. It was a full house. He may no longer have been popular with a lot of people, but notoriety was just as effective at drawing a crowd. He'd never been much of a speaker in his younger days. It was a skill he'd cultivated in his years in the Presidency and especially in the years since. He took a deep breath. The spokesman for the Confederate Society for Prosperity and Industrialization was finishing his introductory remarks.

"And now may I present former President Thomas Jackson!" The hall erupted into polite applause. If he had opponents in the crowd they were at least giving him the honor due to a former Confederate President. The shouts of "Stonewall!" that rang out let him know that he also had some veterans in the hall. Jackson made his way out onto the stage and to the podium. He shook hands with the CSPI spokesman and then turned to face the audience. A massive Blood Stained Banner, the national flag of the CSA hung from the rafters behind him.

"Just over twenty-five years ago, the Confederate States of America secured their independence for the foreseeable future. The War of 1869 showed the world that we would not be dictated to by any foreign power and it taught the United States a lesson that they will never forget. Our northern enemy is still suffering the effects of the blows we visited upon them in that brief but bloody conflict. I submit to you my fellow countrymen, that a new threat has emerged to our beloved South, and it is not an enemy that may be resisted by force of arms alone. It is the threat of economic ruin. It is the threat of an internal conflict that could tear our Confederacy apart one day. It is a threat that could stab us in the back should we ever find ourselves at war with the Yankees again. The threat I am speaking of, is the institution of slavery..." Suddenly a heckler called out.

"If you're gonna set the niggers loose than what the devil did we fight two wars for?" Jackson met the challenge head on.

"We fought the wars to defend our homes against an aggressive invader and for the right to *decide for ourselves* what our course of action should be, and for the right not to be dictated to on the issue of slavery or any other issue by a dictatorial federal government. Slavery has been around since the book of Genesis and it will always exist on the earth in one form or another. As a Christian man I hold no love for it whatsoever. Now, I freely admit that there was a time when slavery was the best available structure for the co-existence of the white man and the negro on this continent. There was a time when our very way of life depended on the institution of slavery. But I submit to you here today that slavery has now become a danger to our way of life, a danger that far outweighs any advantage that might be gained by retaining it. The outside world abhors us. Cotton sales this year are the lowest they have been since the height of the War of Confederate War of Independence, when our coasts were blockaded by Yankee warships. As any cotton planter in the country will tell you, the cost of feeding and supporting his slaves has increased, while the profit from cotton sales has decreased."

Another heckler called out.

"I'm not paying taxes so that some rich planter can set his niggers loose!" Several shouts of agreement rang out. In principle, Jackson agreed with them. It was not fair to ask poorer tax payers who had never owned slaves in their lives, to pay the wealthiest men in the CSA to emancipate their slaves. Jackson's time as President, however, had turned him into a political realist. Without compensation, wealthy planters would never be willing to turn their slaves loose.

More hecklers called out their disapproval. A few called Jackson names. From there it got more complicated as several veterans started swinging fists and canes at those who had dared disrespect Stonewall.

As he had from the train car, Jackson cried out "Enough! As you men have so aptly demonstrated the institution of slavery also threatens the internal unity and stability of our nation. Many of you young men dream of one

64

day owning slaves for yourselves. But many of you also want to find work other than working on farms and in the fields. With the emancipation of the slaves, will also come a new wave of industrial development. Many of you, like me, want to see our great nation be able to manufacture all the goods that it needs so that we are not dependent on the outside world. The prosperity and living conditions of people throughout the Confederacy will be greatly increased."

"It's not worth letting the niggers be our equals!"

"No one is suggesting that," said Jackson. *At least not right away.* Jackson sighed. *Sooner or later I have to formulate a more specific plan for what to do with the negroes once they have been emancipated.* Jackson filed the thought away, then proceeded to the end of his speech.

"Finally, let me remind you of a fact that I and the older generation are well aware of. The Yankees still heavily outweigh us in industry and numbers. If the slavery issue is left unresolved it could explode into a crises at the worst possible moment. You young men have never had to fight battles outnumbered three to one. You don't know how many times in the late conflicts our nation's defenses hanged by a thread. You don't know how many times we drew perilously close to defeat. Like Robert E. Lee before me, I championed a plan to impress negroes into the army in the event of another War with the United States, and to grant such negroes freedom in return for their service. I viewed the plan not only as prudent but also as vital to the security of our Confederate States. When and if we fight the United States again we will need every available man. The Yankees will not repeat their mistakes of the past. We must therefore be ready for them. As you know I got my plan passed during my Presidency..." In fact it was the only substantial anti-slavery measure Jackson had managed to pass during his presidency. "...it made me more political enemies than any man in the office President should ever have to face. I would have gone further, had I not been blocked at every turn. Mark my words, if we do not act we will come to regret our inaction in our lifetime."

As he looked out on the crowd, for the first time Jackson thought he saw people nod in understanding and even agreement. As he finished his speech, a polite applause came from a little over half the people in the room. Some applauded because they approved. Others simply because he was Stonewall, and it was the polite thing to do. After the applause the entire auditorium erupted into conversation as people began to heatedly discuss the issues. Jackson stared out at the crowd in surprised approval.

At least this time I didn't start a riot.

VIII

Major Antonio Vega made his way up the spiral steps and through the narrow passage of Morrow Castle. When he had first arrived from Spain he had fallen in love with the beautiful fifteenth century fortress. He had since discovered that living in it was a much different experience than he had originally imagined. It was hard to move around inside of it. The passages had all been built with the mindset of defending against a siege and so the corridors were only wide enough for men to pass through them in single file. In many places the ceilings were also exceedingly low. He'd learned painfully to keep his head low when moving within the Castle. Morrow Castle did, however, have one very excellent attribute, aside from its beautiful Spanish architecture. Its thick stone walls kept out the glaring rays of the tropical sun.

Back in Spain, visitors from other parts of Europe often complained about how hot it was. Antonio like any native Spaniard had laughed them to scorn. Now that he was stationed in Cuba, he was learning the real meaning of the word "hot," and he was not laughing about it. He tugged at the collar of his sky blue uniform coat. The army's "tropical uniform" consisted of a long sleeve coat, and long trousers. The higher ups allowed the enlisted men a certain amount of latitude with the uniform code, but General Valeriano Weyler insisted upon strict protocol amongst the officers.

Antonio reached the end of his climb and stepped onto the upper ramparts of Morrow Castle. A cool ocean breeze was blowing from the north, and Antonio breathed a sigh of pleasure after taking in a breath of fresh sea air. Above him, the red and gold la Rojigualda flew proudly in the wind. A lookout stood at the edge of the rampart, staring out to sea with his binoculars.

"Any sign of the Confederados, Corporal?"

"No, Major."

In the aftermath of the destruction of the CSS Mississippi, the Confederacy was threatening war. Spanish garrisons in Cuba and elsewhere were on high alert.

"Is it true what they are saying, senor?"

"That the Confederados have had the arrogance to demand that Spain surrender Cuba? Si. The Gueros have been plotting to steal this island from us for a long time. Now they have their excuse."

"If they show their miserable faces here, then we will blow them out of the water," said a voice from behind them.

Antonio turned to see Major Elian Ortega. The artillery officer was a swarthy man who was as mean as he was heavy. He wasn't obese by civilian standards, but by army standards he was fat. Antonio was amazed he could fit into his uniform.

"The Confederados haven't got the cojones for a fight with us," said Ortega.

Antonio looked at the cannons that lined the ramparts. They were all antiquated smoothbores. Antonio knew that they were seriously lacking in range and accuracy.

"I watched the Mississippi sail into Havana before she exploded. She was armed with twelve inch rifled guns. If war erupts, our coastal defenses will be heavily outmatched with regards to artillery."

Ortega's complexion darkened even further.

"What do you know about it you defeatist swine? I should report you to the General!"

Antonio pointed at a stack of iron cannon balls that were piled up by one of the artillery pieces.

"I know that those will never pierce the hull of an armored warship."

Now Ortegta smiled savagely.

"Ah, but you are forgetting the guns on the La Cabana." He pointed at the massive fortress on the hill just north of Morrow Castle. It too was antiquated, but it was still larger and more formidable than any fort in the Caribbean. And it did have some enormous guns, some of which were rifled.

"I just wish Madrid would send us some modern artillery," said Antonio. "Before I left Spain I saw the cannoneers of the Royal Guard. They had guns that could match anything the Confederados have."

"We'll do fine with what we have," sneered Ortega. "In any event, it's not your problem. Your concern is infantry. Leave artillery matters to those of us with brains."

Antonio wanted to laugh in his face. While it was commonly thought that only the least academically inclined officers entered the infantry, and that only the best and brightest became artillery officers and engineers, Antonio also had it on good authority that Ortega owed his position more to his political connections in Madrid than to his skill with artillery. As for Antonio, he'd graduated near the top of his class and then requested to be posted to the infantry.

Adventure. More adventure. That's what I thought. What a zonzo I was!" Antonio did not think it wise to let on what he knew about Ortega. Or to tell the pompous arrogant fat man what a zonzo he was. What Antonio did say was, "I'm just glad we have our Mausers." The vast majority of the Spanish infantry had been equipped with state of the art rifles from Prussia.

"You will not need them," said Ortega. "At least not in defense of our fortifications. The guerros will never get within rifle range."

"Shall we bet on it, Major?" said Antonio. "Say a bottle of Rioja?"

"You will certainly lose," said Ortega. "It is agreed. I can taste my wine already."

"Vega, Ortega!"

The two Spanish officers snapped to attention at the sound of Colonel Diego Gonzales' voice.

"We're putting together an expeditionary force to deal with the rebels that have been raiding the sugar plantations outside Matanzas. Our orders are to patrol the area in force, and relocate all the villages in the area to Colon."

"Villages, senor? Entire villages?" Antonio had heard that the army had been forcibly relocating rural Cubans to special camps in an effort cut off the rebel's base of support. He hadn't known how serious to take the reports. He'd only been in Cuba a couple of months. He'd also heard other things...

Things too horrible to be true... Antonio pushed the things he had heard out of his mind. *They couldn't be true.*

"These are General Weyler's orders, Major Vega. Tomorrow morning you will report to the Mantilla Garrison and take command of the Seventh Infantry Company."

"Si, senor."

Gonzales then turned to Ortega.

"I'm sorry to say that there are major rebel uprisings outside of Santiago de Cuba. General Weyler has sent a large portion of our forces to the west to deal with the situation. Because of the crisis with the Estados Confederados, those forces are being brought back east immediately."

"What about the rebel uprising in the east?" asked Ortega.

"For the moment we will simply have to fortify Santiago de Cuba and a few other major strongholds and yield control of the rest of the eastern provinces to the rebels for the time being. In the meantime, our western forces are shorthanded. You and half of your artillerymen will also report to the Mantilla garrison, and temporarily supplement the infantry, besides—it looks like you could use the exercise."

The look on Ortega's face was priceless. Antonio wouldn't have believed it possible but he turned several more shades darker. He looked like he was so enraged that his head would explode, yet at the same time he looked sick to his stomach at the prospect of doing infantry work. Under any other circumstances the thought of Ortega having to slog along as a common foot soldier would have been enough to fill Antonio's heart with an almost sadistic joy. But with the fires of rebellion sweeping across the island, the bulk of their forces in the east, and the danger of a Confederate invasion in the west, the idea of depleting Havana's already meager defenses seemed outrageous. Ever so cautiously he asked, "Colonel, if I may respectfully ask: If we are willing to leave most of the eastern provinces under rebel control for the time being, then why are we so worried about a few raids in Matanzas?"

"Vega, I had no idea you were in line to join the General Staff," said Ortega with a derisive laugh. A sharp look from Gonzales silenced him. To Antonio's surprise the Colonel answered his question, and to his greater surprise the answer actually made sense.

"Shut up, Ortega. I like having officers that think strategically. You may indeed make the General Staff one day senor Vega. Our real reason for taking the risk of moving against the villagers outside Matanzas at this time is so that we can draw out the rebel cells in the area. We have reason to believe that the destruction of the Confederate warship may have been caused by rebels from around Matanzas. We want to capture as many rebels as possible and interrogate them. If we can learn who is responsible and properly punish them, then we may be able to avoid war with the Confederados. Comprende?"

"Si, Colonel." *We are looking for sacrificial lambs to feed the Confederados.*

Antonio had planned on attending the bull fights that afternoon. He wouldn't have the time now. He had much to gather and to prepare before the following day. There was, however, one engagement he utterly refused to miss.

After Colonel Gonzales had departed, Antonio took his leave of Ortega and made his way out of Morrow Castle himself. He walked down a steep stone path that took him to the shore of the channel that connected Havana harbor with the ocean. As much as he loved the architecture of the castle, the walk down to the channel took him past a part of the fortress that he did not like at all. It was a large stone wall that was stained red in many places and marred by bullet impacts. It was often used to execute captured rebels by firing squad. Antonio crossed himself, as he always did when walking past the place of execution.

A small rowboat was tied up at a rickety dock manned by a young private, who promptly ferried Antonio across the channel so that he could go into the old city. As usual Havana was bustling with activity. In that respect the looming threat of war made no difference. The threat, however, was impossible to ignore. The greatest proof of it was sitting off one of Havana's largest docks.

Antonio's walk took him immediately past the docks where the twisted and devastated hulk of the CSS Mississippi was sunk at her moorings. He hadn't seen the explosion, but even within the thick walls of Morrow Castle he had heard it. A squad of Spanish soldiers stood guard on the docks beside the wrecked battleship. The Confederate States had sent a team of engineers to investigate the wreck. Antonio had read in the newspaper that their official report back to Richmond confirmed the testimony of survivors from the Mississippi that a strange man impersonating a Confederate officer had made his way onto the ship, and then dramatically jumped off of the ship barely a minute before the explosion. The explosion had originated in the ship's powder magazine. If not for the survivors' testimony, Antonio would have thought it likely that the destruction of the Mississippi was nothing more than a tragic accident.

In any event, the Confederados are convinced that someone intentionally blew up their battleship and killed nearly a hundred of their men. They are determined to make somebody pay for it. God, please help us catch the people responsible! Or at least some bloodthirsty rebel on whom we can pin the blame!

At last he reached his destination. All was quiet as he entered the church. It was only Friday, but none the less there were a few parishioners sitting in the pews and praying silently. He waited patiently outside of the confession booth, until an elderly and penitent man pulled aside the curtain and emerged from the booth with his head bowed. Antonio, entered the booth, closed the curtain and sat down. He crossed himself and addressed the priest:

"Bless me father, for I have sinned…"

IX

Richmond Virginia, the capital city of the Confederate States of America, was bursting with activity. The Confederate capital was one of the most prosperous cities in the Confederacy. It had swelled in population since the CSA had gained its independence. Over a quarter million people lived within the city. As a result, Richmond was over three times as large as it had been only a few decades before.

Smoke belched from the massive Tredegar iron works and the many factories on the south side of the James River. Happy and prosperous people crowded through the streets. Behind them, their slaves carried their parcels and packages. Other slaves drove their masters around the city's commercial markets. At the docks, more black slaves worked to load rice, corn, tobacco and cotton onto waiting ships that were docked on the James. Still more negroes were busy unloading manufactured goods that had come in from Europe and that were ready to be distributed throughout the Confederate States. Though Confederate industry had increased greatly, the CSA was still unable to completely supply its own need for manufactured goods.

From the window of his coach, John Wilkes Booth, the head of the Confederate States Secret Service watched the happy and prosperous people of Richmond go about their business. He nodded in approval, conscientious of the fact that he had helped make this glorious future of the CSA possible.

The city was in high spirits. Red and White patriotic bunting seemed to hang from nearly every building, almost all of which also sported either a large Confederate Battle Flag or the Blood Stained Banner, the national flag of the Confederacy. Such levels of patriotic décor had not been seen in Richmond since the War of 1869.

Booth watched from his carriage as he passed the Confederate Capitol Building sitting atop a hill at the heart of Richmond like an ancient Greco-Roman temple. Immediately thereafter, they passed the impressive equestrian statue of George Washington and the larger and more impressive equestrian statue of Robert E. Lee. At last the carriage came to a halt in front of Confederate Hall, the former customs house that had long since been used as the headquarters of the executive branch of the Confederate government.

Booth climbed down from the carriage and made his way up the front steps of Confederate Hall. His legs hurt slightly. At fifty-seven years old, he'd begun to feel aches and pains that weren't there even a few years earlier. Two gray clad Confederate soldiers stood guard at the entrance to Confederate Hall. They recognized Booth, and raised their model 1891 C.S. Richmond Rifles in salute. The bolt-action, magazine fed, repeating rifles were brand new and had been adopted by the Confederate army four years earlier. Booth was greeted at the door by Samuel Lamont, one of President John Marshall Stone's many secretaries.

"Good afternoon, Director Booth. The meeting has already begun. I'll show you into the President's office immediately, sir."

Booth hardly needed the young secretary to show him the way to the President's office. Booth had been the Director of the Confederate States Secret Service for over twenty-five years and had served four Confederate Presidents. Nevertheless, he politely followed Lamont and allowed him to show him into the Executive Office.

The President was in in the middle of addressing his cabinet and advisors. Booth quietly made his way to a seat beside General Porter Alexander.

"Gentlemen, I have been assured by congressional leaders that all I have to do is ask for a declaration of war against Spain and they will give it to me on a silver platter. What I need to know, is how will such a declaration be received in Europe?"

Thomas Holt, the Secretary of State, scowled.

"I'm afraid, Mr. President, that with the exception of our allies, the European nations are more or less taking Spain's side in this matter. Never mind that Spain destroyed one of our warships and killed over one-hundred of our men! Never mind that Spanish cruelty and incompetence has allowed a dangerous powder keg to sit eighty miles off of our shore! All those self-righteous European snobs can talk about is 'the expansion of slavery!' It is the worst in Britain! France of course is on our side. Napoleon IV has assured our minister in Paris that the Empire of France will stand by us. Also Portugal is on our side, but that has more to do with the Portuguese animosity with the Spanish rather than any love for us. Austro-Hungarian Emperor Franz Joseph has also issued a statement in our support."

President Stone nodded. That was no surprise. The CSA had spent the better part of two-decades fighting Mexican revolutionaries south of the Rio Grande alongside the French to make sure that Franz Joseph's brother, Maximillian, remained Emperor of Mexico. Holt continued in somber tones.

"The rest of Europe, however, is almost unanimous in their condemnation of us and their support for Spain. Prussia, Sweden, Russia, Denmark, Belgium, the Netherlands, Greece, and Italy have all issued statements in Spain's support and opposing any moves on our part against Spain. Prussia has actually threatened to declare war on us if we invade Cuba!"

"Not surprising, considering the family relationship between King Leopold and King Wilhelm," said the President.

General Alexander suddenly rose to his feet.

"If I may, Mr. President. The only European nation we need to be worried about right now is Great Britain. Prussia's navy is limited, and if they were so foolish as to declare war on us, they would immediately find themselves at war with France. Only Britain has the power and the reach to actually come to Spain's aid directly, and only they won't be cowered by French."

The President turned back to Holt.

"What exactly is the position and mindset of the British?"

"As I said, Mr. President, the British are opposed to our annexation of Cuba because they view it as an extension of slavery."

The President sighed heavily and shook his head.

"It always comes back to that issue doesn't it? I've honestly begun to wonder whether or not Stonewall has been right all along."

If any of his advisors disagreed with him, no one spoke up. Like it or not, the CSA's peculiar institution was coming back to haunt it yet again.

"The British are also offended by our close military alliance with the France," said Holt.

"Then they should have thought twice before being against us diplomatically and economically over an issue that's none of their business," said General Alexander.

The President looked his Secretary of State in eye.

"I want your considered opinion, Thomas. Will Britain intervene on Spain's behalf?"

The Confederate Secretary of State removed his glasses and rubbed his eyes.

"According to our minister in London, there is a strong movement in the British parliament to severe diplomatic and economic ties with us completely if we declare war on Spain, but his report also states that the British are reluctant to threaten direct military intervention because they feel it could easily lead to war with France, Austria-Hungary, and Mexico as well as with us. My gut tells me that if we declare war on Spain, they'll carry out their diplomatic and economic threats, but I do not believe they will intervene militarily on Spain's behalf. Of course, I can offer no guarantees."

Beside General Alexander, Booth was simmering in hatred. *How dare these fools condemn my nation! They will pay!"* He had already been planning several *operations* in Britain meant to deal with British abolitionists and politicians hostile to the CSA. In his mind he was expanding both their number and their intensity.

"So there is an extremely high chance that this war will finally tip the British over the edge of severing their commercial relations with us?" asked Stone.

"I would say the chance is almost certain, Mr. President," said Secretary Holt. A loud murmur went through the assembled men. Such a move would hurt Britain's economy, but to the already struggling Confederate economy, it would be devastating.

"Perhaps it is time to throw the British a bone," said the President. "I will use my authority to activate the Negro and Slave Conscription Act. With cotton and slave prices as low as they are, there will be plenty of our slave owning citizens ready to emancipate their slaves in exchange for government capital. The army will get several regiments of expendable troops, the economy will get a much needed influx of cash, and we get to show the British that we are taking the first steps towards finally emancipating our slaves. If we can frame this war as being a step towards the end of slavery, then perhaps they will be less likely to rashly break off diplomatic and economic ties with us."

Like many white men in the CSA, Booth was not fond of the Negro and Slave Conscription Act. He'd almost taken, *drastic,* steps to stop it from being passed back in the 1870s. It had cost President Jackson all of his political capital, but he had been able to pass it. Now President Stone, who was as Pro-

Slavery as a Confederate President could be, was finding a use for the conscription act that even Booth had to admit was clever. The conscription of a few thousand slaves would hardly put a scratch in the institution itself, but it could be just enough to keep Britain from carrying out its diplomatic and economic threats. Still, the idea of putting guns in the hands of negroes, sickened Booth and several others to their stomachs.

"Opinions, Gentlemen?" said the President. "Come on let's hear it."

Booth was about to express his disapproval, but before he could, General Alexander spoke again.

"I was hesitant to bring this up, Mr. President, but since you have expressed your willingness to allow negroes to be conscripted into the army, I think that a report from the War Department's Medical Division bears consideration. The Medical Division believes that if we invade Cuba, the vast majority of our losses will not be to enemy action but to disease, specifically tropical illnesses such as malaria and yellow fever. The Surgeon General of the Army of Northern Virginia believes that because the negroes originally come from the tropical jungles of Africa that they will be largely immune to such diseases. Utilizing negro troops in Cuba could save thousands of our soldiers from dying of yellow fever."

Nods and grunts of approval came from most of the assembled men. Even Booth found it difficult to come up with an objection to that particular point. Difficult or not, he spoke up.

"I still must protest, Mr. President. Slavery to the white man is the only proper place for the negro. We already have far too many free niggers in the Confederacy as it is. If we do this it will mean freeing thousands of more slaves."

"I'm afraid slavery is on its death bed, Mr. Booth. It has been for a long time. Our task is to make sure that it ends on our terms— specifically with as little damage to the nation and its economy as possible, with minimal inconvenience and alarm to our citizenry and with certitude that in the aftermath the negro will be in a controllable and subservient position to the white man."

Before Booth could respond, Vice President Ronald Keith made an interjection of his own.

"Might I suggest, Mr. President, that we do two further things to increase the chance that the British will view this as a genuine move towards emancipation and not as a mere political maneuver aimed at placating them?"

President Stone motioned for him to go on.

"First, I suggest that, in addition to their freedom, we grant all negro conscripts a land grant in Cuba. This will show the British that we are willing to help the negroes start lives as freemen after the war, and it will have the added bonus of keeping these newly freed negroes on Cuba and away from the mainland Confederacy."

More nods and words of approval came from the cabinet and advisors.

"That is a brilliant idea, Ronald. What's the next?"

"That we give Britain and other European nations a guarantee that we will not spread slavery back to Cuba."

"I'm afraid that's not possible my friend," said the President. "You know as well as I do that our constitution guarantees the right of slavery in every state and territory of the Confederacy."

"In every state and territory, yes..." said Keith. "But what about a commonwealth? Instead of fully annexing Cuba, why not simply grant them a limited self-government under Confederate hegemony? We'll reap the economic and strategic benefits of controlling the island, the Cubans get to govern themselves in large measure, we keep all those negroes and mulattos confined to the island and we can promise the British that slavery will not return to Cuba. Think about it, gentlemen. Nearly half the population of Cuba is either negro or mulatto already. Does anyone here really want to make Cuba a Confederate State? Mr. Booth, sir, you are worried about a few thousand negroes being set free by the conscription act, but just think about the fact that directly annexing Cuba will itself bring over *half a million* free negroes and mulattos into the Confederacy overnight."

Many of the men in the room looked stunned. They had never actually thought about annexing Cuba in those terms. Even Booth had no reply.

"You make some excellent points, Ronald," said Stone. "And you can be assured that I shall give them serious consideration. I agree with your first proposal entirely. As for the second, we shall have to wait and see. Now, gentlemen, before we dismiss, are there any other suggestions on how to further entice the British not to break off all relations and trade with us the moment we go to war with Spain?"

"I have, Mr. President," said Booth. He opened his satchel and pulled out several papers. "My agents have confirmed several reports that the Spanish forces in Cuba are committing horrible atrocities. I have reports on mass executions, forced relocations of entire populations, thousands of people being made to starve to death in internment camps as well as rape, murder and pillaging by Spanish troops. If these things are made known to the world, perhaps the high and mighty British will think twice before giving the Spanish the high moral ground in this conflict. Perhaps we might even be seen as liberators in the eyes of the Cubans and the rest of the world."

"I very much doubt it," said Holt. "Reports like that have been coming out of Cuba for years. They are so horrible and fantastical that no one really believes them. Even if you say you've confirmed it, we'll just be accused of spreading propaganda."

"Unless," said the Vice President, "it is corroborated by independent journalists from neutral nations. What if we issue an open invitation for foreign war correspondents from interested neutral nations—by which I specifically mean Great Britain—to accompany our army into Cuba and see the Spanish atrocities for themselves?"

"I don't like the idea of foreign reporters following around our army," said General Alexander. "But if it will keep Britain from cutting of her commerce with us, then so be it."

Sudden silence pervaded the room. At last President Stone turned to Vice President Keith.

"Call a joint secession of Congress into secret secession. It's time to make some serious decisions…"

X

Captain John J Pershing rode at the head of a cavalry troop headed south.

"Press on!" he said. "They can't be far!" They'd been pursuing a gang of ruthless outlaws for two days. So far there had been no sign of them.

Pershing admired the terrain around them. Southern Iowa was beautiful in its own way. The area was dominated by luscious green farmland and green trees. In many ways it reminded Pershing of Missouri where he had been born. That was no wonder since he and his men were right on the border with Confederate Missouri. Off to his left, Pershing sighted a farm house with a weather vane. A large red barn stood not too far away. On the other side of the dirt road to Pershing's right he spotted an old cemetery. He raised his hand to signal his cavalry troopers to rein in.

"We're less than a mile from the border," said Lt. Richard Paddock his second in command. Pershing spit to show his disdain for what Paddock had said. He hated being reminded that his home state was now part of another nation— a nation which he despised and hated with every fiber of his being. Paddock was not only Pershing's second in command, he was also his best friend and brother in law.

"How's Lorain doing?"

"She's doing fine John. I got a letter from her a week ago. She should arrive in Des Moines by next week." Pershing nodded. Lorain was actually his half-sister but he had always been extremely protective of her. He was glad she had married his best friend.

"She asked me about you, John."

"Did she?"

"She wants me to find you a wife."

"She always was a busybody," said Pershing. Paddock took off his hat and fanned himself.

"John, I think they've probably gotten away. They must be over the border by now." The outlaws they'd been hunting hadn't been that far ahead of them—no more than a day. Pershing had been certain they could catch up to them before they reached the border. He looked around with the eyes of a hawk. His gaze settled on the farm house.

"I don't think they've crossed the border yet." He drew his army revolver and brought his horse around to face his men. He sent seven of them around and behind the farm. He, Paddock and the rest of the men then fanned out and approached the farm from the front. Ever since the USA and CSA had parted ways for good, bandits and outlaws had used the new international border to their advantage—committing crimes on one side and taking refuge in the other. As far as Pershing could tell the vast majority of crimes were committed on the US side and the vast number of criminals took refuge on the Confederate side. His stepfather, Cain Strickland had been a US Marshall. Pershing remembered him cursing up a storm about it till the day he had died. The situation on the border with Missouri had grown so bad that the US army had detached units from northern Iowa that had been sent there to fight Sioux Indians, and sent them to southern Iowa to help protect the border.

Pershing and his men slowly but cautiously approached the farm house with their guns ready.

"What is it, John?" Pershing pointed to a spot on the ground about twenty feet in front of the farm house. A young teenage boy lay dead on the ground with a double barreled shot gun clutched in his cold hands. Not far away, an older man lay dead with a hoe in his hand.

Pershing's mind was suddenly filled with the image of a burning farmhouse. He remembered as a boy how he had watched his home burn to the ground with his brothers and sisters inside. The fire had been set by Rebel raiders. Only John and his mother had survived.

"John… John! Are you alright?" Pershing snapped out of it. He realized he was sweating and on the verge of hyperventilating.

"I'm fine. Let's get on with it." As they neared the farmhouse, Pershing noticed that the front door was slightly open. Suddenly a rifle shot rang out. One of Pershing's troopers fell from the saddle dead. The remaining US cavalrymen opened fire on the farmhouse with their revolvers and lever action rifles. Bullets slammed into the house's wooden siding and shattered its glass windows. More shots came from within the farmhouse but the fusillade of fire from the blue uniformed cavalry troopers kept it to a minimum. While his men gave him covering fire, Pershing charged up the front steps of the house onto the front porch. Paddock was right behind him. The front door had already been kicked in and was slightly open. Pershing dropped to one knee while Paddock went to the side of the door. With his arm, Paddock pushed the door completely open. A bullet cracked through the air just inches above Pershing's head. Pershing fired his revolver and dropped the outlaw that had fired at him. He and Paddock then rushed into the house together. It was a wreck. The outlaws had obviously been in the process of looting it. Suddenly they heard a woman scream.

"It came from upstairs!" said Pershing. He rushed up the stair case. As he ascended the stairs, he heard more gunshots below and more feminine screams above. No sooner did he reach the second story than a bullet slammed into the wall to his left. The bullet smashed a black and white photo of an elderly couple. The man who had fired at Pershing had done so from the end of the hall. Pershing fired at him with his revolver but the outlaw ducked into one of the rooms to his left. With his gun ready, Pershing made his way down the hallway. Paddock was still right behind him. As he neared the door, he heard the sound of glass breaking. Pershing stormed into the room brandishing his revolver. Two women let out screams of horror. One looked to be in her forties the other in her late teens. From their stripped, bruised and bloody bare bodies, Pershing could tell that they had been raped. A roaring rage built up inside of him. The bandit had busted the window and gone through it. Making his way to the window, Pershing saw that the outlaw had leapt from the window to the ground beneath and was limping towards the woods. Pershing fired at him but he made it to the tree line just in time.

Where are the men I ordered to the backside of the farmhouse? Pershing considered leaping down from the window himself but didn't want to chance hurting himself. He turned to face Paddock who had followed him into the room. Paddock was helping the women. He had given them blankets to cover themselves and was busily checking the injuries on their faces. "Come on Richard, he can't get far!" Pershing charged back down the stairs and discovered that his men had killed another outlaw in the kitchen. One of his troopers addressed him.

"Sir, there was another one that got out the back door, jumped on a horse and galloped off. The men are after him."

"Another one leapt out of the upstairs window and made for the woods," said Pershing. "There are two women upstairs. They've had dreadful and indecent machinations worked upon their bodies. See to them!" With that, Pershing stormed out the front door. He'd intended to mount his horse, ride around the farmhouse and try to find a way to pursue the outlaw that had escaped from the upstairs window into the woods. As it was, his quarry did the work for him. A gunshot rang out as soon as he stepped out of the farmhouse. It missed him by several inches. The outlaw had come back around to the front of the house and taken a horse. After taking the shot at

Pershing, he spurred his horse and galloped away from the farm and off towards the south.

Pershing leveled his pistol at the outlaw and pulled the trigger. The revolver clicked but did not fire. Pershing swore loudly and profanely. He ran to his own horse intending to take off after the outlaw. Paddock took several shots at the fleeing bandit but failed to hit him. He then hastened after Pershing.

"Wait up, John! You can't go after that murderer alone!"

"Watch me!" The two cavalrymen leapt onto their horses and went charging after the outlaw.

"We're less than a mile from the border!" said Paddock. "If we keep after him we're gonna wind up in Reb territory!"

The word Pershing used to tell him how much he cared turned Paddock's face red. Five minutes later, when Paddock was certain they had crossed the border into Confederate Missouri, the two US troopers crested a small hill. Down below they could see the fleeing outlaw. He was a good hundred yards off from them. Pershing leapt off of his horse and pulled his rifle from the saddle holster. He worked its lever to chamber a round and then took aim at the fleeing bandit. Pershing squeezed the trigger and the rifle barked. The outlaw fell from the saddle. Paddock whooped in glee.

"You got him, John!" Pershing nodded. He remounted his horse and they trotted down the hill to where the outlaw had fallen. As they made their way towards him, Pershing reloaded his revolver. He again dismounted and walked over to the fallen fugitive. The man was moaning and groaning in pain. His gun lay beside him. Pershing kicked it away and then used his booted foot to turn the bandit over. He wasn't mortally wounded.

"What are we going to do with him, John?" Without saying a word, Pershing took his revolver, cocked it, leveled it at the outlaw's head and pulled the trigger.

"We're going to leave him for the vultures," said Pershing coldly. Holstering his weapon he turned to go back to his horse, leaving Paddock to stare at the corpse. Paddock took off his hat and scratched his head. He then replaced his hat and hurried after his brother in law. They had just remounted their horses, when they were startled by a voice.

"You men shouldn't be here." The two startled US army men jerked their mounts around to face the one who had spoken. It was a woman about their age. Pershing pointed towards the corpse.

"We had unfinished business with that." He refused to give the outlaw the dignity of human status.

"And he earned the cold blooded way in which you killed him how?" she asked. Clearing his throat, Paddock answered her question.

"Among other things ma'am, robbery, murder and the raping of two innocent women just over the border a couple of miles." The answer seemed to satisfy her.

"I believe you," she said. "But you need to get back. I won't report you to the Confederate authorities, but you need to hurry. Rebel cavalry patrol this area all the time." Pershing eyed her.

"I take it by your tone, that you disapprove of Rebels being in Missouri."

"I take it from your accent that you are no Yankee," she replied. "Your accent is unmistakably from Missouri." Pershing dismounted and took off his hat.

"Captain John Pershing, ma'am, of the 6th Cavalry, United States Army. And yes, mam, I was born in Laclede. My mother and I left right after the Confederacy stole Missouri." The woman nodded.

"My name is Jennifer Harper, and to answer your question Captain, I am not at all happy with Missouri being in the Confederacy, but the world is as it is and not as we would have it." Pershing took her hand and kissed it—and at the same time noted that she wore no wedding ring. He looked her in the eye.

"I've always believed that if the world is not as we would have it, then we should change it."

"And how would you propose to do that Captain? Start another war?"

"Maybe not today," he said more than half seriously. Her reply was very serious.

"If you don't get back to your side you might get one today if the Rebels find you here, whether you want one or not."

"She's right, John," said Paddock. Pershing bowed to her and then remounted his horse. He started to ride north but then reigned in and brought his mount around to face her again.

"Miss Harper, may I have your address that I might write you?"

XI

Captain Blake Ramsey stared at the battleship *CSS Texas*. The three-hundred and eight foot long Confederate warship was tied to her moorings in Galveston harbor. Her menacing, twelve inch guns were raised into their firing position. The entire crew was assembled on the deck in their dress grays. They stood at rigid attention awaiting the arrival of their new commanding officer.

Flanked by Commander Ray Brisk who would serve as his executive officer, Ramsey started up the gang plank. A bugler on deck began playing martial notes to announce Ramsey's approach. As soon as Ramsey set foot on the deck, a naval band started blaring Dixie. As the Confederate national anthem played, the Blood Stained Banner was immediately run up. The national flag of the Confederate States billowed proudly at the battleship's stern. Ramsey turned and reverentially saluted the flag. He then turned and saluted the officer of the deck.

"Permission to come aboard," he said.

Returning the salute, the officer said, "Permission granted, sir." A red carpet ran from the end of the gang plank to where Admiral John McIntosh Kell waited on deck. While the naval band played a light march, Ramsey followed the carpet towards the Admiral. The carpet was flanked by the ship's officers, who brought their hands up in salute as Ramsey passed by. Ramsey gravely returned them before halting in front of the Admiral and saluting again.

"Captain Blake Ramsey, reporting as ordered, sir." The Admiral returned Ramsey's salute. In his sixties, Admiral Kell was well past retirement age. But he had served with the famous Captain Raphael Semmes on the *CSS Alabama* during the Confederate War of Independence and had commanded a commerce raider of his own during the War of 1869. The medals and ribbons on his chest bore testimony to his deeds and accomplishments during those two wars. And so he would remain an Admiral until he became senile, or more than likely even after he became senile. Admiral Kell pulled out a piece of paper and unfolded it.

"On this date, May 14th, in the year of our Lord 1895, by order of President John Marshall Stone and the Navy Department, I hereby assign command of this vessel to you." Ramsey again saluted the Admiral.

"I relieve you, sir."

"I stand relieved," replied Kell saluting one last time. Ramsey turned to his new crew.

"Dismissed!" While the Petty Officers set the crew back to their duties, Kell led Ramsey through a hatchway in the side of the superstructure which led into the wardroom. It was well furnished with mahogany furniture. Among other things there was a large clock, a chronometer and a portrait of Admiral Mallory, who had been the first head of the Confederate Navy. Removing their caps, Kell and Ramsey took seats opposite one another at one of the fine wooden tables.

"I must admit I envy you, Ramsey," said Kell. "You're getting command of a fine new warship just before a new war heats up."

"So it's definite?" asked Ramsey.

"It is. Congress has already voted in secret session to declare war on Spain. It will be made public tomorrow. My task today, is to brief you on our preparations and plan of invasion."

"Cuba?"

"Cuba." Kell pulled out a map of the Gulf of Mexico and unfolded it on the table between them. He pointed to Mobile. "We are concentrating ships here to form a battle group for the assault on Cuba. Your orders are to set sail next week along with the rest of the Galveston squadron. You'll be escorting a squadron of transports. You'll stop at Biloxi to pick up a contingent of Marines and a special contingent of troops before joining the rest of the battle group at Mobile where the Army is also assembling several divisions."

"Will we have enough ships to transport them?"

"They will have to be transported in two waves. The first wave will make the initial landings and capture Havana. They will then push east while the transport ships return to Mobile to pick up the rest of the troops."

A yeoman entered the wardroom, carrying a tray and two cups of coffee. He handed the admiral his coffee first, and then set the second in front of Ramsey. Kell brought the steaming cup to his lips and took a cautious sip, waiting for the yeoman to withdraw before continuing.

"As soon as the orders from Richmond come through, the fleet will set sail from Mobile to commence the attack on Havana. A task force from Charleston is standing by to set sail and cover the sea approaches to Cuba, to fend off any advances by the Spanish navy. The Texas will sail ahead of the main force with a small screening force, just in case any Spanish ships get passed the Charleston task force." Kell then handed Ramsey a large book. "This book has been provided by the Secret Service. It contains detailed drawings of Spanish warships. Have your lookouts study them in detail."

Ramsey nodded. Kell took another sip of his coffee before continuing.

"As you are the highest ranking survivor of the Mississippi, you will have the honor of firing the first shots at

Havanna and avenging the Spanish treachery and the murder of our comrades."

Ramsey thought back to that fateful night. He remembered the scarred face of the man who'd called himself "Commander Smith." That face and scar was burned into his memory. Ramsey knew with every fiber of his being that that man was responsible for the destruction of the Mississippi, though who he had truly been working for remained a mystery.

Officially, the Spanish were to blame. Ramsey, however, knew that there were many who thought that the saboteur had been working for some other power. After the bombing, Ramsey had been summoned to Richmond to give depositions to the Navy Department and before the Confederate Congress. At first he feared that he'd be made the scapegoat for the destruction of the Mississippi. He'd been wrong. In the weeks since the explosion, Spain had been vilified by the Confederate government and by every newspaper in the Confederacy. While he was in Richmond, Ramsey had even been interviewed by the head of the Confederate Secret Service, John Booth and by President Stone himself. They had made him into a national hero of sorts—a poster boy for the Confederacy's war rhetoric against Madrid and a reminder of Spain's treachery. Ramsey was certain that was the primary reason for his sudden promotion to Captain and his being given command of such a prominent warship.

His thoughts returned to the identity of the bomber. While in Richmond, Ramsey had heard many theories. Behind the scenes, many suspected the United States or even Great Britain of being behind the bombing of the Mississippi. It had even been speculated openly in a few Confederate newspapers that Cuban nationalists were actually behind the bombing in an effort to goad the CSA into declaring war on Spain.

In which case, the Spanish are still to blame for allowing a powder keg to sit under our country. They should have ceded Cuba to us long ago. In any event, the Spanish would be paying the price for the destruction of the Mississippi. One other thing Ramsey knew. He would never forget the bomber's face. If he ever saw him again, he would not hesitate.

"There's another thing you need to know," said Kell. From the sound of his voice, Ramsey could tell that it was something that was agitating him. "The transports you will be escorting will be picking up a special unit of troops in addition to the Marine force."

"What kind of troops, sir?"

Kell took a deep breath and exhaled loudly. The admiral looked Ramsey dead in the eye.

"Do you remember the Negro and Slave Conscription Act?"

"Of course, sir," said Ramsey. "It would be hard to forget it." Ramsey's words were an understatement. Former President Thomas Jackson had spent most of his second term fighting for it to be passed by the Confederate Congress. It had earned him many political enemies. Many people in the Confederacy had opposed it. At one point, South Carolina had even threatened to secede from the Confederacy, though Ramsey and most other people didn't think they had been serious. Despite all the political turmoil, Jackson and his supporters had just barely managed to get the bill passed. The measure had passed the house by three votes and the senate by one. The act allowed for the conscription of negroes, both slave and free, during time of war, in order to supplement the Confederacy's manpower.

"They are actually going to put it into effect?" asked Ramsey. He wasn't necessarily against it, he was just surprised that the unpopular measure, though on the books, would actually be invoked.

"Surprisingly, everyone in Richmond seems blasted eager to put it into effect. Its proponents are saying that the niggers are better suited to tropical conditions than the white man, since, their ancestors come from the jungles of Africa. The egg heads are all saying that they'll be more resistant to Malaria, yellow-fever, and other tropical diseases."

"What about those who oppose the act?" asked Ramsey. "Why are they suddenly clamoring for President Stone to put it into effect?"

"They've always argued that niggers are too cowardly to fight. Since this isn't going to be a big enough war to free a substantial number of negroes, they figure this is a perfect opportunity for them to be proven right. In any event, the President has made his decision and there's going to be an entire regiment of negro troops waiting at Biloxi for your transports to pick up." Suddenly, Kell swore derogatorily. "I still maintain that the only reason that Jackson was able to pass that blasted bill is because it was Robert E. Lee who authored it." Lee had written the measure in secret during the height of the War of 1869, when the Confederacy's manpower had been stretched nearly to the breaking point. That war had come to an abrupt end and President Lee had passed away shortly thereafter. Jackson had wisely waited until he had finished out Lee's term and been elected to one of his own before he submitted the bill. On that one point, Ramsey, agreed with Kell completely. Only the facts that the measure had been authored by Lee, had been heavily approved of by the Longstreet War Department and because the man power shortages of the War of 1869 had still been fresh in the public mind, was the bill able to be passed. In the years since, it had largely moved out of the public mind—though it was about to make a dramatic return.

Folding the map back up, Kell said, "I'll leave you to familiarize yourself with your ship and get acquainted with your crew. He handed Ramsey a sealed manila envelope. "Here's the formal copy of your orders."

"Thank you sir." Ramsey accompanied the Admiral back to the gangplank. Once Kell had gone, Ramsey found Brisk still issuing orders on the main deck.

"I want an officers meeting in the Ward Room in one hour," Ramsey said.

"I'll see to it sir," replied Brisk. Ramsey then proceeded to take a tour of his new command. The Texas was essentially a sister ship of the late CSS Mississippi, but there were some superficial differences. Ramsey started at the rear of the ship. Her steam engines were impressive. Working his way forward he toured the coal bunkers and furnace room, the rear armory, the chart room, the crew's quarters, the officer's quarters, the forward armory and the forecastle. As he made his way through the ship, busy sailors dropped what they were doing, leapt to attention and saluted him, though in each instance Ramsey quickly waved them back to their duties. Returning to the main deck, he inspected the primary and secondary gun emplacements. He was very impressed with the twelve inch guns and looked forward to seeing them in action.

After touring the ship, he went to his office, opened the manila envelope and reviewed the formal copy of his orders. He scanned over it. It was more or less exactly what Admiral Kell had told him. Suddenly a knock came at his cabin door.

"Come in," said Ramsey. "Sorry Captain. Just wanted to let you know that the officers are assembled in the wardroom as you ordered. Ramsey, nodded. As he gathered the orders back into the envelope and headed out the door, he wondered how his first mate was going to react to the news that negroes would soon be serving in the Confederate military.

Knowing Brisk, not very well... Then Ramsey asked himself another, more important question. *How will the whole of the Confederacy react?* He feared he knew the answer: *Not very well.*

XII

"But why can't you let someone else go!" Helen Allen's voice was as loud as Cole had ever heard before. It was not loud with anger. They never fought...*or almost never.* It was loud with frantic fear. Either way, her voice resounded through the entire house. "Now that the Confederacy has declared war on Spain, Cuba is going to explode like a powder keg! I don't want my husband there when it does!" Cole pulled several pairs of socks out of his chest of drawers and tossed them in the leather suit case on the bed. Outside the sun had long since gone down. Out in the living room, the Grandfather clock struck eight.

"Darling, I am the only one at the Gazette who has any experience as a war-correspondent. I wouldn't feel right sending anyone else."

"Yes, but you were seventeen years old."

"I was eighteen. What does it matter?" He looked at her with mock hurt. "Are you trying to say that I'm old?" At twenty-nine, his beautiful wife was far closer to that wondrous age of eighteen than he was at forty four. Still, Helen's statement hit far too close to the mark for his comfort. He knew that he wasn't as young and spry as he once was. He was still trying to convince himself that the reason he was going to Cuba was not to relive the glory days of his youth.

"Of course I don't think you're too old," she said. "But you didn't have a wife back then either. I just don't want my husband getting shot at again." Not for the first time, Cole regretted telling Helen about his experiences during the War of 1869. He'd told her many of the more exciting things while courting her. He'd wanted her to think him brave. After marriage he'd opened up to her about some of the more terrifying aspects of what had gone on during that horrible conflict. It was as if by sharing it, it wouldn't bother him as much. Now he was paying the price.

"And I'm not all that pleased at the idea of your travelling through the Confederacy," she said. "What if the Southerners imprison you?"

Cole smiled.

"The United States are not going to war with the Confederate States. President Cleveland has made it abundantly clear that this is none of our business. They have no reason to arrest me. Besides..." he held up a wire "the CSA has invited foreign journalists from neutral nations to accompany their forces into Cuba so that there will be independent witnesses to the atrocities the Confederates claim that the Spanish are committing against the Cubans."

"The Confederates don't care anything for the Cuban's," said Helen. "They are just trying to find more ways to justify their new war to expand their territory and keep down international opposition. Besides…I'm pretty sure the Confederates didn't have reporters from the USA in mind when they issued a call for foreign journalists to go into Cuba with their army."

"Darling, I'm going to Cuba because I want the people of the United States to get good reliable information about what goes on in this war. There are hotheaded editors of other newspapers demanding that we get involved and support the Spanish. If we do, it could easily drag us into another war with the Confederacy. Maybe if enough people are reminded about how horrible war actually is, we'll be less likely to get involved in another one."

"So this is all about making sure we stay out of war?" Cole sighed again.

"It's also about finding out the truth behind these claims of Spanish atrocities. You know I can't stand the Confederacy and what it stands for. But it's not just the Confederates making these claims, Helen. Reports have been coming out of Cuba for years that the Spanish are doing things, horrible things to the inhabitants of Cuba. We need to know if these things are true. If they are, people need to know. I don't want us involved in another war. But I certainly don't want us in a war allied to a nation that is committing such horrible atrocities against men women and children."

At last she did not come back with an immediate reply. For a moment, Cole thought that he had finally won the battle, and that Helen was reconciled to his going. But then she pulled out her secret weapon—a weapon wives had been using against their husbands since time began, a weapon against which there was virtually no defense. She started crying. By the light of the gas lamps in their bedroom, Cole could see the tears streaming down her face. While he was convinced most women could turn their crying on and off to manipulate their men and get what they want, the sadness in her eyes showed that these were real and they stabbed into his soul like a hot knife.

He sat her down on the bed. He put his hand under her chin and lifted her face up towards him. He took her face in his hands and wiped the tears away with his thumbs. Then, still holding her beautiful face in his hands, he brought his own face down to hers and kissed her, long and tenderly. He got up just long enough to blow out the gas lamps and the room was engulfed in darkness. They made passionate love. Afterward, they lay under the covers. She had fallen asleep in Cole's arms, her head resting against his chest. He kissed her forehead, stroked her hair, and caressed her face.

I am a fool indeed, he thought, *to leave this angel behind just to stare at death and destruction again.* But then his mind drifted back to what he thought of as his duty. *I admit it, part of me does want to relive the glory days of my youth, but it's not just that. It is my responsibility to report the truth. The people of this country need to hear about what goes on down there, so that they will not be tempted to forget what happens when we forsake diplomacy and resort to guns.* Cole never wanted his country to suffer through another war. He was convinced that the best way to keep it from happening was to keep its horrors fresh in the people's minds. Before getting married, he would have been restless all night, especially with the excitement of the days to come. But the intimate warmth of his wife's body and the steady rhythm of her breathing quickly lulled him to sleep.

Cole awoke to the sweet smell of coffee and bacon. Outside the sun had only just risen. He got dressed, and quickly finished the packing he'd begun the night before. As he entered the dining room he glanced at the grandfather clock. It was six-thirty. He was normally walking into his office at the Gazette about that time.

As usual, Helen had a full breakfast waiting on him in the dining room. He patted his stomach. Even though he was thirty-nine, his stomach had remained relatively flat. He'd always been a slender man. Since, getting married, however, he'd begun to develop a slight girth. Helen was an excellent cook. She was still in the kitchen. He walked over to her, slipped an arm around her and kissed her. "Good morning, darling."

"Good morning, dear," she replied and handed him a steaming cup of coffee. They then sat at the table and started eating breakfast together. Neither of them said anything at first. Cole had no desire to resume their battle of the previous day and he was grateful to see that neither did Helen. When she finally spoke, there was not a hint of combativeness.

"What time did you say your train was leaving?"

"Eight O'clock. I've got just enough time to swing by the paper."

She nodded by way of reply.

"I'm sure George will do a good job running the paper while you're gone."

Cole nodded.

"I wouldn't leave him in charge otherwise." George Stetson was a good man and Cole's best reporter. He'd made him the assistant editor a year earlier. Cole had known him since the War of 1869, when Stetson had served in the 3rd Kentucky Infantry. Cole had accompanied that regiment as a war correspondent throughout the war. Stetson had taken a minie ball in the leg outside Frankfurt. He'd walked with a limp ever since.

When Cole had finished his breakfast, he rose from the table. His wife rose with him. Cole put on his coat and grabbed his hat and suitcase. Helen waited for him by the door.

This is not going to go well, he thought, bracing himself for what would no doubt be a tearful goodbye on her part. But she just stood at the door.

Either she's accepted it, or she resents me for leaving her. Cole had built up an expectation that she would continue to try and stop him by crying. In some strange way, Cole felt that tears would somehow show that she was not really angry with him. But her almost cold silence made him uneasy. Cole took a deep breath and headed towards her.

"I don't have to tell you how much I will miss you," he said. She smiled and kissed him. Cole felt more at ease. She looked him in the eyes.

"You won't miss me for long." Not knowing how to take that remark, Cole stooped down and kissed her again.

Does she honestly think I won't miss her or is she just saying that for spite? He embraced her and kissed her one last time, then headed out the door.

The walk to the Covington Gazette was short and brisk. The old adage "When the Cat's away the Mice can play" worried Cole slightly, but when he walked unexpectedly into the offices of the Gazette, Cole was glad to see that everyone was busy as usual. He hadn't informed them he'd be stopping in that morning. The workers of the Gazette had presumed him gone. George Stetson was shouting loud and ferocious orders as good as any newspaper editor could. Cole knew he'd picked the right man to fill in for him.

"What are you doing here, chief? You're going to miss your train."

"I just figured I'd stop in one more time," said Cole. Stetson smiled.

"Well as long as you're here boss you should know that this morning we have a story bigger than yesterday's"

"What could be bigger than the CSA declaring war on Spain?"

George Stetson turned around and grabbed a folded newspaper of his desk and then tossed it to Cole.

"The morning edition, hot off the press, you should find it interesting." Cole stared at the headline on the front page.

CONFEDERATE STATES ENLIST NEGRO TROOPS. BLACK SOLDIERS PROMISED FREEDOM & LAND.

"Word came in over the wire last night just after the evening edition shipped out," said Stetson. Cole had gone home early the day before so he could spend some time with Helen. "We would have let you know, but I knew you needed to be with the wife."

Cole looked up at Stetson in surprise.

"I never thought I'd see the day that the South would free…well…*some* of its slaves. I certainly never thought I'd see the day they'd give them guns."

"Neither did, I," said Stetson. "This war is already making history. I'm just glad we're not a part of it this time around."

For a moment, Cole saw his friends hand stray to the spot on his upper leg where he'd taken a bullet back in 1869. Cole put his hand on Stetsons shoulder.

"And we're going to make sure that we stay out of it!"

The veteran nodded.

The clock on the walled chimed and Cole looked over at it.

7:30! "Good job men," said Cole.

"Thanks, now get out of here boss, before you really do miss the train." Cole tucked the paper under his arm and rushed out of the office and headed towards the train station. He got there just in time. After checking to make sure he had his ticket, and to remind himself what his car number was, he made his way out onto the crowded train platform. It didn't take him long to find his car. Right after climbing aboard, the railroad worker hollered "All aboard!" Moments later a steam whistle sounded, and the train lurched forward. Slowly but surely it chugged away from the Covington Station, leaving a billowing trail of smoke behind it.

It took Cole some time to locate his seat. He wasn't used to travelling on trains and certainly not used to walking on one that was not only moving but also accelerating. He stowed his leather suitcase in the overhead rack and took a seat beside a large glass window. A fellow passenger sat across from him whose face was completely hidden by a large open newspaper. Cole gave a slight scowl when he saw that it was the Covington Daily Mail, one of his chief rivals, and in his considered opinion, not a very good newspaper. He was about to read his own copy of the Gazette but was suddenly fascinated by the view from the train window.

He watched the buildings of Covington go by rapidly as the train made its way through the city and towards the river. When the train started across the long bridge that connected Covington with Cincinnati Ohio, Cole found the view of the Ohio River, which they were crossing, absolutely breathtaking—if also a little disconcerting. They were rather high. Cole had read enough stories in his own newspaper over the years about train wrecks and collapsed bridges to make him rather wary. He turned away from the window. He glanced at the front page of the Covington Daily Mail that his fellow passenger was reading. The headline read: REBS ARM NEGROS. That was one reason he didn't like the Daily Mail. It was often biased and opinionated in the way it reported the news, not objective and neutral they way Cole's late Uncle Perry had taught him to be. Cole had no problem with opinions in editorials—that's what they were for. As an editor he wrote them all the time. He wouldn't have objected at all if the editor of the Daily Mail had referred to the Confederates as "Rebs" in an editorial, but like it or not the Confederate States had been an independent nation since the 1860s and "Reb" a short form of the word "Rebel" used to deride the inhabitants of the South just resounded with too much personal animosity to be used in an area that was supposed to go by the motto, "just the facts." Cole had no great love for the Confederacy, rather the opposite, but he was very passionate about what his Uncle had called "journalistic integrity."

A man about Cole's age with a hook for a hand suddenly walked past and Cole remembered something he had forgotten. The editor of the Daily Mail was a veteran of the War of 1869 and had lost his own arm during the conflict. Thinking on that, Cole decided he was willing to forgive the slight breach of journalistic protocol.

Cole opened up his newspaper and started reading. Unsurprisingly, the citizens of the CSA were heavily divided about the freeing and arming of negroes. He found it interesting that the Confederacy had promised their negro troops land grants in Cuba for their service, in addition to their freedom. After a moment he thought he had figured out why.

They want to do their best to keep these newly freed negroes in Cuba and away from the mainland CSA. The rest of the paper contained little new news about the conflict. The Kingdom of Spain had been informed by the CSA that if they wanted to end the war, they would have to unconditionally cede the island of Cuba to the Confederate States. The Spanish had responded that they would never surrender the island and that they would defend "every inch" of Spanish soil. Thus far no fighting had begun but most experts believed that fighting on the high seas would begin soon and that a Confederate invasion of the island would not be long in coming. There were a couple of other stories as well. These were located in the "International News of Interest" section.

Out west, the Republic of California and the Mormon Nation of Deseret were still saber rattling over the disputed Nevada territory. Nothing new there. Most experts didn't think it would go any farther than that. The two-petty nation states had been threatening war with each other for over twenty-five years.

Over in Europe, however, another dangerous situation was brewing. The Kingdom of Prussia was doing some saber rattling of its own. Leopold, the King of Spain, was himself a native Prussian who had been given the Spanish throne in 1870. The Spanish King's blood relationship with Wilhelm the King of Prussia could easily start another war between Prussia and France if the French joined their Confederate allies in their war against Spain. Napoleon IV was on record as desiring the Spanish possessions of the Philippines in the Pacific and Puerto Rico in the Caribbean. Many believed he was on the verge of declaring war on Spain to get them, but the Prussians were trying to deter him by threatening war. In response the French Emperor had sent more troops into his puppet state the German Confederation and massed troops along the French-Spanish border. He had also had his ally, Austrian Emperor Franz

Joseph, mobilize the Austrian Hungarian army in preparation of coming to France's aid in the event of war with Prussia.

By fighting a protracted war in the 1860s and 1870s that had established a strong Hapsburg monarchy in Mexico, led by Franz Joseph's brother Maximillian, France had been able to form an firm and lasting alliance with the Emperor of Austria that had kept the small but upstart nation of Prussia contained.

But Prussia was not a nation to underestimate. From what Cole had read it had one of the finest and most disciplined armies in the world. But Cole doubted that they would risk another war against both France and Austria-Hungary. They had tried in 1877 and had been soundly defeated by the combined French and Austro-Hungarian armies. In that short war the then twenty-one year old Napoleon IV, had masterfully commanded the French armies at the battles of Wissembourg and Dusseldorf, defeating the Prussians and humiliating Bismarck. The young French Emperor had proved that he was a force to be reckoned with and respected in Europe and that he had much more of his great uncle's military genius, than had his father Napoleon III.

The other two great European powers, Britain and Russia had not yet taken a position on the Confederacy's war with Spain. London had taken no official stance on the Confederacy's new war against Spain other than to state its opposition to any expansion of slavery. Cole imagined the British were waiting to see if there was any truth to the reports of atrocities by the Spanish against the Cubans. But the British had condemned the buildup of French troops in the German Confederation.

Britain and France had been growing apart for years, ever since France invaded Mexico in 1863, allied itself with the slaveholding CSA against the United States in 1869, assisted the Confederacy in invading and seizing the Isthmus of Panama from Columbia in 1888, and most especially, since Napoleon IV had begun a massive expansion of the French fleet in an effort to rival the Royal Navy on the high seas.

Britain was still considered by most to be the most powerful nation in the world, but together Richmond, Paris, Vienna, and Mexico City formed a serious challenge to that power— especially with a strictly neutral and isolationist United States not bothering to get involved. There was talk of a new alliance between Prussia and Britain. But Cole reflected that it would take an alliance between Britain and the United States to pose a serious counterbalance to the Confederates, French, Mexicans and Austro-Hungarians. That was not an alliance that Cole envisioned happening any time soon, nor was he sure if he would want to see such a thing.

Two such powerful alliances at each other's throats could end up causing the largest war in the history of the world... All of a sudden, his task to remind the people of the USA of the horror and futility of war seemed more urgent than ever. *We must remain neutral. We must not allow ourselves to be drawn into these world conflicts!*

After finishing his reading, Cole pulled out a pen and paper and started to write three editorials: one to express his opinion about the Confederacy's use of negro troops, another about the political situation in Europe, and a final one about the need to maintain scrupulous neutrality in the USAs foreign relations.

The train rode remarkably smooth, so he was able to write quite easily. The words flowed from his mind as water from a fountain. He was quickly lost in his thoughts and his writing. Suddenly, a familiar feminine voice snapped him back to reality with a jolt.

"Hello darling," said his wife. Cole was so startled and surprised that he nearly jumped out of his seat.

"Helen! Wha....how.....what are you doing here!"

XIII

"Move it you Cuban scum!" cried Major Elian Ortega at an old woman who wasn't moving fast enough to suit him. The gray haired woman was trying to carry several rolled up blankets and a wood weave basket that she had crammed full of as many personal belongings as possible. When she failed to move faster, Ortega kicked her from behind. She toppled forward like a rag doll, landing face first in the mud. Her possessions scattered everywhere.

"Get up you old hag," cried Ortega. "And leave most of that junk where it is! You were told to bring only a blanket and a few clothes."

"Leave my grandmother alone!" came a wild and angry young voice. A twelve year old Cuban boy charged Ortega— *Bam!*

The boy went down with a crushed bloody nose and several missing teeth. Ortega had bashed in his face with the butt of his rifle.

"That's enough, Ortega!" cried Antonio Vega. He'd been checking one of the village huts to make sure no one was left inside when he'd heard the boy's cry. "We have orders to relocate these people, not grind them into the dirt."

"That's exactly what they are," said Ortega and spat on the boy as he writhed in pain. "They are dirt! They are traitors! They've been aiding the rebels!"

"I'm telling you to back off!" said Antonio.

"I don't take orders from you, Vega!" Things might have gotten out of hand at that point, but suddenly a cavalryman came riding up and shouting, frantically.

"Rebels are attacking a sugar plantation just over three miles east from here! We need infantry support!"

"We're on our way!" said Antonio. "Vega, you and your men finish the evacuation and keep these people secure! Squads one through nine, head east—move it!" With that, Antonio double timed it towards the fighting.

Antonio hated to leave the villagers at the hands of Ortega and his men, but they were the last people he wanted at his side in a fire fight with Cuban Rebels. Ortega and his scum were good at bulling helpless old women and boys, but were ill suited for fighting an infantryman's war. He still had his doubts about their artillery skills, though for Spain's sake he hoped he was mistaken.

His company followed a muddy path through the forest. After a few minutes, Antonio stopped just long enough to consult a map that he pulled from his sky blue uniform coat.

According to this we are just about to the plantation. We should be hearing the gunfire by now! "Be on your guard!" He replaced the map and readied his own Mauser rifle. When at last they emerged from the forest, they caught sight of several warehouses, one of which was on fire. About a dozen Cuban negroes and mulattos had a bucket chain going and were trying to put out the fire. Spanish cavalrymen trotted here and there with their horses. On the ground there was a handful of dead Cubans but the battle looked to be over.

"What happened here?" demanded Antonio.

"It was the strangest thing, senor. One moment the rebels came into the camp, screaming loudly and firing their weapons. They killed a few mayates, set the warehouse on fire, and then fought with us just long enough that we thought we would need reinforcements. They withdrew shortly after that. They could have fought much longer than that. They had the numbers. Had we known they were cowards who would slink back into the forest so quickly we would not have troubled you, Major Vega."

Antonio glanced around again. He noticed that most of the dead rebels were as black as the plantation laborers they had bushwhacked. All rebels considered anyone who worked on the sugar plantations as traitors to Cuba—regardless of color.

Why didn't they stay longer and do more damage to the plantation if they had the numbers to do so? They could have burned down more than half of it in the time they had. Suddenly, his strategy prone mind came to the answer.

"Back to the village!" he cried at the top of his lungs. "Back to the village! Double time! Move!"

Back at the village, Ortega watched the continuing forced evacuation with a vicious scowl.

How dare that Vega, presume to order me around?
Ortega turned to look for another Cuban to vent his rage and
frustration at. His eyes settled on a young teenage girl and a
wicked smile spread across his face.

"Get these people into line! For final inspection. We
don't want any contraband brought to the camp."

Using bayoneted rifles, the Spanish troops forced the
Cuban villagers to stand in five ranks, while sergeants went up
and down the line searching their belongings. Ortega made his
way to the young girl who seemed to be standing with her
mother. He smiled at her.

"What is your name?'

She said nothing. He pulled his sword bayonet from his
belt and put the tip at her throat.

"I said, what is your name?"

"Anna Maria," she said in a voice filled with terror.

"Anna Maria," he said. "And is this your mother?"

She nodded.

"And where is your father?"

"He's not here."

"Where is he?

She said nothing.

"I said, wear is he!"

Suddenly, the look in her eyes went from fear to rage.

"He's off fighting you Spanish pigs, along with my
brothers!"

Ortega gripped the hilt of his sword bayonet tightly,
tensing in rage as though about to plunge it into her throat.
Suddenly he relented smiled a sadistic smile. For women, there
were some fates that could be worse than death. Ortega looked
forward to personally showing that to the hot headed young
Cuban girl. But first, he intended to humiliate and degrade her
in front of everyone.

"Sergeant Gomez! I think this little Cuban puta might
be hiding something. Strip search her!"

"Right here, Major?"

Ortega swore, loudly and profanely and followed it up with a blasphemy. "Yes, right here! And turn her around so everyone can see." He then laughed derisively while the Sergeant and a private practically ripped the clothes from off of her, until she stood with her young naked body exposed to all. There were whistles and loud obscene comments from most of the Spanish troops. To Ortega's consternation, Anna Maria's face radiated neither fear nor shame, but the same stubborn defiant pride she had shown before Ortega had tried to humiliate her. She looked him dead in the eye.

"Viva la Cuba!" she shouted. Then she spat on his uniform. Ortega's face grew dark with rage. He hit her with his backfist, knocking her to the ground. He then grabbed her by the hair of her head and forced her back to her feet.

"We'll see if you still have that little attitude when I'm done with you. Gomez, keep an eye on this scum. Anna Maria and I are about to get to know one another much better." More coarse laughter erupted from his men as he started to drag the naked girl towards one of the abandoned huts by the hair of her head. "When I'm done, then the rest of you can have a go!"

Suddenly gunfire erupted all around them! In the chaos of the ambush, Ortega was momentarily distracted. Though he still held her by the hair of the head with an iron grip, Anna Maria twisted painfully and kicked Ortega between the legs as hard as she could. Ortega fell to the ground and curled up into a fetal position, grasping his private area with both hands. Anna Maria made a dash for the forest. The Spaniards were all too busy dealing with the ambush to stop her. Several of the other villagers likewise made a break for it. Others simply dropped to the ground to avoid being hit by the flying bullets.

Antonio and his men heard the gunfire shortly before they were halfway back to the village.

I knew it! The rebel attack on the sugar plantation had been little more than a diversion meant to draw his forces away from the village. *It worked too.* Antonio cursed himself for not figuring it out sooner. *I only hope we are not too late.*

When they were half a mile from the village, Antonio suddenly called his men to a halt. He knew there was a high probability that the rebels had laid another ambush along the path, meant for he and his infantry. He had no intention of giving them the chance to spring it. He quickly issued his orders.

"Squads one through four to the right. Squads five through nine to the left. Move! And be on your guard!" He set out at the head of the first four squads, leading them off of the muddy trail and into the forest to the right. It was much slower going through the trees, but the sound of gunfire let them keep their bearings. As he surmised, there was a small band of rebels waiting in the woods near the road. The would-be ambushers instead found themselves ambushed from behind.

What followed was a chaotic and haphazard battle. The small rebel party guarding the road was quickly dispatched, but when they moved on towards the village they found themselves in a cross fire with their own forces. The rebels fought tenaciously, but in the end superior numbers on the part of the Spanish prevailed and the surviving rebels fled back into the forest. Antonio didn't dare order a pursuit. He'd already lost far too many men to risk sending more into the forest. The Spanish force decided to lick its wounds and then carry on with its task. Nearly half of the villagers had escaped but they still held a large number captive. They had also managed to take seven Cuban Rebels prisoner. That fact alone made the loss of half the villagers superfluous. Taking some Rebel fighters prisoner had, after all, been the main point of interning those particular villages. Antonio had to restrain his men from killing the Rebel fighters, and issued strict orders that they were to be kept alive so that they could be taken to Havana and properly interrogated.

After the battle, Antonio spotted Ortega laying on the ground. For a brief instant a kind of morbid excitement arose in him, but he quickly suppressed it, and sent a petition of forgiveness to the Almighty, for presuming to hope for the death of a fellow soldier. It turned out Ortega was wasn't dead—in fact he didn't even look to be wounded.

Ortega stood to his feet and had a look of murderous rage on his face. He drew his pistol and made his way towards the remaining prisoners, looking to see if Anna Maria or her mother were amongst the remaining captives. He swore loudly when he saw that they were gone and stormed off to see to his men.

After securing the wounded, the Spanish expeditionary force compelled the remaining Cuban villagers to force-march to the internment camp, which was located twenty miles south of Havana. They smelled it, long before they ever saw it.

Antonio had never seen one of the internment camps and he prayed to God that he would never have to see one again. He'd smelled the stench of death before, but never to such an overwhelming extent. To his horror there was a field outside of the camp where over one thousand dead bodies had simply been dumped and piled up. The bodies were so thin that they looked as if they were little more than skeletons with skin on them. Flies swarmed everywhere, and ravenous birds descended on the corpses. The sight was even too much for Ortega, who vomited at the sight and the smell. As horrified Antonio was, he saw an even greater terror on the faces of the Cubans he had brought to that hellish place. Antonio crossed himself.

A large wooden wall surrounded the small town that served as the "internment camp." Several guard towers also ringed the camp. The main gates were opened and the Cuban villagers were herded inside. Antonio went inside just long enough to officially hand them over to the camp's commandant. What he saw would haunt him the rest of his life. He saw thousands of men, women and children who were literally starving to death. Like the bodies outside the camp, these people were little more than walking skeletons. Antonio knew that most of them would likely be added to the pile of the dead in the near future. There were literally thousands of people crammed into the small camp. Starvation and disease were rampant. Since coming to Cuba he'd heard whispered rumors that camps such as this existed but he hadn't believed it. He did now. Did he ever.

How could General Valeriano Weyler allow this? How will he stand before God? How will I stand before God? Antonio felt as though he would faint. He wanted to take a deep breath of air but he didn't dare. Killing rebels in battle was one thing. This…this was…

Hell. This place is hell. The air positively reeked. Only when they had left the camp and gotten several miles away was he able to suck enough oxygen into his lungs to try and clear his bewildered and overwhelmed mind. He was overwhelmed with grief and guilt. He searched desperately for a way to rationalize what was happening.

How many more camps like that are there? He suddenly felt an overwhelming sense of guilt that he had delivered the Cuban villagers to that place. *But I had no choice!* He lifted his eyes to the heavens. *Holy Mother I am innocent! I am a soldier! I must follow my orders!* Somehow, his conscience did not seem to agree with him. Nor did his petitions to heaven seem to bring any relief to his sense of guilt.

Upon his return to Havana he presented his seven rebel prisoners to Colonel Gonzales.

I wonder if he knows the full extent of what is going on in the internment camps?

Antonio expected Colonel Gonzales to order the immediate interrogation of the prisoners. But that is not what happened.

"There is no longer any need," said Gonzales. He handed Antonio a folded military communique. "The Estados Confederados have declared war on us."

Antonio was stunned. He had known that it was a possibility but he hadn't expected it to be so soon.

"What shall I do with the prisoners?"

"They are traitors to Holy Spain. And they shall die the death of traitors. Assemble a firing squad and shoot them before sundown."

Antonio felt little guilt about what he was about to do. Shooting them was more merciful than sending them to one of the camps. Antonio had seen that with his own eyes. These men were not innocent woman and children, they were men who had fought against his country and his king. Suddenly, the images of the camp came back to his mind.

It is your fault! Those women and children are suffering because of you, for taking up arms against your rightful rulers! And for not fighting honorably! As far as Antonio was concerned King Leopold ruled by Divine right. To fight against him was to fight against God Himself. He reflected further that it was the rebel tactics that had forced the Spanish to take such drastic action with the camps. The Rebels lived off the peasants and villagers. When finished with their attacks, the Rebels simply blended into the civilian population until ready to strike again. The internment camps were the only way to stop them from doing that. Antonio suddenly wished that he could send the Rebel fighters back to that camp.

Shooting is too good for you! By this line of reasoning, Antonio was at last able to deaden his aching conscience. For the moment at least, his normal sense of certitude had returned.

A Spanish soldier played a death march on his drum as the seven Cuban fighters were made to stand against the blood stained and bullet ridden wall of Morrow Castle that was used for executions. Two of them were negroes and two of them were Mulattos. The other three looked as if they could have come from Spain itself.

Fourteen Spanish soldiers stood at the ready with their Mausers loaded and ready to fire. Antonio drew his sword.

"Preparen!" Each soldier brought up his rifle, worked their bolt, and chambered a round. They worked in near perfect unison. "Apunten!" As one, the squad of soldiers leveled their rifles at the seven condemned Rebels. "Fuego!" Flame and smoke belched from the fourteen rifles as they were fired

110

simultaneously. The seven condemned rebels were cut down by the hail of bullets. No sooner had their bloody bodies hit the ground than Antonio's certitude left him like a flock of birds that flies off and away. He felt as though the earth had opened beneath his feet and he was sinking down to the bottomless pit of perdition. A moment later he looked down at the dead rebels, lying in a massive pool of their own blood. Their eyes were still open and they seemed to stare…not at him… but through him… into very depths of his soul… as if from the very fires of hell, they were waiting for him to join them.

He left the fortress in a near panic, desperate to reach the only place he might fight refuge and solace. He felt as though his hands were literally covered with blood and that no matter what he did he would never be able to wash the stain away. He rode himself across the channel and then ran through the streets of Havana like a madman. He stormed into the church, ran down the aisle and fell down on his knees at the statue of the blessed virgin. Tears of desperation, grief, and shame flowed from his eyes and down his face. At last a firm comforting hand grasped his shoulder from behind. Antonio turned and gazed up at the priest through tear filled eyes.

"Bless me father, for I have sinned!" *And sinned and sinned and sinned!*

XIV

The sound of negro spirituals resounded through the air at Twin Harbours plantation which sat directly on the Mississippi river. The sun had risen and hundreds of slaves, men and women of all ages, from toddlers to those in their sixties were making their way to the fields. Many carried hoes or bucket yokes as they walked from their drab village of shabby cabins to the fields for the day's work. Many went to the fields where corn and other foodstuffs were grown. Most, however, headed for the cotton fields. For his own part,

Ebenezer had been assigned by Mansel Dumas to work in the workshop.

Ebenezer left the small cabin he shared with Cap, and headed for the workshop. Ebenezer had wanted to keep Cap out of the fields as well, and had asked Mr. Dumas' permission to have Cap work with him. To Ebenezer's astonishment, Dumas had given permission for Cap to work with him on Tuesday's, Thursday's, and Saturday's. It was Tuesday, so Cap was trouncing along beside Ebenezer that morning.

Ebenezer found Twin Harbours a very different place than Sharpstone. The slaves seemed happier—not happy, but happier than the poor souls who were cursed to be at Sharpstone Plantation. There were overseers (white men on horseback with whips were never far away on a plantation), but after being at Twin Harbours a week, Ebenezer had not seen a single slave whipped. The path to the workshop took the two negroes past the Dumas' Mansion—"de' Big House" as the slaves called it. Florence Dumas, Mansel Dumas' wife, stood on the front porch of the mansion issuing orders to several female slaves who would be working in the gardens and flowerbeds that surrounded the mansion and that lined the main driveway which led from the mansion to the main gate of the plantation. She went by the name Flossy.

"Mo'nin Mis' Flossy," said Ebenezer as they passed by the mansion. He simultaneously removed his straw hat. Cap did likewise.

"Good morning, Ebeneezer," said Florence. "And to you as well Cap." She smiled pleasantly at them. Ebeneezer was surprised she had learned their names and faces so quickly. All the other slaves talked about how kind she was. She was a very small and slender lady in her forties. She'd had a stroke a few years earlier and so one of her arms hung limp and useless. She also walked with a hobble, but most of the time without the use of a cane. "I hope you are both settling in well in your new home. We're so happy you've come to be a part of our family."

"Thank you very much, ma'am," said Ebenezer. Cap, thinking on his woman Jemima, and his little boy Zeke, whom he'd been forced to leave behind at Sharpstone, lowered his head in sadness. Tipping his hat to the mistress of the plantation again, and taking Cap by the arm, Ebenezer set out again for the workshop. Suddenly, young Mitchell Dumas came running up excitedly holding a copy the Natchez Post that had come in the mail that morning.

"Mama! Mama! War! We declared war on those dirty sneaky Spaniards! I gotta' tell Daddy!" he stormed past his mother and into the house. A half second later, he came back out, kissed her on the cheek, then ran back into the mansion.

As Ebenezer and Cap continued on towards the workshop, they neared the stables. Two little girls came skipping, hand in hand, out of the stables and headed towards them. Dumas' daughters, Nancy and Connie were nine and seven years old respectively. Nancy was wearing a pink dress and Connie a yellow one. The two little girls separated and danced around the two negroes.

"Where you gowin' Ebeneza'," said Connie. The little white child spoke with the same slave accent as a little black child.

Not surprising, thought Ebenezer considering she was growing up surrounded by it. Nancy suddenly rebuked her little sister.

"Connie, Daddy and Miss Fields say we're not supposed to talk like niggers."

"You used to too," said Connie indignantly (simultaneously switching dialects).

"Yes," said Nancy in a very grown up voice, "but now I've had schooling—and so have you. We're supposed to talk like proper Southern ladies."

"I's gone talk hows' I likes!" said Connie and stuck her tongue out at her sister before taking off running. Nancy chased after her and started hollering at the top of her lungs, "Momma! Connie's talking like a nigger!"

When Ebenezer and Cap finally reached the workshop, the first thing they did was get to work on a wagon that had been brought in late in the afternoon the day before. One of its wheels was broken. Ebenezer grabbed the tools and went to work on getting the broken wheel off.

"You shouldn't of let Miss Flossy see you lookin' so sad and bothered," said Ebenezer to Cap. "She liable to think that you not happy wit bein' here. That liable to get you in trouble."

"I's sorry, Ebenezer. I's can't help it. I's jut miss Jemima and Zeke. I canst stand bein' here, where de white folks is so nice and they's back there at Sharpstone." Ebenezer put his hand on his friend.

"I know Cap. And I's sorry too. I knows it hurts. But there ain't nothin' you can do 'bout it. You gone have to makes a new life here." There were plenty of pretty negresses on Twin Harbours plantation. Cap shoved Ebenezer's hand away angrily.

"I's don't want a new life. I wonts my woman and my son."

Keeping his calm, Ebenezer looked him straight in the eyes, and said again, "There's nothing you can do."

"I's can git outa here, go back to Sharpstone, get dem' and git up north."

Ebenezer glanced quickly out of the open door of the workshop to make sure no one had heard that remark. Kinder or not, no white person would allow that kind of talk to go unpunished. Ebenezer stared him hard in the eyes again.

"You talk like that, you gone get us both in trouble! Even if you do what you just say, dey likely to shoot you and Jemima and lil' Zeke. And just where do you plan to go?"

"North," said Cap.

"I hates to tell you dis' Cap, but de' Yankees, dey don't like niggers any mo' then white folks here. Dey either shoot you or dey sends you back." Ebenezer was partly right. The United States officially considered runaway negroes from the CSA "foreign nationals." Official US policy was to turn back negroes at the border or, if caught well within US territory, turn them over to the Confederate Department of Servitude. In reality, negroes caught trying to cross into the United States were often shot by border patrols. Many Northerners blamed negroes for the division of America into two nations (though Ebenezer could hardly see how he was to blame. His ancestors hadn't very well had a choice about coming over from Africa). Those negroes who were residents (citizens would not be accurate) of the United States were generally registered in their state and carried papers on them stating that they had not originated in the CSA and therefore could not be deported. In short, the United States offered little hope for the enslaved millions of the south. But regardless, there were still a few in the U.S. who cared for their plight.

"What about de' underground railroad. Dey helps niggers get farther north den da Yankees. They helps us git to a place called Canada. Dey's let niggers in."

"You gots to find them first Cap. And I don't know about you but I's don't know how to find 'em."

Cap turned away. Ebenezer quickly noticed that tears were flowing down his face. He hated to dash his hopes, what negro didn't dream of being free? But he had to stop him from getting himself killed. A few moments later, he managed to get the broken wheel off and carried it over to the work bench. He then started to mend it.

"It gone need a couple a new spokes..." Suddenly, Mansel Dumas walked into the workshop. Ebenezer's heart leapt in fear. *Did he hear what we talks about?* "Massa Mansel! Good mo'nin suh!"

"Good morning, Ebenezer," he said. He then turned to Cap. "Good morning...uh..." He looked quizzically at Ebenezer.

"Cap, Massa..." said Ebenezer.

"Yes... Cap. Good morning Cap."

"Mo'nin Massa," said Cap almost in a whisper. His voice was hoarse from crying. In fact his face was still wet with tears. Suddenly embarrassed and alarmed, Cap reached up and wiped his face. Mansel Dumas looked very confused but turned back to Ebenezer.

"You've done some fine carpentry work in the short time you've been with us." He turned and examined the wheel that Ebenezer had removed. "I understand you're also a blacksmith."

"Yes, suh," replied Ebenezer.

"None of my other niggers know how to do blacksmith work. And my hired man recently left to seek new employment." Dumas had caught the man stealing various things off the plantation and let him go, but he didn't tell Ebenezer that. "I want you to shoe one of my horses."

"Yes Massa, that won't be no trouble at all."

"Follow me."

Ebenezer followed his master out of the workshop and a short distance to the stables.

"This is General."

"Hello Genral'," said Ebenezer and patted the animal softly on the side.

"You know where the blacksmith shop is?" asked Dumas.

"Oh yes, suh," said Ebenezer. "I find it de' other day. It right over 'dere."

"Good, just put him back in the stable when you're done."

Ebenezer then started to lead the horse towards the blacksmith shop.

"One moment Ebenezer." Dumas voice was suddenly hard and firm.

Ebenezer, turned to face Dumas who proceeded to ask him a pointed question.

"What was wrong with that boy over there? Grown men aren't supposed to cry like that, even niggers are supposed to be more manly than that. What did he do, hammer his finger?" Duma's voice held more than a little suspicion. Ebenezer looked down then back to his master. He decided to tell him (part) of the truth.

"No Massa, nothin' like dat. He cryin over his woman and youngin. Dey's back at Sharpstone. He hurtin' somethin' bad, he sho is suh."

Mansel's face softened slightly.

"That's a shame," he said shaking his head. "It surely is." He suddenly looked back at Ebenezer with sharp eyes. His voice again growing firm and hard. "He's not thinking of running off is he?"

"Oh no suh Massa!" lied Ebenezer and hoped he didn't sound too desperate in his answer. "Ole Massa Fitch, he is, beggin yo' pardon massa…" Ebenezer hesitated. For a negro, it was an *extremely* bad idea to say anything bad about a white person at all.

Fool! I is a fool! It turned out that he didn't have to decide whether or not to finish his sentence. Mansel Dumas finished it for him.

"He's meaner than a snake."

Ebenezer nodded.

"Comin here, suh, we feels like we come to de promised land. Yall suh, Yall is such good people." Ebenezer was exaggerating how happy he was to be at Twin Harbours. No matter how much better it was than Sharpstone, he was still a slave. But he hoped by playing on his master's ego slightly he could make him less suspicious of his friend. It apparently worked.

"Well he'll get better in time," said Dumas. "There's plenty negresses here for him too. When he has another youngin' that'll help, and who knows, if old Fitch Haley keeps running his Plantation into the ground I just might end up buying Cap's family too." Dumas then looked sharply again at Ebenezer. "Don't tell him I said that, you don't want to get his hopes up."

"No, suh."

"And you keep an eye on him. If he starts talking fool talk you let me know. It'll be a lot better for him than if he runs off, I promise you that."

"Yes, Massa, I keeps my eye on him suh."

Mansel Dumas then left, and Ebenezer found himself wondering whether he had betrayed his friend, or done him a favor.

XV

Nathan Audrey walked down the front steps of the California War Department in Sacramento. The small, square brick building was a relatively new edition to the city, and was rather unassuming to be the headquarters for the army of an independent country. But as Audrey had told the Sheriff of Pine City, California didn't have a very big army. Audrey found himself thinking about the Sheriff's words about the folly of California going its own way after the disaster of the Second War of Rebellion.

Perhaps he's right. Audrey had delivered Pine City's official request for armed protection from the army. An uninterested clerk in the War Department had assured Audrey that their request would be given "due consideration." Audrey wasn't holding his breath.

He pulled a cigar from his coat pocket and stuck it in his mouth. Then he scratched a match against the sole of his boot, and got his cigar going. He exhaled a small cloud of smoke, then sighed. He looked across 10th Street at the Capitol building. A massive Californian flag flew from the building there. To Audrey's mind it just seemed unnatural. As a child he'd grown up being taught to honor and reverence the flag of the United States. As a young man at West Point he'd sworn allegiance to the Stars and Stripes. Now he lived in one of three lands that had totally forsaken them.

The world has gone crazy! He suddenly found himself wishing that the South had never struck the blow that shattered the United States. He felt that, somehow, if they hadn't been so prideful and selfish or if the U.S. leaders had gotten their act together back in the early 1860s and won the First War of Rebellion, the world would be a much better place. Even if the

Confederates and Mormons had broken away, California hadn't had to follow suit. Audrey reflected that of the seceded nations, California had possessed the most legitimate cause to break away from the USA. The Union was supposed to provide protection and security for its states, but during the Second War of Rebellion the USA had virtually abandoned California. The people had had good cause to be angry, but the more he thought on it, the more he came to agree with the Sheriff of Pine City that California had acted rashly. Of one thing he was convinced, one strong unified nation was a lot better than four, selfish sectarian ones.

One nation...He threw his half smoked cigar away in angry frustration. That was a dream long dead. As he'd told the Sheriff, "water under the bridge." He cursed himself for mooning over a past that he could not change. The world was as it was, and they had to make the best of it. The reality was, California was an independent nation-state, now it would have to shoulder the responsibility of defending itself and its citizens, small army or not. Audrey didn't think the War Department was going to act quickly enough, so he resolved to try and light a fire under them. The people in Pine City were good people. They deserved the protection of their *nation*.

Audrey headed towards the telegraph office which was located not far away from the Capitol. Horse drawn coaches, wagons and carriages rolled past as did pedestrians. Just about every man that Audrey passed wore a six shooter on his belt, most entirely unselfconsciously about it. It might have made people back east a little nervous, but out west it was just a part of the reality of life. Audrey scarcely noticed it all. What he did notice were the shouts of newsboys on the street corners, holding their newspapers aloft and shouting at the tops of their lungs EXTRA! EXTRA! CSA DECLARES WAR ON SPAIN, READ ALL ABOUT IT! Audrey wasn't normally one to read newspapers, but in this case he made an exception. Tossing one of the boys a nickel, he grabbed a copy of the Sacramento Chronicle and folded it up under his arm before continuing to the telegraph office.

Audrey was pleased to see that the office was not busy. He walked straight up to the clerk.

"May I help you, sir?"

"I'm a California Marshal." The clerk eyed the silver badge on Audrey's duster jacket.

"What can I do for you, Marshal?"

"I need to know if the wire to Pine City is working yet or not."

"I'm not sure, sir. But I'll find out for you real quick." The clerk reached down below the little counter where he did his work and pulled out a map and unfolded it between them. Audrey noticed that it showed all the telegraph lines in the Republic of California. "Now where is Pine City, sir. I'm afraid I'm not familiar with it."

"It's in the eastern territories," said Audrey. He moved to point to it but before he could the clerk folded up the map and started to put it away.

"I can tell you then sir, that the line is definitely not open. All of our telegraph lines going in and out of the Nevada territory are down. Most of them have been down for weeks. It's very strange."

"I was in Pine City just over a week ago. The sheriff told me they'd been cut off. Have you sent anyone out to check the lines?"

"Oh yes, sir," said the Clerk. "Unfortunately none of them have returned."

Audrey tipped his hat to the Clerk.

"Thank you."

Audrey walked out of the telegraph office. He leaned against a wooden post right outside and ignited another cigar. He then unfolded the newspaper. He glanced over the article on the new war between the CSA and Spain with only passing interest. It wasn't long before another article caught his eye, one that struck far closer to home. MORMONS ISSUE ULTIMATUM! The Mormon minister in Sacramento had delivered a communique from Salt Lake City which stated that if the Republic of California did not recognize Deseret's claim to the whole of the Nevada territory within ten days "dire consequences would ensue." Audrey couldn't believe that that was not the top story in the paper. Then he read the editorial, which relegated the Mormon threat to nothing but bluster and ho hum of the type the Mormons had been spitting out for twenty-five years. The fact that all the telegraph lines to the disputed territory just happened to be down, indicated to Audrey that the threat was more serious than the paper made it out to be. The newspaper article didn't even mention the severed telegraph service to the border towns like Pine City. Audrey nearly threw it aside in disgust. Instead he headed towards the courthouse.

Someone has to light a fire under these idiots. There was only one person with whom Audrey had influence that might be able to make a difference. The Courthouse was located behind the capital. A large clock was built into the front of the Courthouse. The time was nearing noon. Sure enough three condemned murderers stood on top of the gallows that seemed to be a permanent addition to the Courthouse lawn. A large crowd had turned out to see that week's hangings. Had Audrey not shot Black Dog back in Pine City, the outlaw would be up there with the others that very day.

Audrey did not care to witness the hangings. In his violence filled life he'd already seen more death than he ever cared to. But the crowd around the gallows was massive, and he could not easily reach the courthouse. Up on the gallows a minister in a black suit and hat was reading a few verses from the Bible. A moment later he led the assembled crowd in a verse of Amazing Grace. After that one of the court clerks read the crimes and sentences of the condemned out loud to the crowd, while the minister went and prayed with each criminal in turn. Black hoods were then placed over their heads. Less than a minute later, a lever was thrown, and the three criminals fell through trap doors in the gallows which had suddenly opened. The ropes went taut and there were three simultaneous cracking sounds as the necks of the condemned criminals snapped. In the dead silence that followed, the assembled crowd watched the three strung up bodies dangle lifelessly from the gallows above.

As the crowd dispersed, Audrey was able to make his way to the courthouse. As he walked towards the front steps that led into the building, he noticed that the second story window of the Judge's office was open. Judge Hingle was still standing there. He'd watched the hangings from on high, like the Almighty passing judgment on the world. He spotted Audrey just as he started to climb the steps. Audrey nodded to him. The judge nodded back and motioned for him to come up.

Audrey made his way into the courthouse. He walked through the foyer and climbed the large oak staircase that led to the second floor. He passed several court clerks as went down a side hall and into the antechamber to the judge's office. Hingle's secretary rose from his desk and addressed Audrey.

"The judge is expecting you, Marshal. Go right in."

The judge's office was large and ornate. He had several bookcases filled with books on the law. Hingle rose from behind a fine wooden desk and extended his hand to Audrey.

"Good to see you, Johnson." As usual the judge's office was pervaded by cigar smoke. Audrey loved to smoke cigars himself, but the judge preferred a very expensive tobacco that was so dark it was almost black. The odor was very strong—almost overpowering.

"That's fine work you did in Pine City, with Black Dog. I'd have preferred to send him to the fires of damnation myself, but will content myself in the knowledge that you sent him there a little early." Audrey's eyes went to the large leather bound Bible on the judge's desk—by far the largest volume in the room. The judge had a tendency to view his job in religious tones. He viewed himself as an instrument of God, put in power on the earth to mete out justice. Audrey supposed that made him a good judge.

"It's partly about Pine City that I've come to see you, sir," said Audrey. "Telegraph lines leading to it and other settlements in the eastern territories are out. Many of the locals fear a Mormon attack. They sent me back with a request for the army to send them some help, but when I dropped it off at the War Department I got the distinct feeling that they weren't going to do anything about it."

"And you want me to talk to the President about it," said Hingle. It was well known that judge Hingle and California President Henry Markham were good friends. Hingle had endorsed him during the last election.

"Yes, sir," said Audrey. The judge took a long drag on his cigar and exhaled a cloud of smoke.

"Marshal, I don't let anyone tell me how to do my job, and I'm not about to tell the President how to do his."

"I wasn't suggesting you do that, sir," said Audrey. "I merely felt that the President might not have been fully informed about the situation and that you might bring it to his attention. Particularly the telegraph being out of order."

Hingle took another long drag on his cigar.

"Yes, Marshal, I might just do that. I'm having dinner with him the day after tomorrow. I might bring it up then."

"Thank you, sir. I was also hoping you might send me and some other Marshals to Pine City to give them some protection until the army can get some men out there." To Audrey's professionally trained military mind it was the height of insanity that the Californian Army didn't have some forts in the region already.

Rather than answer immediately, the judge rose from his desk and walked over to a map of California on the wall. He pointed at his with his lit cigar.

"Marshal, do you see this map? I've got less than 50 marshals, including yourself, to cover it all. I'm tasked with keeping law and order in this country and I can't afford to send my men to do something that's not our job."

"I thought our job, sir, was to protect the innocent." The judge suddenly waved his hands frustratingly at Audrey, who knew he'd scored a point.

"You know what I mean, Johnson. It's the army's job to protect the people from outside dangers and our job to protect them from themselves. Even if I let you and a few others go to

Pine City, what about the other towns? There's over a dozen towns in western Nevada that need protecting and I'm not about to play respecter of persons and give special protection to one and not the others just because you've got a soft spot for Pine City!"

The frustrated judge sat down and started shuffling through the papers on his desk trying to calm down. Suddenly, a memory came to his mind, and he forgot his frustration. He looked up at Audrey.

"Come to think of it Marshal, you might have another friend that can help you more than I can."

Audrey was pleased the judge still considered him a friend. Their relationship went back over a decade. Hingle had given him his Marshal's star, and hadn't asked too much about his background. But Audrey had learned the hard way that Hingle was easily angered even by those closest to him. This wasn't the first time he'd locked horns with the judge. But Audrey had no idea what friend he could possibly be talking about.

"You never told me you were a veteran of the First War of Rebellion or that you had fought at Gettysburg!"

Audrey's heart froze in his chest.

"I should have known though," continued Hingle, "You're too brave and good with a gun."

Someone's recognized me... after more than twenty-five years... Audrey forced himself to remain calm. Whoever it was obviously hadn't given him away completely. The judge reached into his desk, rummaged through some files and pulled out a piece of paper.

"You remember of few weeks ago when we hung the Leman brothers?"

"Yes, sir," said Audrey. Hingle had ordered him up onto the gallows and presented him to the crowd as the lawman that had captured the two notorious bank robbers being hung that day. Now Audrey at least knew how he'd been spotted. The judge continued.

"An army general recognized you and the next day he came to see me. He says he served with you over twenty-five years ago in the U.S. Army and that you fought together at Gettysburg. He was certain you were the same Nathan Johnson he'd known back then." Audrey relaxed a little.

Either he doesn't want to give me away or he's mixed me up with someone else. To know which, Audrey would need to know more.

"What was his name, judge?"

Hingle looked down at the paper.

"General William Goldwyn. He left this address for you, and asked that you call on him as soon as you are back in town." A chill went down Audrey's spine. He knew Goldwyn. Despite the fact that it had been well over twenty-five years since he'd laid eyes on him, in his mind he could see him as plain as day. He had served with him at Gettysburg but more importantly than that, Goldwyn had been there when Audrey had killed George Armstrong Custer.

He knows who I am. He knows what I've done. Why hasn't he turned me in? Audrey decided the only way to find out was to go and see him. The only other option he could see was to go on the run again. He couldn't stand the idea of that.

"Thank you, judge," said Audrey and accepted the paper with Goldwyn's address from Hingle.

"I have a nagging suspicion that he wants to steal you from me," said the judge. "If he does, rest assured you'll always have a place here...Marshal."

"Thank you, sir."

Audrey left the courthouse as quickly as possible and made his way towards Goldwyn's address. Hingle's paper said that he lived at 22 Webster Street. Audrey fetched his horse from the stables, so that he could get out there faster. It was a prosperous area. The homes were large and extravagant.

Goldwyn's done well for himself, thought Audrey. He seemed to remember that Goldwyn had been the son of a rich man. He'd probably come into his inheritance. He guided his horse along Gibson Avenue and then onto Webster. Number 22 was a large red brick home. Audrey hitched his horse to the hitching post and then walked up the stone pathway to the front door. He lifted the large heavy knocker and banged three times. A moment later, the door opened and Audrey found himself face to face with a well-dressed servant.

"May I help you, sir."

"I'm here to see General Goldwyn."

"Are you expected?"

"He left word that he wanted to see me at my earliest convenience."

"And your name, sir?"

"Marshal Nathan Johnson."

The servant eyed the silver badge on Audrey's duster and then opened the door wide for him.

"Please, come in Marshal. If you'll wait right here in the foyer, I'll let the General know that you are here." Audrey stepped into the house. The foyer had a couple of comfortable looking chairs, but Audrey remained standing. He eyed himself in a large mirror in the corner.

How did he recognize me? The hair of Audrey's head and beard was longer and grayer than it had ever been. His once smooth skin had become rough and weatherworn, his face lined with wrinkles that bespoke a lifetime of hardship. Suddenly the servant returned.

"The General will see you immediately."

Audrey followed the servant through the house. They proceeded through a lavish living room and then down a long hall way which led to the General's study. The servant opened the door for Audrey and then after he had entered, closed the door behind him.

The study was large and spacious. It was well lit by large windows on both the north and south sides of the room. But Audrey didn't see Goldwyn. Suddenly Audrey's eyes caught sight of a large open wooden cabinet. Inside a blue U.S. officer's uniform with Colonel's eagles on the shoulder straps was proudly displayed. He walked over and examined it.

"Captain Nathan Audrey," came a voice from behind him. Audrey spun around to face Goldwyn who'd been standing out of view in the corner of the room. "It's been a long time."

"Yes, it has," said Audrey. "Though for some of us, not long enough."

Goldwyn walked towards him. He was dressed in the forest green wool uniform that had been adopted by the Californian Army. Audrey noticed that time had been a lot kinder to Goldwyn than to himself.

"Now is that anyway to greet an old friend," said Goldwyn. "Especially one who has kept your... shall we say spotted past... from being discovered."

"My only question is why," stated Audrey. "You were there the night I blew Custer's brains out and then shot my way out of the camp."

"Yes. You did, in the heat of the moment, what a lot of us would have loved to have done personally. But you should know that during your escape you wounded several other troopers, among them Thomas Custer."

Audrey hung his head. He'd always wondered whether he'd hurt anyone else in his desperation to escape.

"Did any of them die?"

"No. The only serious injury was to Tom Custer. After you killed his older brother one of your bullets hit him where the sun doesn't shine—if you follow what I mean." Audrey looked horrified for a moment but then any feelings of guilt disappeared. Custer's men had raped and murdered plenty of Indian women. It was ironic justice that one of Audrey's bullets had robbed Tom Custer of the ability to ever ravish another woman.

"Is Tom still alive?" asked Audrey hesitantly. Goldwyn nodded.

"Unfortunately, old Tom Custer managed to keep himself alive throughout the Second War of Rebellion. I wish the same could be said for thousands of his men. As far as I know, he's still in the U.S. Army." Goldwyn looked Audrey in

127

the eye. "Nathan you should know that he hates you with every fiber of his being, both for killing his brother and for unmanning him. If he knew you were here he would stop at nothing to hunt you down. He had a bounty out on you for years, but I'm pretty sure he's given you up for dead."

"I wouldn't count on it," said Audrey. "Hate is a powerful thing."

"Isn't that the sorry truth," replied Goldwyn.

Audrey eyed the man from his past who had come so suddenly out of nowhere as if to haunt and torment him. *What does he want?* Audrey remembered that he had been a lot like himself. Someone who'd been forced to fight along Custer and his butchers but didn't enjoy it.

"What do you want with me, William?" he said in a voice like ashes.

"Don't worry, Nathan. I have no intention of turning you in, or letting dear old Tom know that you're still alive. I just wanted to see you. As I said, It's been a long time. I also wanted to ask you if you would be interested in accepting a commission in the Army. California desperately needs qualified professional soldiers and there are almost none to be had. We believe that the Mormons plan on attacking us any day. President Markham has directed me to very quietly assemble as strong a force as possible to head east, but we have very little time." Goldwyn's proposal hit Audrey like a ton of bricks. Judge Hingle had suspected that very thing, though Audrey had given it no thought. He was also pleased to know that the leaders of his small country that destiny had given to him were not as hapless as he'd thought. Audrey took a deep breath and gave Goldwyn his answer.

"I am at your service, General."

XVI

Joseph Whitmore watched the ticking grandfather clock in the antechamber of the President's office with increasing frustration. The secretary had invited him to sit in a comfortable chair in the corner of the room. Much to the secretary's annoyance, the rich tycoon paced the room back and forth impatiently. At times he even held his gold capped walking stick like a sword. Whitmore was not a patient man and he was used to getting what he wanted when he wanted.

What could possibly be so important that Cleveland is keeping me waiting? Whitmore was used to politicians practically groveling at his feet for his financial support. He'd supported Cleveland during the last Democratic Convention. He'd supported him for the following general election as well, (not that that really mattered, no Republican had won since 1868).

The point is, I deserve a more punctual reception!

Whitmore's personal assistant, David Lovejoy had taken one of the proffered chairs. He accompanied his employer just about twenty-four hours a day. The reason was because he was more than just Whitmore's personal assistant; he was also his body guard. He kept a loaded revolver in his coat at all times. Lovejoy was quite amused by his employer's impatience, though he kept it well hidden. He was fairly certain he knew the reason the President was keeping Whitmore waiting. One of the things Cleveland had been elected on was a promise to combat cronyism in the Federal government. He might well have been sending Whitmore a not to subtle message that even though the business man was rich and powerful, Cleveland was the President and would not be unduly influenced. Thinking on how Whitmore had audaciously demanded an on the spot audience with the President a few weeks earlier, Lovejoy was suddenly certain that Cleveland was making Whitmore wait, for no better reason than to put the eccentric multi- millionaire in his place.

After another fifteen minutes, during which Lovejoy was afraid that Whitmore might actually grow agitated enough to complain, or possibly walk a hole into the floor from his impatient pacing, a Presidential aide stepped out of the Executive office.

"Mr. Whitmore, sir. The President will see you now."

"Bout bloody time." Whitmore marched past the aide and into the office of President Grover Cleveland. The aide then closed the door. Lovejoy would remain in the antechamber until the meeting was over.

"Ah Mr. Whitmore how good to see you." Cleveland came around his large desk and extended a hand. He sounded excited and sincere enough, but Cleveland, like a lot of politicians, had struck Whitmore as the kind of person who could turn on joviality and friendliness with a flip of a switch. Nonetheless, Whitmore accepted the President's proffered hand without hesitation. Cleveland motioned Whitmore to an overstuffed arm chair before returning to his own seat behind his executive desk.

"I'm sorry I was unavailable when you first came to see me, but as I'm sure you understand, the Presidency requires a great deal of me. Had you made an appointment with my staff you would have saved yourself trouble."

"I am well aware of that Your Excellency, however, the matter I wished to discuss with you—and still wish to discuss—came about quite suddenly and unexpectedly, and I felt it my urgent duty as a leading citizen of the country to come to you immediately."

A servant then entered the office carrying a brass tray with two steaming cups of coffee. He first set a cup in front of President Cleveland and then in front of Whitmore.

"And what might that urgent thing be, sir?" asked Cleveland.

"What is so urgent?" asked Whitmore in genuine surprise that Cleveland even needed to ask. "The urgent matter of the war-mongering of that slave-holding monstrosity to the south of us!"

"You mean the war between the Confederate States and Spain."

"Yes, exactly!" said Whitmore.

"Forgive me, Mr. Whitmore, but I fail to see how a conflict between two foreign nations is of any matter to the United States."

"Forgive me, Mr. President, but I was under the impression that you wanted the United States to be a strong and powerful nation again. If we are to do that, then we must take a leading role on this continent. We mustn't sit idle while our greatest enemy further expands its sphere of influence."

"Sir, I'm sure I don't have to give you a history lesson for you to know that the last time we tried to assert ourselves on the Confederacy it ended up costing our nation the most humiliating defeat in our history. Even though a quarter of a century has passed, the shame of that defeat and the pain of it, is still very much a part of this nation's consciousness."

"All the more reason to stand strong now," said Whitmore. "Until we vindicate ourselves, we will never be rid of the shame of the Second War of Rebellion."

"Mr. Whitmore, even if I wanted to involve us in this dispute between the CSA and Spain, the Congress and the people would never go along with it."

"You are a strong leader, Mr. President. If you handled it right, I'm certain the nation would follow you."

"We cannot face the Confederate States alone," said Cleveland emphatically.

"On that point I must respectfully disagree, Your Excellency. We have the population and the industrial might to crush the CSA. Our problem is that in both previous wars we either failed to utilize those advantages or else we suffered from incompetent leadership. With the right leadership and organization, the United States would be unbeatable. But I digress, I'm not even asking you that we face the Confederates alone, though it is my strong conviction that we could."

"Then what are you asking of me, Mr. Whitmore."

"I'm asking you to build a coalition against the Confederacy. There is no need to oppose them alone. They have arrogantly thumbed their nose at the entirety of western civilization by their continued keeping of slaves. Reach out to the British, Mr. President. The vast majority of the British despise the Confederate States because of slavery. If the United States and Britain were to act in concert on Spain's behalf, the Confederates would be forced to back down."

"No they wouldn't," said Cleveland and took a quick sip of his coffee. "The Confederates are a proud and as you pointed out *arrogant* people. They'd cut their nose off to spite their face, and they'd certainly go to war against both us and the British before they would yield to an ultimatum."

"Well then you are making my case for me," said Whitmore. "They could not hope to prevail against us both, and arrogant as they are I don't think they would choose to fight both the British and us. Take my word for it, they'll back down but if they don't, we'll pay them back everything they gave us in the Wars of Rebellion."

"You seem to be forgetting a very important factor," said Cleveland. "The Confederacy has allies of its own. The Empire of France is not about to sit idle while we and the British go after their North American ally. You can bet Napoleon IV doesn't care whether or not the Confederates keep slaves. All he cares about is growing his own power and influence, and the CSA helps him keep his puppet state in Mexico propped up. The Confederates and French fought together in Mexico for ten years to make sure Mexico stayed a monarchy with a European Habsburg on the throne. I will be very surprised if France doesn't very soon declare war on Spain as well. You can bet Napoleon's going to get his piece of the pie. The point I'm driving at, however, is that if we and the British involve ourselves in this, we could wind up embroiling not one but two continents in war."

Whitmore sighed. Though he hated to admit it, Cleveland had a point.

No, he has half a point. If the United States and Britain did end up setting off an Intercontinental War, he was confident that the British could handle France and that the United States—if properly led and organized—could handle the Confederacy. But Whitmore knew that as far as President Cleveland was concerned, the USA would never again challenge the Confederate States alone.

"Mr. President, if I may ask," if you don't want the United States to take a proactive role in the security of this continent and hemisphere, why did you lead the Congress into modernizing and upgrading the Navy? Why did the Federal Government recently pay my company to build some of the most powerful battleships afloat? Why is the Congress even now contemplating having me build more? What's the point in having strength, if you're not going to use it?"

"Mr. Whitmore, I want us to have a powerful Navy, not so we can get into affairs of other nations, but so that we can keep them out of ours. There is something to be said for armed neutrality." The President then looked at the clock on the wall. Whitmore could tell he was growing tired of the discussion.

Well too bloody bad. "Allow me to make another suggestion, sir. Since we are unwilling to help Spain directly, might I suggest that we help them indirectly. We could easily supply them with arms and materiel on credit. My shipyard has just finished two state of the art battleships for the Navy. They are larger, faster and stronger than anything the Confederate Navy has in the water. Why don't we sell them to Spain on credit at cost of production? We could easily sell Spain enough rifles and ammunition and artillery and shells to make taking Cuba more costly than the Confederates are willing to pay."

"I'm afraid that would be seen by Richmond and Paris as unfriendly acts on our part to say the least."

"Do we not have the right to trade and do business with whom we wish?"

Cleveland did not answer the question. Instead he looked again at the clock and then turned back to Whitmore. He spoke politely but firmly.

133

"I'm sorry Mr. Whitmore, but I'm afraid that's all the time I have for today."

You just want me out of your hair.

"You can rest assured though, sir, that I will give all your proposals serious thought."

As soon as I'm gone, you'll do your best to forget everything that I've said. With great reluctance, Whitmore rose from the comfortable seat, shook Cleveland's hand politely and then exited the Executive Office.

David Lovejoy rose to his feet and followed his employer out of the Executive building. They walked down the stone steps towards Wall Street and their waiting carriage.

"How did it go, sir?" asked Lovejoy.

"He is a fool!" said Whitmore. "A stupid, isolationist, spineless, visionless fool!"

The driver came down from his seat and held the door of the carriage open for the fuming millionaire. Whitmore climbed in followed by Lovejoy. The driver returned to his seat, flicked the reins and the carriage was off.

"Are we returning to the hotel, sir?" asked Lovejoy.

"Only long enough to pack a few things, then we go to the train station. I want to be in Philadelphia as soon as possible."

"What are you planning, sir?"

"I'm going to show Cleveland, our country, and the whole world, that the Confederates are not invincible."

Lovejoy found himself concerned, but overwhelmingly curious, about what his employer's latest scheme was.

Meanwhile, back in his office, President Cleveland had seated himself at his desk. He pulled a dark brown Colorado from the gold cigar box on his desk, struck a match and got it going. He took a long thoughtful drag on the cigar, then exhaled a small cloud of smoke. He stared into space lost in thought. Finally, he set down the cigar and picked up the candlestick telephone. He held the ear piece to his ear and brought the receiver close to his face so that he could address the operator.

"Get me the British embassy!"

XVII

Joseph Whitmore arrived in Philadelphia the following day. Though Lovejoy was younger than Whitmore by more than a decade, he found it difficult to compete with the man's tenacious energy. It seemed they had been on the move non-stop since the day before. On the train trip from New York, neither of the men had slept much. Nonetheless, Whitmore insisted that they immediately go to the place that was his reason for coming to Philadelphia—the Spanish Embassy.

The embassy was located on Cherry Hill Rd in southwest Philadelphia. Whitmore had sent a telegram that they should expect his arrival, but had not bothered to wait for a reply that they were interested in seeing him. Lovejoy decided that he shouldn't be surprised. If his employer had the audacity to demand an on the spot audience with the President of the United States, he would think nothing of doing the same with the Ambassador from the Kingdom of Spain.

The carriage pulled up to the front of the Spanish Embassy at close to noon. It was a beautiful building that looked to be made of sandstone. From the top of the building, there flew a very large red and gold flag with the coat of arms of the King of Spain. An iron fence separated the embassy's small front court yard from Cherry Hill Rd. A guard in a very fancy red uniform, with lots of glittering gold braid all over it stood at attention at the front door of the embassy. He also wore a bright red and gold hat with a big blue feather sticking up from the front of it.

"I hope that's not what they plan on wearing when they fight the Confederates," said Whitmore to Lovejoy quietly.

"This fellow looks like he belongs in an army from the Napoleonic wars," replied Lovejoy.

Whitmore shook his head.

"No, he looks like he belongs in a circus marching band." They walked up to the closed iron gate. There was no bell to ring, and since the Spanish guard in the fancy uniform didn't seem to want to move, Whitmore went ahead and opened it and walked boldly up to the front door and the waiting sentry.

"I am Joseph Whitmore. I believe your superiors are expecting me?" The guard was still at perfect attention. Suddenly he turned his head slightly to look Whitmore in the face. The guard spoke something that to both Whitmore and Lovejoy was unintelligible. "Perfect," said Whitmore. He looked at Lovejoy. "I don't suppose you speak Spanish?"

"I'm afraid not," sir.

Whitmore rounded on the sentry again. He pointed at the front door with his cane.

"Go inside, and tell them to send someone out here who speaks English." Whitmore was aware that he sounded annoyed and bossy but he was tired pesky minutia getting in the way of his carefully laid plans. The guard spoke again in Spanish. Once again, Whitmore didn't understand any of it but he was relieved when the guard did an expert about face and then climbed the steps to the front door and entered the building. A few minutes later he returned followed by another man in a very exquisite suit. The man had dark hair and eyes and an almost swarthy complexion. The man spoke in perfect but heavily accented English.

"Gentlemen, I am Enrique Dupuy de Lome. And you, sir, are Senor Whitmore?"

"I am. And it is a pleasure to meet you Mr. Ambassador. Allow me to present my associate Senor Lovejoy."

De Lome nodded politely to Lovejoy then said, "Welcome to the Spanish embassy, gentlemen. Please come this way." De Lome led them past the sentry and into the embassy building. It was beautifully furnished. The carpets were all red. Several paintings and tapestries adorned the walls. There were even a couple of suits of armor. Most prominent was a massive portrait over the fire place. It was a portrait of a stern looking older man decked out in royal robes and wearing a crown. It was

Leopold, the Prussian descended King of Spain. Ambassador De Lome motioned for them to take seats on a fine red velvet couch.

"What can Spain do for you today, Mr. Whitmore?"

"Actually sir, I am here to let you know what I can do for Spain. I would like to offer you my services in your war with the Confederate States."

For one brief second, a fierce look of anger came over De Lome's face at the mention of the Confederates.

"We have already asked your government to aid us. Your President has told us that this is impossible."

"I know," said Whitmore. "I spoke with President Cleveland yesterday to try and make him see reason, but I'm afraid that his mind is quite made up."

"Then forgive me, Senor Whitmore, but I fail to see what you can do for us."

"Senor De Lome, as you no doubt know I am a very wealthy and powerful man. I own factories, and shipyards and railroads. I could very easily supply you with rifles, ammunition and artillery to aid you in your fight against the Confederates. But I am willing to do much more than that. I want to raise, equip and arm a paramilitary force of American volunteers—a force that would be equipped with the latest and most advanced weapons available in the industrialized world. If I did so, would your government be willing to take us into its service?"

"As what? Mercenaries?"

"More or less."

"This has been considered before. The French have long used a Foreign Legion in their army, and I know several officers in the army who have before discussed the possibility of a Spanish Foreign Legion."

"Then you will agree?"

"I can make no promises. My superiors in Madrid will have the final say. I must ask though. Why are you willing to do this? What do you get out of it?"

Since the ambassador had asked a two-fold question, Whitmore gave two answers. "First, I'm doing this because I want a group of Americans, armed with American weapons to face off against the Confederates (that the Confederates also called themselves Americans never crossed his mind). I want the people of the United States to see that we can face those blasted Southerners and win. I want my people to see that the Confederates can be defeated."

Ambassador De Lome nodded. Whitmore continued.

"I would also expect Spain to see to it that the volunteers are adequately provisioned once we are on the field."

"We?" said De Lome. "Do I take that to mean that you intend to be one of these volunteers?"

"Well of course," said Whitmore. "If I'm going to raise an army out of my own pocket, you'd better believe I'm going to be its General!"

"*Si Senor,*" said De Lome, momentarily lapsing into his own language. The Spanish ambassador found the eccentric millionaire's proposal almost absurd, if he wasn't so obviously serious. Even if he was serious, how did he plan on raising such a force in time? "Senor Whitmore, the Confederados could attack at any time. How do you propose to raise this force in time to be of use?"

"I have a number of friends in the War Department and in the Congress. I plan on pressuring them to allow me to recruit a number of highly trained volunteers directly from the U.S. Army. There will also no doubt be plenty of older men who served in the Second War of Rebellion who are itching for some payback. Those two groups will form the core of the force that I have in mind and will help to train the raw recruits that will come in. I plan on starting immediately. I have already arranged for a training camp to be set up on my property in New York."

"How can you be certain that President Cleveland will allow this?"

"In the first place I am not breaking any laws. I don't need his permission to spend my money on what I want and to use my property for what I want. In the second, if he gets in my way, I'll cause him plenty of trouble in the election next year and he knows it. They say no Republican will ever be elected President again. By Jove I'll put that theory to the test after I spend a couple of million dollars backing whoever the Republicans nominate and spend another million letting everyone know what a coward Cleveland is."

De Lome nodded. He'd seen how ugly American politics could be. He thanked heaven every night that Spain was ruled by a King, the way any proper country should be.

"I will get you an answer as soon as I can, Senor Whitmore. I'm positive that my government will be interested in any artillery, rifles, and ammunition that you can provide us. As for the rest, we will have to wait and see."

"Good. If your country is going to hold on to its prize colony, you're going to need all the help you can get."

Ambassador De Lome's face grew suddenly hard and stern.

"Senor Whitmore. We do not consider Cuba to be a colony. We consider it to be a province of Spain itself. As much a part of our country as the soil on which the Royal Palace in Madrid sits. We will defend it to the last drop of Spanish blood."

Whitmore nodded but said, "Let's hope it doesn't come to that Your Excellency."

XVIII

John Wilkes Booth studied the large maps of North America, South America, and Europe that hung on the wall of his massive windowless office in the basement of the Confederate Treasury Building. Different colored pins represented different types of agents that he had spread around the world. Black was for assassins, green for provocateurs. Red was for saboteurs, and brown was for spies. But a very few of the pins were gold. Those represented very special agents with a multiplicity of talents. Those agents were the best that the Confederate Secret Service had.

Booth had been so busy for the past several weeks that he hadn't had time to update his map. One needed correction in particular stood out to him. He pulled one of the golden pins off the map that had been stuck on Havana, and moved it up to Richmond.

Suddenly, the clock on the wall chimed. Sighing, Booth pulled out his own pocket watch to double check the time. Now that they were at war with Spain, the President was holding meetings nearly every day, and he wanted constant intelligence updates from the Secret Service. Booth was proud of his network. He'd spent the better part of a quarter-century building it. In his opinion, the Confederate Secret Service was the best and most ruthlessly efficient intelligence service in the world. But even he couldn't provide up to the minute intelligence on a daily basis. Booth opened the iron reinforced door to his personal sanctum, turned off the electric lights and exited the office. After closing the door he locked the three massive bolts locks with his key. The sanctum contained files on every agent that the Confederate Secret Service had in the world. Booth was the only one who had a key to that room and the only one in all the Confederacy with access to its files. He headed down the corridor. He passed up the stairwell that led to the Treasury buildings upper floors and approached another iron reinforced door. After opening it with his keys, he went down yet another flight of steps that took him even further below the surface. He made his way through an underground that was also lit by electrical lights. The tunnel went under Ninth Street and attached the Treasury Building with the War Department. There were also tunnels that connected the Treasury basement with Booth's massive home behind the Treasury building, and that connected the War Department with the office building that housed the massive Department of Servitude. Only a select few people knew of the tunnels existence and even fewer had access.

Booth tried not to ever depart or return to the same point more than twice in a row. The tunnel system (which had taken the Confederate Army's Corps of Engineers two years to excavate) allowed him to keep any foreign agents that might be in Richmond from easily following him. One day he hoped to have every major government building in Richmond connected to the tunnel system. To make matters even harder for enemy agents, he had a number of drivers who drove identical looking coaches around Richmond. Even the individual drivers didn't know on which days they would actually be riding Booth around Richmond. Sometimes Booth even utilized body doubles of himself in an attempt to further mislead enemy agents.

On this particular day he used a coach that was waiting for him at the back entrance of the War Department. It carried him through the busy streets of Richmond, past Confederate Hall, past the Capitol building and up Shockoe Hill to the official residence of the President of the Confederate States. The three story gray mansion was surrounded by a tall cast iron fence and guarded by an entire company of Confederate troops. Booth was quickly shown into the main parlor, where President Stone was already meeting with the Secretaries of State and War, as well as General Porter Alexander and several other officers and officials from the War Department.

"Mr. President, this is absolutely outrageous!" said Thomas Holt, the Secretary of State. Booth wondered what had the former North Carolina Governor in such an uproar.

"We must have our minister in Philadelphia protest in the strongest possible terms and demand that Cleveland intervene in this outrage!"

Booth took a seat in one of the large overstuffed armchairs next to General Alexander. While Secretary Holt was still shaking the room with his angry voice, Booth leaned over to the Confederate General in Chief and asked him, "What is this about?"

Alexander handed Booth a copy of the Richmond Examiner. YANKEE MILLIONAIRE RAISES MERCENARY ARMY TO FIGHT FOR SPAIN.

"This constitutes an act of war!" declared Holt.

John Marshall Stone beside the fire place at the front of the room, leaning upon the mantle and warming himself by the crackling fire. Above the mantel hung a portrait of Jefferson Davis. Stone stared at the portrait almost as if the first

President of the Confederacy could let his counsel be known. Stone found himself wishing that he really could seek Davis' guidance in this situation. Davis, Lee, and even Jackson had borne enormous responsibilities during their administrations. He hadn't appreciated the weight responsibility until taking office. He turned to face his enraged Secretary of State.

"Calm down, Thomas, before you give yourself a heart attack."

Holt took a deep breath and then sat down.

"I had a meeting with US Minister Runyon this morning," said President Stone. "He assures me that this Mr. Whitmore is an eccentric crackpot and that he has no sanction or support from the United States Government."

"Yet they are still allowing him to recruit people into his illegal army," said General Alexander.

"The United States Constitution, like our own, guarantees its citizens the right to keep and bear arms. Since this Yankee is technically breaking no US laws, Cleveland claims there is little he can do."

"A likely story," said Holt.

"He has assured us that while on U.S. soil, Whitmore and his Yankees will not be allowed to take any action against us. Should Spain formally accept the services of this mercenary band, President Cleveland has assured me the United States will not hold us responsible for anything that should befall them, so long as we treat them in accordance with the rules of war."

"What business is it of theirs?" demanded Holt. "This Whitmore is proof that there are still plenty of Yankees who think that they can lord it over our country!"

Ignoring the bombast of his Secretary of State, President Stone turned to Booth.

"Mr. Booth, did the Secret Service have any notion about this man Whitmore and his raising a private army?"

Booth looked up from reading the newspaper article and addressed the President.

"No, sir, not directly. We of course have kept a close eye on Whitmore and his company. He builds warships for the Union navy and supplies rifles and artillery for the Yankee army, but Minister Runyon was not exaggerating when he called Mr. Whitmore an eccentric crackpot. This is the kind of bombastic, spur of the moment idea that he is well known for, so there was little chance we could have seen it coming. Rest assured, however, that we will be giving Mr. Whitmore's private army quite a bit of attention." Booth had several spies in Whitmore's factories and design firms tasked with stealing plans, blueprints, trade secrets and construction schedules. Most of them believed they were merely working for rival corporations. But Booth had never considered it necessary to get an agent close to Whitmore himself.

An oversight, soon to be corrected...

"I don't want anything to happen to him on U.S. soil," warned President Stone. Booth had a reputation for being very zealous when it came to hunting down enemies of the CSA abroad. "If he is so foolish as to join up with the Spanish, then our armed forces will make him sorry he ever considered this venture. But I do not wish to antagonize the rest of the United States over this issue by... over reacting. Understood?"

"Understood, Mr. President," said Booth. *But the second he is off U.S. soil I will show him no mercy...*

"Now, General Alexander," said President Stone, "would you please give us an update on the invasion plans for Cuba..."

Booth listened only half-heartedly to Alexander's presentation. He was already making plans on how to deal with Whitmore and his mercenaries.

I know just the man for the job...

When the meeting was finally over, Booth made his way out of the Presidential Mansion along with the other officials. He placed his top hat on his head and then climbed up into his coach. The driver flicked the reins and the carriage sped out of the Presidential Residence's iron gate, and again wound its ways through Richmond's busy streets. Booth again unfolded the newspaper, intent on rereading the article on Whitmore's mercenaries. The carriage dropped him off at the Department of Servitude, from which Booth took an underground tunnel to the War Department, another to the Treasury and a final one to his own home.

Like the Presidential Residence, Booths own home was surrounded by an iron fence. He virtually never left or entered his home by its main gate. After climbing the flight of stairs that lead from the underground tunnel to his own basement, he proceeded up two more flights of stairs to the second story of his home. He paused at the door to his personal study to catch his breath. Using the tunnel system all but insured he could not be followed, but at his age the distances and the climbs were beginning to take their toll. His feet were killing him and he was practically hyperventilating.

He entered his study and flipped a switch that activated the electrical lights. This study was more for his personal meditation and reflection. It was a place where he could sit, think, and plan out things in his mind. He never kept anything sensitive or classified there, he just didn't view the house as secure enough. Everything important was kept in his personal sanctum underneath the treasury—or in his mind. What the office did have was a candlestick telephone. With it, he could make a coded call that would summon the agent that he needed. He picked up the phone put the ear piece to his ear, and brought the receiver close to his mouth. Before he could utter a word, a sudden voice spoke out from within the room.

"Good afternoon, Director."

Booth was so startled he jumped. He turned to face the man that had been standing out of sight in the corner of the room. Booth slammed the telephone down onto the desk.

"Connery! I've told you not to do that," said Booth irritably. The Confederate agent fixed his boss with a brazen and arrogant stare. The man was tall with dark hair. A vicious scar made its way down his face.

"Aren't you going to congratulate me on the work I did in Havana?"

Booth's eyes narrowed to small slits. He stared at Roger Connery like a pit viper.

"You were seen," said Booth. "The first officer of the Mississippi was able to describe your face to me in exacting detail."

"The detonator I was given was faulty," said Connery. "I had to *improvise* in order to set off the explosive charge in the ship's powder magazine. I barely had time to get off the ship with my life. I couldn't exactly take my time about getting off."

"That doesn't change the fact that he saw you and could identify you!"

"If it's that big a problem, why not eliminate him?" said Connery coldly.

Booth shook his head.

"Enough of our own people have died for this scheme," said Booth. *It was a necessary sacrifice...* He kept telling himself that over and over again. The Confederacy needed Cuba. Booth had taken it upon himself to supply the CSA with the excuse it needed to take the island. *I had no choice. Those fools here in Richmond would never understand! They would never have had the audacity for what needed to be done!* Booth's agents had informed him that both the United States and Britain had made offers, far beyond what the CSA could have ever afforded, to purchase Cuba from Spain or to lease a section of the island for a naval base. Booth had had to manufacture an undeniable excuse for the Confederate States to seize the island, and so he had taken steps...

"Am I still going to London?" asked Connery.

"No," said Booth. "President Stone has come up with his own plan to forestall the British breaking off trade relations with us. The London assassinations can wait. I have another assignment for you." Booth tossed Connery the newspaper containing the story about Whitmore and his mercenary army. "You're going north..."

XIX

Biloxi was packed with marines, soldiers, and sailors. The entire Gulf Coast seemed to be packed with marines, soldiers and sailors. Corporal Jefferson Case of the Confederate States Marine Corps., reflected that a transport was supposed to have come and picked up his unit almost a week earlier. Like a lot of things it was running way behind schedule. The whole of the Confederate military seemed to be behind schedule. Newspapers around the Confederacy had taken to calling the new war with Spain the "phony war" because nothing seemed to be happening. As far as Jeff was concerned, the Confederate military could take all the time it wanted. A skeleton garrison of army regulars had taken the Marines' place on Ship Island. Jeff hoped he never saw the miserable island or the fort that sat on it again. He was particularly glad that his unit was waiting in Biloxi, even if it had become a little too crowded.

Being in Biloxi meant that he was much closer to his…*sweetheart?… girlfriend?… lover?… fiancée?* Jeff wasn't sure how he'd classify Ellie. He knew how he'd classify her if she was a full White. He'd parade her around on his arm as his intended and write a dozen letters home to his folks about her. Regardless of what anyone thought, he wanted to call her his fiancée, the only problem was it wasn't even legal for him to marry her. There wasn't a state in the CSA that would allow such a thing. Since she was a Mulatto girl, they had to be extremely discreet in seeing one another—both for her safety and his. Racial laws required that she only be allowed to marry a negro or another mulatto. As it turned out his military duties insured that they hadn't seen each other too often. Most of the time he barely found the time to go by her clothing stand to spend a few brief moments with her.

Jeff roused from his tent at the sound of the morning bugle call—actually bugle *calls* was more accurate. A half-dozen regiments were encamped just north of Biloxi and they

146

all seemed to sound reveille at the same time every morning. Case lined up for the morning inspection along with his fellow marines from Fort Stick. Captain Fordice walked amongst the formations of his men. Jeff stood out because of his black-felt, big-brimmed hat. The Sergeants had screamed bloody murder about it until they found out it was on Dr. Richardson's orders that he wear it. Jeff was so fair-complected that without it his hide would cook in the sun like a steak over an open fire. That didn't mean the Sergeants gave him an easy time about it. Being different in any way made you stand out from the crowd. Standing out from the crowd was usually the last thing you wanted to do when it came to Sergeants. Jeff thought the they paid undue extra attention to other things about him because of it, but what could you do? Thankfully, he got through the inspection without any problems that morning.

After morning inspection it was time for breakfast. Unfortunately, the food wasn't much better now that they were on the mainland. Jeff ate a bowl of grits and a couple of biscuits that could easily have done justice as rocks.

"I'm tired of sittin' around," grumbled a Private named Jenkins. He swore and then said, "When are we gonna get this dang blasted war started!" Several others muttered their concurrence. Jeff thought back to some of the things his father had told him about the War of 1869. More than anything he thought about his father's missing arm.

I don't think I'm quite that eager to see the Elephant. I don't recon these boys would be either if they knew what it was likely to do to them. Suddenly he winced. Thinking about his father had made him think about what his father and mother would do if they found out he'd taken up with a Mulatto girl. They'd disown him. They'd hate him. They'd never forgive him. This was one of those things his brain had warned him about when his heart went off on this crazy venture. His mind told him to forget her, but just thinking about such a thing made his heart hurt. *Maybe the Spanish will kill me and put me out of my misery...*

Suddenly Case heard several loud and blasphemous curses. They weren't being said in anger so much as they were in total shock and surprise. Case and Jenkins rushed to the edge of the camp to see what all the fuss and shouting was about. When he caught sight of what had caused the stir, Case blasphemed himself loud and long. There, before his eyes, was something he'd never seen before in his life—something he never thought he'd ever see. A column of negro troops in Confederate uniform, with shouldered rifles. The uniforms weren't much—gray trousers, white cotton shirts, and gray slouch hats. Neither were the rifles much to look at. They looked to be ancient muzzle-loaders from the War of Confederate Independence. They were certainly no match for the bolt-action, magazine-fed rifles that Case and his fellow Marines carried. A large Confederate battle flag floated at the head of the column of black troops. Beside Case, Jenkins swore loudly and profanely.

"They've done gone and given niggers guns! What has this world come to?"

Case himself was lost in thought. If the Confederate States was willing to arm negroes, how long would it be before they allowed, at least half-negresses (or as Case liked to think of Ellie—a half white) to marry a white man. Case thought he knew the sad answer.

A very long time.

Suddenly Case caught site of a white officer on horseback. He galloped up the line of negro troops and took his place at the head of the column. Finally he shouted the order: "Company, halt!" Instantly the column came to a halt. "Right, face!" As one they pivoted on their feet to their right and went from a column of fours into a wide battle line. Case whistled loud and long. It wasn't the smoothest moving bunch of soldiers he'd ever seen, but he'd seen plenty of white troops that were a lot rougher in their movements.

"All right you mangy curs, stop starin' at the nigger's and go get your rifles! We've got bayonet training today and then we've got a field march. Can't have you boys getting soft on us before we fight the dagos!"

Case still hadn't fully recovered from the beating he'd taken a couple weeks earlier. Nonetheless, he still performed adequately enough for the Sergeants. When it came his turn to stab the straw dummy with his bayonet, he did so with ferocious intensity. In his mind he saw not a Spanish soldier, but one of the men that had attacked Ellie.

"That's what I want to see, Case!" After mortally wounding the straw "Spaniard," Case thought about those men that had attacked Ellie. They'd neither heard nor seen any of them since that night.

They must have been sailors and they must have left port. It was the most likely explanation. *They must be gone for good, but if they every hurt her again I'll kill them...*

During the field march, Case thought he was going to die, his side hurt so much. The company marched from a position just north of Biloxi to a position just north of Gulf Port. They then marched down through the streets of Gulf Port itself to the tune of Stonewall Jackson's Way. As in Biloxi, the city of Gulf Port was decked out in red and white patriotic bunting with Confederate Battle Flags and the Blood Stained Banner flying from every house and building. The citizens lined the streets to cheer them. They marched clear through Gulf Port and then headed east back towards Biloxi along the beach. Case's heart leapt as they neared Biloxi, for he caught sight of Ellie at her clothing stand. She scanned the ranks of the Confederate Marines as they marched past, looking for him. Then she spotted him. Their eyes locked for a single moment.

The day had nearly been spent when Case's company marched back into the regimental camp. He had barely collapsed in his tent and gotten a few minutes rest when the bugle sounded, summoning him once again to assembly. As he fell into formation with his fellow Marines, Captain Fordice stepped out of his tent and stood before them.

"Boys, our ship has finally arrived. We set sail at 3PM tomorrow."

Suddenly, the men let out a fierce cheer! Most of them were ready to get to Cuba and whip the Spanish. The Captain then continued.

"Ya'll have worked hard these past weeks, and that's a fact. Every man's on leave until eight o clock tomorrow morning. Go into town, have some drinks, spend time with your sweet hearts or whatever, but back here by eight in the morning and be fit for duty. Any man that's not back here on time in the morning will wish he was never born. Understood?"

"Sir, yes sir!" they chorused.

"Dismissed!"

Finally free from the monotony and brutality of his military duty (if only for a night), Case headed back into town. Biloxi was alive with an almost celebratory spirit. Fireworks were being set off at the beach. An impromptu dance was being held in the town square. Gray uniformed young men who would be off to war the next day, danced away with beautiful young women in hoop skirts. He wished he could take Ellie out on that dance floor, but it was socially—and legally impossible.

Case made his way to Randall's restaurant. It had a lot of customers. Nearly every table on the wooden deck was taken up. Case was greeted by the same negro who'd waited on him the last time.

"Good to see you again, suh! Will you be dinin' alone tonight?"

Case shook his head. He handed the negro a five dollar gray-back.

"I'd like an order for two to go, please," he said. "And a bottle of red wine."

"What would you be wantin' suh?"

"I'm in a hurry, so whatever you have ready will be fine. You can keep the change."

The negro looked at the five dollar note and smiled.

"I see what I kin do suh."

He returned a few minutes later with a basket filled with several pieces of fried chicken. There was also an entire casserole dish full or Randall's famous cheese casserole and as requested a bottle of red wine. It had cost him most of half a week's pay, but if he couldn't take his girl out on the town, he could try to bring something from the town to his girl. With basket in hand he set off for Ellie's house. The sun had fully set, but Biloxi was very much awake. Gas lamps lit the streets and most of the buildings. It grew darker as he neared the beach but the moon was nearly full and there was not a cloud in the sky. A cool ocean breeze blew from the south that carried with it the smell of the sea. Above, he heard the sound of sea gulls. Case passed more than one young couple walking the beach in the moonlight. He yearned to take Ellie on such a romantic outing and cursed the world for not allowing it. He passed the place on the beach where Ellie was accustomed to set up her clothing stand and then turned north. When he neared the clap board house that Ellie lived in he looked around carefully. Thankfully, the cabin was not on any type of main thoroughfare, and there were no other houses right next to it. Ellie had told him that the nearest neighbors were free negroes but Case didn't want them seeing him either. White men entering the cabins of black or mulatto women were usually only there for one reason and Case didn't want Ellie's reputation tarnished by any vicious lies.

If I could court her publically like a proper gentleman I would... Since he couldn't—he quickly walked up the plank stairs, onto the front porch and knocked on the door. After a tense moment in which he thought his heart would explode, she finally opened the door. He stepped in and she quickly closed the door behind him. Case set the basket on the table and uncovered it. The aroma of the food quickly filled the small cabin. He turned to Ellie, took her in his arms and pressed his lips to hers—but something was wasn't right. Though she let him kiss her, she seemed distant—almost cold.

"What's the matter?"

"Nothing," she replied. She walked over to the table and began to fix them some plates. Her eyes widened when she saw the chicken, the casserole, and the bottle of red wine. "This must have cost you a fortune." He shrugged.

"This will be our last time to be together for a long time. I wanted it to be special." She let out a long sigh. After they had eaten they each had a glass of the red wine.

"Do you really think there will be another time, Jeff?" she asked suddenly.

"What is that supposed to mean?"

She sighed again.

"Jeff, I believe you when you say you're coming back for me. I believe you when you tell me you love me. But what can we do about it? What future can we have?"

"I don't care!" he said firmly.

"Well I do! No matter how hard we try to hide it people will eventually learn that we are together and when they do you'll be disgraced. It will cost you your entire family. I'll be lucky if I'm not killed."

Case's heart felt like it had stopped. He was willing to give up his family and reputation for her. He was willing to risk anything for her—but he hadn't thought about the risks she faced. With tears in his eyes he said, "Ellie, I love you and I just can't stop loving you. I will do anything and give up anything to be with you. If the only way we can be together is to leave the Confederacy, then we'll leave the Confederacy."

Now it was her turn to look stunned. After a moment she asked, "Where could we go?"

"I don't know but I'll figure it out. When this war is over we'll go." He looked into her eyes. "Will you come with me?"

Rather than answer him with words she all but ran to him. Their arms wrapped around one another and their lips pressed passionately together. In that moment all his cares, worries, and doubts disappeared. Before long the lights were out and they were in the bed together, locked in the most intimate embrace a man and a woman can share. Afterwards, as they lay together, her head resting on his chest, he thought about taking Ellie and leaving the following morning—making a run for it and skipping the war. He quickly pushed that thought from his mind. As flawed as it was, he loved his country and he was loyal to his comrades. It wouldn't be right abandoning them. Besides, desertion in wartime carried the penalty of death if he were caught. He also reflected that he still had no idea where they could go.

He went to sleep with his arms around the woman that he loved. The next day, he would be off to war…

XX

Joshua Winslow awoke to the sound of his father's amused voice. "I see Medical School hasn't kept you in the habit of rising early." Joshua sat up in bed and looked out the window. The sun had fully risen and its rays were streaming into the bedroom. Joshua was both embarrassed and annoyed. Having grown up on a farm, he'd spent most of his life rising with the breaking of the dawn and the crowing of the rooster. His medical classes in Chicago started early in the morning, but not by the standards of a farm.

"Father, why didn't you wake me earlier! It's my place to help you with the morning chores."

Jethro smiled.

"I saw you up late last night, reading your books by candlelight. If I wanted you milking cows and feeding hogs, I wouldn't have paid tutors to come out here and teach you nor would I have sent you off to Chicago. You're meant for more than this. Besides: the Bible itself says that much study is a weariness of the flesh. Studying to be a doctor is hard work—as hard as being a farmer and don't you let anyone tell you different."

Suddenly Joshua sniffed the air. His eyes grew wide with delight and he virtually leapt out of bed.

"I see being around all those cadavers and medicines hasn't dulled your sense of smell."

"I could smell Momma's pancakes a mile away!" As father and son came down the stairs, Obadiah was already at the table.

"Well look wat' da' cat done dragged in…" said Obadiah. "Hangin' round all dem' fancy white folks done made him soft."

Joshua took his seat and paid Obadiah no heed. He was in no mood for the farm hand's teasing. It turned out, however, that Obadiah had only begun to warm to his theme.

"You too good to work out in the fields wit' da' niggas is dat' it?"

"That's enough!" snapped Jethro. Realizing he had gone just a bit too far, Obadiah hushed and stared at his empty plate. It wasn't long before Lilia came by with a griddle stacked high with pancakes. She served her husband and son first, then gave Obadiah a generous stack of pancakes for himself. Jethro said grace and all four of them began to eat. Obadiah glared momentarily at Joshua's plate. He'd gotten nearly twice what Obadiah had. Of course, Obadiah reflected, Joshua had also gotten about twice what Jethro himself had gotten. Deciding it was nothing more than motherly coddling, Obadiah dug into his own pancakes. He had plenty.

"I'm riding into Lancaster to go to the General Store, care to come along son?"

"Certainly father!" Living in Chicago, Joshua had become accustomed to having access to newspapers on a daily basis. The telegraph allowed news from all over the continent to be wired across the country. Thanks to 19th Century technology, news could and did travel fast. Joshua was particularly eager to hear news about Cuba and whether or not the CSA had managed to bully Spain into giving it away.

"I'll hitch up the wagon," said Obadiah as he finished his breakfast.

"Good," said Jethro. "Then you can get to work mending the south fence while Joshua and I go into town."

"We nearly out'a nails!" complained Obadiah.

"You've got enough to keep you busy for a while. Just use up the nails you have. I'll get more in Lancaster and you can finish tomorrow. Once you've done all you can on the fence, your other chores will keep you plenty busy till we get back."

Obadiah looked on the verge of some curt remark, but he kept quiet. He rose from the table and headed out to hitch the horse to the wagon. A while later Jethro and Joshua were on their way up to Lancaster. Joshua kept quiet for the first hour of the trip. He admired the wide open country side as it slowly rolled by. Here and there they passed farms. At the entrance to one farm, they passed an elderly white woman working in a flower bed. Jethro tipped his hat, smiled pleasantly and tried to give her a friendly wave. The woman took one look at their black skin and then she turned and ran back towards her house as terrified as if she'd seen two monsters. Jethro simply shook his head. A while later they passed another farm. A middle aged white man looked to be busy mending his own front fence. As before Jethro tipped his hat and waved. The white man didn't run away—he didn't wave or smile back either. What he did do was glare at them with a look similar to what a gunman might have had looking at his target over open gun sights. The farmer took his corn cobb pipe out of his mouth and spat in their direction. Both Joshua and Jethro felt hot flushes come up in their faces. Their dark skin hid them. The farmer continued to glare until they had ridden past and then he turned back to his work.

"Why do they hate us, father?"

"You've asked me that question a thousand times since you were a boy. My answer hasn't changed."

"I know," said Joshua. "We look different and people are afraid of anything that is different."

Jethro nodded.

"That is, unfortunately, the way of the world."

"It shouldn't be though, father. I know for a fact that underneath the skin, white men and black men look identical—I know I've seen."

Jethro held down a shudder and felt momentarily sick to his stomach. His son had a valid—and very interesting point. But the picture of his son skinning human beings to see what was underneath was still a bit too much for him. He'd skinned and gutted animals himself plenty of times and had no problem with it, but for some reason the idea of doing it to people— even dead people for the noble goal of advancing medical science—made him sick.

Maybe it's because of all the wounds and mutilation I saw in the war... Try as he could, he could not get the picture of what the Apache and Merecat Indians had done to the bodies of captured Calvary troopers in New Mexico and during the Utah campaign out of his head. During his time as a Buffalo Soldier, Jethro had seen—to his great horror—that on the inside black men and white men and red men all looked the same. His son had seen too. Jethro was thankful that he hadn't gained that particular piece of education the same way he had.

Lord, may my son never know such horrors... After sending his prayer heavenward, Jethro looked at his son. "You're right son. We are all the same. But until the majority of people realize that we are all made in God's image, we must remain patient and forgiving."

"It's hard to forgive when people look at you like you're an animal or worse."

"Just remember that it could be worse, son. Down in the CSA people would do more than look at you like an animal. They would treat you as an animal. You would be property— owned and used in the same manner as the beasts you labored alongside of. The USA isn't pleasant—white folks here don't like us anymore than the ones down in the CSA—but at least they can't own us here."

"You're right, father."

Jethro put his arm around his son. "It's my hope that because of the blessings and opportunities you have available to you, that you will be able show the world that we are people and that as people, we are worthy of respect and capable of great things."

Joshua nodded. "I want to help our people father. Both here and everywhere else—including the CSA."

"I know you do son. And there is no doubt in my mind that you will."

They reached the outskirts of Lancaster at about noon. The road became almost completely clogged with traffic. They quickly realized that the city was much more crowded than usual.

"Looks like we picked a bad day to come to town," said Jethro. Joshua nodded.

"I wonder what's going on." It took them an extra forty minutes to get into Lancaster. When they finally reached the General Store, they got their first indication as to what all the commotion in town was about. A nearby sign read: CATTLE SALE 2PM. Nebraska had become one of the primary providers of cattle in the United States. It supplied the hungry population centers in the east with beef. Since Lancaster was the major east-west railroad hub at the heart of the country it was the perfect place to auction off cattle.

After hitching the horse in front of the General Store, Jethro said, "Stay with the wagon. I'll be as quick as I can."

"Sure you don't need any help?"

"Oh I could use the help. I just don't fancy coming out of the store and finding the horse and wagon missing."

Joshua nodded. While Jethro went into the General Store, Joshua got out of the wagon and stretched his legs. Nearly four hours of sitting in the wagon had left him with leg cramps. Suddenly, he heard the cry of a newsboy hawking his papers.

"EXTRA EXTRA READ ALL ABOUT IT: SPAIN OFFICIALLY ACCEPTS WHITMORE MERCENARIES AS THE SPANISH FOREIGN LEGION. WHITMORE SEEKING VOLUNTEERS! READ ALL ABOUT IT!"

Joshua suddenly remembered why he'd been so anxious to come to town. He tossed the boy a dime and took one of the papers. He then leaned against the wagon as he opened up the newspaper. His eyes grew wide as he read the main editorial.

Despite angry protests from the Confederate States and vocal opposition from the U.S. government, Mr. Joseph Whitmore—private citizen, philanthropist, industrialist and now mercenary soldier, has persisted in his plan to raise a personal army and take up arms against the Confederate States on behalf of the Kingdom of Spain. Complicating matters further for the United States government, is the fact that Spain has announced its intention to formally receive the mercenary army under the unoriginal but very apt title: the Spanish Foreign Legion, and utilize them in their war with the Confederate States. Since the initial news about Whitmore's plan nearly two weeks ago, many in the United States, Europe and even the Confederate States, have done nothing but laugh. They have brushed aside Mr. Whitmore as an eccentric crackpot that is not to be taken seriously, and his army as little more than a practical joke meant to draw attention to his ever starving ego. No one is laughing now. The grounds of Mr. Whitmore's private mansion in northwestern New York has become a veritable armed camp. Abolitionists and free negroes from across the United States have flocked to his banner as have a number of much older and disgruntled veterans from the First and Second Wars of Rebellion who are seeking pay back for decades of humiliation and ridicule. There are even reports of Abolitionists from Great Britain who have crossed the Atlantic for the express purpose of joining Whitmore's Legion. While the exact number of recruits is unknown, a conservative estimate would be at least two thousand volunteers. And if anyone doubts that Mr. Whitmore can adequately arm such a large group, let the reader be reminded not only of his vast wealth, but also of the fact that his company is one of the largest manufacturers of rifles, cannons, and ammunition in the nation. The one thing that "Whitmore's Legion" is short on is surgeons. While there is seemingly no shortage of angry and adventurous young men eager to shoulder a rifle and march off to war, there is a shortage of qualified physicians to care for them if and when they are wounded. It must be remembered that contrary to popular opinion it is disease and not bullets that kill the most in war. This is all the more true, in the tropical climate of Cuba, where yellow fever annually kills thousands…

Joshua looked up from reading the paper. He had a new burden on his heart and a crazy idea in his mind.

"Come give me a hand, son." Jethro was at the door of the General Store. Joshua tossed the paper into the wagon and then rushed to help his father. The two of them loaded a large box of nails, two massive bags of sugar and flour, a can of kerosene, a bolt of cloth, a new hammer and hoe, and a new pair of work boots for Obadiah.

"He's a hard worker," said Jethro as he climbed back into the wagon after they had finished loading. "He deserves some decent boots. I know he gives you a hard time, but he doesn't mean anything by it."

"I know, father," replied Joshua as he unhitched the horse. He then climbed back into the wagon. Jethro flicked the reins and they started home. Getting out of Lancaster was slightly easier than getting in had been. When they finally reached the open road, Jethro pulled out his pocket watch.

"We'll be close to an hour and a half late getting home. Your mother is going to be worried sick."

Unsurprisingly, the idea of his mother being worried reminded Joshua of his crazy idea.

Father, you'll understand won't you? You of all people… He held the paper tightly and stared down at it intensely.

"Was there something interesting in the paper, son?"

"Here father, let me take the reins I've got something I'd like you to read."

For the next ten minutes, Joshua drove the wagon while his father read the article. Jethro read in silence and without a trace of emotion on his face. When he had finally finished he laid the paper down, took a deep breath and let out a long sigh. Then, as if reading his son's mind, he spoke.

"You're not a doctor yet, son."

"No, sir, but I have had three years of medical school. Dr. Forrester—one of my chief instructors—was a surgeon during the Second War of Rebellion. He says that after seeing the way many doctors were incompetent in dealing with war wounds that he thinks it mandatory that medical students learn to deal with those types of injuries. I have far more training than many doctors did in the Wars of Rebellion. I've learned to remove bullets and treat wounds, I could do amputations…" Joshua stopped speaking, for he noticed that his father had begun to cry.

Jethro reached up and felt the back of his head. There was a nasty scar at the base of his skull where no hair would grow anymore. He'd taken a spent bullet in the back of the head that had knocked him unconscious in the middle of a battle in the Utah campaign of the Second War of Rebellion. He'd awoken to find that he was the only survivor of his regiment. His commander and all of his comrades had been slaughtered.

I've never told him what I went through… I've never told him what war is like… perhaps now I should…

"Father, please forgive me…I didn't mean to upset you…"

"It's not your fault, son. But you talk about wounds and amputations like it's an academic subject. It's not the same when you see it with your own eyes. You have no idea what it's like, and it's been my prayer that you never would."

"Father, I want to make a difference for our people. Spain freed all the negroes in Cuba and its other colonies years ago. If the CSA conquers Cuba, those negroes face oppression, possibly even re-enslavement. Large numbers of the recruits in Whitmore's Legion are negroes from our own country. They're going to need qualified surgeons to treat them when they are injured…" Joshua stopped for his father had once again begun to weep. A moment later the older man lifted his face to the sky and stared at the heavens with tear filled eyes.

Thy will be done…

XXI

Former Confederate President Thomas Jackson found the Kings Street Hotel in Charleston South Carolina quite worthy of the name. The Presidential suite in particular was as elegant and fancy as any royal personage from Europe would like. But Jackson found it too gaudy for his spartan military tastes. He found that its size, however, easily accommodated large meetings. On that day he was meeting with two leaders of South Carolina's budding anti-slavery coalition. South Carolina was the only state in the Confederacy, in which the Confederate Society for Prosperity and Industrialization did not have a fully organized division up and running. Jackson hoped to change that.

"Gentlemen, I thank you for coming today, and I hope that together we will be able to increase support for compensated emancipation here in South Carolina…"

A young but influential planter named Terry Sledge brought him up short.

"Mr. President, I am very interested in emancipating my slaves in exchange for government compensation. I would very much like to build a tool factory."

Jackson nodded.

"It would be the first of its kind in South Carolina and one of very few in the entire Confederacy," said Jackson. "It would be an enormous advantage to the nation. I commend you for your vision."

"Thank you, Mr. President, but you will find that until the CSPI clarifies its position on what to do with the negroe after he has been emancipated that you will find little support here in South Carolina, no matter how horrible the economy and the cotton industry have become, or how low the value of slaves falls" Sledge was the owner of nearly seven hundred slaves. "My family have been planters for over two hundred years. But because of soil depletion and the blasted boll weevil my crops have been dismal. What I have managed to produce I've barely been able to sell thanks to competition from India and the present hostility of foreign markets. I haven't made a profit in three years."

The other planter, T.C. Ruckman nodded agreement.

"I'm in the same situation. I've had to mortgage the plantation that's been in my family for over two centuries just to stave off bankruptcy. The bank barely gave me half of what my plantation was worth only ten years ago—slaves and all!"

"Do you find that most of your fellow planters are in similar situations?" asked Jackson.

Ruckman nodded.

"Most of them have realized that the time has come to switch from agriculture to industry. The problem is that no one has any money. Keeping our plantations running, even though they are relatively unproductive drains what little we have. Many like us would be willing to go along with this compensated emancipation scheme but both they and the common people want to know what the negroes place will be in society once they are emancipated. They want to make sure there are effective plans to keep them in their place."

"That is something we begun to formulate," said Jackson. Though he recognized the need such a policy, he loathed the position they had had to devise in order to make compensated emancipation politically viable. The vast majority of people wanted to keep the black man in a permanently repressed and subservient roll. Jackson found it unchristian and unconscionable but saw little way around it. *One thing at a time,* he thought.

"I say we ship them all back to Africa!" said Ruckman. Sledge all but rolled his eyes. Jackson nearly did the same, but for diplomacy sake retained a mask of composure. Thankfully, Sledge took care of most of the argument.

"Mr. Ruckman I've heard this proposal before. First of all it would be extremely impractical not to mention expensive. It is estimated that there are over ten million negroes in the Confederacy, that is a third of our country's entire population. We have close to one-hundred ocean going ships in our entire navy—now you do the math sir. Even if we could pack one-hundred negroes onto each ship and then have them all make round trips to Africa once per month it would take over eighty years to send them all back. To realistically send the negroes back to Africa we would have to build hundreds—if not thousands of more ships or else pay private ships from a dozen nations more money than they would earn doing their regular business to do the job for us. Either way it would be a gargantuan financial undertaking requiring a large portion of our national budget. We simply cannot afford it."

Ruckman was a much older man than Sledge. At first he'd looked affronted that the younger man would dare to disagree with him. But as the reality of the facts set in, Ruckman deflated like a balloon. Finally he said, "I hadn't thought of it quite those terms." He sat quietly a moment in deep thought, then spoke again. "If we cannot ship them across the ocean, then perhaps we can deport them over the land—say to Mexico. The Empire of Mexico is little more than a puppet of our French allies. It should not be too difficult to get Napoleon IV, to *convince* Maximilian to open his borders to our negroes. And I might add that railroads are far more efficient than ships. We already have a sufficient infrastructure and building a few extra lines across the border would be cheap enough. I know for a fact that you can fit sixty cattle in a railroad stock car. We could easily fit a hundred niggers in the same space. That would be six thousand negroes per train. We could rail them all into Mexico in just under two years."

"I must say I never considered that," said Sledge. "It could work."

Jackson winced slightly and rubbed his eyes. He was beginning to get a headache.

"I'm afraid, gentlemen, that that is also not a practical plan."

"And why not?" asked Ruckman, his voice tinged with hostility. Sledge, though more friendly, nodded agreement with his fellow planter.

"Logistically it could work, sir," said Sledge.

"The problems," said Jackson "are not logistical; they are political and strategic."

"Please explain, sir," said Sledge. Ruckman, though guarded, also motioned the former President to continue.

"We spent the better part of two decades fighting alongside of the French in Mexico putting down rebellions and helping Maximilian's government secure the whole country. We spent a decade after that pouring foreign aid that we could not really afford into Mexico to try and help develop it into a more respectable and powerful country—it has been an enormous investment. Our own nation and France and to a smaller extent Austria-Hungary, are determined to develop Mexico into a more stable and economically powerful country. We are doing this because we want a solid and dependable ally on our southwestern flank. A nation that could come to our aid in the event of another war against the Yankees."

Both Ruckman and Sledge nodded. Towards the end of the War of 1869, Maximilian's forces had been on the verge of total defeat because of U.S. aid to Mexican revolutionary Benito Juarez and his forces. At the end of the War of 1869 Juarez's forces had actually seized Mexico City itself and Maximilian had barely escaped with his life. Only complete victory against the United States by the CSA and France and the subsequent flood of support from those two victorious powers allowed Maximilian to regain his capital. It had taken most of the 1870s for the combined French and Confederate forces to defeat the Revolutionaries. The 1880s had been spent building a "better" Mexico.

"If you ask me, Mr. President," said Ruckman "I say Maximilian and the Mexican's owe us. It's only fair that they should be willing to take our niggers off our hands for us." He then blasphemed. "All the aid we've given to Mexico is part of the reason we're in this economic mess to begin with."

Jackson fixed Ruckman with an icy glare.

"Do not take my Lord's name in vain in my presence, sir." Jackson's voice was so harsh, and his gaze so sharp that Ruckman recoiled slightly. Jackson then eyed both of the planters with a serious glare. "We must always be looking forward to the next war with the United States. Only a fool would believe that we will never again face them in battle."

He then tossed Ruckman a copy of the Charleston Sentinel. Its front page article detailed the growing mercenary army in the north that a Yankee businessman was raising to fight for Spain.

"Those people hate us. We will face them again and when we do, it will take every ounce of strength we can muster to defeat them. We'll need every ally we can get. That means getting the albatross of slavery off of our neck. It means having a Mexico that will be able to join us in the fight against Yankee tyranny. To flood Mexico with ten million negro refugees would throw the entire country into chaos and undo all we have labored to accomplish for the past thirty years. Besides all that, our French Austro-Hungarian allies would never go along with it. Both Frenchmen and Austrians have been immigrating to Mexico in droves. They are determined to turn Mexico into a European nation on the American continent. Napoleon would never condone what you propose. To even try would be to risk losing the most important ally we have."

Jackson took another deep breath, and looked both planters dead in the eye.

"Gentlemen, you must accept that for better or for worse the negro is here to stay. The goal of the CSPI has been to formulate a policy concerning the negro's place in Confederate society that is both practical, acceptable, and beneficial to the nation. No matter how much you may desire it, we cannot get rid of them. And if we claim to give them freedom and then continue to repress and oppress them to the extent that many in our nation presently do, we are doing nothing but placing a hostile enemy behind our own lines and preparing a powder keg that could blow apart our entire nation."

Now it was Ruckman that eyed Jackson with an angry glare.

"If you are suggesting that we in any way, form, or fashion offer the nigger equality with the White Man, then you can consider our relationship over here and now, sir. And you can certainly forget about any support for compensated emancipation in South Carolina and I'd wager also in the rest of the Confederacy as well!"

"Have you ever heard of Saint Domingue, Mr. Ruckman?" asked Jackson. From the look of horror that came over Ruckman's face, Jackson could see that he had. "Let me refresh your memory, sir. In 1798 the slaves of Haiti revolted against their White masters in the city of Saint Domingue and threw the entire colony into turmoil and civil war. The vengeful slaves pillaged, raped, tortured, mutilated, and killed. Now imagine, the millions and millions of slaves in our beloved Confederacy rising up in the same fashion. Even if we managed to put them down think of the cost. Think of the destruction. Your plantations would certainly go up in flames and you yourselves would be lucky to escape with your lives. That is the inevitable outcome if we allow the negro to be ruthlessly persecuted and neglected. In such a situation the Yankees would undoubtedly seize the opportunity to invade and subjugate us, is that what you want?"

"Of course not!" said the planters almost in chorus. Jackson had hit them in a very tender spot. It was a weak spot that every sensible White person in the Confederate States had, though they rarely spoke of it openly: fear of an open and all out slave revolt.

Sensing blood, Jackson moved in for the kill.

"Let me make you preview to another piece of information gentlemen. Speaking as the former President of the Confederate States, I can assure you that there is no shortage of fanatical foreign abolitionists trying to instigate the nightmare scenario I just outlined to you. During the ten years that I was the President of the nation, the Secret Service devoted enormous resources to intercepting seditious material meant to incite our slaves, foreign instigators and even shipments of weapons meant to arm negroes. Unless we take action now to effect change, it will happen."

"So you are proposing that we grant the negro not only freedom but equality," said Sledge. By the way he made the statement, Jackson thought the planter was on the verge of vomiting in disgust. But Jackson shook his head.

"Not in the manner you are thinking. I'm realistic enough to know that the people and the states will never accept such a thing."

"Then what are you proposing?" asked Ruckman.

"I'm proposing that we be beneficent masters. I believe it is possible for the negro to occupy a productive and positive place in Confederate society. The segregation of the races that we presently enjoy must and shall continue, let there be no mistake about that. Political authority in this nation shall remain in the hands of white men where it belongs, let there be no mistake about that. But we can preserve these things without tyrannizing and oppressing the negro. We can be separate but equal in all other things. We can afford them the protection of law. We can build them schools and hospitals. We can help them to establish their own farms and businesses. We can build them nice places to live separate and apart from where we live. We can even allow them supervised self-government within their own separate communities. In short, gentlemen, if we treat them well, while at the same time keeping them separate and under our leadership, we need not fear revolt, nor do we need fear the chaos of some futile attempt to integrate races that are too different to live together on an equal basis. Please do not misunderstand, gentlemen. In the Confederate States of America the white man is going to govern the black man, but he must do so paternally, not tyrannically."

"I think I understand what you're saying, Mr. President," said Sledge. "You're saying that the "paternal dictatorship of the white man" will lead to loyalty and respect, and that the "tyrannical dictatorship of the white man" will lead to resentment and rebellion."

167

"Exactly," said Jackson.

"So you're not advocating giving the negro any political say in the states or the Confederacy in any way?" asked Ruckman.

"As I said," replied Jackson "they would be granted limited autonomy over their own communities. They would of course be allowed to elect their own leaders in those communities. They would not, however, be allowed to hold state or confederal office, nor to vote in state and national elections—that is the responsibility of the white man."

At that Sledge and Ruckman nodded vigorous agreement. Jackson continued.

"However, because we will not allow them true representation in the state and national governments..." *At least not right away...* "...we will see to it that the negroes of our nation are treated benevolently. We will see to it that they are given all that they need to live happy and prosperous lives, if they will work hard and obey the laws of our land. To do any less would mean to be hypocritical and to sow the seeds of resentment and discontent instead of gratitude and contentment. We want the negro population of the Confederate States to be secure, content, and contributing to the good of the nation. This can best be accomplished by treating them with benevolence and Christian charity. Who knows?" said Jackson. "Slavery has existed in our land for nearly three centuries. Perhaps after another two or three centuries of living separately but in peace, then we will finally be ready to live together."

When the infernal regions freeze over, thought Ruckman. Aloud he said, "What your proposing will cost the nation a fortune, and to many people it will seem a waste to spend so much money on niggers, but it is better than Saint Domingue."

Sledge nodded.

"And you may be right about that last part, Mr. President," said Sledge "though I'm glad to say that I won't be there to see it. As for the rest of what you have said...I must agree—more or less. If this is the position of the CSPI, then you have my support."

"And mine as well," said Ruckman.

Jackson then rose to his feet. The other two men followed in quick succession.

"Gentlemen, I think that is enough for today. We will reconvene tomorrow and discuss the particulars of how best to start organizing our Society in this state. Good day."

"Good day, Mr. President," they chorused. After shaking Jackson's hand in turn, they headed out of the door.

After they had gone, Jackson brought his hand up to his forehead. He did indeed have a headache.

"Sandie…"

His aid, Sandie Pendleton, came bounding into the room.

"Yes, sir?" A half second later he added, "Are you alright, sir?"

"Please fetch me a glass of lemonade, Sandie."

"Yes, sir. You should know also, sir, that there are two Englishmen waiting down stairs to meet with you. I told them you were indisposed but they insisted on waiting until your meeting was finished. They've been waiting in the lobby for two hours. Shall I tell them to return tomorrow?"

Jackson exhaled long and loud.

"No. Get me the lemonade please, and then send them up."

Pendleton rushed to get Jackson the lemonade. He downed it gratefully while Pendleton went to fetch the two Englishmen. They walked into the Presidential suite just minutes later. The first man was tall and thin. He had a thin mustache and auburn hair. The second man was much shorter and plumper. Both were dressed in immaculate suits.

"Ah…Mr. President!" said the tall man extending his hand. "I am Sir Reginald Barret and this is my associate Mr. Phillip Simmons."

Jackson shook both of their hands.

"I am pleased to meet you two gentlemen. What may I do for you?"

"Sir, we represent the United British Society for the Abolition of Slavery. We have come to the Confederate States first of all to meet you and to tell you how much we support your initiatives."

Jackson nodded politely and feigned a smile. His headache had grown considerably. The Englishman continued.

"Sir, as you must know, it is illegal in your country for foreigners to purchase negroes and set them free. Under Confederate law such negroes are to be re-enslaved upon the departure of their foreign owners—without compensation. We are aware of your practice of purchasing slaves in order to set them free. We have come to offer you a donation of five thousand gold sovereigns for use in purchasing the freedom of negroes. Half of this money was donated by Queen Victoria herself. The rest has been painstakingly raised by our Society. The sum has been given to us to entrust to you. Your honorable and noble character has been known and appreciated on both sides of the Atlantic for over three decades. We entreat you sir, to take this money and use to purchase liberty for as many negroes as you can."

Jackson sighed.

"Gentleman, I am truly honored and grateful for your efforts. However, I must respectfully decline."

Both of the Englishmen looked stunned.

"May I ask why, sir?" The Englishman's voice held a mixture of disbelief and indignation.

"Allow me to be candid, gentlemen. This affair concerns the Confederate States of America and only the Confederate States of America. Britain has no business whatsoever in trying to coerce us diplomatically or economically to change our systems and institutions. We will deal with slavery ourselves, in our own way and in our own time. We are in fact already dealing with it. Your Society and others like it back in Britain are turning British textile companies against doing business with my country. You are at this very moment trying to convince your government to severe diplomatic ties with us and to boycott all trade with us. In effect sir, you are waging economic warfare on my country, and you expect me to accept your help? No. Go home. And leave us to settle our own affairs."

At that Simmons started to leave but Sir Reginald motioned for him to wait. He addressed Jackson.

"Mr. President, your Confederate States are fiercely proud of their independence. Being British, I can understand this. Britain is not in the habit of being dictated to herself. But if I may make an observation. You, sir, are known for your honor and integrity and also as being a pious Christian man."

At that Jackson hung his head in genuine humility. The Englishman continued.

"As a Christian man you have professed your opposition to things such as spirituous liquors, gambling and other immoral practices. In fact you tried with various degrees of success to have such things outlawed in the CSA during your time as President, did you not?"

"I did," said Jackson.

"Now, would it be safe to say, Mr. President, that you personally would not associate with a person who habitually practiced such immoral things. Do you ever go to taverns, or brothels, or casinos?"

"Of course not. What is your point?"

"My point sir, is that I and the vast majority of my countrymen find slavery to be a moral evil. And as a nation we have the right not to associate with nations that we believe to practice things we find to be morally wrong. Furthermore, as British subjects we are perfectly within our rights to influence our own country as we see fit and we choose that we do not want our country to associate with a nation that holds human beings as property. We have not tried to coerce you by force, nor do we ever intend to do so. All we have done is exercise our right of conscience. Now like it or not, the economic problems of your nation that we have had a part in bringing about have helped your personal cause to free the negroes. Do you believe that emancipating the negroes is what is best for your country?"

"Yes," said Jackson through gritted teeth. He did not like to be argued with and liked it even less when the other fellow had a point.

"Then take our money."

"Sir Reginald, even if I agreed to take your money, when it got out that I have accepted foreign money to free slaves then I will lose credibility throughout the Confederacy. I would be seen as your pawn."

"If keeping the fact that we have aided you in freeing slaves secret will help the cause of ending slavery in the CSA, then we will gladly keep it secret. In fact I will do better than that. If you will accept the money, then I promise that upon returning to London I shall announce publically that you rebuked us but claim that we found someone else to take the money anonymously. That should allow us to continue raising funds and bolster your position here. And you still get the money! You will get the best of both worlds."

At first Jackson found the scheme dishonest and distasteful. But the Englishman's proposal was strategically sound and very audacious. Jackson admired audaciousness.

"There is still one problem, Sir Reginald. When I start purchasing slaves with British Sovereigns, it will be the same as publically announcing our relationship. The effect will be the same. I will lose all credibility."

Now it was Sir Reginald that sighed.

"Well then sir, though it pains me to think of the images of our beloved Queen Victoria eventually being melted down to make Confederate coins, if it will help set men free, we shall take the Sovereigns to the bank of Charleston and exchange them for their Confederate counterparts. The gold you use to set negroes free, will have the face of none less than Robert E. Lee himself engraved on them. If that's not irony, then I don't know what is."

"President Lee, was a great and good man," said Jackson. "He abhorred slavery and wished to see its end."

"Then instead of ironic, let us say appropriate. Do we have a deal President Jackson?"

Jackson nodded.

"We have a deal."

XXII

John Pershing stood atop Fort Halleck in Keokuk Iowa. With a pair of field glasses he peered across the Des Moines River into Confederate Missouri. Keokuk had once been a very small and insignificant town. Now it was a very large town on the verge of being a city. John Pershing had seen bigger places. During his cadet days he'd seen New York City itself. Nonetheless, he found himself amazed by the rate of the town's growth. But Keokuk was important for more than just its booming size. Its strategic location on the international border between the USA and CSA made it a vital post for the United States Army. Fort Halleck, located at the corner of 5th and Johnson Streets was a massive brick fortress that bristled with cannons. To the south, the US Army had also constructed fortifications along the shore of the Des Moines River which separated Iowa from Confederate Missouri. Keokuk was situated at the place where the Des Moines joined with the Mississippi. To the east, across the Mississippi, another massive US Fort stood sentinel on the Illinois side of the river. To the south of Keokuk, however, a massive Confederate fort held a vigil of its own.

Alexandria Missouri was nothing when compared to Keokuk Iowa. The Missouri town was little more than a village. The massive fort flying the Blood Stained Banner, however, was as formidable and menacing as either of its US counterparts across the rivers. Keokuk was booming and prosperous, but it sat under the shadow of massive Confederate guns that could smash it to ruin in little time at all. Pershing eyed the Confederate Fort with gritted teeth.

His gaze then swung eastward. The US intercontinental railroad ran parallel along the riverbank on the Illinois side. It then turned west and crossed the Mississippi by way of a massive bridge and passed right through Keokuk. This was the real reason for Keokuk's economic success and growth. After Missouri had been ceded to the Confederate States at the end of the Second War of Rebellion, the United States had been forced to re-route their inter-continental railroad around Missouri and through Iowa. What angered Pershing was the fact that they had done so perilously close to the Confederates.

The railroad should have diverted farther east and north, he thought. *The next time we fight the Rebels they're going to blow the bridge and the railroad to hell and gone with the first shots of the fight and practically cut the United States in half in the process.* He cursed the politicians in New York... *or Philadelphia or wherever those cowards are hiding these days!* The last Pershing had heard, the new US capital city wouldn't be finished any time soon.

He tried to calm himself by taking a deep breath. There were other rail-lines further north, though their distance and layout made them very inefficient for military use.

This is the main line! It should have been built with an ounce of common sense! He swore, loudly and profanely.

"Is something the matter, Captain?"

Pershing spun around to see a Corporal, not much younger than himself.

"Nothing but your common run of the mill civilian idiocy. What is it, Corporal?"

"Sir, Colonel Jensen wishes to speak with you immediately."

Without another word Pershing left the Corporal and descended the stone steps into the bowels of the fort, making his way towards the Colonel's office. On his way, he was self-conscious enough to admit to himself the real reason he was in such foul mood.

I've written Jennifer three letters and she has yet to respond even once... Mail between the USA and CSA took a good while, even when they didn't have to travel very far geographically. *Still she's had time to have responded to at least the first one…*

As he reached the Colonel's office, Pershing tried to push the Missouri woman from his mind. He removed his broad-brimmed hat and took a moment to straighten his blue uniform coat. He then knocked on the rickety wooden door that led to Jensen's office.

"Come."

Pershing walked in and came to rigid attention, bringing his arm up in a precise salute. Jensen returned it.

"At ease, Captain."

Lieutenant Colonel Henry Jensen was a large man. He stood well over six feet tall. Unfortunately, he had a girth to go with his height. Pershing was surprised he could fit in his office chair. Pershing sniffed the air ever so subtly. Sure enough, he smelled whiskey. Jensen was over fifty and nearing retirement. Like a lot of US army officers of his generation, Jensen was an alcoholic. They'd lost two wars in a row and lived with the shame of those defeats for more than twenty-five years since. During that time, the nation had done nothing but ridicule and blame Jensen's generation. It was common for newspapers and magazines to depict US Army officers as drunken buffoons in their political cartoons. Much of that animosity stemmed from the close of the Second War of Rebellion. Ulysses S. Grant had been drunk at Cold Harbor when the Confederate Army of Northern Virginia had counterattacked and trapped the decimated Army of the Potomac. Pershing had studied that battle in detail at West Point.

Grant could have been as sober as a Baptist preacher on Sunday and it wouldn't have made one bit of difference! It was Grant's bull headed and outdated strategy that was at fault.

One thing was clear to Pershing. The US Army needed a younger generation in charge, one that was not stained by defeat, shame, cynicism and tactical ideas that dated back to the days of Napoleon I and George Washington.

"Have a seat, Pershing."

"Thank you, sir."

"What I have to tell you today is absolutely confidential. It is not to leave this room. Understood?"

"Absolutely, sir."

"Are you aware of the mercenary army that is being raised in New York to fight for the Spanish?"

Pershing nodded.

"Vaguely, sir. I've had little time to read newspapers recently."

"Yes, patrolling the border has kept you quite busy. Well, Captain, allow me to get straight to the point. Officially the United States opposes the formation of this mercenary group and discourages all US citizens from enlisting in it. Unofficially, however, the War Department is very interested in seeing a core group of our officers serve with 'Whitmore's Legion.'"

"Why, sir?"

"Because, Captain, the Army is running low on officers with combat experience. We haven't fought a real war since 1869 and my generation is on the way out the door. The Confederate Army on the other hand has had a lot of recent experience down in Mexico and Panama. And they are about to get even more by fighting the Spanish. This is not good. When an experienced veteran army goes up against an inexperienced army it doesn't usually turn out that well for the latter. Ever since the disaster in sixty-nine the politicians have kept us out of military conflict at all cost. Other than chasing bandits and redskins the army hasn't had much to do, so we need to find a way to get some of our officers some real combat experience. Are you interested?"

"What all would be involved, sir?"

"Well first of all you'll have to resign your commission. Officially speaking, no US military officer is permitted to associate with Whitmore's group."

"Sir, I've work hard my entire life to be an officer in the United States Army. Going to West Point was…"

Jensen held up a placatory hand.

"Captain, the Army offers you a private assurance that upon your return you will be welcomed back with open arms and at a higher rank I'd wager. This could put your career on the fast track. And it will give you an opportunity I've wanted for over twenty-five years."

"And what is that, sir?"

"A chance to kill some Rebs again and get away with it."

Pershing nodded.

"I won't let you down, sir."

Jensen smiled.

"Very well, Captain. I'll expect your resignation from the Army of the United States to be on my desk by morning." Jensen then reached into his desk drawer and pulled out an envelope. Handing it to Pershing he said, "This will tell you where you're supposed to go and what you're supposed to do. We'll send a discreet wire to New York to let Whitmore know you're coming but you'll have to hurry. You'll need to leave tomorrow. As of right now you are on leave to get your affairs in order. Make sure you leave your uniforms and gear behind and remember—this is confidential. As far as anyone knows, you're making this decision on your own and against our recommendation. You are not to discuss this with anyone is that understood?"

"Understood, sir."

"Good luck, Captain. You're dismissed."

Only after he had stepped out of the Colonel's office did the reality of what he had done sink in.

What have I done? Orders or no, I have to tell Richard and Lorain. He suddenly remembered he was supposed to have dinner with them at their home that evening. *I'll tell them tonight.*

His first order of business was to procure some civilian clothes. He made his way out of the fort and headed towards the water front where many of the best stores were. He walked down the street that ran along the river bank. It seemed almost

a contradiction. To his left, along the shoreline were gun
emplacements that the Army had built. In the event of war with
the CSA cannons and Gatling guns would be placed in those
positions. The Confederacy had similar positions prepared on
their side of the river. To Pershing's right was a line of stores
and businesses that faced the waterfront. As he headed towards
the clothing store he passed the bridge that connected Keokuk
Iowa with Confederate Missouri. The Stars and Stripes and the
Blood Stained Banner flew at opposite ends of the bridge.
Beside their respective flags, soldiers of blue and gray also
stood sentry. Ever since the Second War of Rebellion, the
border between the United States and the Confederate States
had been officially closed. Both nations had attempted to
control the border in an effort to keep spies, saboteurs, (and in
the CSAs case, slave provocateurs) from entering their
respective territories. Crossings had to be made at specific
locations and those crossing had to have a valid passport.
While this was the official policy of both nations, the reality
was that USA and CSA shared over 1,500 miles of border,
from the Atlantic ocean westward all the way to the Rocky
Mts. Neither nation had the will nor the money to fully patrol
and regulate the entire border and so only major crossings such
as the one in Keokuk were actually guarded.

Pershing noticed that the blue uniformed guards on the
US side of the bridge had halted a woman trying to cross into
Keokuk from the other side. At first he looked away but then
he quickly swung his gaze back in her direction.

Jennifer! It's her! Pershing rushed towards the bridge.
One of the guards—a staff sergeant—was speaking to her in a
brogue Irish accent.

"I'm sorry ma'am, but Confederates are not allowed
into the United States without a passport."

"I just told you I'm not a Confederate," she said
sharply. "I am a citizen of the United States."

"You were a resident of Missouri in 1869 and you did
not go to live in a US state before January first 1872, correct?"

"That's right. I've lived in northern Missouri my entire life."

"Then ma'am, you are legally a citizen of the Confederate States of America, regardless of where you claim your loyalties lie. I'm very sorry.""

"I can vouch for her, Sergeant," said Pershing. "I assure you she's on our side."

The two guards snapped to attention and saluted Pershing.

Returning the salute he said, "At ease."

"You eh... know this girl do ya, sir?"

"I do."

"I'm very sorry sir, but ya know the rules well... there the rules, sir."

"Sergeant, I've been writing this beautiful young lady for a month hoping to court her into being my intended. Now that she's actually come to see me, I'd really appreciate it if you could just...look the other way? What do you say?"

The sergeant smiled and suddenly turned towards the river.

"Look Watkins! Is that not the most beautiful water fowl you've ever seen!"

"I do believe it is, Sergeant..."

Smiling, Pershing offered her his arm. She accepted it and as they stepped off the bridge together the sergeant called after her.

"Welcome back to the land of the free, lass."

She turned and smiled at him.

"Thank you, Sergeant." She then turned and walked away with Pershing.

"Your intended?" asked Jennifer with a smile. "Moving just a little fast don't you think Mr. Pershing? Your letters were very flattering and presumptive, but I don't recall an offer of marriage."

"Well, I learned at West Point that all the great military men of history were... bold..." He turned and looked her in the eyes. "When they saw something they wanted they went after it."

She blushed—just for a moment then turned away suddenly.

"I am truly sorry to disappoint you Captain. But I'm afraid I did not come to Keokuk to see you."

At that he feigned injury and melodramatically pointed his nose up in the air. The smile returned to her face.

"But I am grateful for your help just now."

He nodded.

"So why did you come here?"

She hesitated several moments before finally answering.

"My mother and brothers were killed when I was just a little girl. Rebel raiders invaded our town. My father raised me alone—that is until he died of a fever two years ago."

Inwardly, Pershing winced. They had more in common than just being from Missouri. He wanted to tell her that he knew exactly how she felt, having lost most of his own family in the exact same way, but he did not interrupt her as she continued.

"Put simply, Captain, I have nothing back in Missouri. I've read in the newspapers about a group being raised in New York to fight the Rebels. "I'm going to sign on as a nurse… Captain, are you all right?"

"I'm fine…" he said as he composed himself. She had caught him off guard. He'd been so startled he'd swallowed and choked.

Is this destiny or cruel fate? He wasn't sure what to think or how to feel. He knew he'd begun to develop feelings for Jennifer, and the thought of a woman on a battlefield—even as a nurse—was appalling to him. At the same time he understood her need for vengeance all too well. Being a woman, she could not take up a rifle and march off to war. This was her way to fight back after all these years. He sighed.

"Captain, what is wrong?"

"Nothing," he said. "It's just that we have a lot to talk about. And please...call me John..."

XXIII

Agent Roger Connery of the Confederate States Secret Service peered down at the mansion of Joseph Whitmore in northwest New York State through his pair of binoculars. The grounds were covered in tents and uniformed men. From his position atop a wooded hill just south of Whitmore's property, Connery was also able to spot a rifle range, a drill field, a supply depot, and what looked to be an ammo dump. He zoomed in on the rifle range. There were a large number of men undergoing rifle training and target practice. There was an enormous volume of fire coming from the rifle range.

They must be using magazine fed rifles. This Whitmore isn't fooling around. If Connery had had his way, he would have been on a mission to eliminate the enemy millionaire. As it was, he had explicit instructions that nothing was to happen to Whitmore on US soil. He also noted that there was no smoke coming from the range.

They're using smokeless powder then...

With a grunt, he swung his binoculars over to the entrance of the mansion's main drive. The entire grounds were encircled by a tall cast iron fence with a base of stone. As he zoomed in on the main entrance he noticed four guards holding a small crowd at bay. From their pads and pencils they looked like reporters.

It's far too crowded for me to get in through there. Connery put up his field glasses, shouldered his field pack and hiked down the hill, trying his best to stay on the very edge of the wooded area so that he could see the mansion grounds but remain hidden from any eyes that might see him. A large portion of the perimeter fence touched the wood line. At first he examined the fence to see if he could climb over it. Unfortunately the iron fence was topped with pointed spires.

Undaunted, he hiked for nearly half a mile along the perimeter of the fence, keeping an eye out for an auxiliary entrance. Eventually he reached the back part of the property and his suspicions were proven true. A small one man gate stood unguarded but securely locked. Connery made his way from the edge of the wood to the gate so that he could examine the lock.

He swore profanely. He was skilled at picking locks and had the proper tools but the gate was locked from the other side. There was no key hole on his side. He tried to reach through the iron bars of the gate and pick the lock backwards but the space between them was too narrow. He swore again.

All right. I'll do it the hard way.

Connery retrieved a set of files from his field pack and set to work on the lock. It was not easy. There was very little space between the gate and the main fence for him to get at the iron latch. He was forced to use his smallest files. After an hour and a half of filing away at the latch he had made it about two-thirds of the way through. But he had worn down two of his three files. Grabbing his final file, he set to work again. His hands ached terribly but he pressed on. Only when he'd completely worn away the teeth on one side of the file did he flip it and use the other side. After another forty five minutes he'd just about filed through the entire latch when his file broke. He uttered a blasphemy. He held one half of the broken file in his hand. The other had fallen onto the other side of the fence. Connery took a deep breath to try and calm himself and then re-examined the lock. He'd filed most the way through. Very little of the latch remained. He hefted himself off of the ground and then with all of his might he kicked the gate. Then he kicked it again and again and again! On the final blow, last remnants of the latch snapped and the gate swung open with loud bang.

Not exactly as inconspicuous as I'd had in mind.
Connery put up his files and made his way quickly through the gate, hoping no one had heard him force his way in. He found himself in a small apple orchard. From the poor state of the

orchard it looked as if it had been picked clean by Whitmore's recruits. Only a few apples remained. The orchard itself was surrounded by a white washed lattice barrier with an arched un-gated entry that led to the rest of the mansion grounds. He hesitated by the opening, trying to determine what his next course of action would be. There was very little cover in sight and there were a lot people about the grounds—most of them in khaki uniforms. Suddenly, he was startled by a voice from behind.

"Who are you?"

Remaining calm, Connery put a big smile on his face and turned around. He found himself staring at a Khaki clad mercenary soldier no more than twenty years old. He wasn't pointing his rifle at Connery, but he was holding it at the ready.

"My name is Robert Smith. I'm with the Baltimore Harold. I've come all the way from Maryland to interview Mr. Whitmore and do a story on your group."

The boy relaxed slightly and let his rifle down to his side.

"The General doesn't give interviews without an appointment and no one is allowed on the grounds without his permission and an escort. I'm afraid you're going to have to leave."

The General? Connery had read about Whitmore's bombastic personality when preparing for the mission. *I'm surprised he's not calling himself the Grand High Marshal.*

"You're just going to let me go? Shouldn't you take me prisoner and let *the General* decide what to do with me? I did break into his property. I could be a spy."

The young mercenary grinned.

"You're just trying to get that interview." He pondered it a moment then said, "Why not?" He pointed towards the mansion. "That way."

At that instant Connery kicked him in the groin. The young mercenary went down hard, dropping his rifle and then clasped himself in a very indecent fashion. Connery leapt atop him, put his hands around the young man's throat and proceeded to strangle the life out of him. It was over in about two minutes. Connery let go of the soldier's lifeless body and stood to his feet. He then looked around for a place to hide the body. He started to drag it towards a row of bushes at the back of the orchard by the iron fence but about half way there he stopped. He eyed the body, taking in the dead soldiers measurements with a glance.

It'll be a little tight but it should fit. He quickly set about stripping the soldier of his uniform, boots, and accoutrements. A few minutes later he had put on the uniform himself. Connery examined the uniform's hat. It was a well manufactured "visored" or "peaked" cap.

Considering the cut and color of these uniforms it looks as if Whitmore has bought his uniforms from the British. Connery further reflected that Whitmore's mansion was not far at all from the border British Canada.

After hiding the body in the bushes, Connery transferred the contents of his field pack into the soldier's haversack. He then hid the field pack in the bushes with the body. Next Connery retrieved the soldier's rifle and examined it taking mental notes for the report he'd send back to Richmond. The rifle looked to be one of Whitmore's own manufacture. It was about forty inches long, bolt action with a five clip magazine. Connery used the bolt mechanism to eject one of the cartridges.

Brass casing, 30 Caliber. He then headed out of the orchard and walked towards the mansion along a flagstone path. The mansion grounds were spacious and well kept. Whitmore owned vast amounts of land. All total, Connery estimated the land surrounding the mansion at over two hundred acres. Whitmore seemed to be fond of gothic statues, for they had been erected all over the property.

A large encampment stood between Connery and the mansion. As he neared the encampment, he began to pass other mercenaries. Most were dressed just as he was and carried identical rifles. He noticed very quickly that those mercenaries considered officers wore rank insignia virtually identical to those of the US army. He made certain to salute them when he passed them. As he made his way into the encampment, he was able to get a good look at the supply depot. Several of the crates were painted with the British Union Jack.

He's definitely getting a lot of his equipment from the British. Suddenly, he spotted something that made his blood boil and his jaw clench in fury. A group of negro mercenaries carrying rifles came walking by. Connery's finger itched to pull the trigger on his rifle with it aimed straight at them.

Nigger's carrying guns! When he thought about the fact that even his own side had begun to arm negroes, it made him still angrier. One of the blacks waved to him. Connery forced himself to offer a brisk nod in return. After making his way through the encampment, he was finally able to get a good view of Whitmore's massive home.

The mansion itself was gothic in style. It consisted of two wings in an L formation. One of the wings was two stories high and had a flat roof. The other was three stories high and had a large pitched roof. Black iron work adorned both. Each wing had two double chimneys. The front door was made of fine mahogany wood and was accessed by large stone steps.

I'll need to create a diversion—a big diversion if I'm going to be able to get in there and have time to find anything. His eyes suddenly settled on the ammunition dump. A vicious smile spread across his face. He checked his pocket watch.

Less than two hours till sundown—perfect. In the meanwhile Connery busied himself with inspecting the camp. He found the strange mixture of Yankee, British and negro accents very disturbing and avoided speaking as much as possible. He'd learned to alter his accent, but it wasn't perfect. He could always claim to be from Maryland, Kentucky or Missouri, but he'd just as soon not take a chance.

When the sun had set, Connery cautiously made his way towards the ammo dump.

They think that here in the United States, right on the Canadian border that they are safe and beyond the reach of their enemies. These fools haven't even bothered to post guards. They've got a lot to learn about soldiering. When he had safely made his way into the stacks of ammo crates and was out of sight, he reached into his haversack and pulled out a bundle of dynamite with a wind up timer and detonator. *It will be my pleasure to further their education.* He set the bomb on top of an ammo crate and set the timer to ten minutes by turning the small twist key on the side ten times. He then flipped the small metal switch that started the timer clicking down to the moment that it would ignite the dynamite. Connery quickly made his way out of the ammo dump and as close to the mansion as he could get without drawing attention to himself. Most of the mercenaries were either lined up to get their dinners or else had already seated themselves in front of their various tents to eat. Connery seated himself behind a large statue of a gargoyle that used a large stone block as a base. He pulled out his pocket watch and waited.

The detonator worked perfectly. The explosion shook the grounds. Several of the mansions windows shattered. Flaming debris and shards of wood and metal flew in all directions. Several men screamed in pain. It was not a gargantuan explosion such as when he'd planted a bomb in the powder magazine of the CSS Mississippi, but it was big enough to throw the entire camp into chaos. Shouts of alarm and panic seemed to come from every direction. Mercenaries ran back and forth unsure what to do. Connery smiled at the havoc he'd caused. He turned and looked at the mansion. It was less than a minute before an elderly man came out of the front door waving his cane angrily and shouting orders.

That would be Whitmore. Another man came out immediately after him. To Connery's eyes it seemed he tried to convince the millionaire to go back inside. Whitmore would have none of it. He shoved his way past his protective aid and proceeded towards the heart of the disaster. The other man followed right on his heels. Connery saw his chance and he took it. He dashed over to the mansion, up the front steps and through the front door.

He passed through a foyer and into a vast conservatory. Fine red carpets covered the flagstone floor. There was a massive fireplace to the right from which the majority of the room's light came. A massive portrait of Whitmore from his younger days hung above it. Much of the room was cloaked in shadow. Book cases lined the most of the walls. Two large stair cases led to the upper floors. He was beginning to have second thoughts about his plan—the mansion was far vaster than he'd anticipated.

I'll never have time to search this place. It'll be sheer luck if I find anything. He noticed a large cluttered writing desk in the corner of the conservatory. There was an ornate gas lamp mounted on the wall immediately beside it just barely producing light. Connery turned the small brass knob on the underside of the lamp and the light increased, greatly illuminating the entire desk area. He quickly began rummaging through the many papers on the desk. Suddenly he heard a noise. He spun around quickly but didn't see anyone. There were undoubtedly servants in the house. Even though it was late, the explosion undoubtedly had them up and about. He had no time to search through the papers in detail. He grabbed as many as he could and stuffed them into his haversack. Suddenly he heard another noise, louder and closer than before. It was a woman's voice.

"Do you know what's going on, Mr. Longworth?"

"No, Mrs. Beasley, I have no idea!"

Connery had no time to go out the way he came. He rushed through an archway and into a large dining hall just as a butler and maid—both elderly—came into the conservatory from the east wing. The sound of their voices seemed to grow closer and closer as did the sound of steps on the stone floor. Connery drew a knife out of his haversack and poised himself to strike.

"I say, look at that!" said the butler.

"Gracious heavens!" said the maid.

When neither of them came into the dining hall, Connery chanced a glance out of the archway. The two servants were on the other side of the conservatory, staring out of a shattered window at the chaos outside. Their backs were to him, but he dared not try to sneak past them. He looked around the dining hall. There was a fine raised panel wooden door at the far end. When he opened it, he discovered that it led to what seemed to be a large storage room for tablecloths, napkins, plates and glasses. To the left was another door.

If I've guessed the layout of this place correctly that should lead to the outside.

He unfastened the door chain, unlocked the bolt lock and opened the door. He was right. He dashed out the door and found himself behind the mansion. There was a path that led to a large square building which he guessed housed the kitchen. He turned right, and hiked around from behind the mansion as quickly as he could. After about a minute he came back into sight of the encampment. Everything still seemed to be in a state of pandemonium. As tempting as it was to head towards the chaos to try and gauge how much damage he'd done, he knew he needed to get out of there. Before heading north towards the apple orchard he took one more relishing glance at the carnage.

This is only the beginning!

XXIV

The *CSS Texas* crested a wave. Her armored hull crashed through the swell, throwing water up on the main deck. The Confederate Battle Flag flying from her bow was whipping violently in the wind. In the sky, dark clouds were on the horizon. Within those clouds, thunder rumbled and lightning flashed. Outside a light rain had already begun to fall.

"Looks like a storm is coming," said Captain Blake Ramsey. His XO, Commander Ray Brisk stood beside the helmsman, peering out of the forward viewports.

"I'd hate to be up in the crows' nest right about now," he said. As if on cue, the bridge telephone that connected the bridge with the lookouts in the crows' nest rang. The bridge had two of the state of the art devices. In addition to the one that linked directly to the crow's nest, there was another that connected with a shipboard switchboard and from there to almost any compartment in the ship. Ramsey picked up the earpiece and put it to his ear and then shouted into the wall mounted receiver.

"Bridge."

Through the sound of howling winds and the inevitable static, Ramsey was just barely able to make out what the lookout was saying.

"Land ho' Captain, we've spotted Key West. We can see fort Zachary Taylor, sir."

"Right," said Ramsey. "Ya'll buckle down up there. It's about to get a lot rougher."

"Aye aye, sir."

Ramsey replaced the receiver.

"We're in position, Mr. Brisk."

The XO nodded and made his way over to the chart table. According to the navigator's markings they were right off the coast of the Florida Keys. He sighed and shook his head slightly.

"I just wish the rest of the fleet was with us. I don't like being this far ahead."

"Somebody's gotta scout ahead of the main battle-group," said Ramsey. "Besides, it could be worse. At least we're not alone." He pointed out the bridge's starboard porthole. The Armored cruisers *Tallahasee* and *Jacksonville* were in formation with the *Texas* off her starboard side. The rest of the fleet and invasion force was still a good distance to the northwest. The two armored cruisers weren't as heavy as the battleship. They were having a much harder time in the rough seas.

"If we do run into the Spanish, at least we'll get the first shot at them," said Ramsey.

Brisk nodded.

"I'm all in favor of that. But I'd still prefer to have a few more ships."

Ramsey then walked over to the map table and stood beside Brisk to examine the chart for himself. He pulled out a cigar and stuck it in his mouth, struck a match and got it going. A moment later he exhaled a small cloud of smoke and pointed at the chart with his cigar.

"This is our last stop."

Brisk nodded. They weren't supposed to be putting in at Key West, it was merely a way point and staging area for the fleet before the final leg to Havana. But with a coming storm...

Suddenly another large wave crashed into the *Texas*. The ship listed hard to port before righting herself.

"Maybe we should put in," said Brisk. "It sure would make it easier to weather this storm."

Ramsey shook his head.

"We've got to remain on station in case the Spanish come poking around."

"Begging your pardon, Captain, But I don't think the Spanish would have the guts to poke their noses into our home waters."

Ramsey turned to the navigator.

"Mr. Carson, as soon as the rest of the fleet arrives..."

Suddenly, the telephone rang again. Ramsey again picked up the earpiece and shouted into the wall mounted receiver.

"Bridge!"

"Captain! We've spotted a couple of ships bearing 180, range 9 miles. They're definitely military ships."

"What flag are they flying?"

"Can't make out a flag yet, sir. But they look a lot like the pictures of Spanish ships we were given."

"Understood. Keep a sharp eye for any more ships!"

"Aye aye, sir!"

Ramsey hung up the receiver and quickly issued his orders.

"Mr. Brisk, sound general quarters! Mr. Sorvino, signal the *Tallahassee* and the *Jacksonville* that we've spotted two possibly hostile contacts. They are to set an intercept course."

"Aye aye, sir," they chorused. A moment later, klaxons were sounding throughout the ship. At the ship's stern the Blood Stained Banner was raised. On the starboard side, signal flags were run up. A minute later both escort cruisers raised their affirmative pennants. Their smoke stacks belched black smoke as they picked up speed to full steam. As soon as they had changed course to the south, Ramsey issued orders to his own helmsman.

"Seaman Donaldson, hard to starboard. Make your course 180.

"Course 180, aye." As the helmsman spun the large spoked wheel hard over, Ramsey picked up the ear piece of the other telephone and spun the crank on its side. He then shouted into the cone shaped receiver on the wall.

"Get me the Engine room...Engine room, we're going to need full speed ahead."

A minute later the *Texas'* own smoke stack was belching black smoke. Ramsey could feel the awesome power of her steam engines vibrating through the deck. The *CSS Texas* was much slower than her escorts, but that was due to the thickness of her armor, not the size of her engines. Suddenly the phone to the crow's nest rang again.

"Bridge," said Ramsey.

"Red, Gold, Red Captain! It's definitely the Spanish. They've picked up steam and are headed right for us, so they must have spotted us. One of the ships is mighty big. I recognize her from that book of Spanish ships, sir. From her shape I'd say it's the *Vizcaya.*"

"Understood." He hung up and turned to Brisk.

"Fetch me the intelligence report on Spanish ships." Brisk headed through the hatch in the rear of the bridge and down the gangplank towards the ships wardroom. He returned barely a minute later with a large volume in his hand. Ramsey took the book, set it on the chart table and opened it up to the pages about the *Vizcaya*. Brisk stood at Ramsey's side so he could also examine the data on the enemy ship. He let out a loud long whistle.

"She's about sixty feet longer than we are," said Brisk. "Faster too."

Ramsey took a long drag on his cigar as he studied the enemy vessel. He exhaled a small cloud of smoke before replying.

"But we have bigger guns and thicker armor. If she's foolish enough to engage us then we'll make her sorry she ever entered Confederate waters."

Brisk raised his binoculars and peered out of the forward viewports.

"There she is." He passed the binoculars to Ramsey. "It's definitely the Vizcaya." He then panned right slightly. "And there's her escort. Looks like a destroyer." Suddenly they heard a distant boom from the direction of the Spanish warships. Ramsey thought it might be thunder, but a moment later a shell splashed into the sea about a hundred yards to the *Texas'* port.

"If that's the best they can do, this should be easy," said Brisk. Ramsey said nothing. The howling winds were undoubtedly playing havoc with the aim of the Spanish gunners. The flip side of that coin was that Ramsey's own gunners would face the same difficulty and from the look of things it wouldn't be getting any easier. The light rain had become a steady downpour. The waves had grown in size. A moment later another shell came crashing down. This one landed about forty yards of the port bow of the *Jacksonville.* The *Jacksonville* responded in kind and sent a shell screaming back at the Spanish. It obviously missed, but Ramsey didn't see where it crashed into the sea.

They don't have the range, he thought. *But we do.* "Mr. Brisk, order our forward twelve inch gun to fire at will!"

From their position in the bridge, Ramsey and Brisk could see the large armored turret with the menacing twelve inch gun swivel to the port. They then watched as the barrel was elevated to the appropriate firing arc. When the main gun fired it sounded like the end of the world. Fire and smoke belched out of the guns muzzle as the 870 pound shell erupted out of the barrel at a speed of 2,100 feet per second. The force of the main gun rocked the entire ship. The shell exploded into the water to the starboard of the *Vizcaya*. It was a miss, but the Confederate gunners had gotten a lot closer than their Spanish counterparts.

Ramsey watched as the *Texas'* main gun changed its elevation by a few degrees and swiveled slightly to the starboard. It fired again. It was so loud that Ramsey thought his eardrums would explode. This time the shell crashed into the sea much closer to the Spanish warship.

By that time, the *Jacksonville* and the *Tallahassee* had moved well ahead of the *CSS Texas* and were finally within range to fire at the Spanish and have a chance of hitting them. Both cruisers opened up almost simultaneously with their ten inch guns. The shells landed nowhere near the target. The Spanish warship returned fire. The shell slammed into the side of the *Jacksonville.*

Ramsey zoomed in on the wounded Confederate cruiser with his binoculars. Black smoke and flames were coming out of the gash in the side of her hull. Neither of the Confederate escort ships had the armor that the Texas did. Wounded or not, the *Jacksonville* showed no signs of slowing down. A moment later she returned fire.

"Looks like the *Jacksonville's* still in the fight," said Brisk.

Ramsey nodded.

"At Mobile, Captain Monclure had the nickname dauntless."

The *Texas* fired again. This time her shell screamed through the air and slammed into the superstructure of Spanish warship. The entire bridge crew let out a cheer. A few moments later the *Vizcaya's* gun announced that she too was still in the fight. The Spanish shell struck the *Texas* a glancing blow on her port side. The battleship shook with the force of the impact.

"Order the six inchers to open fire, and get me a damage report!" ordered Ramsey.

Brisk nodded and headed below. A few moments later, the two six inch guns on the *Texas'* port side added their own thunderous noise to the battle. The forward twelve incher also fired again. This time the shell struck the *Vizcaya's* turret that housed its main forward gun. It went up in a spectacular fire ball. The *Vizcaya's* smaller guns sent a few more desperate shots at the Confederates but the *Texas* had struck the decisive blow. The *Jacksonville* and the Tallahassee sent shells of their own crashing into the *Vizcaya's* superstructure which had become little more than a fiery wreck that billowed black smoke. The *Texas'* twelve inch guns fired several shots that struck the Spanish ship near the waterline. Shortly thereafter she began to list. Flames and smoke had engulfed most of her deck. Spanish sailors were leaping into the angry sea, desperately trying to escape the fires.

Peering through his binoculars, Ramsey watched the Spanish ship strike her colors.

"Cease fire!" he ordered. He nodded gravely and respectfully. The *Vizcaya's* crew had fought bravely and honorably. The *Vizcaya* had been large and fast but had been outmatched by the armor and firepower of the *CSS Texas*.

Brisk then reentered the bridge.

"The armor held, Captain. Only moderate damage to the outer hull."

"Very well, Commander. Prepare for rescue operations."

"What about the other Spanish ship?"

Ramsey pointed in the direction of the destroyer that had never managed to get in on the fight.

"They've apparently decided that discretion is the better part of valor." She was headed south at full speed. Ramsey looked again at the burning hulk of the *Vizcaya*. "If we can help get those fires out then we can tow her into Key West..."

Suddenly the *Vizcaya* exploded violently. Wreckage and flaming debris were thrown in all directions. Whether it was her powder magazine, her coal bunker, her boilers, or all three—the *Vizcaya* had, by and large, ceased to exist. Her shattered remains quickly flooded and sank into the sea.

XXV

The southbound train screeched to a halt at the Confederate border, just north of Harper's Ferry and just southwest of Frederick Maryland.

"This is the end of the line folks. Make sure you have your passports ready."

Cole and Helen Allens rose from their seats and made their way out of the train along with the rest of the passengers seeking entry into the Confederate States of America. From the number of drawls he heard, about half of the passengers were Confederates returning home from the United States. It was an extremely short walk to the border post. In fact, the Union rail platform was connected to its Confederate Counterpart. Two small Customs houses stood caddy corner to one another. Cole and Helen stood in the line that led to the one flying the Blood Stained Banner. When they reached the end of the line they found themselves facing a gray uniformed Confederate customs official. They handed him their passports. He was polite enough. Most Confederates were.

"My I ask the purpose of your visit to the Confederacy, sir?"

"I'm a reporter for the Covington Gazette. I have an appointment with your War Department in Richmond."

The official seemed unimpressed. He stamped their passports and returned them.

"Mr. Allens, Ma'am, welcome to the Confederate States. We hope you enjoy your stay. Next please."

They then boarded a southbound train for Richmond. While Cole read a newspaper he'd picked up in Pennsylvania, Helen stared out of the train at the passing Virginia country side.

"The South is so beautiful," she said. "It's a shame we couldn't get along."

"Irreconcilable differences, darling," said Cole over the paper with a pipe clenched in his teeth.

"Like I said, 'a shame.'" She glanced at the newspaper. "What are you reading that's so interesting?"

"It seems there was some type of explosion at the training ground of Whitmore's Legion. A lot of people don't think it was an accident. They're accusing the Confederacy of sabotage."

Helen looked around quickly to make sure no one was paying attention. She wanted to remind her husband that at that very moment they were in the Confederate States on a train largely filled with Confederates. If someone overhead Cole, it might lead to unwanted trouble. She tried to shift the subject slightly.

"Are you sure it wouldn't have been better to go to New York. Perhaps we could have attached ourselves to Whitmore's Legion the way you accompanied the 3rd Kentucky."

"I've thought about it," said Cole. "Based on what I've read, Mr. Whitmore is not fond of reporters and I'm not convinced they're ever going to get to Cuba—at least not in time to do any good."

"Why do you say that?"

He handed her the paper.

"Check out the front page."

CONFEDERATE FLEET SINKS SPANISH WARSHIP OFF THE FLORIDA KEYS.

"The Confederates are going to be invading Cuba soon. Cuba could be conquered before Whitmore's Legion gets there."

"So you want to get to Cuba as soon as possible?"

"I do."

Helen suddenly noticed that he was staring at her with that same look that he'd been staring at her with since they'd left Covington. It was a look that said "I don't want you here, but part of me is glad that you are." But there was something else—worry. They hadn't been married that long, but she could tell he was worried for her safety. She took his hands in hers.

"I know you're worried about me being along," she said. "But my place is at your side, where ever you go. It's going to be fine, I promise."

"I hope you're right," he said.

The train finally reached Richmond. Cole and Helen were amazed at how large it was. Most people in the United States had made the Confederacy out to be a backwards undeveloped agrarian nation. But Richmond was a sprawling modern city. It had factories, and iron works and many other modern buildings.

The train station was located near the center of the city, not far from the Confederate "Capitol Hill." As they debarked from the train Cole could clearly see the backside of the Confederate Capitol building just to the south and east. Inside the train station, there was a small booth that sold maps of the city and other souvenirs. He purchased two maps for five cents using a US Liberty Head Nickle. Confederate and Union paper monies were not generally accepted in each other's territories accept at border areas. However, since both nations minted coins to the same standard of precious metals, most people had no problem accepting coins from the other side.

Cole pulled out his pocket watch and scowled. They were supposed to have arrived in Richmond three hours earlier.

"I've got to get to the War Department before I miss my appointment. Go to the Hotel and wait for me there."

"I'll check us in. But after that I think I'll look around a bit," said Helen.

Cole sighed.

"Just try to stay out of trouble, darling."

"Don't worry, Cole dear, I promise I'll be waiting for you at the hotel when you get there."

No sooner had they left the train station than they came face to face with further evidence that Richmond was a modern city. Electric trolleys ran down the center of the street. Though Covington was not one of them, Cole knew that several US cities had had them installed. It cost a dime for both of them to ride, but the thrill was worth the price.

The wonders of the 19th Century never cease to amaze me. As the trolley made its way through the city, Cole and Helen took in the sights. They got a much better view of the Confederate Capital building. It sat atop a hill like a Greco-Roman Temple with the Blood Stained Banner floating proudly above it. They passed a massive equestrian statue of Robert E Lee. The trolley ran down the center of the street. Traffic moved one direction to the trolley's left and the opposite direction to the trolley's right. They passed pedestrians, men on horseback, and lots of horse drawn carriages. They also passed a handful of horseless carriages. The fancy contraptions drew the attention of everyone who passed them.

The city itself was decked out with patriotic decor. Red and white bunting was everywhere and Confederate flags flew from nearly every building. It reminded Cole of Covington back in 1869.

They love their country, there is no denying that. Cole suddenly realized that for the first time he had mentally given legitimacy to the Confederate States. All his life he'd thought of Confederates as Rebels that hated their own country. Now for the first time he thought of the Confederacy as a separate nation. It had cost hundreds of thousands of lives but for better or worse the CSA had achieved its goal.

To Cole the Red and White bunting that lined many of the buildings looked strange. He supposed they left off the blue so that there patriotic decor looked different than that of the US, but he still found it odd. Richmond was also decked out in flags. Some of the buildings flew the Confederate Battle Flag, most, however, flew the Blood Stained Banner. As he studied the Confederate National Flag, Cole decided that color scheme of the Confederate patriotic bunting made a certain amount of sense since the majority of their flag was red and white. Only the star belted saltier in the canton was blue.

A few moments later, Cole was reminded that the love of one's country was often accompanied with hatred of one's enemies. A small but angry crowd at the corner of tenth street were burning King Leopold I if effigy. Cole again wondered if the Spanish King's Prussian background would be enough to bring Prussia into the war. He didn't think so. He'd studied enough European history to know that blood relations between monarchs were neither an impediment to war nor a guarantee of assistance. The crowned heads of Europe and their petty nation-states had been fighting one another and playing politics against each other for centuries regardless of family ties.

Now the petty nation-states of North America gets to do the same, thought Cole cynically.

When the trolley reached Franklin street, Helen disembarked. Cole was thankful that he could see the Jefferson Hotel from the trolley. She would not have far to walk.

Though she's likely to go out site seeing any way. Cole would have bet good money that his wife would soon be exploring Richmond's art museums. He sighed. *By all accounts this is a safe city. She should be fine.* He wondered if it was normal to worry so much about his wife. He decided it was simply because he loved her.

As the trolley continued on its way through Richmond, they came near a large, red brick building that was surrounded by a cast iron fence. It stood out to Cole because of its unique flag. It did not fly the Blood Stained Banner, but the British Union Jack.

Undoubtedly the British Embassy...

The trolley stopped in front of the embassy building and two young men dressed in the khaki uniforms of the British Army got on. Cole wondered what the young Englishmen thought of the CSA in general and of Richmond in particular. In recent years the British had been the most vocal opponents of the western hemispheres last slave holding nation. There in Richmond, they were positively surrounded by it. The capital of the Confederacy was positively bustling with negro slaves. They were driving all the coaches and wagons. They were loading and unloading ships at the docks. They were carrying people's luggage at the hotels. They were cleaning the buildings and houses. They were constructing buildings. They were carrying groceries and parcels. Just about everywhere in Richmond one could see negro slaves toiling away at something.

Of course, Cole reflected, *they aren't all slaves.* He knew that some of them were free negroes. The CSA had more free negroes than it had ever had before. *And if it's true that they are emancipating thousands of slaves to serve in the war against Spain, then there will be still more. Maybe slavery's days really are numbered...*

Cole continued to ride the trolley until it reached 9th Street where he disembarked. To his surprise, the two young British army officers also got off the trolley.

"I don't suppose you two gentlemen are heading to the war department?" he asked. The two young officers were momentarily startled—not by his having spoken to them, but by the accent of his voice.

"I infer sir," said one of the young men "that you are yourself a visitor to Richmond, and I'd dare say to the CSA." The young man spoke in the flowing elegant English of Britain.

"You are correct," said Cole. "I am a war correspondent from the United States. I've come to observe the Confederate army in Cuba."

"Then sir, we are on the same errand, for we ourselves have been assigned to the same task. The War Department is right this way." The three men walked along 9th Street until it intersected with Bank Street. Cole was please that he had no trouble keeping up with the quick strides of the much younger British soldiers. The Confederate War Department was on the corner, across from the massive treasury building. It was a large four story brick building. Two gray uniformed soldiers with rifles stood guard outside. Cole decided to let the uniformed British officer's be the first to deal with the Confederate sentries.

"Hello, gentlemen," said the officer with whom Cole had conversed. "We are Lieutenants Churchill and Barnes. We have an appointment to talk to someone about military press passes and transportation."

"These fellers sure do talk funny Joe," said the younger of the two soldiers in the most southern country accent that Cole had ever heard.

"They're British, you dummy!" said the other soldier. He then looked at Cole. "And are you with these English fellers?"

"No sir, my name is Cole Allens. But I do also have an appointment about getting a military press pass."

The two Confederate soldiers were visibly startled by the sound of Cole's voice.

"It looks like we've got ourselves a Yankee here," said the older soldier in a very hostile and suspicious tone.

Cole thought about telling them that he was actually from Kentucky (though being from Covington he actually did have more in common with the 'Yankees' of Ohio) but decided against it. He'd heard that a lot of Southerners viewed Kentuckians who had sided with the Union as worse than Yankees. Not for the first time, Cole was thankful that the Union had been able to hold on to Kentucky during the Second War of Rebellion, even if they had suffered disasters on every other front. Of course, Cole reflected, a large portion of Kentucky was still under the martial law of the US army. The United States was not about to risk another secessionist uprising in Kentucky. The downside was that the occupation kept hard feelings from the uprising alive. If the United States and the Confederate States ever came to blows again, Cole would bet money that the US would have to deal with another uprising in Kentucky.

"A Yankee! We can't (he pronounced it cain't) let no Yankee in the War Department!"

"What did you say your name was?" asked the other soldier.

"Allens, Cole Allens."

"Keep an eye on these three, Johnny, I'll be right back."

While Joe entered the War Department, Cole stood waiting with the two British officers, and found himself hoping that the Confederate bureaucracy was more efficient than what he was used to in the US. His appointment had been confirmed by telegram before he'd left Covington. If they claimed to have never heard of him, he was unsure what he'd do.

A few minutes later a Confederate Lieutenant emerged from inside the war department. Whereas the common soldiers had spoken with what Cole could only describe as the accent of Southern hicks, the Confederate officer spoke with the smooth drawl of a Southern gentleman.

"Welcome, gentlemen, right this way, sirs."

The guards looked disappointed but they allowed Cole to pass along with the two British officers. The interior of the Confederate War Department had the feel of a clean orderly office building, save that virtually everyone Cole saw was dressed in a military uniform. Cole was surprised to see that the building had electrical lighting.

The Confederate Lieutenant led them to the left and down a hallway. It was lined with portraits of Confederate military heroes. One of them was Nathan Bedford Forrest. Cole still remembered his meeting and interview with "the Scourge of the South" over twenty-five years earlier. It still sent chills down his spine.

At last they reached an office at the end of the hall. The door was already open but the Lieutenant still knocked politely.

"General Patton sir, these three gentlemen are here for military press passes. They have appointments."

"Thank you, Lieutenant, send them in."

They stepped into the office. General Patton was an older officer who had to be in his early sixties. He stood and extended his left hand to all three of them. In turn, all three men awkwardly shook it. The General's right arm was gone just above the elbow.

Here's a man that no doubt knows the terrible price of war first hand, thought Cole. He wondered what the two British officers were thinking. They looked way too young to have ever seen action.

"Please have a seat, Gentlemen"

As he sat down along with the British officers, Cole took in the office. It was small but extremely neat and organized. The primary decorations were two flags behind the General. The Blood Stained Banner was on a pole to his right and the Confederate Battle Flag on a pole to his left. Cole suddenly noticed a young boy about nine years old playing with gray and blue toy soldiers in the corner of the room. From the look of the battle, the gray troops had slaughtered the blue ones.

"I'm General Lee!" said the boy.

Cole smiled at him. Lieutenant Churchill tussled the hair on the boy's head.

"My Grandson, George," said General Patton. "He's my little namesake. Well let's get on with it. Mr. Churchill, Mr. Barnes, everything has already been prearranged and approved. You both should report to Fort Zachary Taylor in Key West Florida. From there you will eventually be able to accompany our forces into Cuba." He handed them two press passes. The General then turned to Cole. "Mr. Allens, I understand that you also want a military press pass?"

"Yes, sir."

"I have to tell you, sir, the Confederate Army is not in the habit of granting such passes to journalists from the United States."

"With due respect, General, your government issued the call for journalists from neutral nations to come and observe the campaign in Cuba."

"You'll forgive my being blunt, Mr. Allens, but I have a hard time viewing the United States as "neutral" when it comes to my country. I understand why they are here," he said, pointing at the two young British officers, "and I understand why my superiors want them to see what goes on in Cuba. But this is not your war, so I want to know what your interest is in this. You'll have to give me a pretty good reason if you want the pass."

Cole nodded.

"Sir, I lost my father and older brother in the First War of Rebellion...excuse me... in the Confederate War of Independence. I also had two uncles who fought on the Confederate side."

Now Patton nodded.

"The border states had it bad, Kentucky probably worst of all. What is your point?"

"The point, sir, is that I know firsthand the terrible cost of war. In the War of 1869 I was a war correspondent covering the fighting in Kentucky. I saw the suffering and death of that war with my own eyes. I saw not only war, but shameless butchery on both sides. I don't want people—North or South— to forget, lest someday we revisit the horror of the 1860s."

For the briefest instant, Cole thought he saw Patton's eyes glance down to where his right arm should have been. He saw indecision on the General's face. It looked very out of place. Cole still had two more arguments to make.

"Also, General, if Spain is committing the atrocities that you and others claim, it needs to be reported in the USA as well. The final thing I ask you to consider General is that the Spanish may try to accuse the Confederacy of brutality. You have my word that I will report what I see in Cuba objectively. I understand there will be other neutral correspondents there, but if a US journalist were reporting on the honorable conduct of the Confederate forces, no one back in the USA could believe the claims of the Spanish for even a moment." In reality, Cole was not entirely convinced that the Confederates would fight "honorably" if there was such a thing. He remembered the brutal tactics of Nathan Bedford Forrest during the Second War of Rebellion (as well as those of the

Union army). In Cole's eyes neither side had been clean but he was willing to give the Confederacy the benefit of the doubt in the new war with Spain if it would help get him to Cuba.

Without another word, Patton reached into his desk, pulled out a form and began to fill it out.

"I'm granting you a provisional pass. Your best bet to get to Cuba is to join these gentlemen in going to Key West Florida. I'm not sure what the situation will be when you get down there but whatever it is it will be up to the commander of Fort Zachary Taylor as to what to do with you. You'll report to him when you get to Key West and then you'll abide by whatever he decides. Understood?"

"Understood, sir. And thank you."

Cole, Churchill, and Barnes shook hands with the General again as they rose to leave. Cole looked over at General Patton's grandson.

"George, say goodbye to our guests," said the General.

The boy eagerly shook hands with the two British officers. But instead of offering his small hand to Cole, he pointed one of his toy cannons at him instead.

"Die Yankee!" Even though it came from a nine year old child, Cole felt there was something eerily serious about the way the boy had said it.

"They learn young, do they not," said Churchill quietly, as he headed out the door. For his part the General simply smiled.

"Come on George. We're supposed to be meeting General Mosby for lunch and we're late."

XXVI

Civilian and private citizen John Pershing sat across from Jennifer Harper. They were so transfixed on each other that they hardly noticed the jostling of the train or the passing green scenery of rural New York State. Pershing felt out of place in the tan wool civilian suit Jennifer had picked out for

205

him. Army blue had been a part of his life for so long that he felt like a different person without it. Jennifer had assured him that he looked very handsome in his new clothes. The way she was constantly beaming at him, let him know that at least she believed it.

"I think I like you as a civilian better. You look so grave and grim as a soldier.

"Ever since I was a boy, I've dreamed of running the Rebs out of Missouri and paying them back for what happened to my father, my brothers and my sisters."

"And that's why you joined the Army?"

Pershing nodded.

"I figured that another war with the Confederacy was inevitable. I wanted to make sure I was in a position to be a part of it."

"Is that why you're joining Whitmore's Legion?"

Pershing nodded. He noticed that the way she was looking at him had changed. It had gone from obvious romantic admiration to…

Sympathy? Concern? He liked the previous look much better. "What did you mean I look grave and grim as a soldier?" His voice was not particularly harsh or suspicious but his tone obviously disturbed her.

"I didn't mean to offend you," she said. "It's just…I remember the way you killed that bandit—the look on your face—it's almost like you enjoyed it."

"He was nothing but Rebel scum. He deserved what he got."

"Yes, John, he deserved it. And I'm proud of you for pursuing him over the line for the sake of justice. I just don't want to see you hurt, or so burned up by hatred and the thirst for revenge that it consumes you. You are such a good hearted man."

"You said yourself that you are here because you want to do your part in fighting the Rebs," he said.

"I know. I'm not saying you're doing the wrong thing. I really think you're doing the right thing." She then took his hands in hers and stared into his eyes. "I just want you to know that there is more to our lives than getting vengeance. When most my family was killed my father and I stayed in Missouri because we had nowhere else to go. Ever since he died I've felt…lost. When I read about Whitmore's Legion I felt I had finally found a place to go and a way to fight back. But meeting you again… and the time that we've spent together the past few days… has made me realize that there's a lot more in this life that I want. Let's do our part. And then let's get on with our lives."

They continued to hold hands and stare at one another like a couple of star crossed lovers. Even that modest display of affection was enough to cause a couple of older ladies gossiping and loudly "coughing" in protest. Public affection was considered to be in bad taste. Eventually Pershing pulled out the newspaper he had picked up during their last stop in Chicago. The headline was not encouraging.

CONFEDERATE NAVY SINKS SPANISH BATTLESHIP IN FIRST ENGAGEMENT OF THE WAR.

"How exactly does Whitmore plan on getting his forces to Cuba?" asked Jennifer.

"He'll have to do it by ship. But as to what ships, and where and when the departure is set for he's very wisely keeping quiet. The Confederate navy will undoubtedly try to intercept him." He then held up the paper with the ominous headline. "And it doesn't look like the Spanish fleet is up to the task of escorting his ships to Cuba."

"We're going to be on those ships!" said Jennifer in a startled tone. "I knew this was going to be dangerous but I never thought about getting blown out of the water before we even get to the war!"

"It's not too late for you to…"

Suddenly there was a commotion further back in the train car. Pershing caught the sound of a harsh and mocking voice.

"Looky what we have here folks! A big ugly nigger in a fancy suit."

Joshua Winslow sat quietly. His face seemed as still and resolute as stone, though within he was seething with rage like a smoldering volcano. His dark skin hid the burning flush of anger coming up in his face. He took in deep slow breaths trying to keep his self-control. He then looked ever so calmly into the face of the white man mocking him. For the first time, Joshua noticed that the man had a glass eye.

"Have I done something to offend you, sir?" he asked. Joshua spoke in a deep rich voice that testified to his great education. It contained not a hint of the intonations of slavery that afflicted the speech of the vast majority of North America's negroes.

The white man tormenting him was at first taken aback by his response. He rallied quickly.

"As a matter of fact you have done something to offend me, nigger. Your being here offends me." The man pointed to his glass eye and a hideous scar that went from his eye and across his temple. "If it wasn't for you niggers the Wars of Rebellion would never have happened. We'd still be one country, I'd still have my eye, and a whole lot of good men would still be alive. You don't belong here. You should all go back to Africa!"

"I assure you, sir, my African forefathers had no desire to come here. I am no more responsible for your injury than I am for the color of skin with which I was born. Now please, sir, kindly leave me in peace." With that Joshua opened up his copy of Grey's Anatomy and began reading. The one-eyed white man turned back towards his companions enraged.

"Did you hear that boys? Did this fancy nigger just talk back to me?" He turned around and snatched the book from Joshua's hands. Instinctively, Joshua leapt to his feet. Because of his great height he towered over the white man who was momentarily startled by his size. But with the courage that only a bully with a bunch of friends at his back could possess, the man did nothing but point the book at Joshua's face. The man's friends had all leapt to their feet. The cramped train car looked as though it were about to be the scene of a brawl.

"That's enough!" came the commanding voice of John Pershing. He may have been dressed like a civilian, but he spoke with all the authority of an officer of the United States Army. The harassers turned to face him, momentarily startled by his stern command. Pershing had taken off his coat and stood with his hands on his hips, staring at the four men like a rifleman over his gun sights. The man with the glass eye gazed menacingly at Pershing. His companions weren't so confident. They were busy eyeing the army revolver that was in the holster on Pershing's belt.

"This man has done nothing to you."

"You need to mind your own business, Mr. nigger lover."

"And you need to stop being so driven by sheer hate, anger, and ignorance that you go looking for a fight with a man who has done you know wrong, just because you don't like the color of his skin. Now I'm just going to tell you this once..." Pershing placed his hand on his revolver. "Move along. Find another car and don't let me see you in this one again or its going to get very ugly. You understand me?"

The man with the glass eye glared angrily at Pershing, trying to decide whether or not he was bluffing.

"Come on Gus, lets go," said one of his companions. "It isn't worth getting killed over." The man with the glass eye let Joshua's book fall to the floor. Then, giving Pershing a look that bespoke fierce hatred and rage he turned away.

"Let's get out of here! I don't want to be in the same car with a filthy nigger any way."

After the four hateful men had withdrawn from the car, Joshua stooped down and picked up his book from the floor. He then drew back up to his full height and looked Pershing in the eye.

"Thank you, sir."

"You're welcome, friend."

Joshua took mental note that Pershing had called him *friend* instead of *sir.* As he thought about it, Joshua reflected that he had never, in his entire life, heard a white man refer to a black man as sir. But Pershing had come to his aid—apparently out of nothing but good will—so Joshua was quite ready to overlook minor infraction. He had only been called "nigger" about a hundred times on that particular trip. He wasn't about to complain about being called friend.

"May I ask your name, sir?" inquired Joshua.

"John Joseph Pershing. And you are?"

"I am Joshua Winslow."

"Well Joshua, I'm pleased to meet you. If you don't mind my asking where are you going? What do you ah… what do you do for a living?"

You mean: How did I come to be a well-dressed and well educated negro? Joshua didn't fault him for his curiosity. The vast majority of negroes on the North American continent were illiterate slaves that barely lived above the level of farm animals. Even in the United States, though slavery had been ended for thirty years, most negroes lived in abject poverty with no opportunities to be educated or to better their lives in any meaningful way. Once again he thanked God, that he had been given such blessings.

"I am a medical student. I am on my way to Massena to join Whitmore's Legion as a field surgeon—if they'll have me."

A very small world... thought Pershing.

The rest of the trip was relatively uneventful. Massena was on the US / Canadian border, so in many ways it was the end of the line. The closer they got to it, the more passengers disembarked and the fewer people were on the train. In any event, no one harassed Joshua again. When the train finally pulled into the small train station in Massena, there were only a handful of passengers left.

Porters rushed to help Pershing and especially Jennifer with her luggage. As usual Joshua handled his own. A lean clean shaven man in a khaki uniform stood waiting on the platform.

"Mr. Pershing?"

"I am."

"And who are these?" he asked pointing to Jennifer and Joshua.

"Miss Harper has come to volunteer as a nurse. Mr. Winslow is here to offer his medical services as a surgeon."

Mr. Winslow? thought Joshua. In all his life that was the first time he had ever been referred to as Mr. by a white man.

"A negro Doctor?"

"I was given to understand that Mr. Whitmore was allowing negroes to serve in this endeavor," said Joshua.

"He is…they are… but as rifleman. I don't know what he'll say about one… you serving as a doctor."

You're not sure if anyone will want a nigger giving them treatment, translated Joshua mentally. *I wonder if that would matter if you had a bullet in your leg and you were bleeding to death?*

"Do you have any proof that you are qualified?"

Joshua nodded.

"I have brought a letter of recommendation from Doctor Forrester, the chief instructor of surgery, at the Physician's College of Medicine and Surgery in Chicago, attesting to my qualifications. I have come to offer my services in the fight against the Confederate States," said Joshua. "If the only way I can do that is to carry a rifle, than that is what I will do. But let us allow Mr. Whitmore to decide."

The uniformed man nodded.

"Alright, Sambo, sounds good enough to me. Now if you will all step this way, I have a wagon waiting to take us to the mansion."

Suddenly, another man appeared on the platform. He was tall with dark hair. His face would have been handsome accept for a nasty scar that ran down the right side of his face.

"Excuse me. I would also like to sign up."

"And you are?"

"Murphy. Frank Murphy. I've come all the way from Baltimore."

"Baltimore? Do you have any military experience? We don't really have any more time to train raw recruits."

"Yes sir, I served in the state militia. I also have brought a letter. It's from my Captain attesting to my service."

The man in khaki sighed.

"Alright, let's go."

As the five of them headed towards the waiting wagon, Jennifer whispered to Pershing.

"I don't remember seeing that man on the train…"

"Neither do I…"

XXVII

Ebenezer reached up and wiped sweat from his face with a cloth rag. He'd been hard at work for most of the day working on building a new railing for the front porch of the Dumas' mansion. Since it was a Wednesday, Cap was in the fields and Ebenezer was doing the work alone. He'd spent most of the previous day sawing wood for the legs and railing and then using the lathe to carve them into the appropriate shape. He'd had Cap to help with the sanding, though they hadn't finished until nearly sundown. Ebenezer had spent that morning taking down the old railing and hauling it away by hand. He'd then begun the delicate task of constructing the new railing. The posts had to be placed in just the right position or it wouldn't look right. Mr. Dumas would be back that afternoon, and Ebenezer wanted his master to be pleased—not so much because he cared about his owner's happiness but because he cared about his own wellbeing. When a white master was displeased with his black slave, it usually didn't turn out that well for the black slave. Mr. Dumas had shown that he was not as cruel and vicious as Fitch Haley had been, but in the short time that Ebenezer had been at Twin Harbours, he'd learned that Mansel Dumas was a stern man that expected everyone's best work. Ebenezer might have agreed with him, if he were actually being paid for his labor. Nevertheless, for his own sake, Ebenezer did his best. By late afternoon he was nearly finished.

"Ebenezer, you are doing a wonderful job, it looks beautiful!"

"Thank you, Miss Flossy."

The Mistress of Twin Harbours was, in many ways, the opposite of her husband. Mrs. Dumas was exceptionally kind.

"I've asked Rosy here to bring you some nice cold lemonade."

Ebenezer suddenly noticed the beautiful young negress standing behind the Mistress. From her dress and attire, Ebenezer could tell she was a maid. He downed the glass of icy lemonade and sighed.

"Thank you, Miss Flossy. Dat' was mighty fine." As he returned the empty glass to the tray that Rosy was carrying, Mrs. Dumas asked:

"Tell me, Ebenezer, how is Cap adjusting?"

A stab of fear came over Ebenezer. The Dumas' knew his friend wasn't happy and he didn't know what to think about their inquiries.

Are dey' askin' cause dey cares or cause dey think he gwoin' run away? He decided a lie mixed with some truth was the best answer to give. "He still all tore up inside," said Ebenezer. "But I think he gwoin' to be fine. He gettin better."

Mrs. Dumas smiled.

"Well, I don't want you to tell him, because we don't want to get his hopes up, but Mr. Dumas has gone to Natchez today and on his way back he's going to stop at Sharpstone to speak to Mr. Haley about purchasing Cap's family."

Ebenezer didn't know what to say. All that came out was, "Thank you, Miss Flossy!" He was reasonably certain that Mrs. Dumas had had more to do with it than Mr. Dumas.

Suddenly, Mitchell Dumas came riding a horse through the plantation's front gate and up the main drive to the mansion. The eighteen year old boy looked extremely excited.

"Momma! They've activated the county militia! They're looking for volunteers!"

"I'm sure it's only a precautionary measure, Darling," said Mrs. Dumas. "I'm sure there's very little chance of the Spanish Navy sailing up the Mississippi."

Far from being comforted by his mother's assurance, young Mitchell looked almost disappointed he would not be able to shoot at the pride of the Spanish fleet any time soon.

"Maybe the Spanish will show up off the coast, near Biloxi or Gulfport!" he said excitedly. "The militia might see some action if they're stationed there!"

"I should hope not," said Mrs. Dumas. "In any event you won't be there."

"I'm eighteen! I'm old enough!"

"That's beside the point," said Mrs. Dumas. "Now, go wash up for supper. Your Father should be home at any moment. We'll discuss it tonight."

As the Dumas son went into the mansion the two young daughters came prancing out the front door.

"And where do you young ladies think you are going?"

"We want to go see the chicks..."

"Oh no you don't! You get back in that house and wash up."

The girls' loud protests went unanswered as a large black mammy came out onto the front porch and brought the girls back inside the house.

"You heard yo mamma, git in da house!"

Mrs. Dumas and Rosy also withdrew into the mansion, allowing Ebenezer to resume his work in peace.

Just as he had set the last post, and fastened the last segment of railing, Mr. Mansel Dumas came riding into the plantation. A large black slave named Jeffrey went bounding up to take the horse for Dumas.

"Welcome home, Massa."

Dumas handed Jeffrey the reins, gave the slave a pat on the back, and then bounded up the steps and onto the front porch. Ebenezer wanted to know about Caps family, but he didn't dare ask. Dumas did take a moment to look at Ebenezer's work. He gave a nod of approval.

"Very good, Ebenezer. That's enough for today, you can pick up in the morning."

"Yes, suh, Massa."

Dumas then stepped inside the door of the mansion which the well-dressed slave Berry had opened for him.

"Welcome home my dear!" said Florence Dumas as Berry closed the door and took his master's coat and hat.

Mansel kissed his wife and they then walked through the mansion arm in arm on their way to the large dining room. Mansel kept his stride slow so that his crippled wife could keep up. The table was far larger than was needed for the family of four. It could have easily seated twenty people. The mammy had placed the girls across from one another and was watching them like a hawk. Mitchell had seated himself to the left of his father's chair. Mansel Dumas helped his wife into her chair and then seated himself at the head of the table. As the family held hands for prayer, the slaves stood with hands clasped and heads bowed.

"Father," said Mansel, "Thank you for this food, and for all you have provided for us, help me to lead this house, as you have appointed me, forgive us of our sins, protect our soldiers as they go to war, help our great nation to win victory...Amen."

"Amen," said all in the room. Immediately the slaves went to work setting napkins and utensils before the family. Rosy came in carrying plates of corn, and green beans and ham with cherry glaze.

"My dear," said Florence, "how did your business at Sharpstone go?"

Mansel suddenly looked angry and frustrated. He took a sip of wine before answering.

"Let's just say Fitch Haley holds a grudge for the price at which I purchased Ebenezer, Cap and the others. He was not inclined to do business with me at a fair price. Cap will simply have to adjust."

Mansel then dug into his ham like a starving man. Mitchell took the opportunity to change the subject.

"Daddy, they've called up the county militia."

"Yes, I know," said Dumas almost derogatorily. "It is a complete waste of time. The Spanish will never attack here. They are a rotting failing empire whose day has come and gone. It will take all they've got just to try to hold on to Cuba, not that it will do them any good."

Mitchell looked none too pleased to hear that his father's sentiments matched his mothers. Nonetheless, he had one more subject to broach.

"I was wondering, sir, if I might join the militia?" Out of the corner of his eye, he could see his mother smiling. *She knows he'll say no,* thought Mitchell.

"Of course you can join," said Mansel and took a large sip of wine. "A little military discipline will do you some good..." He then held up his glass for a refill.

Outside, Ebenezer had returned the tools to the workshop and begun to make his way towards the small shanty village that was home to the plantation's negro slaves. He was totally exhausted. As tired as he was though, the rumblings of his stomach let him know that his hunger exceeded even his exhaustion. He waited in a line with the rest of the slaves to receive a bowel of stew and a hunk of cornbread. After getting his dinner, Ebenezer spotted Cap sitting by a fire. His friend looked sadder than as ever.

"How yo' day go, Cap?"

"What it matter? Don't matter none. You knows how I's feel and what I thinks about doin.'"

Ebenezer swore under his breath.

"You hush, fool! You gone get yo self into a lot a pain and trouble, if'in you keep talkin' and thinkin' like dat." Ebenezer wanted more than ever to tell Cap what Mrs. Dumas had told him.

But if it don't happen, he be crushed worse den he is now!

Cap then stood and walked away from Ebenezer. With a sigh, Ebenezer decided it was time to turn in. He had another day of work ahead of him. As he approached the shanty that he and Cap had been assigned, a voice that he had not heard in years called out to him from the darkness of the woods to his left.

"Ebenezer!" It was a half shout half whisper. Ebenezer's heart froze. He looked and at the edge of the wood stood an older negro holding a small kerosene lantern. Ebenezer had never imagined he would see him again.

"Caesar! Is dat really you?"

"You bet yo hide boy. Let's get in the cabin fo' someone sees us."

Ebenezer quickly led Caesar into the cabin and then closed the rickety door behind them. Caesar then increased the brightness of the lantern. Ebenezer felt like he was beholding a ghost. The fiery light coming from the lantern lit up the room in a manner that eerily contributed to that feeling.

"How long you been gone from Sharpstone, boy?"

"Not long. Caesar, where you been all dis time? I thought you done run off north years ago!" Ebenezer couldn't believe his eyes. The man that had taught him to read in secret as a child was with him again. The one slave who had ever run away from Sharpstone plantation and eluded capture had somehow returned.

"I went a lot further than just north," said Caesar. "The underground railroad got me out of the CSA, through the United States and into Canada."

"Den why you come back? You are some fool crazy nigger. Dey catch you, dey kill you. Dey catch you wit me, dey kill me too!"

"Listen to me, Ebenezer. After I went to Canada I met a small but devoted group of abolitionists. They are interested not just in helping us sneak more slaves out of da' CSA. Dey wants to help us overthrow the Buckra and free all negroes by force. Some of dem's Yankees and some of dem's British, but dey's both hates da Buckra down here. Dey sent me to England, across da ocean. I done seen things dat I never thought I ever see. But I mets people willin' to do what it takes to make things right. Deys hatching a plan. Real soon, now, a boat full of guns is gone come down the Mississippi. We gone arm ourselves and then we is gone win our freedom!"

Ebenezer was in shock. His heart was pounding. He wanted with every fiber of his being to be free. But he wasn't sure that violence would work. Even if it would, he wasn't sure it was right.

Is that it or am I just scared? As he sat under the piercing gaze of his former tutor, Ebenezer suddenly realized he was scared and couldn't help thinking that beyond his control he was now being drawn into something that would ultimately end in his death or worse.

Lord, help me...

XXVIII

Nathan Audrey stared at the mob of raw recruits that stood on the fields of Camp Kibbe, outside of Sacremento. They ranged in age from gray headed old men down to boys not old enough to shave. The way they lolled about the field and chatted away with one another showed their utter lack of discipline and military training.

I'm supposed to turn this into an army?

It had been over twenty-five years since Audrey had been a soldier and nearly thirty since he'd been an officer in the US Army. Regardless, Audrey was now officially Lieutenant Colonel Nathan Johnson of the Republic of California Army. Despite the fact that General Goldwyn knew his true identity, he hadn't dropped the alias. The knowledge that there were still people out to capture and kill him, even after all those years, meant that he would never be able to openly use his real name again.

As Audrey rode towards them and assessed the recruits, they stared back at him almost impudently. Despite his Colonel's uniform, they looked at him like he was little more than a cranky old man.

They're nothing but an untrained rabble. That's going to change and quickly.

"Sergeant, get these men into line!" shouted Audrey. Several of the recruits jumped at the harshness of his voice. He was pleased that his voice hadn't lost the edge of command. The Sergeants snapped into action. While the non-coms screamed and shouted profanities at the mob of civilian clad recruits, Audrey shifted uncomfortably in the saddle of his horse. He hadn't worn a military uniform in two decades and he found the forest green coat and khaki pants that he had been issued extremely uncomfortable.

It took longer than it should have, but the sergeants managed to get the recruits into formation. Audrey was displeased that he'd had to order the Sergeants to put the men into line. He had learned shortly after arriving at the training camp that many NCOs of the Californian army were poorly trained themselves. The fact that he, a Lieutenant Colonel, was having to be so personally involved in the training of the troops, showed how little they had to work with. Making a potent military force was going to be difficult.

I need to gauge the quality of the Sergeants. Audrey pointed at the head NCO.

"Stand at attention, Sergeant."

The NCO came to rigid attention.

"What's your name, Sergeant?"

"Matthews, sir!"

"Sergeant Matthews tell me about your military experience." From the NCO's age (he had to be in his mid fifties) and his Brooklyn accent, Audrey would have bet money he was a veteran of at least one of the Wars of Rebellion. He would have won.

"Sir, I signed up in the U.S. Army in 1861. I fought with the Army of the Potomac from Bull Run to Gettysburg."

Audrey nodded. His story was the same.

"Well, Sergeant Matthews, it seems that fate has brought you and I together again. I too fought in the Army of the Potomac. How much soldiering have you done since then?"

"Well, sir, I came to California in sixty-five. I've served as a volunteer in the Militia ever since. I saw a little action in sixty-nine when the Rebs stole the southern part of California. Other than that it's been pretty quiet till now."

Audrey nodded, not in approval but in understanding. The sergeant hadn't done any real soldiering in twenty years.

Of course when you get right down to it neither have I. "Sergeant Matthews, I trust that you still know how to march?"

"Yes, sir."

"Then let's show these green horns how we used to do it in the Army of the Potomac!"

Audrey looked at the other Sergeant and the two corporals.

"And I trust that you men know how to march as well?"

"Yes, sir!" they chorused.

"Good. Fall in with Sergeant Matthews. Audrey turned to the assembled recruits. "Any of you other men veterans that know how to march?"

A few more hands went up.

"Then you fall in as well. You gentlemen are going to demonstrate for our recruits how to march. Everyone else pay attention." Audrey knew he was taking a gamble. If the non-coms proved themselves to be inept, they would lose the confidence of the recruits and their ability to lead. On the other hand, if the non-coms couldn't perform the basic commands he was about to put them, then they weren't qualified to be non-coms in the first place. "Squad, left face!"

The Non-Coms executed pivots and turned to their left in unison. Audrey nodded. They had executed the move perfectly.

"Forward, march!" Over the next several minutes, Audrey demonstrated basic military drill—left face, right face, and about face. He marched them around, demonstrating basic marching maneuvers. He had the non-coms perform flank turns and column turns as well as counter column marches. Finally, he had them deploy into a skirmish line.

"Well, done gentlemen," said Audrey. He was glad to see that his non-coms would be useful after all. "Now, I want you to drill these men until their legs fall off! Until they know and can perform every command flawlessly."

The non-coms smiled savagely. "Yes, sir!" they chorused. A few moments later they had set upon the recruits like Egyptians upon the children of Israel. It wasn't long before they had the formation of recruits marching around the field. Audrey watched them for nearly an hour, not interfering, but taking careful note of which Sergeants seemed to know what they were doing and which did not. The problem was that even if he marked certain NCOs as unqualified, he had no men to replace them. With a sigh he turned his horse and rode towards the rifle range. On his way, he passed a row of artillery. All the pieces that he could see were outdated smoothbore cannons that would not have been out of place in the First War of Rebellion or even the Napoleonic wars for that matter. As far as Audrey could tell, there were no rifled guns among them.

As he neared the rifle range, Audrey saw a line of about thirty men that were bringing their rifles to their shoulders and taking aim at targets about fifty yards down range. The rifles were a mix of U.S. and European breech-loaders. Audrey cursed under his breath in frustration.

We don't have rifles for half the men and those we do possess use different types of ammunition. A moment later he reflected that it could be worse. *They could be carrying muzzle-loaders.*

A grizzled sergeant yelled "Fire!" The rifles barked. Audrey brought his binoculars up and scanned the targets. Surprisingly he found himself nodding in approval.

There seems to be hope for this ravel after all.

"What do you think, Colonel?"

Audrey spun his horse around to face General Goldwyn. He brought his arm up in salute. Goldwyn gravely returned it.

"I think, General, that we have our work cut out for us."
The answer was blunt and direct, but Audrey wasn't one to
beat around the bush.

"You don't know the half of it, Colonel. Ride with me."
The two officers rode towards Goldwyn's command tent. The
Californian national flag billowed in the breeze from a nearby
pole. After they had dismounted, they walked into tent.
Goldwyn handed Audrey a dispatch from Sacramento.
Audrey's eyes grew visibly wider as he read it.

"They can't be serious!"

"We march out in one week."

Audrey reread the dispatch. The Mormons had invaded
the western third of Nevada. They had seized several
Californian towns, including Pine City. In Sacramento
President Henry Markham had asked the Californian Congress
to declare a state of war between the Republic of California
and the Mormon Nation of Deseret. They had obliged him.
Unfortunately, California was ill prepared for the struggle. The
situation was desperate.

"General, these men aren't ready."

"'In a week they'll be as ready as our respective
companies were when we marched off to war in 1861."

"Exactly," said Audrey. I assume you remember the
First Battle of Bull Run, as well as I do?"

"Colonel, I don't need you to give me a history lesson,
these are our orders."

"What about guns, sir? We barely have enough rifles
for half of our force."

"There's a shipment of brand new repeaters waiting for
us at Fort Truckee." Goldwyn motioned Audrey over to a map
table and pointed at a small settlement and fort right across the
line from Nevada. "The regular army will be waiting for us
here. Once we've linked up with them and fully armed our
forces we'll march together into Nevada. If our intelligence is
correct we should have the Mormons outnumbered.

Audrey wanted to swear again, but he held it in. Even if
it was true that they would have the Mormons outnumbered,

Audrey knew from personal experience that that was far from a guarantee of victory. That, however, was not his only concern.

"General, Fort Truckee is just over the line from Nevada. There's no guarantee the Mormons will halt their advance with western Nevada. From what I've seen of our present deployments there is very little to stop the Mormons from invading California proper if they choose to do so. If they overrun Fort Truckee then we won't have those guns."

"Which is why we must move as soon as possible," said General Goldwyn. We'll link up with the regular army at Fort Truckee and retake Carson City, Pine City and the rest of the towns that the Mormons have captured. Trust me. They won't push further into our territory." The General motioned with his gloved hand at the immensity of the Nevada desert. The Mormon supply lines must be tenuous at best. There is nothing but vast desert in between western Nevada and Deseret. They'll not risk a further incursion into our territory."

"I hope you're right, General."

"Take heart, Nathan, I assure you that the Mormons are no better trained and equipped than we are."

"Neither were the Confederates at Bull Run."

Goldwyn feigned injury. "I hope, Colonel, that you have a slightly higher opinion of my military ability that you do of the late General McDowell?

Audrey smiled a disarming smile.

"A much higher opinion, sir." Audrey meant his words. Close to thirty years earlier he had seen not only Goldwyn's courage, but also his cunning in battle against the Sioux and other Indians. That, however, was not Audrey's point. "Even if you were Robert E. Lee himself, General, I would still worry about the coming campaign. The men will be poorly trained, and if the Mormons capture Fort Truckee half of our men won't even have weapons."

Goldwyn nodded. "We'll drill the men as hard as we can over the next few days. We'll make sure they are as ready as they can be. There's little that we can do about the rifles. They are safer at the fort than if I ordered them moved."

"Agreed," said Audrey reluctantly. He gazed down at the map again. His mind went back to the desperate battlefields of his past. Bull Run, Gettysburg, Fort Moultier and many others. It had been over twenty-five years since he had seen and smelled the carnage of war. He'd hoped he'd never know it again. He reached up and felt the crucifix under his uniform, its cold metal pressed against the skin of his chest. He knew he would very soon return to battle.

XXIX

Even riding in the comfort of his personal Pullman car, Joseph Whitmore detested long train rides. Especially train rides where he was uncertain where he was going, who he was meeting, and what he was supposed to do when he got there.

"I find this detestable!" he said. Whitmore then pointed his cane at his personal assistant who was, as far as he could tell, the only other person on the train besides himself besides the black clad Federal Marshals that had commandeered his personal train. "You are absolutely certain that it was John Garrison?"

"I'm positive, sir," said David Lovejoy. "I must say it was rather cloak and dagger the way he found me in town. He spoke to me just briefly enough that I could recognize him and then he handed me the sealed letter which I delivered to you immediately."

Whitmore pulled the letter back out and inspected it for what must have been the one hundredth time. It contained very little information accept that the United States Government strongly requested that he board his personal train at four in the afternoon without announcing to anyone that he was leaving and that the train would be run by special Federal agents. The envelope had the US Presidential seal and the letter had President Cleveland's signature.

Both of which could be duplicated by the Confederate Secret Service, thought Whitmore. The explosion on his property a few days earlier had him seeing spies, saboteurs and even assassins everywhere. The US Marshalls on the train seemed genuine enough, but even their badges, clothing, and weaponry could be duplicated by the Confederates. Only the knowledge that this whole thing had been set in motion by President Cleveland's personal secretary gave Whitmore any comfort. Of course, he reflected, it was only on Lovejoy's word that he had actually received the letter from John Garrison. Whitmore quickly pushed that unpleasant thought aside. If he allowed himself to be overcome by paranoia, than he would cease to be able to function.

"I still wish I knew more about what was going on!"

"Patience, sir. We will no doubt find out soon enough."

The drapes had all been pulled closed and the Federal Marshals had instructed them to keep them that way. That hadn't stopped Lovejoy from pulling out his pocket compass at the start of the trip.

"We're still headed west. My guess is that we're going to Buffalo or maybe even Cleveland."

Whitmore pulled out his gold pocket watch and scowled. It was 9:35 in the evening. A while later the train finally began to slow. When it finally came to a screeching halt, Lovejoy said, "I don't believe we've arrived at a train station. It's too quiet outside for a major station or depot, even at this time of night. It must be a small train stop."

"We haven't made any stops until now," said Whitmore. "We must have reached our destination at last." The elderly millionaire rose to his feet and headed for the door of the car. It opened before he got to it and a black clad Federal Marshal entered. He was quickly followed by two finely dressed men, one of whom was none other than US President Grover Cleveland.

"Forgive all the secrecy and inconvenience, gentlemen but it was necessary. The Confederacy's spy network is incredibly good. We wanted to take every security precaution possible."

Whitmore nodded and quickly motioned for the President and his companion to seat themselves in the Pullman's most luxurious seats. Not a minute later the door was shut and the train started forward again. Only then did the President introduce his associate. The well-dressed man looked extremely dignified in his finely tailored suit. He was an older man in his early sixties with large white side burns.

"May I present, Sir Julian Pauncefote, the Ambassador from Great Britain."

"The pleasure is all mine Ambassador!" said Whitmore with a look of joy and excitement that said he was ready to leap out of his seat. The enthusiastic way in which he shook the ambassador's hand, showed he had the energy to perform such a feat. The President continued.

"After our last meeting I did quite a bit of thinking," said Cleveland. "You made a lot of very good points Mr. Whitmore."

Out of the corner of his eye, Whitmore could see Lovejoy grinning. Whitmore's assistant knew how convincing the old millionaire could be when he was impassioned about something. There was a lot of truth to the claim that the industrialist was eccentric. But there was no doubting he loved his country or that he was sly and daring enough to see things and accomplish things that others could not.

Cleveland looked Whitmore dead in the eye.

"I hope you understand that much of what I have said publically about your mercenary venture has merely been a front to protect the United States."

"Of course, Your Excellency," said Whitmore.

"Now as I'm sure you have guessed, a lot has happened on the diplomatic front since we last spoke." The President motioned towards the British ambassador. "The United States and Britain have come to an agreement on taking joint action in the situation concerning Cuba."

"We have decided to take joint military action?" asked Whitmore expectantly.

"No," said Sir Julian, speaking for the first time. "Nothing so direct."

Whitmore looked from the British ambassador back to President Cleveland.

"Mr. Whitmore, before we continue further I think it necessary to explain a few things. In the past four years, both the United States and Great Britain have made offers to Spain to purchase Cuba. Even though we could both pay much more than the Confederate States, Spain rejected our offers as flatly as they have rejected the Confederates. Subsequently, the United States offered to pay Spain a handsome sum of gold if they would only consider leasing—long term—the port of Guantanamo for us to use as a naval base. As you know Mr. Whitmore, ever since the Confederacy gained its independence and especially since it seized southern California the United States has been completely cut off from central and south America as well as the Caribbean. A naval base at Guantanamo would allow us to project US naval power into the heart of the Confederacy's sphere of influence."

"It would also," said Sir Julian, "put the United States Navy within easy striking distance of the canal that the Confederates and French are building across the Isthmus of Panama along with our own naval forces stationed in Jamaica."

Whitmore nodded in understanding. The canal, if successfully completed, would give the Confederate States and the French Empire an enormous advantage in both international trade and naval warfare.

"Your saying in the event of war, we want to be able to capture or destroy the canal quickly?"

"Exactly," said Lord Julian.

"The Confederacy may well view that as a knife leveled at its throat," said Whitmore.

"As well they should," said Sir Julian. "As should the French. There are those in Her Majesty's government who believe that we cannot allow France and the CSA to reap the advantages of such a canal under any conditions. They want the US and Britain to put joint pressure on the CSA and France to make the canal and international project."

"And having a major US naval base in the Caribbean is more likely to make that happen?" said Whitmore.

"Exactly," said Sir Julian.

"It is also," said President Cleveland "just as likely to start the biggest war in world history—an intercontinental war that would rage on both sides of the Atlantic."

"Which is something neither Britain nor the USA is presently prepared for," said Sir Julian. "Therefore we wish to avoid it at all costs."

"So how does all this play into what's happening now?" asked Whitmore.

"When the CSS Mississippi was destroyed in Havana a few months ago," said Cleveland "Spain and the United States were on the verge of concluding a treaty whereby Spain would lease us Guantanamo for fifty years to use as a naval base."

"I find that highly suspicious," said Whitmore.

"As do we," said Sir Julian. Cleveland nodded his own agreement.

"It's just too convenient that right before we were to sign the deal with Spain the CSA gets a casus belli to declare war and seize the whole island."

"Why haven't we gone ahead and made the deal?" asked Whitmore.

"In the first place, we feared it would be too provocative against the Confederacy. We have no evidence that the destruction of their warship was caused by anyone other than Cuban Rebels. In the second place, the Spanish immediately withdrew their offer unless we agreed to openly support them against the Confederates."

"So what is this joint action that America and Britain are proposing?" Once again, it didn't cross Whitmore's mind that the Confederates also referred to themselves as Americans.

"At first we were hoping that Spain would come to its senses, realize it had no hope of holding Cuba against the CSA, and get what little profit they could by selling us Guantanamo before the Confederates overrun the whole island—but your little scheme to raise a mercenary army, has complicated matters somewhat."

"How is that, Mr. President?"

"You have given the Spanish a false hope that they can hold onto the island," said Sir Julian.

"I'd not call it a false hope, Mr. Ambassador," said Whitmore. "The artillery and rifles made by my company are some of the finest in the world. The Mercenary force I am raising will be one of the most elite in history."

David Lovejoy, who had remained absolutely silent during the discussion now lowered his head and rubbed his eyes as if getting a headache. He knew his employer sincerely meant every word he said about his private army being elite. But he also knew from firsthand experience that it was not. Mr. Whitmore had a habit of seeing things the way he wanted them to be, as opposed to how they actually were. Whitmore's Legion was good, but it would not be enough to stop the CSA from overrunning Cuba. He wished Whitmore would allow himself to see that.

"Are you asking me to withdraw my offer to Spain? If you are I must warn you that I cannot. I have given my word, and I'm not about to back down after all the publicity. People would never take me seriously again."

"No, Mr. Whitmore," said President Cleveland, "we are not suggesting that you withdraw your agreement with the Spanish, nor do we intend to interfere. We're not convinced that you can stop the Confederates from taking over the island. Chances are, you won't even get there in time. But you will make it harder on the Confederates, and make taking the island a lot more costly for them. What we are asking, assuming you make it down there in time, is that you do everything in your power to hold onto Guantanamo and keep it out of Confederate hands. When push comes to shove down there we're going to put all the pressure on Spain we can to get them to sell us Guantanamo. We want you to insure that it stays out of

Confederate hands long enough for us to convince the Spanish to sell it to us. "

"One thing confuses me, Mr. President," said Whitmore. "You have made it clear that you do not want us to wind up in another war with the CSA and that you do not believe we are ready. I'm afraid I don't see how you're going to avoid it. Just how do you plan to take possession of Guantanamo if the Spanish finally do sell it to you at the last moment? The entire area will be crawling with the Confederate Navy."

"That's where we come in," said Sir Julian. "We are prepared to send a naval task force of our own to Cuban waters along with the task force the USA sends to take possession of Guantanamo. The Confederate Navy will have been weakened by its war with Spain, and confronted with a combined US / British fleet I doubt they would be so foolish as to try and intervene by force."

"I wouldn't be so sure, Sir Julian. Some might be counted on to react rationally in such a situation but not the Rebels. They are a proud and arrogant people."

Sir Julian continued.

"We are also taking other measures to insure that both the Confederates and the French have other reasons to not force a confrontation over Guantanamo."

"I was just about to ask about the probability of French involvement."

"Let's just say that both the French and Confederates are in for some distractions," said Sir Julian. "Her Majesty's Secret Service has been extremely busy. If all goes according to plan, the French are going to have a major problem with Berber tribesmen in Algeria, the Confederates are going to have a slave rebellion in the heart of their home territory and both the Confederates and French forces in Panama are going to be dealing with attacks by Columbian guerrillas. Suffice it to say, they will be very angry at the situation, but I'd wager they'll not risk war with so many unpleasant things going on elsewhere."

"But what if it does come to war?" asked Whitmore.

"Then," said Sir Julian, "the United States has the assurance of the British Empire that we will stand beside you."

Whitmore nodded. He then rose from his seat and walked over to the Pullman's counter and personally poured four glasses of brandy. Lovejoy leapt to his feet to carry the drinks over to the President and British ambassador. Whitmore held his glass high.

"A toast gentlemen, to the United States of America finally taking a stand against her enemies and to our friend Great Britain for her courage in standing beside us!"

The assembled men drained their glasses. As he set down his empty glass, Lovejoy found himself wondering if an intercontinental war was in their near future.

XXX

As Captain Blake Ramsey starred at the city of Havana from the deck of the *CSS Texas,* he found his thoughts going back months earlier, to the fateful night when the *CSS Mississippi* had been destroyed. Now he had returned with a fleet of Confederate warships behind him, to take bloody vengeance. Standing on the forecastle deck, and gazing through his binoculars, Ramsey was able to make out the shoreline, the city, the entrance to the harbor, and most of all, the fortifications that guarded the entrance to the channel. The fort on the western side of the channel was small by modern standards. It looked like a miniature castle with a few fortified gun emplacements. The eastern side, however, was much more formidable. A much larger stone fortress, Morro Castle, sat atop a two hundred foot hill along with an even larger fortification known as the La Cabana which was one of the largest military forts in the Caribbean. A massive red and gold Spanish flag flew atop the fortress.

As Ramsey surveyed the city, his first officer Ray Brisk ascended the forecastle, walked along the large anchor chains and stood beside him.

"Good to be back at Havana," he said. "This time it's my turn to go ashore."

Ramsey smirked as he stared through the binoculars.

"We'll have to earn our shore leave this time, Ray." His eyes came to rest on Morro Castle, the La Cabana and the massive cannons that bristled all over them. Brisk raised his own binoculars to his eyes. He uttered a blasphemy.

"Those are some awful big guns."

"They look intimidating, but don't be fooled," said Ramsey. "Those guns are as antiquated as the castles they are defending. They're nothing but big ugly smoothbores." He lowered his binoculars and turned to stare at his battleship's own twelve inch guns. Mounted in armored deck turrets, they had already been brought to bear on the enemy fortifications.

"Most of those fortifications date back to the 1500s," said Ramsey. "Our own guns should make quick work of them."

"I'm surprised they turned down our terms of surrender," said Brisk. The day before the Confederate fleet had sent an envoy into the city by boat under a white flag, asking that the Spanish declare Havana an open city, and spare it and the people inside the unpleasantness of an attack. Unsurprisingly the Spanish hadn't accepted.

"The Spanish view Cuba as a province of Spain itself, not as a mere colony," said Ramsey. "They won't give up Havana without a fight, of that you can be sure."

"Well, the fleet is in position and the Admiral has made it clear we get the opening shot."

Ramsey nodded in reply. He and Brisk had barely escaped the explosion that had destroyed the *CSS Mississippi*. It was only fitting that they be allowed to fire the first shots of the Confederacy's campaign to conquer Cuba. At Ramsey's command a yeoman in a dress gray uniform came forward carrying a reverently folded Confederate Naval Battle Flag. It was the same flag that had flown from the bow of the *Mississippi.* It had rips and tears, as well as burn and scorch marks on it. Nonetheless, Ramsey and Brisk personally raised it on the flag pole at the bow of the *CSS Texas.* The torn and heavily damaged red flag with the star belted blue saltier fluttered in the ocean breeze. Ramsey turned to Brisk.

"Fire at will." A few moments later, the *Texas'* main guns thundered to life. They belched fire and smoke with a sound like the end of the world. They fired twelve inch explosive shells which screamed through the air and came crashing down on the Spanish fortifications. They impacted violently, throwing shrapnel and stony debris in all directions. Shortly thereafter, the entire fleet opened fire. The Confederates relentlessly rained death down onto their Spanish adversaries. The gunners did their best to target only the military fortifications, but in such a massive bombardment, it was virtually impossible to prevent collateral damage. Several shells overshot their targets and exploded into the heart of the city. Rising smoke indicated that several fires had begun, but not all of the smoke was a result of Confederate shells. Fresh bursts of smoke and a sound like booming thunder showed that the Spanish were replying in kind with their own cannons. As Ramsey predicted most of the cannon balls slammed into the sea far short of the Confederate fleet. A few, however, landed dangerously close to the *Texas* and her sister ships.

So they do have some rifled guns, thought Ramsey. He and Brisk made their way up the stairwells on the sides of the ship's superstructure and to the bridge. Ramsey made his way over to the chart table and shouted orders over the roar of the main guns. "Engines ahead one third! Helmsman come right to course one-zero-one."

"One-zero-one, aye, sir." Even over the thunderous noise of the main guns, Ramsey could both hear and feel the power of *Texas'* steam engines as the ship headed south east towards the Cuban shoreline. As the battleship began to move, the turreted gun emplacements readjusted to compensate. The ship's rate of fire was barely effected. Ramsey nodded in approval.

"Where are we headed, Captain?" asked Brisk. Ramsey pointed to the chart.

"It would be suicide to make a run down the channel as long as the forts are in enemy hands. We can damage them, but we'll never knock out all the guns that they have trained on the channel." Ramsey pointed at the shoreline to the west. If we landed troops here the enemy would have the advantage of fighting from behind a sea wall. Even if the marines breeched it, they'd be forced to immediately fight in the city streets—a defender's dream. So, command has decided that the main landing will be made here on the shore to the east of the channel and of the primary fortifications. Our orders, are to get in close enough to the shore and knock out any defensive positions and artillery that the Spanish may have set up, before the Marines go in."

"If we get in that close than any guns they have on the shore will be able to open up on us."

"But we'll have the added firepower of the six inch guns. We've got to make sure to soften up the beach for the leathernecks. Once they're ashore they'll drive west and take the forts from behind."

"They'll still have to fight a tough battle to take those forts," said Brisk.

"I know, but if the forts fall, then Havana itself is as good as won. I don't envy them the task."

Not for the first time, Brisk was glad he was a naval officer and not a marine. The marines would pay a heavy price to take the Spanish forts. Ramsey continued relating the plan. Regular army troops will be landing right behind the Marines. They'll be pushing inland. If they can move fast enough they can swing around Havana and block the retreat of the Spanish Army."

"That means we might win the war right here," said Brisk.

"That's what command hopes, but I wouldn't count on it."

"What about the niggers? Are they going ashore too?"

Ramsey nodded. Brisk shook his head.

"Well I guess we're about to find out just what kind of fighters they make. You mark my words, they'll be cowardly. I just hope they don't get our boys killed."

"That's enough," said Ramsey. "Our only concern right now is to soften up the shore defenses..."

Shortly thereafter *Texas'* main guns fell silent as they moved out of range of the Spanish forts. It wasn't long, however, before the turrets swung around and the main guns began to fire on the eastern shore. Ramsey again raised his binoculars to his eyes. As he scanned the beach he spotted several fieldworks and gun emplacements that the Spanish had constructed. From that distance, the Spanish troops manning them looked like small sky blue ants. Shells from the *Texas'* twelve inch guns slammed into the beach throwing great plumes of smoke and sand into the air. As they drew even closer to the shore, the battleship's six inch guns added their own fire to the rain of death. None of the Spanish artillery returned fire.

They know they don't have the range so they aren't wasting ordinance. Ramsey admired their discipline. After the *Texas* had cruised down the entire target beach, she came about and started to head back along the same route only this time in a westerly direction. The main gun turrets swung back around and resumed the shore bombardment for the return trip.

"Make your course, three-eight-zero helm. I don't want us getting too close to those forts."

"Three-eight-zero, aye." The helmsman turned the ship's spoked wheel and adjusted the *Texas'* course. A minute later, several of the cannons on the La Cabana and Moro Castle opened fire. The cannon balls splashed into the sea not far away, but they were still just barely out of range. The Texas' own guns swung around and resumed the bombardment of the elevated fortifications. Suddenly the telephone that connected the bridge with the crow's nest rang. Ramsey picked up the ear piece himself and spoke into the wall mounted receiver.

"Bridge!"

"Captain, there's three Spanish warships coming out of the channel. Bearing two-seven-five."

"Understood." Ramsey replaced the earpiece and rounded on the bridge crew. "Look alive, Mr. Brisk." They again brought up their binoculars. It wasn't long before they spotted the warships—a battle ship and two armored cruisers—steaming out of Havana harbor with flags flying and guns blazing.

"Are they coming out to challenge the fleet?" asked Brisk. His tone said he thought they were insane.

"More likely their trying to break out," said Ramsey.

"From the amount of smoke coming out of their stacks they're at full steam," replied Brisk.

"Bring the forward guns to bear, I don't want them getting away from us!"

"I don't think that's going to be a problem Captain," said Brisk. "They just turned straight for us!"

Ramsey brought his binoculars back up. Sure enough, the Spanish warships had changed course and were trying to slip away from the Confederate fleet to their north by heading east along the shore.

But they have to deal with me first, thought Ramsey. "Fire at will, Mr. Brisk! They're not getting past us."

"It's three against one Captain. I don't like those odds."

"The odds are a little better than that." Ramsey pointed west. "Several of our other ships are closing in from the other side. If we hurry, we'll have them boxed in. They'll have nowhere to go!"

The *Texas* opened up with everything she had. Her shells slammed onto and around the oncoming Spanish warships. The Spanish warship returned fire. Most of their shells overshot the *Texas* and landed in the sea. One, however, struck against the forward gun turret and exploded violently. The whole ship shuddered with the impact.

"Damage report!"

Brisk stared out of the bridges forward viewport.

"The foredeck's a mess! Looks like the main forward turret took a hit but the armor held. A moment later the sound of the main gun returning fire let them know that though the gun had been hit, it wasn't out.

Suddenly, shells started screaming down all around the Spanish ships. The bulk of the Confederate fleet had diverted their fire from Havana's fortifications to the three Spanish ships trying to escape. The Confederate ships coming in from the other side had come close enough to also open up with their six inch guns. A few moments later the *Texas* opened up with her own auxiliary guns. The beleaguered Spanish ships were being pummeled by Confederate fire. The enemy vessels sent a few more haphazard shots towards the *Texas* but within a few minutes they had taken so many hits all three of them were crippled. Most of the smoke now coming from the Spanish ships was not coming from their guns but from fires that raged on deck and within the ships. A few moments later all three struck their colors.

"Cease fire!" ordered Ramsey. Through his binoculars he spotted several Spanish sailors busy battling fires with hoses. Others were leaping into the sea to escape the hellish flames. A few of those had been on fire themselves. "Signal the enemy vessels we're coming to their aid. All fire crews on deck. Get the pumps ready. I want those ships captured! Prepare to receive both wounded and prisoners!"

"Look, Captain!" Brisk was pointing out of the starboard viewport. To the south east the landings were about to begin. Marines and soldiers—both black and white were disembarking the troop ships and headed for the shore in long boats.

Suddenly an explosion sounded from the direction of the crippled Spanish ships. At first Ramsey thought they'd started firing again but he quickly realized one of the cruisers had exploded. Ramsey let out a long sigh.

This war is just getting started...

XXXI

Jeff Case's heart was pounding. From the deck of the *CSS Aurora* he had watched the bombardment of Havana by the Confederate fleet. As his troop ship had made its way towards the shore, he and his fellow marines had also been able to watch as three Spanish ships were practically ripped to shreds by enfilade fire from surrounding Confederate battleships. The sight of burning men leaping into the sea to escape the flames of their doomed vessels made Case sick to his stomach, even if the unfortunate men had been Spaniards. Now his own baptism by fire was approaching. He hoped that for him, it would not be as literal as it had been for the enemy sailors. Case took off his black broad brimmed hat, and ran his hand through the mop of red hair on his head. Instantly he felt the blazing heat of the sun on his pale skin. He quickly replaced the hat.

It seemed as if every battleship, cruiser, and destroyer in the Confederate navy was participating in the bombardment of the enemy coast, city, and fortifications. Over the thunderous noise of the fleet's guns, the Sergeants were shouting and swearing.

"Man the longboats! Move it! Time to whip the dagos, boys!"

Twenty gray-clad marines crammed into each of the boats. It was a tight fit. Each man carried a rifle and had a field pack on his back. Case took his place towards the front of the boat right behind the Sergeant.

Why'd I ever think getting promoted to Lance Corporal was a good thing? He was seated on the port side of the longboat. He placed his rifle to his right so he could use both arms on his oar. After the boat had been lowered into the water, they pushed away from the troopship and positioned themselves to head for the shore as soon as the command was given. The *Aurora* was far from the only Confederate troop ship disembarking marines. While they waited for the rest of the boats to get into position, Case scanned the shore.

Ahead he could clearly see the beach. Though he couldn't see them, he knew that men with cannons and rifles were waiting for him on the shore. Whether it was that knowledge, or the constant rocking of the boat by the waves, it brought his nausea to a critical level. He leaned over the edge of the boat and vomited in the sea. After what seemed an eternity, in which he heaved up all of his guts, he finally managed to sit himself back up. He expected the Sergeant would be angry at him. Instead, the grizzled veteran surprised him by smiling at him. Case reflected that it was the first time he had ever seen the man smile.

"Think nothing of it, boy." The Sergeant then swore loudly and profanely. "If you're not scared when you see the elephant then you're a fool." A few minutes later someone behind Case began reciting the Lord's prayer. Case and everyone else reverentially joined in—even the Sergeant. Never in his life had he uttered the words with such intense sincerity. But he meant them now—did he ever!

As they came to the end of the words, *Thine is the kingdom and the power and the glory forever, Amen,* there was a boom like thunder, then a sound of something shrieking through the air, and finally a large splash in sea several yards ahead of them.

"Just the dagos taking pot shots at us!" said the Sergeant. "We're out of range for now. Let them waste there ammo."

Out of range or not, the thought of a hundred pound iron ball, flying through the air at a hundred miles an hour was almost enough to send Case wrenching again.

At least it's not canister fire. Explosive shells would have detonated in the air and sent thousands of pieces of shrapnel flying through the air. That would have made things very unpleasant for the Confederate marines. Case suddenly realized that his hands were shaking. He closed his eyes and tried to think of Ellie and being with her. For that moment at least, all his doubts and worries about their relationship vanished. In light of what he was about to face, the fact that his beloved was a mulatto girl seemed miniscule and insignificant as did all thoughts of what his family back home would think. Just the thought of her in his arms, the warmth of her body, her lips pressed against his, was enough to give him a measure peace in the face of the closest thing on earth to hell itself. *I have to make it. For her, I have to make it.*

Finally, the entire line of longboats was ready to head for the shore. Off to his left, Case could see Captain Fordice in the adjoining boat. Behind him, a color bearer carried a Confederate Battle Flag that billowed in the breeze. Captain Fordice blew a whistle. The Sergeants responded by blowing their own whistles. The signal cascaded through the line of longboats and they all began to row forward with a fury.

Adrenaline rushed through Case as he worked his oar. He kept his eyes fixed on their target. The shore ahead was level with the sea. As he looked to the west, Case noticed that the land sloped upwards until it became a large hill on which sat massive Spanish fortresses. The cannons in the fort still seemed to be throwing their ordinance at the besieging Confederate fleet. The cannons on the beach, however, were more preoccupied with the approaching Confederate marines. Cannon balls crashed down into the sea all around them. The impacts sent sea spray up into the air. Off to the left, Jeff watched as a cannon ball crashed into one of the other longboats. The longboat and the twenty marines inside of it just seemed to explode. Shards of wood, and pieces of men seemed to go everywhere. After the impact the boat just seemed to break up—its survivors left thrashing in a bloody patch of sea. Over their screams and calls for help, Case could still hear the thunder of big guns. It came not only from the Spanish cannons on the shore, but also from the gun emplacements of offshore Confederate warships. The Confederate fleet was still trying to soften up the shore for the landing forces.

I just hope that they stop the bombardment before we get there! As far as Case was concerned, he hoped the naval bombardment sent every last Spaniard on Cuba straight to the infernal regions. But he also knew that Confederate shells were just as lethal, if not more so than their Spanish counterparts. They shrieked overhead and crashed down onto the beach. Case could make out the fire at the center of each explosion. As much as he hated having Spanish cannon balls rain down around him, he would have hated much more to be on the receiving end of what the Confederates were giving the Spaniards on shore. Nonetheless, the Spanish defenders on the beach continued to work their guns and fire at the oncoming wave of Confederate boats.

"Row harder, boys!" cried the Sergeant. "The sooner we get ashore the sooner we can start killing these dago bastards instead of being shot at like ducks in a pond!" Case agreed with the Sergeant. If he was going to be shot at, he at least wanted to be in position to shoot back. The marines now worked their oars with renewed determination. As they drew closer to the beach, they began to hear hissing noises in the air. The Spaniards on shore had begun to fire at them with rifles. The Spanish artillery may have been antiquated, but their infantrymen were armed with state of the art Mauser rifles that had been manufactured in Prussia.

Suddenly there was a sound like a wet slap. Case found himself absolutely covered in blood. He went into a momentary panic. His heart started pounding in his chest so hard he thought it would explode.

It doesn't hurt anywhere... Suddenly the Sergeant fell backwards into the boat and onto his men. He'd taken a bullet in the throat and it was still spraying blood. Case rounded on the other Marines in the boat.

"Put pressure on that wound!" he said to the man closest to the Sergeant's head. "If we don't stop the bleeding he's a dead man!" Case thought the Sergeant was a dead man anyway. He'd lost an enormous amount of blood. The front of the boat looked like a butcher shop and smelled the same. The metallic scent of blood filled Case's nostrils. He was completely drenched in the other man's blood. At first he wanted to heave up what was left of his guts but he felt a sudden burning in the pit of his stomach. His disgust was suddenly transformed into a violent and resolute rage. Case once again turned to face the hostile shore.

He pulled in his oar and then brought his own rifle to bear on the shore line. As a corporal he had been positioned in the front of the boat for this very reason. The senior corporal to his right did the same. They were entering the most dangerous part of the landing. Not only had the boats entered into the range of enemy small arms fire, but any Spanish artillery that had survived the shore bombardment would now have a much easier time shooting at them. As if to punctuate his thought, there was a sudden boom like thunder. A second later a cannon ball splashed into the sea less than ten feet away. The spray from the impact came down on Case's boat.

We've got to silence those guns! The more lead we put in the air the better! Case worked the lever on his Richmond rifle, chambered a round, and then started firing, trying his best to target the Spanish shore batteries. The corporal to his right did the same. After eight rounds he removed the magazine and replaced it with a fresh one from his haversack.

At first Case couldn't really make out anything or anyone on the shore, though puffs of smoke and flame let him know where the Spanish had working artillery emplacements. A short while later he was able to make out the men in sky blue uniforms who were sending bullets in his direction. Many of them had hastily dug shallow firing pits in the sandy beach while others had constructed makeshift fieldworks. Case leveled his rifle at a blue clad Spaniard that was trying to dart from one position to the next. Case squeezed the trigger, the rifle barked, and the enemy soldier fell face down in the sand. A second later a cannon boomed and Case felt a rush of air as the projectile shot over the Confederate landing boat, perilously close.

The waves started to white cap as the longboat approached the shore. It was time to get out of the boat and begin their bloody work. For a moment Case turned to look back at the Sergeant. The non-com was dead. To Case's right the senior corporal was silent. Now that the Sergeant was dead the Senior Corporal was in charge of the squad, but it was time to move and he wasn't issuing any orders. In a situation like that, time was blood. Case took the initiative.

"Move it!" yelled Case. "Everyone out! Watch your gear!" Case leapt out of the longboat holding his rifle high to insure it remained dry. The last thing he wanted was to be on a hostile beach with men trying to shoot him and not being able to shoot back. The other members of the squad (including the Senior Corporal) followed his lead. The seawater came up nearly to his torso. He splashed forward as quickly as he could. He could see muzzle flashes ahead and hear the sound of bullets whirring through the air. To his right, the Senior Corporal took a bullet in the leg and collapsed into the water. Case swore. He hung his rifle over his shoulder and across his chest and then rushed to where the Corporal had fallen. He grabbed his fallen comrade and started to pull him ashore. Bullets continued to whirr through the air and splash down around them. A moment later there was the boom of a cannon and a cannon ball spashed into the water, raining sea water and sand down on the entire squad. For the briefest moment, Case heard a man scream in pain.

Case dragged the wounded Corporal up the shore and through the wet sand until they reached the dry beach. He didn't want the man to drown while waiting on a medic. Case quickly pulled his knife, cut off the Corporal's pants leg and tied it tightly around the wounded leg so that (hopefully) he wouldn't bleed to death.

As he looked around, Case saw that the squad was in chaos. They were pinned down by enemy fire. It was also apparent that several more men had gone down. Suddenly a cannon ball crashed down only a few feet away from him, throwing up a large plume of sand.

If we stay here we're dead! About a hundred yards to his left, Case could make out the Confederate Battle Flag that marked the command squad. Captain Fordice and his men were pressing forward. Case looked at the fieldworks ahead. Case knew that if the Sergeant were alive, he'd be ordering them forward too. His heart was pounding. He took a deep breath. He couldn't just order a charge and expect the men to do it. He had to lead if they were to follow. He pulled his sword bayonet from its sheath and affixed it to the end of his rifle. "Fix bayonets!" He made sure to put a fresh magazine in his rifle and then gripped the weapon tightly. "Alright boys! We're taking this beach! Get up and move it!" He leapt to his feet and let out a screeching Rebel Yell. As he had hoped, the others joined him. They charged wildly at the Spaniards, howling like wolves and firing their rifles. Case made sure to shoot at the Spaniards manning the nearby cannon. He wasn't the only one. The Spanish artillerymen were mowed down by a hail of Confederate bullets.

The other Spanish defenders stood their ground for a few moments and three more marines from Case's squad were cut down by their rifle fire. However, Case's squad was hardly the only one on the beach. A small horde of gray clad marines and soldiers had come ashore. The bulk of the Confederate landing force was wheeling right and trying to sweep away the Spanish shore defenses in a flank attack. By all appearances it was working.

The Confederate marines charged straight into the Spanish defenders like wild dogs. Case leveled his rifle at one of the enemy soldiers and pulled the trigger. The bullet blew a large hole in the Spaniard's chest. Case rounded on another, leveled his rifle and pulled the trigger—it jammed. Case had no time to clear the cartridge. The Spaniard had raised his own rifle. Case dove for the ground just before the Mauser fired. The bullet passed over him. Case executed a roll, came up, lunged forward and thrust his sword bayonet straight into the stunned Spaniard's gut. The man's face contorted with a strange mixture of surprise and pain. His stunned eyes bulged and locked with those of his killer. Case wrenched his bayonet loose from the man and then kicked him to the ground.

Suddenly there was an enormous burst of rifle fire from the treeline just south of the beach. Case heard a bullet crack right past his head. A few dozen sky-blue clad Spanish infantry came charging out of the tree line and towards the Confederates. They let out a war cry that was the match of any Rebel Yell Case had ever heard. Case worked the lever on his rifle, brought it back up and fired. A few other survivors from Case's squad did likewise, but it looked as if they were about to be finished off by the charging Spaniards. Case fired his rifle until it was empty and then readied himself for a fight to the death.

Suddenly, another squad of Confederate troops came charging in from the right. To Case's utter shock they were a squad of negro troops. With a fluttering Confederate Battle Flag above them, the black Confederate soldiers pitched into the Spanish flank ferociously. Case ordered what was left of his squad forward and side by side with their negro comrades they met the Spanish counter attack head on. As quickly as it had a moment before the tide of battle turned again. The soldiers in sky blue had no desire to die where they stood. Some of them ran into the thick tropical forest just north of the beach, but most of them began to flee uphill and towards the relative safety of Morrow Castle and the La Cabana. The Spaniards had offered tough resistance, but, now that they had satisfied their pride by not yielding the beach without a fight, they were perfectly content to withdraw to the heavily fortified high ground and let the Confederates come to them.

The Confederates continued to fire at them as they fled up the hill. They managed to gun down a few more. Every so often one of the Spaniards would turn and fire back at them, but for the most part, they were content to merely run as fast as their legs could carry them.

"Where's Sergeant Anderson?"

Case turned to see Captain Fordice. He came to attention and brought his arm up in salute.

"He was killed in the landing, sir."

Fordice looked over what was left of Case's squad, and the position that they had helped take from the enemy. He then turned his gaze back to Case.

"You've done well, Corporal. I think you've earned yourself another stripe or two. But for now you've lost over half your squad. Fall in with Sergeant Gates' squad."

Suddenly a bullet hissed through the air. The shot had come from the tree line to the north. The Spanish were sniping them from the cover of the trees. Captain Fordice detailed off a squad to flush them out. Case was thankful he wasn't part of it. The idea of fighting in a thick tropical jungle had no appeal for him. Captain Fordice then started to issue orders to the rest of the squad commanders. "We've got the dagos on the run! But the job's not done until we take those forts. Move your men up the hill!"

Moments later the screeching sound of the Rebel Yell was sounding from the throats of thousands of men—both white and black as they charged up the hill towards Morro Castle and the La Cabana.

XXXII

Major Antonio Vega crouched behind the east facing stone ramparts of the La Cabana. Every minute, three to four Confederate shells came shrieking through the air and exploded into the fortress sending deadly shrapnel and bits of stony debris in all directions. Every so often (and not near often enough as far as Antonio was concerned) the massive cannons of the La Cabana would boom and throw cannon balls back at the Confederate ships besieging them. Unfortunately, the antiquated cannons lacked the range to seriously threaten their tormentors.

As bad as the bombardment was, Antonio knew that the poor souls manning Morro Castle were getting it even worse. He was thankful that he and his men had been reassigned to the La Cabana barely a day before the Confederate fleet had arrived off of Havana. The Confederate navy had all but smashed the sixteenth century fortress to rubble. Antonio shed a tear, not only for the destruction of the beautiful castle, but also at sad cruel irony. In the 1500s Spain had been strong, a mighty Empire that was the most powerful nation on earth. Now, just over three hundred years later they were a mere shell of their former glory, so weak that even a back woods, upstart nation like the CSA could attack them with impunity.

Another shell came screeching in. This one burst in the air. One of the soldiers huddled next to Antonio took a piece of hot shrapnel in the chest. The man's blood sprayed everywhere and he screamed like a damned soul, before falling lifeless on the stone floor of the rampart. Antonio loosened his iron grip on his rifle just long enough to reach into his sky blue tunic and pull out the silver crucifix that he wore around his neck. He kissed it reverently, muttered a Hail Mary, then gripped his rifle again as though holding on for dear life.

Dear God, please kill these Confederados for doing this to us! A moment later he added an amendment to his petition. *More than that, please keep me alive!* The bombardment seemed to go on forever. Suddenly, a call came from the look outs.

"The Confederados are on shore! The Confederados have landed!" Summoning his courage Antonio brought himself to his feet and peered over the edge of the stone rampart with his binoculars. He wasn't near as high as the lookouts, but he was high enough. The La Cabana (or what was left of it) sat on the top of a hill. Antonio was able to look over the tops of the thick palm trees that covered the upper slopes of the hill and at the beaches beyond. An army of gray clad invaders had come ashore by boat. It was hard to hear over the sound of the bombardment, but he could just make out the sound of rifle and cannon fire on the beaches to the east. The small line of defenders clad in sky blue were doing all that they could to hold off the invading Confederates.

Suddenly, Antonio dropped back behind the rampart at the screeching sound of another incoming shell. Another nearby soldier wasn't as prudent. The shell burst and a piece of shrapnel ripped into the man's back. He fell forward, off of the rampart to the green ground below the fort. Antonio looked frantically over the edge to see if by some miracle the man might be alive. Mercifully, he was not. Antonio crossed himself, then rose back up to gaze at the battle on the beaches. It didn't take much time for the Confederates to sweep away the defenders and seize the beaches and it wasn't long after that the tattered remnants of the shore defense forces started coming out of the tree line and shouting at the base of the fort to be helped up. Antonio ordered the soldiers manning the ramparts to throw over a couple of rope ladders so that their comrades could climb up.

"Vega! You idiota!" came the cry of Major Ortega. Antonio turned to see the fat man's sweaty face nose to nose with his own. "The Confederados could be here any minute and you've thrown down a ladder for them!" Ortega's breath smelled as foul as his mood.

"That's enough, Ortega!" came the voice of Colonel Gonzales. Both Antonio and Ortega came to rigid attention. "What would you have him do, leave the men down there to die? We can cut the ladders if the enemy breaks through the trees unexpectedly, but as I see it they've not yet reached the base of the hill."

Ortega scowled hatefully at Antonio, but he didn't dare say anything further. A moment later half a dozen Spanish troops ascended the rope ladders and took positions on the ramparts alongside their comrades. Colonel Gonzales craned his neck and listened intently.

"It sounds like the bombardment is letting up."

"They could be low on ammunition," said Ortega. Gonzales shook his head.

"More than likely, they have stopped firing because their troops are about to try and storm us." The Spanish commander rounded on Antonio. "Lieutenant Vega, are the men all up?"

Antonio glanced once more over the edge and then turned back to the Colonel.

"Si, senor. But there could be more behind them."

The Colonel brought up his binoculars and stared eastward.

"The Confederados have reached the hill and begun to ascend into the tree line. We can't afford to wait on a handful of men. There are hundreds of enemy soldiers right being them. We have to make the most of the time we have to kill as much of the enemy force as we can before it reaches the fort. Major Ortega! Have the cannons open fire!" Ortega grinned savagely, and made sure to take a second to direct his smirk directly at Antonio.

Gilipollas! thought Antonio. Gonzales was only doing what was militarily necessary. He took no pleasure giving an order that might result in the death of some of their fellow Spaniards. The fact that Ortega could take spiteful pleasure in such a thing, made Antonio loath him all the more.

A few moments later, and the cannons up and down the ramparts began to rain steel down the wooded slopes of the hill. Unfortunately, because of the thickness of the trees, it was impossible to see how much affect they were having.

Not much in any event, thought Antonio. Most of the Spanish artillery pieces were antiquated smoothbores. Most of their ammunition consisted only of solid shot. They had precious few explosive shells. Nonetheless, Ortega had them keep up a steady barrage of fire. The Confederates advancing up the hill and through the trees would not do so unopposed.

Suddenly, there was a shrieking sound in the air. It was not as loud as earlier incoming shells but had a much higher pitch. Suddenly, a shell exploded almost directly on one of the Spanish gun emplacements. The cannon was wrecked by the impact and the gun crew was killed. Colonel Gonzales swore loudly and profanely as he brought his binoculars back up to his eyes.

"The gilipollas have deployed Whitworth cannons!"
The Colonel made the word Whitworth into a swear word. The
British designed Confederate cannons were breach loaded,
rifled guns, which were accurate to within a few inches and had
a range of one thousand-six hundred yards. They were, in
effect, sharpshooter artillery. They were not very effective
against infantry, but they were deadly when used for counter-
battery fire. Gonzales started shouting angrily.

"Ortega! Take out those Whitworths!" The Spanish
artillerymen all trained their guns on the advanced Confederate
artillery just beyond the base of the hill and started to open fire.
Antonio's heart sank in his chest when he saw all of their
rounds fall far short of their targets. As if to mock the Spanish,
the Whitworths fired again and eliminated two more artillery
emplacements on the east facing ramparts of the La Cabana.
Colonel Gonzales swore even more vehemently. All the
fortresses larger cannons (those that hadn't been wrecked by
the Confederate naval bombardment) were in fixed positions
facing the sea. The Colonel rounded on Antonio.

"You and your men be ready, Vega! The Confederados
will be coming out of the trees at any minute.

Antonio prepared to repel the enemy infantry that
would soon be upon them. Once again he gripped his rifle so
tightly that his knuckles turned white. The Spanish cannons
may have been obsolete, but his Prussian made Mauser rifle
was state of the art.

"Fix bayonets!" he cried. If the Confederates tried to
storm the ramparts he wanted to give them a taste of cold
Spanish steel. He drew his own bayonet and affixed it to the
end of his rifle. Suddenly, bullets started to slam into the stone
ramparts and one of them zipped over his head. That was the
cue. "Fire at will!"

Antonio and the rest of the Spanish infantry positioned
on the ramparts rose up and began to blaze away at the tree line
with their rifles. Here and there he could see muzzle flashes up
and down the tree line. Antonio tried to target them. A couple
of times bullets cracked past his head, perilously close. With

every fiber of his being, Antonio wanted to duck completely behind the stone rampart and stay there. But Spain needed heroes, not cowards and he had to set the example for his men. He just hoped he didn't get his head blown off in the process.

Several squads of Confederates emerged from the tree line almost simultaneously. They carried large ladders. Antonio fired his Mauser until the clip was empty, taking extra care to target the men carrying the ladders. He ducked back down behind the stone rampart before ejecting the clip and slapped in a fresh replacement.

Bravery is good. But there is no sense staying in the line of enemy fire if there is no need. After loading the fresh magazine he worked the bolt, rose back up and resumed firing. The Confederates in the tree line were sending a hail of lead at the ramparts, trying their best to give cover to the storm squads carrying the ladders. Several of the Spanish defenders went down clutching bloody wounds. The only thing that could be heard through the bark of rifle fire and the boom of the cannons were the torturous screams of the wounded. Down below, the ground at the base of the fort had become littered with bloody gray clad bodies. Colonel Gonzales once again yelled at Ortega.

"Forget the Whitworths! Train your remaining guns on the tree line!"

"Si, Colonel!" cried Ortega. "Elevation down 8 degrees!"

Antonio wished they had never wasted the time and ordinance in the hopeless endeavor of silencing the Confederate Whitworths. He wished even more that the remaining Spanish cannons could be brought to bear on the Confederate storm squads that were almost at the very base of the fort. Unfortunately the Spanish cannons were unable to achieve that level of declension. As the Spanish artillerymen worked feverishly to bring the muzzles of their cannons to bear on the Confederates in the treeline, the CS Whitworth artillery continued their own barrage of the La Cabana. Several more shells came screaming in and exploded into the Spanish batteries. Three more cannons, including the one at the southern end of the ramparts were wrecked by the precision Confederate explosive shells.

A few seconds later, there was an enormous explosion at the southern end of the ramparts. The sound of it was absolutely deafening. The fortress shook as though it were being rattled by an earthquake. The shockwave knocked Antonio from his feet, and he bashed his head against the stone rampart. Dozens of men perished in the explosion. Many were thrown from the ramparts and fell to their deaths. The detonation sent fiery debris up into the air that rained down on and around the La Cabana. It also engulfed the entire upper ramparts in a thick choking cloud of smoke and sent a plume of smoke high into the sky.

Antonio forced himself to his feet and wiped blood from his injured brow. He coughed and tried to access the situation through the smokey haze, wondering what could have caused such a massive explosion.

One of the gunpowder case offs must have taken a direct hit! There was an almost incoherent babble of panicked Spanish coming from the surviving defenders. No voice of authority cut through it to try and restore order. Antonio looked around desperately for Colonel Gonzales but the smoke had not yet cleared enough for him to see if his commander were alive or dead. He spared only a fraction of a second to think of Ortega. He hoped the artillery commander were alive for Spain's sake, but would not shed a tear if he were to discover that the cruel man had gone down to the flames of perdition where he belonged.

Suddenly, Antonio had more pressing concerns than the destiny of Ortega's soul. The tops of several ladders slammed against the tattered stone rampart. Almost simultaneously, several grappling hooks landed on the ramparts and caught firm on the stone edge.

"Stand by to repel attackers!" he cried. Antonio began to shout orders frantically. "Push those ladders over! Someone cut the ropes on those grappling hooks!" There was still chaos on the ramparts, but a few of the soldiers heeded his orders and rushed to his aid. Together they tried to push over the massive ladders. Antonio and a young private took hold of one and tried to shove it backwards. It was extremely heavy because so many Confederate soldiers had already begun to climb it. The ladders were wide enough for two rows of men to climb at once. Unable to shove the ladder backwards, Antonio and his comrade tried to slide it to the right.

If we can push it over it will crash into another of the Confederados' ladders which will then crash into another...a domino effect! At first the ladder lurched to the right but suddenly it came to a halt. Every few feet the underside of the ladder had been fitted with small iron spikes designed to catch onto whatever ledge the ladder was placed against. Antonio swore loudly and profanely. Suddenly the young private next to him took a bullet in the head. The boy's skull exploded throwing blood and gray brain matter all over Antonio. Antonio fell backwards, just barely avoiding the storm of Confederate bullets. He rebounded and put himself in a crouched position just behind the rampart. He gripped his rifle tightly and waited like a coiled spring. When the first Confederate came over the ledge, Antonio fired his rifle at close to point blank range. The bullet exploded into the Confederate's chest, and the gray clad soldier fell backwards off the rampart. A second Confederate came over only a fraction of a second later. Antonio shot him too.

Suddenly to his right, another Confederate popped his head over the rampart. This one had ascended one of the rope ladders affixed to a grappling hook. Antonio sent a bullet through the man's ear and his head exploded like a Casaba melon. He then turned back to the ladder to see two Confederates come bounding over the edge and down towards him. The Confederates fired their rifles. One of the bullets cracked past Antonio's head. The other one grazed his arm. Antonio shot the Confederate on the right. The wounded enemy soldier then lunged vengefully at him with his bayoneted rifle. Antonio parried with his own rifle then spun around and brought up the butt of his rifle into his enemies face. He then struck him in the face again. The Confederate fell backwards and landed on his back. Finally, Antonio brought his own bayonet down into the man's chest. Antonio had no time to savor his small victory. All down the rampart line, the Confederates were coming over the edge. Another two Confederates had already come over the top of the ladder in front of Antonio. To his right, more were on their way up the rope ladder.

"Fall back!" he cried. Antonio began a fighting retreat away from the Confederates, but he never once showed them his back. He walked backwards along the rampart, continuously firing his rifle at the enemy. Only when he reached the place where the rampart turned west and he was hid from Confederate view did he turn and run west along the northern ramparts. It also allowed him the first opportunity to actually worry about his wounded arm. His right sleeve was stained with blood. Antonio shouldered his rifle and clasped his left hand over his wounded right arm to try and stop the bleeding.

I must rally more men or the La Cabana is lost! In his heart he knew that it's fall was now all but inevitable. Most of the fort's infantry garrison had been stationed on the eastern ramparts. The northern ramparts were deserted. Off to his right Antonio could see Morrow Castle or rather what was left of it. It too was under attack by Confederate troops, though they looked to be having a harder time than those attacking the La Cabana. The Confederates may have blasted the old castle to rubble, but the remnants of the Spanish garrison were fighting tenaciously from the ruins. Antonio rounded the next corner and turned onto the western ramparts just as the first Confederates started firing bullets down the length of the northern ramparts. At last he ran into a group of soldiers. They were jumping off of the west facing edge of the fort trying to land in the Havana channel below. They were risking death by doing so. The water below was dotted with rocks and boulders. At least one fleeing Spaniard had missed the water and landed on a rock. His broken and bloody body lay sprawled atop a boulder. The gruesome sight didn't deter others from trying. Several had managed to land in the water and were swimming west across the channel towards old Havana. Beyond the channel the city of Havana itself seemed to be in chaos. Parts of it were on fire. Antonio wondered if it was because of the Confederate bombardment or because his own forces had set fire to the city arsenals and other facilities to deny them to the enemy.

"Stop you men!" cried Antonio. The panic stricken soldiers stopped in their tracks and turned to look at him.

"We must not abandon the la…"

Suddenly the high pitch yell of the Confederate battle cry came resounding from both the south and north.

The blasted Confederados have flanked both sides of the fort! The wolf like howls of the approaching CS troops were enough to send the few remaining Spanish troops over the edge of the ramparts. Some landed on the rocks and some in the water. For his own part, Antonio had to make up his own mind about what to do. His first instinct was to bring his rifle to the ready and shoot the Confederates as soon as they came around the corner.

Going out in a blaze of glory is not what I had in mind. There was a corridor to his left that led down into the bowels of the fort. *I'd be trapped inside. I would either be killed or taken prisoner.* His only other options were to surrender or to follow the others over the edge. When the Confederates rounded the corner and the first bullets flew past him he made up his mind. He ran and leapt over the edge of the rampart.

The fall seemed to last an eternity in which he thought his heart would explode. He hit the water hard. The impact nearly knocked the wind out of him. If it had, he would have drowned. Letting go of his rifle, Antonio kicked and clawed with all of his might towards the surface. The pain in his wounded arm was tremendous but sheer adrenalin and the will to live overrode his agony. He erupted onto the surface and filled his burning lungs with fresh oxygen. He then made for the western bank of the channel.

The swim seemed to take forever. All around him he could hear the sound of explosions and of artillery and rifle fire. The air smelled heavily of smoke. When at last he splashed ashore the western bank of the channel, he finally collapsed from exhaustion. He lay there breathing heavily for several minutes before finally forcing himself to sit up. When he did, he sat gazing back at the La Cabana. Much of the once proud fortress had been broken and smashed by the enemy bombardment. Several areas were on fire and most of it was engulfed in smoke. Through the smoke he caught sight of the la Rojigualda. The red and gold banner was smothered within a veil of choking smoke. Suddenly it was lowered and in its place rose a Confederate Battle Flag. A tear made its way out of the corner of Antonio's eye and streamed down his face.

A few moments later another Spaniard came splashing ashore. It took a moment for Antonio to recognize him. When he did, he did Antonio yelled at him mockingly, "Ortega, you owe me a bottle of Rioja!" The artilleryman fixed him with a murderous glare.

Suddenly, a shell exploded into the shore throwing lethal shrapnel in all directions as well as sending up a plume of sand and rocks into the air which then came raining back down. Antonio leapt to his feet. Two Confederate armored gunboats were making their way down the channel and had begun to bombard the shore. He looked around for Ortega. The artilleryman had taken hot shrapnel in his face, throat, chest, gut and groin. Incredibly he was still alive and conscious. A gurgling sound came from Ortega's throat and blood bubbled up out of his mouth. Antonio couldn't tell whether he was trying to scream in anguish or beg for the mercy of death.

Antonio crossed himself, muttered a prayer for the man and then ran west towards old Havana as fast as his legs could carry him. He wasn't alone. Several other soldiers who had escaped the La Cabana were running with him.

"You men, halt!" came a commanding voice.

Instantly, discipline returned to Antonio. He stopped running and turned to face a Spanish Lieutenant Colonel on horseback. The officer was leading a small line of men from the ruins of the small fortress that had once guarded the west side of the channel entrance. Antonio came swiftly to attention and brought his arm up in salute.

"The Confederados have taken the La Cabana," said Antonio in a voice like ashes. The Colonel nodded.

"A large enemy force is also moving around the city in an attempt to cut off our avenue of escape and trap us in Havana. We must act quickly. Our orders are to withdraw and regroup. Organize as many of the stragglers as you can and then head south-west for Artemisa. The battle for Havana is over. The battle for Cuba has only begun!"

EPILOGUE

Ebenezer awoke to the sound of roosters crowing. The first golden rays of sunlight were already creeping their way through the holes and cracks of the rickety cabin in which he lived. He got up off of the floor and stretched.

"Cap! Time to git up. You helpin me today. Massa Dumas, he want dat' fence whitewashed by noon." Not a sound came from Cap's side of the room. "Cap! You dere?" Ebenezer suddenly realized that he was alone in the cabin. He looked around in confusion. Cap was not an early riser. *Heaven hep me! He done run away!* Ebenezer opened the door of the cabin and hollered loudly. "Cap! You out dere!" A couple of other slaves gave him brief looks as they trotted off towards the fields shouldering their hoes and other farming implements.

I gots to stay calm! Dere's still a few places he could be! Ebenezer went to check the outhouses. When he didn't find him there he went to check the creek. Then just to be sure, he ran down to the fields to see if by some miracle Cap had woken early and forgotten it was his day to help Ebenezer instead of working with the other field hands. There was no sign of him at the fields.

Lord, I don't need dis right now! Ebenezer was still a nervous wreck from his meeting with Caesar a little over a week earlier. He hadn't seen the old renegade negro since, but his revelation that there was a slave revolt in the works in that part of the country, had him on edge as never before. One day soon he was going to have to make a dreadful choice. He hated being a slave. But he hated the idea of dying more so. *We's all gone get killed.* A moment later he thought, *Cap is for sure gone get his crazy nigger self-killed!*

Ebenezer cursed allowed. Cap had put him in a difficult spot. He had intentionally run away on a day when the overseers would not be looking for him in the morning count at the fields. *He's hoping I don'ts run and tell da Massa right away...* Ebenezer swore again, this time more loudly and profanely. Cap had put him in a terrible spot. If he went and told Dumas right away he'd feel as though he were betraying his friend. If he didn't tell Dumas, then the Plantation owner would very likely accuse him of aiding and abetting Cap's escape. *Dat git me punished too.* Ebenezer's mind was suddenly overcome by the scorching and painful memories of the many floggings he had received back at Sharpstone at the hands of Fitch Haley and his overseers. His back, which was a labyrinth of scar tissue, bore witness to the many whippings he had received in the past. Since coming to Twin Harbours, he'd not so much as seen or heard a whip crack. The overseers had whips, but they didn't use them. Back at Sharpstone, when a slave ran away that slave was stripped naked, whipped with seventy lashes from the base of his neck all the way down to his ankles and then branded. As if that wasn't bad enough, Haley would have the overseers give every other slave: man, woman and child five lashes as punishment for the runaway's offense. Ebenezer didn't think that Mansel Dumas would go that far—he hoped he wouldn't—but he was reasonably certain that his white master would be furious. He waited another twenty minutes before making the walk up to the mansion. His footsteps were heavy as though his feet were made of lead. As he reached the mansion he caught sight of young Mitchell Dumas riding his horse. The planter's teenage son was dressed in a brand new gray uniform with gold buttons and a golden sash. He wore a large, gray, broad brimmed hat and shiny black boots. A sword hung at his side.

"Mornin Ebenezer!" he said with a smile on his face.

"Mo'nin Massa Mitch. Yo daddy about?"

"I'm right here, Ebenezer," came the voice of Mansel Dumas. He had come out of the front door of the mansion and was making his way down the front steps. "Why aren't you on the east grounds whitewashing that fence yet?"

"I is very sorry, Massa but der is a problem. I cain't find Cap. I done look all over da place, suh. Der ain't no sign of him."

Dumas swore and blasphemed loudly.

"Are you telling me that boy's done run off!"

"Yes suh, I thinks so suh."

Dumas pointed an angry finger at Ebenezer.

"Ebenezer, you were supposed to keep an eye on him."

"I tried Massa. I swear! He must'a snuck out in da middle of the night. He didn't tell me nothin! I swears!"

"He won't get far," said Dumas. "I know where he's going. When I catch him he'll wish he'd never been born. The planter rounded on his son. "Get down to the fields and get Melt, Greg and Philip. Tell them to get their horses and their guns. Then ride over to Matt's and tell him we're going to need the dogs. We're going to run that nigger to earth."

"You're not gonna hurt him are ya, Daddy?"

"Don't question me, boy. You do as I say!"

Young Mitchell spurred his horse, and then galloped off towards the fields.

"Please be merciful, Massa. He really is a good nigger. If it wasn't fo' his woman and youngin I swear he wouldn't have done this."

"I don't want to hear it, Ebenezer. You get your black hide back to the east grounds. I want that fence whitewashed by the time I get back, or I'll have your hide along with his."

"Yes, Massa. I sees to it." With that, Ebenezer scampered away.

Mansel charged back into the house. His wife was in the process of ordering the little girls, Nancy and Connie up stairs. When they had gone, she rounded on her husband. She pointed at him with her one good arm.

"Mansel, I could hear you cursing and swearing all the way in here. Whatever is the matter that you would use such foul language where our little girls can hear."

"One of the niggers has done run off."

"But we haven't had a runaway in years. It's Cap isn't it? Oh dear, if only we'd been able to buy his family none of this would have happened."

"It's no excuse, Flossy," said Mansel as he removed his hunting rifle from the wall. "You sound just like Ebenezer."

"You weren't harsh on that poor boy were you? He works so hard and this isn't his fault."

Mansel started loading cartridges into his rifle. Afterwards he let out a loud sigh, then turned to face his wife.

"I consider myself a fair man. I treat my people well, and all I ask in return is hard work and loyalty to this family and this plantation. Cap has violated our trust, and he will have to be punished to set an example to the others."

"We haven't had to whip any slaves in years either" said Flossy sternly. Mansel took a deep breath. His face then softened slightly and he looked his wife in the face.

"It will be alright, my dear. I'm not gonna kill him if I can help it. But when I get done with him, I promise he will never run away from this plantation again! But if I don't catch him before he gets to Sharpstone, Fitch Haley is likely to shoot him on sight."

Ten minutes later Mansel Dumas rode out of Twin Harbours plantation on horseback at the head of a large band of armed men. A small pack of ferocious hound dogs ran ahead of them. It wasn't long before one of them let out a vicious howl.

Ebenezer hauled several buckets of white paint over to the eastern grounds, all by himself. He then set to work whitewashing the fence. His mind was afire with several overwhelming emotions. Fear, guilt, shame, anger… He felt dirty and rotten that he had betrayed his friend's absence so quickly.

"It not fair!" he said aloud, though there was no one there to hear it. Then he literally broke into tears. *Cap, all you done is make things worse fo yo self.* Ebenezer supposed that he should count himself lucky that he wasn't clasped in irons awaiting a beating that would bring him within an inch of his life. He could only hope that Mansel Dumas would show mercy. The hours slowly creeped by. As much as he wanted to push it from his mind, Ebenezer's thoughts inevitably returned to Caesar. He tried to imagine himself, with a rifle in his hand. He tried to imagine himself shooting white folks. He tried once again to shove away the thought but found that he could not. He also found that his heart was racing. Not with, fear, but with excitement.

Maybe dat's what I'm really scared of. That I would enjoy it. But theys deserves it! He lifted his tear filled eyes to the heavens, *they deserves it!*

Somehow, Ebenezer finished the paint job by noon. His black hands were covered in white paint. He put the brushes in the buckets and then carried them towards the creek to wash them out. His route to the creek took him past the front of the mansion.

Just after he had passed the big house, Mansel Dumas and his armed party came riding in through the plantation's main gate. They had Cap in tow. They had bound his hands with rope and then made him run behind one of the horses. Cap wasn't sure how long and far they had made him run, but when they finally reined in, Cap collapsed to the ground in exhaustion. His breathing was loud and labored. Dumas leapt from his horse.

"Greg, take Cap down to the slave quarters and tie him to the post. Melt, call all the niggers in from the fields and from their work, then go get your whip."

"Daddy, please don't do this!" said Mitch. "He's sorry! He's real sorry! He won't do it again will you Cap?" Cap looked briefly at Dumas but said nothing. Greg then led him away towards the slave quarters and a whipping post that hadn't been used in over a decade.

"Daddy, please!"

"I'm sorry, son. But this has to be done. You'll understand one day."

"No, sir, I won't. Why does this have to be done?"

"Don't you take that tone of voice with me, young man," said Dumas. "The negroes must be kept in line. There are times when a Master must be harsh in order to maintain order and discipline. We cannot afford to show weakness. Now the matter is closed for discussion. I don't want to hear another word."

"Mitchell," came the voice of Florence Dumas from the front porch of the mansion. "Come up here with me, dear."

"No," said Dumas. "It's time for him to become a man. He needs to toughen up and learn how to be hard when necessary. Weakness is something he cannot afford, especially, if he's going to wear that uniform."

A few minutes later Cap was stripped naked and chained to the whipping post. Like Ebenezer, his entire back was a mass of scar tissue from dozens and dozens of previous whippings. At the sight of it gasps and cries of fear erupted from many of the assembled slaves. Even Mansel recoiled. A look of genuine sorrow and regret appeared on his face, and for a moment, he wanted to end the whole thing. But suddenly his face became hard and resolute.

"I do not want to do this," said Mansel Dumas loudly. "But Cap has given me no choice. Everyone knows that I treat my people well. I feed you, house you, and care for you, and I expect hard work and loyalty in return. What Cap has done is wrong and cannot be tolerated. It hurts me to have to do this, but this lesson must be taught, for Cap's sake—and for yours. Dumas nodded at the overseer with the whip.

Crack! went the whip. Cap let out a pain filled yelp at the first lash then clenched his jaw tightly. *Crack! Crack! Crack!* There were shrieks of fear and terror from the assembled negroes. Tears forced their way out of Cap's closed eyes. *Crack! Crack! Crack!* With each crack of the whip, Ebenezer jerked uncontrollably. Tears poured down his face as he watched the suffering of his friend. A pain filled cry erupted from Cap's throat. *Crack! Crack! Crack! Crack!*

The overseer stopped. He was huffing and puffing and covered with sweat. Cap's legs had given out from under him and he was hanging by chains from the post. Twenty bloody lashes and whelps striped his back, his buttocks, and the back of his legs. He let out a long loud anguished cry, filled with sorrow and despair.

Mansel Dumas stared at him with just barely concealed regret and shame. "Cut him down," said Dumas. The overseers undid the chains and Cap collapsed completely to the ground. At Dumas command, several negroes dashed forward to help Cap. Ever so carefully they took him by his arms and lifted him to his feet.

"Take care of him," said Dumas. He then turned and walked slowly back towards his mansion.

The negroes carried Cap away to a cabin where several negresses would take turns tending to him throughout the day and night.

The rest of the day went by in a blur for Ebenezer. Despite a whole days work, he didn't feel like eating at supper time. He went to the cabin where they were keeping Cap. He lay naked on his stomach. Two negresses were at his bed side. One lightly dabbed his wounds with a cool wet cloth while the other fanned him with a small hand fan. Ebenezer started to speak but one of the women shook her head and brought her finger up to his mouth. Ebenezer nodded. If they had managed to get him to sleep, he didn't want to wake him.

Ten lashes. That was nothing compared to what Fitch Haley used to give out, yet for some reason that didn't make Ebenezer feel any better. *It's not right. It's just not right...*

As Ebenezer approached his cabin, he noticed a small amount of light coming from the inside. Somehow, he knew exactly who was in his cabin. He slowly opened the door and stepped inside, and sure enough, Caesar was sitting inside with a small kerosene lamp in one hand and a rifle in the other.

"It almost time, Ebenezer. We got a hundred of dese' hidden by the river and dat's just here. In a couple days, we is ready to rise up and claim our freedom! We's gone purge dis' land with blood and fire! I jes' needs to know are you wit us or not?"

The day before Ebenezer probably would have said no. After what had happened that day...

Ebenezer reached forward and took the Enfield from Caesar. He then held the weapon in his hands feeling its smooth wood, its cold steel and most of all the sense of power that it filled him with. He gripped it tightly and looked Caesar in the eye.

"I am with you."

**The Saga of the Spanish Confederate War will be continued in:
"Reaping the Whirlwind"**

**Billy Bennett hopes to have Reaping the Whirlwind released by November 2014
Read on for a word from the author and special previews of two other upcoming books from Billy Bennett.**

Barbarossa: An epic alternate history novel about a World War 2 where an isolationist USA refuses to get involved in the conflict.

Starstorm: An epic Space Opera where a group of international fighter pilots must defend humanity against

**an alien armada bent on the conquest and enslavement of
mankind.**

A Word From the Author

It has been an exciting adventure writing Rebel Empire and continuing the alternate timeline begun in By Force of Arms. I wanted to take this opportunity to explain a couple of developments that were revealed in Rebel Empire and that will be much further explored in future books.

Astute students of history will notice that in Rebel Empire, which takes place in the year 1895, that there is no united Germany, and that the French Second Empire under "Napoleon IV" is one of the Confederate States primary allies, and one of the major powers of Europe. I would like to explain my reasoning behind this.

This is a perfect example of what is known in alternate history as the "butterfly effect." In the real timeline, at the height of the American Civil War, Emperor Napoleon III tried to install an Austrian prince named Maximillian (the brother of Austro-Hungarian Emperor Franz Joseph I) as Emperor of Mexico. Upon the Confederacy's defeat in 1865 the United States began supporting the Mexican Revolutionaries of Benito Juarez against Maximillian. Napoleon III subsequently withdrew his support of Maximillian in 1866, and the Mexican Emperor was defeated and killed in 1867.

Now those who have read By Force of Arms know that in my timeline Maximillian was not defeated in 1867 nor did the French withdraw their forces. The victorious Confederacy was able to join France in support of Maximillian during the late 1860s which eventually lead to the War of 1869 where the CSA and France dealt the United States a devastating defeat that, among other things, insured the survival of Maximillian's Regime. Now, let's look at the consequences. These events logically tied the CSA, Imperial France, and Maximillian's Mexico into a strong alliance. This alliance would also plausibly be joined by the Austro-Hungarian Empire which was ruled by Maximillian's brother.

Now at this point some are asking the question "what about the events of the Franco-Prussian War?" In my timeline the Franco-Prussian War did not happen the same way that it did in the real timeline and here is why.

In the real timeline the Franco-Prussian War was begun in 1870 when a Prussian prince named Leopold was offered the throne of Spain. Napoleon III, not wanting a Prussian led Spain on his southern border, had his ambassador in Prussia protest in very strong terms. The Prussian Chancellor Bismarck intentionally greatly exaggerated the affair in the press and made it seem as though the French ambassador had threatened certain war if Leopold took the Spanish throne and that the Prussian King Wilhelm had basically responded with "bring it on!" (if I may be allowed to paraphrase). Now why did Bismarck intentionally do this when he knew it would more than likely goad France into declaring war on Prussia? The answer is that Bismarck's ultimate goal was a united Germany. He viewed the best way to achieve that was to have a "defensive war" against a hostile France. In our timeline it worked perfectly, but would such a thing happen the timeline that I set in motion with By Force of Arms?

Several things mitigate against it. In the first place, in my timeline Napoleon III was fresh of a major military victory against the United States in 1869 and his armed forces would have had much more experience because of the ongoing war in Mexico. Both of these factors would mitigate against Bismarck intentionally provoking France into war. But even assuming that he still tried to do so, in my timeline Napoleon III was still so heavily involved militarily in Mexico in 1870 that it is unlikely he would have allowed himself to be so easily provoked into war. Finally, in my timeline it must also be remembered that in 1870 Napoleon III's France had been heavily involved in Mexico for seven years, fighting for the throne and crown of the brother of the Emperor of Austria. This would have meant a much stronger bond between France and the Austro-Hungarian Empire in 1870 than what existed in the real timeline. So in my timeline, for Bismarck to goad France into War, would also have been to invite war with the Austro-Hungarian Empire at the same time. I therefore view it as highly unlikely that events in Europe would have turned out more or less the same as they did in the real timeline, in the circumstances that I have envisioned.

I do recognize that a conflict between Prussia and Imperial France was almost inevitable. In my timeline, circumstances delayed it until the late 1870s giving "Napoleon IV" time to ascend the French throne and perform much better against the Prussians than his father Napoleon III did in the real timeline.

Since in the real timeline the son of Napoleon III was killed at the young age of 23 (under circumstances that would not be relevant in my timeline) "Napoleon IV" is in many ways a blank slate for me, the novelist to work with. I freely admit that I have taken a novelists creative liberty and prerogative in making Napoleon IV a capable and daring military leader more on par with his famous uncle Napoleon I, as opposed to his militarily very incapable father Napoleon III.

It is my goal first and foremost to tell entertaining and thought provoking stories. It is my hope that you enjoy them as much as I enjoy writing them. Thanks to all the fans who have given such tremendous support and encouragement. I do maintain a blog at www.billybennettbooks.wordpress.com and would welcome correspondence and feedback.

Sincerely, Billy Bennett

A special preview of "Barbarossa"
The start of a new Epic Alternate History saga by Billy Bennett.

Prologue
February 15, 1933

The sun was setting in Miami Florida as Giuseppe Zangara made his way down Biscayne Boulevard towards Bayfront Park. The short Italian man drew looks from several passersby. He was short and disheveled. Like a lot of men in the United States he was unemployed. At thirty-three years old he was a young man, but he nonetheless walked slowly and deliberately with his hand on his abdomen. He'd had an appendectomy a few years before and had never been the same since. There was a constant throbbing pain in his gut that never seemed to go away. Work was hard enough to come by in a country and a world that had been rocked to the core by the greatest economic depression in history. For an uneducated bricklayer like Zangara, it was virtually impossible to find employment. He'd spent the entire day looking for work. No luck.

A few years earlier he'd immigrated to America from Italy, hoping to find a new and better life. He now lived in near poverty off of his ever dwindling savings. The occasional odd job he was able to land, barely slowed the outflow of his funds. Soon he would be in abject and total poverty and he wanted the world to feel his pain.

Not just my pain, he thought. *But the pain of all poor people everywhere!* All day long, he'd heard people talking about the event that was going on in Bayfront Park that very evening.

Now is my chance to strike a blow for the poor and the oppressed against the greedy capitalists.

As he neared Bayfront Park it began to get very crowded. Just as everyone had said, the new President Elect was in Miami. Franklin D. Roosevelt had been elected the previous November. In less than three weeks, he would take the oath of office and become the next President of the United States. Even though the election was over, he was travelling the country to let the nation get to know their next President and in an effort to lift the spirits of a people who were suffering such hard times. He had been elected in a landslide, and in Miami, as in all the other places he went, people turned out by the thousands to see him.

Zangara halted on the street at the back of the crowd. Not far away a band was playing "Happy Days Are Here Again." Zangara leaned against a light post with his left hand and held his aching abdomen with the other. After a moment the pain subsided—a little—and he took a deep breath. Zangara reached into his pocket and felt the cold metal of the cheap .32 caliber pistol he had purchased. Not far away, he could hear the calm and intellectual yet authoritative and confident voice of President Elect Roosevelt.

"On this day, my fellow Americans, I am confident that we can look forward to a bright and prosperous future."

Though Zangara could hear Roosevelt, he could not see him. Zangara was only five feet tall, and the vast majority of men and women in the crowd were taller than himself. Making matters worse, was the fact that several held their little boys or little girls on their shoulders so that the children could also get a look at the great man. As Zangara tried to find a way through the crowd, Roosevelt continued with his speech.

"I know that for many of you, times are hard," Roosevelt said in a genuine heartfelt tone. "The present economic situation in which our country finds itself, due in large measure to bad leadership over the past decade, must be rectified, and you may be certain my friends that I will address it with the utmost zeal and determination. Working together, there is no challenge we cannot face, no obstacle we cannot overcome! We will do whatever is necessary, to insure a bright and prosperous future for the United States of America!"

The crowd erupted into cheers and applause.

These people are fools, thought Zangara. *What does a rich capitalist like Roosevelt know about hard times? He's nothing but a wealthy exploiter like all the other politicians and big shots in this country.*

"With hard work, and endurance, we shall see this great country of ours soar to new heights of prosperity, so that we retain that most wonderful right, that our forefathers envisioned would be the right of every American—the pursuit of happiness!"

Zangara looked down at his callused hands. They were course and tough from years of bricklaying. He had no doubt that Roosevelt's own hands were soft and smooth.

From counting money all his life! Who is he to dare talk about hard work! If the poor people of the world would only stand up and fight, we could teach all these capitalists not to exploit us!

Try as he could, Zangara could not get through the crowd. He huffed and then slammed his fist into his palm in frustration. He wanted to scream. He started to try and make his way through the crowd again.

"As I look upon my countrymen today, I see a people ready for change. When I ran for President, I promised you a new deal—I promised you relief, recovery, and reform! Working together we are going to relieve the poor and unfortunate in our nation. We are going to work for a day when every citizen in our country is socially secure. People in our nation should never go hungry because they are too elderly or sick to work. A man should never have to watch his children go hungry, just because there is no work to be had."

Lies! Nothing but lies! thought Zangara. *He cares nothing for the poor!*

"I promise you recovery. We will work to insure that the United States of America has the strongest economy in the world. A good economy means good paying jobs, for hard working American workers! I promise you reform. We will not let the same bad practices and errors, drag our nation into the depths of depression again."

All he wants to do is to line the pockets of himself and the rest of the capitalists with gold! He wants to keep the system rigged that keeps the poor poor and the rich rich!

After failing a second time to get through the crowd, Zangara spotted a small metal park bench off to his right. He made his way over to it as quickly as his aching abdomen allowed him. He climbed onto the bench and at last he could see the President Elect of the United States. Roosevelt was standing in the back of an open topped automobile. Anton Cermak, the mayor of Chicago, and one of Roosevelt's closest friends and political allies, stood immediately beside him.

Franklin Roosevelt looked out at the crowd around him. His legs pained him terribly. The iron braces around his legs that allowed him to stand were far from comfortable. He'd gone the entire presidential campaign without the public ever seeing him in the wheel chair into which he had been forced when he'd contracted polio years earlier. He wasn't about to be seen in it now that he had won.

I must be strong for my country, thought Roosevelt. *A leader must radiate strength and confidence.* When he looked at the sea of faces peering back at him he was warmed by their looks of admiration. But more than that, he rejoiced to see the hope that he had managed to instill in them.

"My friends, our country is not just any country. America is the bastion of democracy and the beacon of freedom to all the world, that is what has attracted millions to our noble shores. I promise you, that in this period of trial and trouble, that our great nation will be an example to all the world. With such a people as ours, our future is as bright as the sun."

Zangara reached into his pocket and took tight hold of his pistol. When he had been little more than a boy, Zangara had served in the Italian army during World War 1. He had been an expert marksman with his rifle. But as he looked over and across the crowd of people surrounding the President elect, he was far from confident he could hit his target. Roosevelt was several yards away, and the cheap pistol Zangara had purchased from a corner store for eight dollars was a lot less accurate than the Carcano he had carried during the war. Complicating matters worse was the fact that the lady in front of him was wearing a large plumed hat. Even on the bench he had to get up on his toes to get a clear shot. He started to pull out the pistol but then he hesitated.

I need a better shot!

He leapt down from the bench and with renewed resolve headed for the crowd. This time he did not try to find a way through or around the crowd. Throwing all pretense of politeness or courtesy away, he began to openly push, shove and squeeze his way through.

"Hey pal watch it!"

"Who do you think you are?"

"How rude!"

"I swear, people these days…"

"No pushing shorty!"

It took several minutes, and angered quite a few people, but Zangara managed to force his way to the front of the crowd. Roosevelt was now right in front of him. As the President elect drew to the end of his speech, Zangara once again gripped the cold hard metal of the pistol in his pocket.

"My fellow Americans, let me close by also giving you this solemn pledge, that I will always lead you to do what I believe to be morally true and just. No matter what hardships or dangers the future may hold, we will face them together, and we will defeat them. May God Bless America!"

The crowd exploded into cheers and applause. Several people started forward trying to get to the car to shake Roosevelt's hand. At that very moment, Zangara rushed forward and pulled out his pistol. He leveled it at Roosevelt who was no more than ten feet away. Zangara fired several shots. Two of them struck Roosevelt in his chest and another in his stomach. Though he had taken a bullet in his right arm, Mayor Cermak caught the President Elect as he fell backwards into the car.

No sooner had Zangara fired his shots than a half dozen men leapt upon him and began to beat him into the ground. In the back of the automobile, Cermak cradled the dying Roosevelt in his arms.

"Franklin! Stay with me Franklin!" He then shouted frantically at the driver. "The hospital! Get us to the hospital!" The dazed driver started the car, put it in gear and then slammed on the gas petal. The crowd parted like the red sea before the motorcar as it rapidly made its way out of the park and towards the hospital.

"Franklin! Don't die on us! Don't give up!" cried Cermak as he tried in vain to stay the bleeding by applying pressure to the wounds.

Roosevelt then spoke in a still and quiet voice.

"Cold...I'm so cold..."

Cermak stared up at the night sky.

God, why him? Why couldn't it have been me? "Come on Franklin we need you. Don't leave us!" Cermak was virtually shouting at his dying friend.

"Sir, we're almost at the hospital!" cried the driver from the front seat.

"We're almost there Franklin!" Cermak took hold of Roosevelt's wrist, trying to feel for a pulse. Try as he could he could not find it.

"Franklin!"

Roosevelt looked up into Cermak's face and with great effort of will he managed to speak.

"Anton, tell Eleanor I love..." At that moment Franklin D. Roosevelt let out the last breath he ever took.

Cermak let out a deep sigh. He once again stared up at the sky. This time he asked audibly.

"God, why couldn't it have been me?"

*****

April 15, 1941

President Arthur H. Vandenberg stared out of the window of the oval office at the White House lawn. The sun was shining and it was a beautiful day—at least superficially. On his desk he had stacks of reports from the State Department. In East Asia the Japanese were waging a war of aggression against China. In Europe, Hitler and his Nazi's had dominated most of the continent. Britain stood alone against them. The German Air Force bombed the British by night, and German U-Boats sank virtually all vessels that tried to bring in food or supplies. Vandenberg shook his head.

They can't last much longer, he thought. Vandenberg looked at the clock on the wall. Lord Halifax, the Ambassador from Britain, would be arriving at any moment. *I must get him to see reason.* Vandenberg then revised that thought. *I must get him to get Churchill to see reason.*

Less than a minute later, a knock came on the door to the Oval Office.

"Come in," said Vandenberg. A secretary held open the door and Lord Halifax walked into the office. He was a tall and noble looking man, with a mostly bald head. He towered over Vandenberg who, with his combed over white hair, thick glasses, and bow tie, looked more like a professor of literature than a President.

"Good morning, Lord Halifax," said Vandenberg. "It is so good of you to visit."

"I wish that my coming here, was merely a friendly social call, Mr. President, but I'm afraid that I have a matter of the gravest urgency to discuss with you."

Vandenberg motioned Lord Halifax to a chair. When both men were seated, the British Ambassador got straight to the point.

"Mr. President, we need your help…urgently."

"I take it that the war is not going well at all." It was a superfluous question. Vandenberg had seen the newsreels, read the papers, and most importantly read the reports from the State Department. He knew the British plight was desperate.

"Mr. President, things are almost at a crisis point. The German U-Boat campaign is strangling our country. We need more destroyers and airplanes to break the stranglehold the

Germans have on us. We are also running low on vital supplies like fuel and food."

"Lord Halifax, the United States has been and will continue to be, open to selling Britain arms and supplies."

"Yes, Mr. President, but as I'm sure you know, your Neutrality Acts forbid your nation to sell war materiel to us except on a cash and carry basis. I'm afraid that our government is running low on gold. We've liquidated all the assets we can, but our coffers are still anemically low. If you will not allow us to buy on credit, we will no longer be able to afford to purchase arms and supplies from you, in which case we are finished."

Vandenberg could hear the desperation in Lord Halifax's voice. The U.S. President was well aware of what the Neutrality Acts said (he had after all helped draft and pass them back when he was a Senator). Now that he was President, he enforced them to the letter, even though several interventionists (mostly left leaning Democrats) in Washington had been screaming for repealing the neutrality acts or at least finding a way around them. Some had advocated an idea called "lend-lease." The Neutrality Acts said nothing about "lending or leasing." As far and Vandenberg was concerned, such an act would be violating the spirit of the law, while giving lip service to its letter. That was the kind of fiendish political trick that so often contributed to the low esteem with which politicians were often held. For some reason he could not explain, Vandenberg's thoughts went to Franklin Roosevelt, now eight years dead.

This lend-lease nonsense, is just the kind of thing that wily Roosevelt would have tried. Besides, it would in effect take us from a neutral position to being a de-facto ally of Britain. It would end up dragging us into the war, that's what it would do. Vandenberg had worked too hard keep the United States out of war, to risk something as dangerous as "lend-lease." He'd done everything in his power to not offend the Axis powers. In the Pacific, he had kept the U.S. fleet stationed at San Diego and San Francisco and he had allowed the oil and scrap metal sales to Japan to continue unhindered. If Japan used that scrap metal and oil to wage what amounted to a war of annihilation against China, well....

That's none of our concern, thought Vandenberg. It was not the place of the USA to meddle in other country's affairs. He therefore wasn't about to risk another war with Germany, just because the British had bitten off more than they could chew.

"Lord Halifax, forgive me, but perhaps it is time for your government to consider other alternatives. Why not simply make peace with the Germans?"

The British ambassador fixed the U.S. President with an icy glare. The look on Lord Halifax's face went, in a matter of seconds, from angry, to resentful, and then finally to sadness and resignation.

"Mr. President, there is no making peace with Adolf Hitler. We tried at Munich in 1938. I was there when we served Czechoslovakia up to Hitler on a silver platter. He took the Sudetenland, and then just a few weeks later he gobbled up all of Czechoslovakia with it. He had promised he would make no more territorial demands in Europe, and yet less than a year after Munich he was demanding land from Poland. No, Mr. President, Adolf Hitler cannot be appeased and his word is worth nothing. You must realize, sir, that we are not fighting for ourselves alone. We are fighting for the very survival of western civilization itself—including the United States."

"Mr. Ambassador, I must be frank with you. I made a promise to my country during the last election that I would keep the United States out of the troubles of the outside world. We cannot afford to enter a military conflict. The United States is not, I repeat, not going to become involved in any way, form or fashion in your war. We are committed to remaining a true neutral nation. I have always believed that the United States should follow the advice of our first President, and remain outside of entangling alliances. It is not the responsibility of America to be the policeman of the world, nor may I say, with the greatest possible respect, is it Britain's responsibility either."

"Mr. President, something had to be done. Germany could not be allowed to simply invade and take over any nation it chose. A line had to be drawn and we drew it along with the French when we declared war on Hitler after he invaded Poland."

And look what it got you, thought Vandenberg. *Several neutral countries occupied, France overrun, Britain's cities bombed, and for all of that, Poland is still no better off.* "Mr. Ambassador, I sympathize with Poland and all the other nations that have suffered under the Nazis. I sympathize with Britain and with the difficult situation in which you have found yourself, but I have a responsibility to the citizens of the United States to keep them out of foreign wars. Our country is still in the midst of the greatest depression in history." *Heaven knows that John Garner's two terms didn't make anything better.* "Not only that, Lord Halifax, but as I'm sure you know our army is very small." In point of fact, the U.S. Army was smaller than that of tiny Belgium.

"So you are, in effect, Mr. President saying that you will not help us." It wasn't phrased as a question. Lord Halifax could plainly see and understand Vandenberg's position. As he continued to study him, President Vandenberg now saw a look of bitter resentment on the face of Lord Halifax.

"I did not say we would not help you," said Vandenberg. "The United States considers Britain to be a close friend. Our country has its origin in yours. We share a language, a common religion, and many other things. We are very willing to help you, though it may not be in the way you had hoped. The United States offers its services in mediating a fair truce between the United Kingdom and Germany."

"Mr. President you say we are friends, and yet you will not even lend us a water-hose when our house is on fire and on the verge of burning down to the ground."

"I'm afraid that is not a fair comparison, Lord Halifax. Lending war-materiel is more like lending chewing gum than it is like lending a water hose. After it's been used, you don't want it back. Nor would lending you a water hose entail the added chance of my own house catching fire. If we openly and flagrantly supply you with arms, it will make us enemy's with Germany and will very likely drag us into the war as well."

Halifax sighed.

"Mr. President, if a man is not inclined to lend his neighbor a water hose, he may find to his great horror, that the fire will surely spread from his neighbor's house to his own. Mark my words sir, if a line is not drawn now, Hitler's Germany will not stop until the entire world, including the United States, has been ground to powder underneath the Nazi jackboot."

President Vandenberg winced inwardly. The British ambassador's comment struck just a little too close to home, but Vandenberg rallied quickly.

"I'm afraid, sir, that our houses are hardly next door to one another. The Atlantic separates us from Europe and its troubles and the Pacific separates us from Asia and its troubles. Now I implore you, sir, make peace with Germany. Let Berlin know that you are willing to sit down and talk. I promise you the United States will be right there at your side, urging a just and equitable peace for Great Britain."

"I am afraid, Mr. President, that one day you are going to find that not even the great waters of the Atlantic or the Pacific will be able to protect your nation. I warn you, if you refuse to help us, then one day the Nazi's will be coming after you, and you will find that you will have no friends to help you, because there will be no one left."

"Lord Halifax, I think that you overestimate Hitler and his thugs. Our War Department tells me that the Germans lack the ships even to launch an invasion of Britain, much less the United States. If they cannot get across the English Channel, they certainly cannot get across the Atlantic. I say again, sir, if you will merely make peace with the Germans your nation will be able to enjoy a secure peace. Your nation need not suffer the hardship it is enduring right now."

"Prime Minister Churchill has made it clear that we will endure as much hardship as necessary," said Lord Halifax.

"I do not doubt, your nation's or Mr. Churchill's resolve," said Vandenberg. "But if you are holding out, at the expense of the suffering of your people, all in the hope that we are going to somehow join you in your war with Germany, then please, sir, let Mr. Churchill know that all of this suffering is in vain. I will say it again, sir. The United States is not going to get involved. We are a neutral, and we intend to remain just that. Now if your government is willing, I would be happy to facilitate some opening discussions of peace by arranging a meeting between you and Ambassador Diekhoff here at the White House."

There was a long pause in which Lord Halifax seemed lost in deep thought. He did not stare at Vandenberg, he stared through him, as if into some grim dark future that lay ahead for the world. Finally, he rose from his seat and headed for the door. Just before walking out he turned to give one last remark to the President of the United States.

"I will relay your offer to Winston. I personally hope that he does not agree, no matter how hopeless it may seem."

"You will feel differently when you see your country at peace and secure," replied Vandenberg. He meant it honestly, but Lord Halifax merely shook his head, and walked out of the Oval Office.

A Special Preview of Starstorm
An exciting military science fiction thriller;

Chapter 1

A crowd of spectators cheered as a group of five jet fighters roared overhead. The squadron of advanced stunt craft was flying in a perfect diamond formation. After completing the low level flyby of the crowd, the squadron pulled up into a high vertical climb. With precision flying, the five aircraft remained in close proximity to one another. The lead pilot signaled his teammates.

"Alright guys, are we ready?"

"I was born ready Jack!" came the reply of a sneer but sure voice. In his mind, Cadet Jack Thunder could see the sly smile on his friend's face. Many things could be said about Cadet Red Styler. That he lacked self-confidence was not one of them. The other squadron members also signaled the affirmative. Jack started the countdown.

"Starburst maneuver on my mark—twenty seconds…" His heart started pounding and he gripped the controls of his plane tightly. "Remember, don't ignite the plasma until you're clear of everyone else!" Red's arrogant voice came back in reply.

"Don't singe anyone's tail feathers, got it!" The countdown ended and the squadron went into action. Jack hit his after burner and shot to a far higher altitude. The others likewise hit their afterburners but split off into different directions. This was a dangerous maneuver that would require precision timing. The five planes would head directly at one another from five separate directions and simultaneously pass within just meters of one another. The second they cleared one another, they would jettison a trail of plasma and ignite it. Jack came about and brought his fighter into a nose dive. His monitor showed that he was on course. Faster than lightning the five jets streaked past one another. Jack ejected the plasma. A moment later he hit his afterburner, igniting it. There was enormous flash of light behind him. He streaked towards the ground with a burning trail of fiery plasma billowing behind him.

Over the radio Jack could hear his squadron members shouting excitedly.

"Yeah!"

"We are on fire!" yelled Red.

"Smokin'!"

Down on the ground the crowds were awestruck. The squadron had performed the maneuver perfectly. An enormous starburst of plasma fire radiated the sky. The spectators cheered and clapped their hands in thunderous applause.

As he cleared the plasma fire, Jack found himself headed straight for the ground at full speed. He pulled back the stick but his aircraft did not start to pull up. An alarm sounded in the cockpit. Somehow one of the primary control circuits had gone out. Fighting down panic, Jack hurriedly started rerouting the controls through the auxiliary circuits all while enduring enormous G-forces. The ground loomed large and ominous in his view from the cockpit. At the last possible second he regained control and he pulled back on the stick and his aircraft pulled out of the dive. He came so close to the surface that his aircraft did another close flyby of the review stands. Jack's fighter roared overhead and the crowd again erupted into cheers. As far as they were concerned it was all part of the show. Red signaled over the radio.

"Jack! Are you alright!"

"Fine Red, thanks for asking."

"Hey, the greatest pilot in the universe has to check on his best pal." Smiling, Jack keyed his mike.

"All aircraft report!" The other squadron members reported in. Jack congratulated his team. "Well done guys. That was great."

"It was a perfect maneuver if I do say so myself," replied Red.

Smiling again, Jack said, "Alright, let's form up again. If we don't hurry we are going to be late." Moments later they were again flying in a diamond formation. "All craft switch over to auto pilot. Prepare to eject in 3, 2, 1..." Jack pulled the ejection lever. The canopy of his stunt craft flew open and he was rocketed clear. His para-glider deployed automatically and its guidance system took him towards the crowd below. He quickly spotted his squad members. The five ejected pilots glided towards the earth in a linear formation. Their stunt crafts, now under the control of the on board computers, peeled off and head back towards the airfield.

"It looks like the graduation ceremony is well under way," said Jack. "There sure are a lot of people down there."

"It's just my adoring fans, who have come out to bask in the presence of my awesomeness," said Red. Jack rolled his eyes. Down below, the crowds watched as the five pilots descended from the sky above. The other academy graduates were already assembled on the parade ground in front of the massive review stand. Almost simultaneously the pilots of Jack Thunder's squadron touched down to the rapturous applause of the crowd. They released their para-gliders and double timed it to their positions in the front ranks of their graduating class. Once there, they came to rigid attention. Commander Warren, the academy commandant took her place at the podium.

"Let's have a warm welcome for the top five students of the class of 2120!" Once again the audience erupted into applause. The commandant stared down at the five honored pilots. "You have represented Condor Space Academy well this day. Those of you who have chosen to serve in the United States Space Force will no doubt be great assets to this nation." Red beamed with pride as did Jack's three other squad mates. The commandant continued. "I have no doubt that all of you will go on to bright futures whatever your chosen path may be." Now Jack allowed himself to beam ever so slightly. Most of his classmates would be joining the Space Force. He, however, would soon be flying civilian space liners to the colonies. He was too independent for the military life.

And though I would never admit it to my friends, I don't think I could take a life, even in war... He was not a coward, but he could not help feeling like one. He returned his attention to the Commandant's speech.

"It is now my distinct honor and privilege to introduce to you our guest speaker for this afternoon…" said the commandant, "Fleet Captain Morton Doran!" The audience again erupted into cheers. A tall man in a blue Space Force uniform approached the podium. His chest was covered in ribbons and medals. He was in his late forties. His dark black hair was streaked with grey. Though already at attention, the assembled cadets stiffened even further. Doran was a legend. He was known throughout the world as the man that had led the Space Force to victory in the Pirate Wars that had raged for most of the previous decade. He was the hero of the epic Second Battle of Jupiter and the man who had defeated the most notorious space pirate in history, Edward Lee.

"Thank you Commandant," said Doran. "And congratulations to your honor squadron for that superb performance. It was a finely executed maneuver. Condor Space Academy has always produced the finest of space pilots. It is among the best space academies in the world and you should all be very proud. I have no doubt that those of you who have chosen to serve your country in the Space Force will continue to make us proud. You honor us with your service."

For the briefest moment, Jack had second thoughts about his decision to not join the Space Force. Red and the others had practically begged him to join with them. He'd thought about it. With the Pirate Wars over he didn't think it very likely he'd be put into a combat position, but he had still decided against it.

It's a civilian life for me, and that's final, he thought, as if trying to convince himself it was true. Doran concluded his address and returned the ceremonies back over to the Commandant.

"I now declare the class of 2120, graduated! Cadets, you are dismissed!" The cadets erupted into cheers. Many of them embraced one another or clasped one another's hands. They'd had four trying years together. Many of the members of the crowd that were in attendance, mostly friends and family of the graduates, started making their way onto the parade ground. Jack started searching through the crowd, looking for a particular face. Jack wished his parents could have made but had known for weeks that they would not make it. The trip from the Mars colony was not cheap. The face he was looking for belonged to a certain young woman. He looked and looked but she was nowhere to be seen. When he realized that she was not coming his heart sank. From behind him, Red spoke.

"No sign of Jen?" Jack shook his head and then let it hang in sorrow. Red put his hand on Jack's shoulder. "Don't worry bud, I'm sure something just came up. You just wait, you'll get a message before the night's over with." Jack pulled out his personal com-link and checked it.

No messages. No missed calls.

Red put his arm around his friend. "Come on Jack. Tonight we celebrate! Let's hit the town! There are thousands of ladies just waiting to be swept off of their feet by the two handsomest, and let's be honest, most totally awesome pilots in the world!" They made their way back to their dorm to change out of their flight suits. "Make sure you wear your academy uniform," said Red. "It will get us into the Stargazer for free tonight." Red then grinned mischievously. "And you know how the ladies love men in uniforms." While Red admired himself in the mirror, fixed his hair and adjusted his uniform, Jack checked his com-link one more time.

No messages, No missed calls... Sighing, he followed Red to his silver solar car.

Red drove much like he flew—wildly. Fortunately, once they left the Academy grounds they were in a predominantly rural area. Jack enjoyed the view of all the open land. They passed several auto farms where robot harvesters were busily gathering in the crops. Red hit the accelerator and the 2116 Corvette sped up to 174 kilometers per hour. Jack glanced at the car's power meter.

"Looks like you're going to need a new power cell in about a month." The Corvette was powered by a Shinara power cell from the planet Mercury. It had run on the same cell for over four years.

"I'm not worried about it," said Red. "I'll be in space in less than a month and I don't plan on coming back here for a long time. This puppy's going in storage. I'd loan her to you but you're moving to the Mars Colony to be near your folks right?" Jack nodded.

"Just as soon as I land a job with one of the space lines." *And as soon as I can get an answer from Jen on whether or not she'll come with me...*

"You know Jack, those space lines can be awful snobby and stuck up. They're real picky about who they let in. You're a great pilot—you're probably the best with the exception of yours truly. But the space lines care more about how clean and well-trimmed your finger nails are than about how well you fly. If you ask me, they're a waste of your talent. You aught to join the Space Force with me and keep the team together. Besides, flying a Star Sword space fighter beats flying a space liner any day."

"Red we've been over this. I'm not..."

"I know, I know. I'm just saying." They drove on in silence. Jack watched the sun set. When they reached the interstate, Red sped up to 260 KPH. After less than an hour they arrived in Birmingham. Three mile high skyscrapers jutted into the sky all around them. Though it was night, the lights of the city made it almost as bright as day. As they entered the city, Red switched the car over to automatic. As much as he preferred to be in personal control, taking the manual authorized routes would have taken far too long. The auto-grid would get them there much *faster*.

The Stargazer Club was a favorite hangout for the cadets of the Condor Space Academy and that night they were out in force. The club was throwing a celebration for the new graduates. As Jack and Red entered the club they caught sight of a band playing rock music wildly on a stage.

"It's the Galactic Cats!" said Jack excitedly. The sight of his favorite rock band lifted his spirits. The sight of all the beautiful young women lifted Red's. He pulled out a comb and ran it though his slick red hair.

The building was an enormous dome. The upper ceiling was alive with a laser lightshow. Holo-screens displayed close ups of the band. The facility was divided into dance floors, a dining area and a gaming area. The gaming area had everything from holographic boxing to fighter pilot simulators. Jack and Red had spent considerable time in latter. In times past that had dueled to the cheers of their fellow pilots. Jack and Red were the best at the game. It was always a close match.

"Come on Jack. I know just how to get Jen off of your mind," said Red. He then headed towards the dance floors like a tiger on the prowl. Jack was glad Red didn't want to fire up the simulator. Red could sometimes be a little too competitive. Suddenly Jack caught sight of a young beautiful blond staring at him. He decided that for once Red was right. Summoning his courage he walked over to ask her to dance. She looked him up and down. The look in her eyes said she was sizing up more than just his uniform. Jack was twenty three but his boyish good looks made him look a lot younger. The fact that he was only 1.6 meters tall only served to make him look even younger. Nonetheless, she accepted his hand and allowed him to escort her out onto the dance floor. Moments later synthesizers and electro vocorders blared. On stage smoke machines and lights went into actions. The Galactic Cats were known for their melodramatic performances but their music was the rave of the younger generation.

The dance floor was crowded but Jack was almost as good at dancing as he was at flying, and the young blond, whose name he did not yet even know, seemed perfectly happy to get as close to him as possible on the dance floor. She was a skilled dancer as well, and matched Jack's lead move for move. When the music changed to a slow dance, she got even closer. Jack was sweating profusely, but it had little to do with the temperature. She had her arms around his neck and her head resting on his shoulder. The rest of her body was pressed firmly against his. Jack wondered if it was himself or his uniform that the girl was more interested in. Red was certainly right about women liking men who were destined to be fighter pilots. He wondered if his dance partner would be so interested in him if she knew he had no intention of joining the United States Space Force. As the dance continued, Jack caught sight of Red. He had not one, but two girls, and he was dancing with both at the same time. Red's eyes scanned the young woman that Jack was dancing with. He gave Jack a thumbs up and a wry grin. Jack wanted to shake his head. Something told him that Red would always be a wild womanizer. Jack, however, wanted something more permanent—and real.

The slow dance came to an end and everyone gave the band a round of applause. Jack was about to take advantage of the interlude to ask the girl her name, but before he could, someone tapped him on the shoulder. Jack turned to see a tall menacing guy looking down at him.

"Move aside shorty. You flyboys think you can just come in here and hog all the women? You're nothing but a little boy in a fancy uniform." He shoved Jack aside and took a step towards the girl. "Why don't you come dance with a man, honey?"

Jack normally considered himself a lover, not a fighter. But he was too chivalrous (and angry) to just abandon the girl to an oversized punk. He leapt back between them and glared menacingly up at the thug.

"Listen, lowlife, I don't think the lady wants your company."

The punk pounded his fist into his hand.

"Is that a fact, lover boy?" The punker grabbed Jack by the collar of his uniform and practically lifted him off the ground. "You can kiss that baby face goodbye, because by the time I'm done with ya, you won't have a face!"

Suddenly, Red came seemingly out of nowhere. He leapt onto the punks back, wrapped his arm around his throat and started to choke off his air supply.

"That's my friend you're messing with, asshole!"

The enraged punker reached up and grabbed Red by the

hair. He then bashed his head backwards busting Red's nose and knocking him clear. The punker turned to face Red, but in so doing he turned his back on Jack. Little or not, Jack had studied Isshinryu for half his life. Jack punched the punker in the kidney and then used a cross kick to hit his leg which subsequently collapsed beneath him. The moment the fight had begun most of the crowd had backed up, trying to get to a safe distance from which to watch the action. Pilots and punkers got in fights all the time, Jack just wished he hadn't been the lucky pilot.

The punker began to force himself back to his feet. Jack could have been merciless, and hit him while he was down, but once again his chivalry got the better of him. Instead Jack circled around him and then helped Red to his feet.

"Come on Red, we better get out of here!"

"Not until I teach this punk-ass a lesson he'll never forget!"

Red's pride had been wounded and when his pride was wounded he was very often blinded by rage. Jack, however, saw that there were three more punkers coming to help their injured friend.

"We can't take on four of them!"

"Watch me!"

Unwilling to abandon his reckless friend (who had recklessly come to help him in his moment of need) Jack fell into a stance and prepared for the worst. Fortunately, five of their fellow pilots from the Condor Academy came charging in and the dance floor erupted into a full scale brawl. Their surprise attack sent the punkers running before Red or Jack could get back into the fight.

Jack watched them flee then turned to look for the young woman for whose honor he had fought. She was nowhere to be seen. His heart sank. Suddenly Red put his arm around his friend.

"You're lucky I'm here to watch your back! Just think of all the excitement you're going to miss by not coming with me!"

Jack sighed. He checked his comlink again.
No messages. No missed calls.

***

Less than a light year away, traveling nearly two-hundred times the speed of light, on a direct course for the Earth's solar system, was the main body of the Imperial Zidian 3rd Fleet. Thirty battle cruisers, 350 attack ships, fifty transport ships, and Commander Akdon's Flagship the "Krusha" which meant "black soul" in the Zidian language. On its bridge, on his platform, overlooking the view screen was Fleet Commander Akdon. He stood seven feet tall, the average height for Zidians. He wore a gray, black and silver armored uniform with many decorations commemorating his past victories. Like all Zidians he had rough, dark brown skin, a tall hard narrow forehead and powerful jaws that resembled the beak like mouth of a triceratops dinosaur.

The lights were dim and the air hot. Below his platform on the main floor was the bridge crew operating the controls of the mighty warship. The view screen was huge. At fifteen feet by thirty feet, it took up the whole back wall of the bridge. On the view screen was a map of Earth's solar system. Akdon studied it carefully.

Another Zidian climbed up to the platform and stood next to Akdon. It was Sub Commander Kaydan, Akdon's second in command. He was ruthlessly efficient and highly intelligent. Unlike most Zidians, he was a scientist as well as a warrior. Akdon always valued his insight.

"So this is our target," said Akdon.

"Yes sir, a mere nine planets orbiting a single star. Only their home world is inhabitable," replied Kaydan.

"What's it worth?" asked Akdon.

"Once we strip mine it of its natural resources it should yield quite a profit in minerals, oxygen, slave labor, and most especially water."

"And what of the inhabitants?"

"They are mentally and physically inferior to us. Intelligence reports that they haven't even reached space yet."

"Good." Pushing a button on his control panel, Akdon changed the image of the view screen from a map of Earth's star system to an image of the Earth itself. "It is a lush world," said Akdon. It will make a fine addition to our empire." He turned back to Kaydan. "What kind of resistance can we expect?" Kaydan inserted an information chip into the main console. The image on the screen changed.

"These images represent the most advanced weapons possessed by the Human inhabitants." The first image to appear on the screen was of a Bi-Wing fighter plane. "This primitive, prop driven, fixed wing air craft is capable only of low level atmospheric flight. It is slow and poorly maneuverable by our standards. It is armed only with rapid fire-fire arms. It has no sophisticated tracking or detection technology. Our fighters will sweep them from the sky." Akdon stared at the image of the aircraft with disdain.

"If that is the best this planet has to offer I'm going to find this quite a boring expedition. Kaydan brought another image up on the screen.

"This tracked armored fighting vehicle is powered by a primitive internal combustion engine. It utilizes liquefied fossil remains as fuel—most inefficient. It fires a large caliber projectile as its primary weapon. A single blast from a beam cannon would be sufficient to melt through its armor."

Staring at the human tank on the view screen Akdon said, "These primitives might just as well be using toys to fight us."

"An apt description Commander," said Kaydan. Akdon eyed the screen with a menacing look.

"Let me see the enemy in person." Kaydan quickly replaced the image of the human tank with that of a Human foot soldier.

"As you can see commander, we are physically as well as mentally superior to the Humans. We are taller, stronger and have greater physical endurance—not doubt do to our homeworld's greater gravity."

"No doubt we also possess a superior courage and strength of will as is true when the Zidian race is compared with any other species."

"Doubtless Commander," said Kaydan, who reflected silently that his commanding officer's unquestioning belief in Zidian superiority might one day prove to be a weakness. While confident of his own race's strengths and manifest destiny to rule the galaxy, Kaydan knew that it would be unwise to underestimate a foe, no matter how primitive or weak they seemed.

Several different forms of human soldiers flashed across the screen. "As you can see Commander, Human warriors are dressed in various colors of clothing made to resemble different types of foliage and terrain found on their planet. Of course this will be completely useless to them when set against our infrared and other sensors. Their weapons consist mostly of primitive automatic firearms whose projectiles will have no chance of penetrating the armor of our soldiers." Kaydan removed the data chip and the image on the view screen and returned to the map of the Earth's star system.

"How old is this information?" asked Akdon.

"According to Imperial Intelligence only five years," replied Kaydan. "Any advancements the enemy could have made should be minimal."

Akdon nodded, reflecting that it would only be a matter of time before the human race, like many other species across the galaxy, were the slaves of the Zidian Empire.

*****

Fleet Captain Morton Doran walked the grounds of Space Force Headquarters in Washington D.C. The grass was lush and green. The buildings were pristine and clean. Doran's good friend, Colonel Ron Travis of the Space Force Marine Corps. walked beside him.

"I'm telling you Morton, these politicians are fools," said Travis. "Dismantling a third of our space-borne military forces, and mothballing another third is nothing but inviting trouble." He swore derisively. "Why can't they understand that strength is the greatest guarantee of peace." The Colonel paused to wipe sweat from his black skinned face. Washington, D.C. that time of year was hot.

"I agree with you," said Doran. "Believe me, Admiral Shirley and I have told the Space Force appropriations committee, the President and the State department that it would be foolhardy to downsize the Force. The Pirate Wars have only been over less than a year. The Japanese and the Russians aren't planning on cutting back their Space Forces anytime soon, you can be certain of that."

"And I'm not entirely convinced that the Pirate threat has been completely annihilated," said Travis. "There are plenty of the ruthless cutthroats still missing and unaccounted for. They may simply be lying low out in the Kuiper belt waiting for the opportunity to reemerge."

"Possible," said Doran. "But unlikely. There have been no pirate attacks reported since we smashed Lee's fleet around Jupiter."

"You mean since you smashed his fleet," said Travis with a smile. Doran shook his head.

"I may have been in command, but it was the brave men and women of the Space Force that carried the day. Without their heroism and sacrifice, we could not have won."

"Spoken like a true Fleet Captain," said Colonel Travis. "So where are you off to now?"

"Back to the Challenger. We're leaving on another routine patrol in a few days. I just hope I don't find out that I'm out of a job when we get back to Earth. I'm a little old to consider a new career."

Travis laughed.

"Don't worry Morton. There's no way they can put the Space Force's greatest hero out to pasture. The Challenger is the most decorated ship in the fleet. If any of the Super Carriers are left in service, she will. An old jarhead like me, though, that's a different story."

"You did plenty to see us to victory yourself," said Doran. It was true. Colonel Travis had just as many medals and decorations for valor as Doran's.

"If I were you," said Travis, "I'd run for President. You certainly have the popularity for it."

"You must be joking!" said Doran. "Those jackals would eat me alive. Besides, I've spent too many years complaining about the blasted politicians to ever become one myself."

Travis laughed. Doran then continued in a serious and somber tone.

"We both know that my family has a major skeleton in its closet that in the eyes of many would be irredeemable. If it ever comes out—and it certainly would if I was foolish enough to enter politics—most people would distrust and maybe even despise me."

"That's ridiculous! We don't control who we're related to Morton. You're a good man, and I for one am proud to have served under you."

Doran nodded appreciatively to his friend.

"Unfortunately, the politicians wouldn't see it that way. They are shameless opportunists. But it doesn't matter. I'm not cut out for politics or civilian government. I have neither the desire nor the inclination. Besides..." Doran looked up into the busy sky. Various drones and hover pods were flying every which way. "I have no desire to be followed around twenty four seven by news bots."

Travis let out a sigh of resignation.

"Can I see you off at the spaceport?"

"I appreciate it," said Doran "...but I'm afraid I have a private call to make on an old friend..."

5287043R00164

Printed in Great Britain
by Amazon.co.uk, Ltd.,
Marston Gate.